⊰⊱ THE ART OF PERSUASION ⊰⊱

"You still haven't said why you're here," Jame said.

"The Sirdan sent me."

"The leader of the Thieves' Guild?"

"Yes. He wants you to come back."

That startled her. "I should think I would be the last person he would want to see again."

"He says, and here I quote, 'If the Talisman does not come, I will rip her old master Penari out of his precious Maze, even if I have to tear it down in the process.'"

"He can't do that!" she exclaimed involuntarily. The Maze was the model of the city itself. To destroy one was to imperil the other.

"There is this too," said Darinby. "That hostelry where you stayed—the Res aB'tyrr?" Darinby looked uncomfortable. He coughed and braced himself. "The Sirdan bade me tell you this: if you don't return, he swears by his blood that he will order not only the Maze destroyed but the Res aB'tyrr torched and everyone who flees it slain on its threshold."

"Sweet Trinity. He wouldn't."

"You know him. Dare you risk it?"

BAEN BOOKS
By P.C. Hodgell

The Kencyrath Series
Seeker's Bane (omnibus)
Bound in Blood
Honor's Paradox
The Sea of Time
The Gates of Tagmeth
By Demons Possessed

The Godstalker Chronicles (omnibus)

By Demons Possessed

By

P.C. Hodgell

By Demons Possessed

This is a work of fiction. All the characters and events
portrayed in this book are fictional, and any resemblance
to real people or incidents is purely coincidental.

A Baen Books Original

Baen Publishing Enterprises
P.O. Box 1403
Riverdale, NY 10471
www.baen.com

ISBN: 978-1-9821-2461-8

Cover art by Eric Williams
Map by P.C. Hodgell

First printing, May 2019
First mass market printing, May 2020

Library of Congress Control Number: 2019000059

Distributed by Simon & Schuster
1230 Avenue of the Americas
New York, NY 10020

Printed in the United States of America

10 9 8 7 6 5 4 3 2 1

· Tai-Tastigon ·

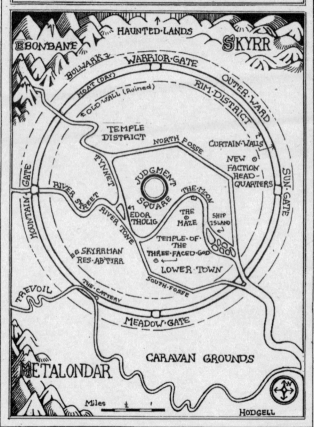

EBONBANE · HAUNTED·LANDS · SKYRR

Miles

HODGELL

By Demons Possessed

Chapter I

Out of the Past
Tagmeth: Spring 60

I

THE HILLS ROLLED AWAY forever and ever. In their hollows, shadows lay tangled. On their crests, thin gray grass wove together in a restless wind that blew this way and that, that way and this.

Ah, it said. *A-ha-ha-ha* . . . and its breath stank like something long dead.

Overhead, a leprous moon tumbled out of tattered clouds, seeming to shred them as they careened past. It was huge, and felt close enough to smell.

Shadows swept past below over the undulating hills. Up and down. Down and up.

Everything was in fretful motion—hills, grass, wind, moon—but without meaning. On and on it all went, on and on. Oh, so weary, the aching muscles that climbed and descended over and over, these never ending nights . . .

Then, suddenly, there was the House.

Jame paused on a hilltop, staring down at it.

I've come the wrong way, she thought, panic catching

1

in her throat. Tai-tastigon lay in the opposite direction, toward the future, toward life. The past was the past, survived, thankfully forsaken, and yet her feet refused to turn away from it.

Child, you were gone so long, whispered the dead, or was that only the grass twisting about her knees? *Remember those whom you left behind.*

What debts had she failed to pay?

Think.

Oh, so many. The inmates of the Haunted Lands keep that she had fled; the few worthy in the House's dark halls like Bender and Tirandys who had tried to help her; her friends in Tai-tastigon left to cope with the mess that she had in part created—in short, all of those, alive and dead, upon whose shoulders she had clambered into the light. Ah, how distant those memories were now, but would she ever outpace them?

"I was only a child!" she cried to the keening wind, to the tumbling moon. "What did I know of consequences, of right and wrong?"

Enough, even then, to know better.

Silent lightning flickered behind the crumbling facade of the House, answered by a witch-glow within its many windows like so many cataract-dimmed eyes glimmering in the night. A grinding sound as if of teeth came from it as, slowly, it dragged itself out of Perimal Darkling into the Haunted Lands. Stones juddered. Mortar rattled down. The dead move, now slow, now fast.

Another verdigris flash.

A skeletal figure stood silhouetted at an upper window. Why did she feel that it was looking out at her?

Another flash.

It huddled in the doorway.

Another.

It stood on a nearby hilltop. Its form, now bulky, seemed surreptitiously to seethe.

He is coming, said a bell-like voice in her memory. *At long last, he will arrive, and soon. Wait.*

Jame woke with a gasp.

The fire had died to embers. The bristling blanket scratched her bare skin and tangled about her legs. Jorin's nut-hard head butted her under her chin as he snuggled against her on this chilly late spring night. She gathered up the hunting ounce and held him close, surprising a grunt out of him and a long, sleepy stretch reaching from above her head to her knees.

It seemed a lifetime since she had fled the Master's House in Perimal Darkling although, ancestors preserve her, it had only been some five years ago. So much had happened since then. Tai-tastigon, Gothregor, Tentir, Kothifir, Tagmeth. . . . So many places. Surely she had left the shadows behind forever. Even the keep in the Haunted Lands where she and Tori had been born had been breached at last on the level of the soulscape, their dead father driven out or, rather, released . . .

"My son, my child, set me free."

. . . and Tori had done so, in the process finally accepting that he was Shanir, of the hated Old Blood. Not that he liked it much. That had become very clear as he had regained his strength after nearly dying of neglected lung-rot. Their quarrels over the past half-season had been legendary. She was here now, at Tagmeth, keeping out of his way, until duty called her back to Gothregor for the Randons' judgment on Summer's Day.

Much, in some ways, was finally going well.

Yet, there was that figure crawling toward her over the dead hills, as it had been since the previous Winter's Eve.

Remember those whom you left behind.

Who?

G'ah. Sometimes dreams were only dreams, even if they came over and over again, drawing ever closer.

Jame fought free of the blanket despite Jorin's grumbled protest, rose, and dressed. Now what? This must still be the middle watch of the night, toward its end. It would be dark outside for hours yet. No one else was up except the guards and the bakers, the day's work barely begun.

How this waiting fretted her. All spring, Summer's Day had hovered like a mountain on the horizon. Now it loomed, only seven days away, but that still felt more like seven years, each longer than the last. She had to do something to fill the endless time. What? Think.

On her desk lay scraps of parchment, a block of ink, and quills. She could write another letter to Tori. He had even answered the last one, after a fashion.

Hello. How are you? I am fine.

Bullshit, as Char would say.

Of course her brother was upset—how not when he had just discovered that he was the very thing their father had taught them both to hate and fear? And he was coming into his powers as That-Which-Creates too fast for anyone's comfort, least of all his own. The last message from his steward Rowan had mentioned prickly weeds erupting from every nook of the keep including the privies, the latter at inopportune times.

She could write to their cousin Kindrie at Mount Alban to ask for his advice. Again.

"Let him sort himself out," Kindrie had said.

That hadn't been very helpful.

Then, too, trouble was brewing in the Kencyrath, started by Lord Caineron's decision to send troops to the Seven Kings of the Central Lands. It was rumored that so far he had dispatched only a token force. The main body would go if the randon allowed her, Jame, to pass the final muster to join their ranks. That seemed like a lot to balance on her shoulders. However, Caldane's obsession with her had only deepened since his defenestration from the Council Chamber, even if was actually Tori who had shouted "Boo!" in his face and sent him bobbing out the window.

If the Caineron did jump back into the mercenary market, boots and all, the other lords would surely follow. Ancestors knew, they needed the money.

The chief danger was that they might lease their Kendar fighters to different masters without safeguarding that they didn't meet each other on the battleground, and the Kings were notoriously free with blood not their own. No one, ever, would forget the White Hills.

The Randon Council liked to say that their warriors' bond transcended that to their lords. That, at least, had been the creed at Tentir, although not always observed. A course on house politics might have been more practical than vague idealism, given what the cadets might face beyond the college doors. However, no one wanted to talk about that. Certainly, the last thing they needed now was Jame under their feet with all of the tangles she had caused. Hence, another reason for her to stay here, out of their way.

In the meantime, though, she fretted at the lack of news. Her spymaster Graykin was on the way north from Kothifir, but he hadn't arrived yet. Even then, it would take him time to establish new contacts, if he even could: this, after all, was the Riverland. Jame worried about her half-breed servant. He was the first after Jorin whom she had bound, if inadvertently, and she had come to owe him so much; but would he ever fit in among the more traditional Kencyr, as he yearned to do? She knew how that need felt. All Kencyr did. That bond was their strength and their curse. Her own place in the Kencyrath was both hard-won and tenuous. What if, at the last moment, the randon deemed her unworthy? What would she do then? Where could she go? What would happen to those who had come to depend on her?

Beyond that, Jame itched to take a hand in events herself. While not yet *the* Nemesis, third face of the Kencyrath's hated god, she was still *a* nemesis and, somewhere, something needed to be broken.

Too restless to settle, she descended from her tower apartment with a bleary ounce trotting at her heels.

A waning gibbous moon hung overhead, casting dark shadows around the edges of the circular courtyard. A solitary candle showed in the bakery, where someone was kneading the morning bread. Slap, punch, slap, punch. The oven would be warming for the first rise. Outside, one's breath smoked on the still air. Spring had been unseasonably cold this year, making Jame wonder if the hill-dwelling Merikit had yet managed to ignite the ironwood sapling that their chief Chingetai had substituted for the usual midwinter log. Without that rite, they said, the season couldn't turn. Wonderful. More problems with the Riverland's scanty crops, more pressure on the lords to feed their people and, incidentally, themselves.

With a cough and a rattle of gear, a cadet emerged from the barracks. It must be the turn of the watch, from middle to last, ending at a still-distant sunrise. Jame remembered that Dar's ten-command was on duty this week.

That was something else she could do: start working out the next ten-day rotation, even if it would be disrupted by cadets leaving for Gothregor a few days from now. However, such planning would require rousing Brier Iron-thorn and, just now, Jame wanted nothing to do with her second-in-command. They had clashed over what the big Kendar saw as the unnecessary risks that Jame took and Jame had flared at her, to the shock of the garrison at large. Dammit, there were some things that only she could do. Well, Marc had warned them that she was (on top of everything else) a Shanir berserker, if of an unusually cold nature. That had set things straight—for a while.

It was natural, Jame supposed, that the Kendar were obsessed with the well-being of their lord or, in this case, their lady. Thanks to their god, they didn't feel whole without a Highborn bond. Tori considered that obscene. So did Jame. But there it was. Of course, only Brier was sworn to her here at Tagmeth (another largely accidental coupling), but Tori had promised that she could bind more once she was established as a randon officer. Were her Kendar thinking about that now? It might come to nothing, of course: Who would want to trade secure service to the Highlord of the Kencyrath for that to his unpredictable, possibly mad sister? But Brier was hers, and the big Kendar had shown herself unnervingly sensitive to her lady's restless mood.

I won't be spied on or coddled, Jame thought mulishly. *I won't.*

Another thing she could do: tell Marc about her dream of the Haunted Lands. She had mentioned them to him before, hoping that his common sense would disperse her dread. Instead, he had taken her seriously.

"You've had dreams before that came true, lass," he had said. "I wouldn't be so quick to dismiss one that comes again and again, much less that progresses."

The cadet met her counterpart by the gate leading into the outer ward. While they stood for a moment, quietly talking, something slipped past them into the shadows of the courtyard.

Jame straightened. Like most Kencyr, her night vision was excellent, but the vivid moonlight made her blink. She could just make out a black-clad figure standing motionless near the southern-most Builders' Gate. The cadets hadn't noticed anything.

Well. After that dream, despite her desire to dismiss it, she had half expected a visitor, but not one who could move with such stealth.

The guards parted, one trudging toward the barracks

for a few hours' sleep before dawn, the other bound for the keep's outer perimeter.

The figure by the wall hesitated. Then Jorin sneezed. Jame felt quick eyes pick her out in the gloom of the doorway. Which way would he go, surrounded by doors, and on what mission bent? Hinges creaked. Open. Shut. *Damn*. He had slipped through the gate immediately behind him.

The cadet had disappeared, and a good thing, too: Jame didn't want it known that the keep's commander was up and wandering about in search of trouble. She crossed the courtyard. There had been a trick stone wall here when the garrison had first arrived, but they had since replaced it and several others with doors of stout, iron-bound wood, usually kept locked. Not so this one tonight. Someone was going to catch hell in the morning. She waited a moment, then entered.

Beyond was a short tunnel that should have led into the body of the shell keep. Instead, a walled garden opened out before her, lush with dwarf fruit trees and date palms. The same swollen moon cast its shadows here, but the stars visible outside its halo were different, and the air was warm.

Jorin's ears pricked. Through them, Jame heard the faint rustle of someone unfamiliar with undergrowth trying to move quietly through it. Then silence. He, too, was listening.

Jame moved closer, flitting from tree to tree. It helped that she knew this landscape very well.

Ahead, again: *rustle, rustle, rustle*.

Someone stood close beside her.

Jame rocked back on her heels so as not to trip over the diminutive figure in a gray cloak.

"There is a stranger in our midst," it said, in hardly more than an articulated breath of air. Bright eyes set in a domed, hairless skull regarded her anxiously. "Should I send for your people?"

"Himmatin. Sorry, I didn't see you. Not yet, but please fetch Chirpentundrum."

It always paid, she had found, to be polite to those far older and much more intelligent than oneself, and that the mysterious Builders certainly were. For millennia, they had preceded the Kencyrath from world to world building temples, but on Rathillien they had apparently all died. It had been a shock to find an enclave of these nearly immortal people living here, where the destruction of their home in the Anarchies had stranded them.

Jorin had slipped away. She followed, to the eaves of the pear trees that lined a small lake. The intruder stood on the sands of the moon-washed shore, no longer bothering to hide. He was scratching Jorin's stomach as the ounce rolled over and over at his feet.

"Hello," he said, straightening up.

"Hello. Are you an assassin?"

"Why, are you expecting one?"

"Not recently, but I believe that they still have me on their books. A spy?"

"Wrong guild."

Ah. That gave her a context, if a surprising one.

"I almost think that I know your voice." And smell, she might have added, now that Jorin was so close.

"And I, yours. Talisman."

"Darinby."

Jame crossed the beach to take his hand. He looked much as he had five years ago—young, handsome, smiling—but also haggard with strain crinkling his eyes and twitching the corner of his mouth.

"You're a long way from home," she said, taking in his travel-stained clothes.

"Apparently farther than I thought." He looked around him in wonder. "Where are we?"

"At an oasis somewhere in the Southern Wastes. We haven't yet explored outside the wall. Y'see, Tagmeth has a ring of step-forward tunnels that lead to all sorts of places. Rathillien is like that, riddled with strange ways to get from one place to another."

"If you say so." He sounded dubious, as well he might. Until this journey, Tai-tastigon had rounded out his world. Now he was trying to fit new pieces into the puzzle, with what appeared to be limited success.

"Don't tell anyone," she added, belatedly, regarding him askance. "It's meant to be a secret."

Darinby gave her a small bow. "Then it is safe with me, whatever it is that you just said."

Ah, she remembered how courtly he could be, a true prince of the Thieves' Guild with his own well-developed sense of honor.

Still, here they were four, nearly five years apart, and what a chasm of experiences now lay between them.

Somewhere in the night, a baby cried. That would be Benj, Must's child. Jame had heard that the Kendar Girt was having trouble with him since his birth and his mother's simultaneous death. Had it been wise to settle the Caineron refugees here in the oasis, neighbors to the stranded Builders? Chirp had so wanted to hold a baby again. So far, suspicious Girt hadn't given him the chance.

"Pleased as I am to see such an old friend," she said, "I have to ask: why are you here?"

He laughed, with a touch of hysteria, and ran distraught fingers through his dark, dusty hair.

"You're a hard person to find, Talisman. We knew you were Kencyr, of course, and heard that you were bound for the Riverland to find your brother. By the way, the Gamblers' Guild laid high odds that you wouldn't survive the Ebonbane, leaving as you did out of season. Gods. I came across this year as soon as the passes opened even a crack, but it was still touch and go."

"Trouble with brigands?" Jame asked, remembering the late, unlamented Bortis.

"Weather, my dear, weather. It's been an uncertain spring. The passes of the Ebonbane were riddled with wyrsan running under the snow. Several of our packhorses fell through into their tunnels, in fountains of blood. So much red snow. I only saw one, when I tripped and tumbled into its burrow. Red eyes, white teeth, rushing at my face. . . . A carter pulled me out." He shuddered, briefly showing the whites of his eyes. "They talk about such things in the city, but I never expected . . . well, never mind. Then there were the margins of the Anarchies. The birds with eyes on their wings. The hungry hills. They are spreading, I hear. The hills, not the birds. Well, maybe the birds too."

He said this with an uncertain laugh. In telling his story, he seemed to wonder anew at its reality.

"Back, then, to civilization," he continued, pulling himself together, "or what passes for it in this part of the world. Did you know that traveling up the Silver is like moving between armed camps? I slipped past your keeps when I could, pretended to be an agent of the Central Lands when I was caught. The first guards I stumbled across gave me that idea. It seems to create a free pass. Finding your brother, though, that took luck. You see, I wasn't looking for a lord. Royalty, are you? And never said a word."

Jame shrugged. "I didn't know for sure then. It seemed as unlikely to me as it obviously still does to you. Did you speak to my brother?"

"That turned out to be unnecessary. Wherever I had word of him, someone mentioned his peculiar sister. Unpredictable, headstrong, always causing trouble . . . that sounded familiar. Of course, you would be at the northernmost end of the Riverland."

"Not quite that. There's a keep beyond Tagmeth, but it's abandoned."

"It would be."

She could almost see his curious look, trying to match the impetuous child she had been to whatever she was now.

"You still haven't said why you're here."

"The Sirdan sent me."

"The leader of the Thieves' Guild?" Not Theocandi, of course: using the Book Bound in Pale Leather he had created a demon known as the Shadow Thief. Then he had lost control and the Book had burned out his brains. "Would this be Men-dalis?"

"Yes. Even though he lost the guild election, he took over after Theocandi's death. No one dared to challenge him, then or now."

"Does he need challenging?"

"No. Of course not!"

His sudden vehemence surprised her. She remembered Darinby as almost militantly apolitical.

"He wants you to come back."

That startled her even more. "I should think I would be the last person he would want to see again, assuming he gives any thought to me at all."

"He says, and here I quote, 'If the Talisman does not come, I will rip her old master Penari out of his precious Maze, even if I have to tear it down in the process.'"

"He can't do that!" she exclaimed involuntarily, then stopped to consider.

How many people knew that the Maze was the model of the city itself? To destroy one was to imperil the other. Trinity, think of the time when Penari and the Architect of the Maze had fought over which could take credit for it. Whole sections of the Temple District had fallen. Would Men-dalis risk that? Would he even care? Remembering him in his smug, demi-god glow, she had no doubts on that score.

"There is this too," said Darinby. "That hostelry where you stayed—the Res aB'tyrr? Men-dalis has kidnapped the innkeeper's wife."

"Abernia?" Jame was startled again, in more ways than one.

"The inn's cook Cleppetania complained to the Five, but Men-dalis denied that he had her. He would only open Ship Island's brig to be searched, he said, if her husband Tubain complained to him personally. So far, for some reason, Tubain hasn't. And the Five are ... preoccupied. The state of the city ... well, you'll see. It's a mess. Also, Abbotir of the Gold Court is currently the Thieves' Guide's representative on the Five's council, and he backs his Sirdan, Men-dalis. The other four hardly want to bring such a case up before him at such a troubled time."

"Then too," said Jame, "we're talking about a potential guild-trade conflict here. Guild wars, trade wars, even temple wars—they all have a place and are taxed accordingly. To cross social boundaries, though, that suggests a loss of order. So the matter wasn't pressed."

Darinby nodded, looking chagrined.

Politics, thought Jame, disgusted.

The Five governed Tai-tastigon, one delegate each from the city's two neighboring countries, who held its charter of independence, and three chosen on a rotating basis from the city's guilds. If a guild prince like Abbotir was involved, yes, he would have an edge on any deliberation, but he would also be bound, at least superficially, by conventions.

Darinby looked uncomfortable. "Be that as it may ..." He coughed and braced himself. "The Sirdan bade me tell you this: if you don't return, he swears by his blood that he will order not only the Maze destroyed but the Res aB'tyrr torched and everyone who flees it slain on its threshold."

"Sweet Trinity. He wouldn't."

"You know him. Dare you risk it?"

Men-dalis was half Kencyr, the son of a temple

prostitute and Dalis-sar, that improbable Kencyr New Pantheon sun god. Jame had never understood the relationship, but she had seen its influence on Men-dalis and his half brother Dally, whose fascination with the Kencyrath may well have led to his death.

Ah, Dally, that sweet, trusting boy who had first welcomed her to the Guild, to the city itself.

. . . sprawling on the Mercy Seat, flayed (alive?) and crawling with flies . . .

Don't think of that.

"What does the Sirdan want with me?" she asked.

"I don't know." For a moment, Darinby looked confused. "He didn't tell me . . . did he? No. Things have gotten seriously strange in the city since last year's Feast of Dead Gods. Afterward, they didn't go away. People say that the dead in general are coming back. Men-dalis certainly believes it. Me, I'm not religious. I go by what I see, but I have seen such things that I—I wonder if I am going mad."

Jame walked a few steps down the beach, considering. Tai-tastigon was in the past, but she still loved it. Such colors, such quirks, such amazing people. Oh, city jammed with so much unexpected life, even when it had challenged and terrified her. Penari had been an eccentric master, but without him little that had happened to her there would have been possible, the good and the bad, but mostly the former. The latter . . . well, she always encountered that, everywhere, usually head on.

The dead are returning.

Darinby is a good man, but he is not himself.

Something needs to be broken.

But not the Res aB'tyrr, the House of Luck-bringers, which had saved her life and given her a home. Tubain, Cleppetty, Ghillie, Kithra, Rothan, even the cat Boo.... She had come to them wounded, stricken with loss, and they had provided the love that she had needed to survive. How could that debt ever be repaid?

Think of those whom you left behind.

But "I can't," she said out loud, still pacing. "In a few days, I have to report to Gothregor where the randon will decide if I'm fit to become one of their officers. That's our warrior class," she added, seeing his puzzled look. "What? Don't you think that I'm capable?"

"Talisman, the gods alone know what you are capable of."

She laughed, a sharp bark. "True. I've just spent a year proving to others and to myself that I can take responsibility, that I can lead. And now you propose that I vanish, just when my people need me the most? If I don't appear at Gothregor, they will suffer. So will I."

"And if you don't go to Tai-tastigon, your friends will die. You have to come with me. Now."

Jorin had rolled to his feet and was backing away.

Darinby stepped toward her.

There was a flurry of movement as shadows danced on the sand, meeting, parting, falling.

Jame withdrew to stare down at her visitor's prostrate form. "You meant to kidnap me? Oh, Darinby!"

Two small figures emerged hesitantly from the trees.

"Is he dead?" asked the one a step back.

Himmatin again, Jame thought, although Builders were often hard to tell apart, especially in uncertain light.

She regarded the faint lift of Darinby's shoulders as he lay face down on the shore. "Fainted, I think, or asleep. Then too, I just used a Senethar earth-moving technique to drop him on his head. He's had a hard time."

"We will bring him something to eat." Chirpentundrum nodded to his colleague, who scurried off. "Food mends much."

"No doubt he will be glad of it." Jame thought for a moment, chewing on an extended nail. Then, with a sigh, she settled cross-legged on the sand, which brought her eyes level with those of the little Builder.

"Chirp, listen. I need to talk to you."

II

SOME TIME LATER, Darinby woke. A bonfire had been kindled next to him, yellow flames snapping over the red glow of branches. Gods, he had been cold for so long, and oh so hungry. Beside him was a platter holding half a loaf of crusty bread. There was also a ewer of water and a bowl of fresh figs, the latter barely familiar from Tai-tastigon's more exotic markets. Someone had dropped a blanket over his shoulders. He sat up stiffly, clutching it to him, and shivered as much from shock as from the evening chill.

Seen in retrospect, the past moon-span presented itself as a vista of madness. The Ebonbane's dire peaks where nightmares erupted from the snow, the shifting, omnivorous Anarchies, the hard eyes of the Riverland . . .

What had he expected when he had left Tai-tastigon?

Nothing that he had found, despite travelers' tales, so easily dismissed in the comfort of home. One thought that one understood reality but then . . .

How big the world is, he thought with wonder, *how terribly strange.*

But the Sirdan had sent him here.

Darinby, dear, dear boy. I have a mission that only the bravest, the most loyal, may undertake. My fate depends on it. Our fate as a guild. As a city. Do you understand?

He hadn't at first, but faced with those luminous blue eyes, that compelling golden voice . . .

And now here he was.

Gods, he must have been crazy. Everyone knew that the Talisman was a superb fighter in that peculiar but oh-so-effective style favored by her people.

She had also . . . changed. Well, people did, even over what felt to him like the blink of an eye. What had he expected? That eager, intense girl in Tai-tastigon, hell-bent on doing what was right if only she could figure out what that was. . . . For her, the truth had always seemed more complicated than for anyone else. He had smiled at that. Such a child's view of the world, he had thought. According to his own code, one simply did one's duty by one's master, guild, and friends.

True, she had never lacked the latter, some highly improbable. Like the Cloudies and the Archiem of Skyrr. Like Gorgo the Lugubrious and his priest Loogan. Like Bane. It had occurred to him before, though, that the Talisman's friendship was sometimes more dangerous than another's enmity.

Oh, Dally, whom she had especially favored. His fate

lingered like a weeping sore. Something there had gone very, very wrong, and warped the world with it.

Darinby was eating figs, trying not to gorge to quell his hunger, when the Talisman returned. At first he saw only the pale oval of her face watching him out of the gloom. Where had she gotten that scar across her cheek? It struck him again that her life since Tai-tastigon had not been uneventful. Then she emerged, black-clad, and sat on her heels on the other side of the fire, arms clasped about her knees, somber eyes gleaming silver.

"I'm sorry," he said. "I think that, for some time, I've been a little insane. I didn't stop to consider: It took me nearly two months to get here over the Ebonbane's passes. We can't possibly get back to Tai-tastigon before Men-dalis carries out his threat against Penari and the Res aB'tyrr."

"Actually," she said slowly, gloved fingertips tapping on her elbows, "it can be done."

He stared at her. Who was mad now? "What? How?"

"Well, I told you that there are many odd ways to get around this world. Consider the gates. There isn't one from here directly to Tai-tastigon, at least that I know of, but one does lead to another step-forward ring under the Anarchies. The gates there connect to most of the Kencyr temples on Rathillien, including the Eastern Lands, or so Chirpentundrum tells me."

She glanced over her shoulder as she spoke, and her words seemed to summon up a small apparition in a gray cloak. Darinby couldn't see its face in the shadow of the hood. *A child*? he wondered, judging from its size.

The Talisman seemed finally to make up her mind. He

saw now that one sleeve of her jacket was full and reinforced for defense, the other tight, for the cut and thrust of attack: she was wearing a Tastigon knife-fighter's *d'hen*—the same, perhaps, that Dally had given her years ago.

"This is hard," she said. "Things could get desperate if I don't return in time. On the other hand, there will be a disaster if I don't go at all. It's going to be tight. No one will forgive me, least of all myself, if I fail either way."

She rose, a lithe, dark shadow, committed if not entirely composed. "Chirp is going with us, at least as far as the Anarchies."

Something in her voice suggested that this last troubled her, but Darinby didn't care. He was going home. Back to his master.

III

RUE WOKE WITH A START. She had been dozing fitfully ever since the middle watch had departed and his earlier counterpart had returned, yawning, to catch a few precious hours of rest. It was still dark outside. No need to rise yet. Rue was very young, lured by sleep. Still, she had had nearly three years of randon cadet training by now, and that counted for something. So, she wondered groggily, what had roused her this time? She thought that she had heard footsteps on the tower stair, as if one could hear that through a stone wall. She would willingly have slept as before in the tower itself, in an alcove off Jame's room or even on the stair itself to keep out intruders—Bear, say, to stop bestial rumors or, worse, the amorous Ardeth Lordan Timmon.

But should she instead say "my lady's room"? Or Ran's? Or Jamethiel's? Even now, the matter of names confused her, as if she hadn't yet quite decided whom or what she served—Highlord's heir, randon cadet, creature of legend, or just plain Jame, whose wardrobe always needed tending and who couldn't remember to eat regularly.

However, her mistress had been restless of late, rising early, retiring after all sensible Kencyr not duty bound were long since in bed.

"No need for you to keep such hours too," she had told Rue with a wry smile, and temporarily banished her servant to the barracks next door.

She just wanted some privacy, Rue had told herself with a shrug, trying not to mind. It hadn't escaped her that the Highlord's sister wasn't used to being waited on.

And she had bad dreams.

Rue hastily fumbled herself into her clothes. So the day would start a few hours early. It was probably nothing.

The courtyard was empty, the only sign of life thudding in the bakery where someone was vigorously kneading dough. Soon the kitchen would rouse, too. Rue's stomach rumbled.

Strange, she thought as she entered the tower, how the smartest people could be so stupid sometimes. Jame had to be reminded to eat on a more or less regular basis, and to dress befitting the occasion, as if neither was all that important. Perhaps those were Highborn traits. Adding to her confusion, Rue had had little to do with the ruling class before her ten-command had crossed paths with the soon-to-be lordan before the gates of Restormir. Highborn women in general were mysteries to most Kendar. They had all thought then (yes, even Brier Ironthorn) that Jame was mad. Many still did.

Here was the familiar third-story apartment. Tangled blankets lay on the floor and the clothes that Rue had carefully laid out the night before sprawled abandoned on the bed. The chest at the bed's foot appeared to have been ransacked. Jame had packed that herself, after several pointed reminders.

("Take what's important to you, Lady. You'll be sorry if you don't.")

No one was there.

Well, thought Rue, fighting panic, *so she's gone out. With Jorin. In the middle of the night. Wearing . . . what?*

There was something on the mantelpiece, a piece of parchment tented so as to catch the eye. Rue unfolded it noting, in an abstract way, that her fingers shook. She wasn't a good reader—few Kendar were. Her lips shaped the words.

Oh god.

She jammed the paper into her pocket and rushed out of the room.

IV

IN THE COURTYARD it was still night, although with a glimmer of false dawn. Soon the garrison would wake. Jame had gathered torches before her return to the oasis and had left them piled before a gate farther to the east along the wall. This door was secured. As Jame bent to pick the lock, someone entered the court from the tower and rushed across the flagstones to grab her arm. It was Rue, her self-appointed servant.

"I went to see if you were awake yet, and you were gone, and there was this note to Brier lying on the mantle. . . ."

In her agitation the tow-headed cadet shook Jame, probably harder than she intended. One tended to think of Rue as small, but that was only in comparison to other Kendar. She could have made one and a half of Jame, by breadth at least.

"Think! They trust you now. If you disappear, will they ever trust you again? And we're so close to becoming a real house—well, a minor one. I want that, oh, so much. Others do too."

Jame detached the Kendar from her arm, compelled to use a pressure point.

"Ow," said Rue, not really noticing. "You can't leave now! I-I'll raise the keep if you try!"

Again, the dilemma caught Jame by the throat. She knew that she was a coward for not confronting Brier face to face. Didn't the Southron deserve that? After all, her fate and Jame's were now intertwined and beyond that, Brier would think of the keep itself. Well, dammit, Jame did too. In defense, for one thing she was in a hurry, which meant that she didn't want to argue. For another, if Brier knew where she was going, the Kendar might follow. Brier loose in Tai-tastigon boggled the imagination. For a third . . .

"Rue, I would rather die than disappoint you, but other

lives are at stake too. I owe them more than I do you. Or Brier. Or anyone else here. Sometimes you have to go back before you can go forward. My honor demands it."

Rue dragged a sleeve across her face, wiping away unnoticed tears and snot. "I don't understand that, but . . . but if it's that important, I'm going with you."

"Oh, Rue. This may be dangerous."

"I don't care."

Jame regarded her helplessly. She knew that Rue was apt to be in the way. Besides, she really didn't want this trusting child to know what she had once been. She couldn't be stopped now, though, even by love.

"All right, all right. Ancestors forgive me. You can come."

The gate's door swung open on darkness deeper than the night. They passed through it just as the garrison began to stir behind them and closed it in the face of a disappointed ounce.

⚔ Chapter II ⚔
The Anarchies
Spring 54

I

THE TUNNEL was long and dark. Torchlight caught the dripping walls and the albino, hands-span crickets that scuttled across them into cracks where they froze, betrayed only by the faint glow of their chitinous shells. Sometimes the way was close and fraught with jutting rocks that must be edged past. Sometimes it led along the edge of chasms in whose depths things stirred and rustled. At one point, foxkin erupted in a black torrent from a fissure and swooped on webbed wings around the travelers. Darinby almost dropped his brand as one landed on his head and began to snuffle curiously in his hair.

"Why is this way so long?" he asked, feigning nonchalance, treading on Jame's heels. "It was only a step into the oasis."

"That gate was built by native architects," said Jame. She was keeping a close watch on her friend, who seemed to be coming apart again. Truth to tell, this place was enough to unnerve even her, and she had come part way down it before. "This tunnel is the work of Chirp and his friends, imitating them. Sorry, Chirp. You didn't quite catch their subtlety."

The little Builder did not answer. He hadn't spoken since their descent, only leading the way in stubborn silence, without the benefit of a torch. Jame wondered again at his insistence in coming. Surely he and his people had been back to their city in the Anarchies since its fall some three thousand years ago, but not to reclaim it. Instead, they had chosen to live far away, in the exile of their oasis garden. What had driven them out, and what lured Chirp back now?

Darinby clutched her sleeve. "What was that?"

Something below had fallen, from the sound of it into deep water. The echo bounced from wall to hidden wall into the remote distance.

"Probably a stone," said Rue.

"We didn't dislodge one. I'm sure of it. What's down there?"

"Trocks," said Jame, without going into detail. She didn't know if the infernal creatures were animate rocks with teeth and claws or if, like omnivorous snails, they simply inhabited flinty shells. They always seemed to be hungry, though.

"Have you noticed?" said Darinby. "Our torches are burning out."

Fire kept trocks back; so, perhaps, did Chirp. They had once been the Builders' pets, useful because they could eat through anything, invaluable, in fact, in constructing such tunnels as this.

Jame peered over the edge of the abyss. Paired points of red light reflected back her torch's crackling glare. However, they seemed to parallel the travelers' course rather than rise to meet it.

The trocks had long since turned feral. Still, they might respect the old bond.

Darinby's brand sputtered out.

"Don't," said both Jame and Chirp, but he had already flung its smoldering remains over the edge at the eyes. They blinked as one. Then an angry chittering rose from the depths.

The Builder extended a long-fingered hand over the chasm. The stir below subsided, but the eyes didn't go away.

They walked on, trying not to run. How long had they been on this benighted path? How far had they come on the step-forward stones? To the southern end of the Riverland? To the Oseen Hills? The Anarchies themselves lay at least a hundred miles beyond that, against the western slopes of the Ebonbane.

Jame began to feel anxious. Judging by her previous experience with such tunnels as this, she had expected a relatively quick journey. Indeed, she had counted on it. Surely hours had passed by now in the sunless dark, if not days. Had this been such a clever idea after all?

"Put out your torch," she told Rue. Darinby, to his distress, hadn't yet been given a fresh one. "We have to conserve our light."

Here and there, fallen debris made the path treacherous. Worse, at more than one point they had to scramble over landslides. Worst, though, was a section where the path had been totally obliterated, forcing them to crawl along a near vertical rock-face for an endless space with the void gaping at their heels. By now, Darinby was panting. Jame felt the pull of muscles in her own legs. Rue said nothing, but seemed to radiate dogged determination. Throughout, Chirp never faltered. Without him to keep them on the true path, they would have been lost a dozen times over.

They burned through what was left of the torches, with Rue's reignited stub saved until last. When its light died, darkness fell, except for the ever-present eyes and a distant rectangle of pale gray light that grew as they approached it.

Stepping through, they found themselves in a subterranean chamber lined with stone and gaping doorways on whose lintels glowing runes were carved. Last season's dry leaves crunched underfoot. More littered steep stairs that led upward toward a brighter light.

"Where are we?" Rue asked. Her voice, even hushed, raised echoes that seemed, oddly, to come from above.

"This is the nexus under the Anarchies," said Jame, also speaking quietly. "Chirp, what door leads onward to Tai-tastigon?"

For the first time, the Builder pushed back his hood. Darinby stared at the little man's bald gray head laced with protuberant blue veins, at his child's face creased with anxious wrinkles. Jame had seen it before.

"Well?" she said.

"Please. You must come with me."

"Chirp, you know that I haven't time. Come with you where?"

"Into the city. To search."

"For what?"

He began to pace, the hem of his robe stirring leaves, brushing patches of moss and causing them briefly to luminesce. An ill-contained anxiety seemed to devour him.

"We returned," he said. "Over and over and over. Our kin had crawled into corners, against walls, under stairs, as if to hide. Their flesh sagged on shattered bones. The lucky ones were dead. What had happened to them? What?"

"I think I know," said Jame, still keeping her voice down. Her mind had flashed back to what she had learned or at least had come to suspect the last time she had been here, years ago. "Your people claimed the Anarchies and closed them to native powers, but this land is home to the rathorn. They returned. The diamantine *imus* above us caught their scream and magnified it. That sound is . . . terrible. Few that hear it survive."

The little Builder made a dart toward her and seized her hands with his long, cold fingers. "But you lived. I was right: you are special, a thing of power. Your people sense this too, but they fear to admit it. You, child . . ."

He spoke to Rue, who had shifted forward at his sudden approach and was now looking apologetic if uncertain. Had she met a Builder before? The small folk shared their oasis with the Caineron *yondri*, but kept out of the latters' way in a wary truce. Word of their existence must have seeped back to Tagmeth, though. The Builders had been presumed dead for millennia, a lost piece of the ancient past. Surely the discovery of such a surviving pocket community couldn't be concealed forever.

"What do you mean?" Rue demanded.

"He thinks that I may be one of the Tyr-ridan," said Jame. Had she admitted that before to any Kendar but Brier? It came hard to acknowledge even to herself. "The avatar of That-Which-Destroys, to be exact."

"Oh," said Rue, blinking. "That explains a lot."

It did? Jame thought that she had done a fair job of suppressing her destructive proclivities, no easy thing while helping to resurrect an old keep or, putting it differently, to build a new one. Someone had told her once that all three aspects of their god would manifest themselves within the Tyr-ridan until its representatives settled into their final roles. Was she destined, in the end, to destroy all that she had worked so hard to create? No, she didn't look forward to that at all.

Ah, think of it later.

"You haven't explained yet," she said to Chirp. "How am I supposed to help you?"

"We never found my mate. That has been hard. For me. For her. Without the final rites, how can either of us obtain peace? So many empty years, feeling the hollow ache, yearning for the lost . . . You must help me find her. Please."

Darinby grabbed her arm. "Think. You can't do this."

Chirp still held her hands. It only lacked Rue seizing her too. Jame bit her lip. She herself felt torn, not just by their demands but by her own gnawing sense of guilt.

Tagmeth depends on you, she thought, *Brier not least. Have you let her down on a fool's errand?*

However, her own people felt much the same as Chirp did about the lost bones of their kin, whom they believed to be trapped in the wastes of the Grayland until fire freed their souls. That was a terrible thing. To refuse assistance, in a similar case, now that she was already here, would be a shameful thing.

"All right," she said to the little Builder, freeing herself. "But I can't stay long. Anyway, Darinby, d'you want to go on in the dark? We need to find replacements for the burnt torches. You can wait for us here, if you want."

He looked around at the circle of dark doorways. Cold, earth-laden air breathed out of them like the ghost of distant sighs. *Ahhhh . . .*

"I'll go with you."

II

THEY CLIMBED THE STAIR, emerging at the top into a circle of standing stones. Each was a nine-foot high lithon of diamantine, that translucent mineral that is one of the hardest substances on earth. In the heart of each, revealed by erosion, was a gape-mouthed *imu*. Each, therefore, appeared to be a tall narrow head with its chin sunk into the ground.

These were not Builders' work. Old, old, they were, erected even before the little people had come here, and each was subtly aglow with stored sunlight. The sky over them was a close, misty lid lit from below and, perhaps, from above. Impossible to tell what hour of day or night it was.

Jame remembered the last time she had been here. The blind brigand Bortis had lured her into the circle by imitating Marc's voice—not well, but she had been desperate to find her lost friend. Then the bandit's weight had fallen upon her and his foul breath had giggled in her ear.

A darkling changer had watched from where he sprawled helpless with exhaustion on top of a lithon.

"And now I think that friend Bortis will amuse himself."

The arrival of the young rathorn Death's-head had saved her but not the life of his dam, encrusted in crippling ivory, whom she had slain for pity's sake.

Trinity. She hadn't thought about that in a long time. Rathorn ivory continued to grow throughout the life of its host. Mares became encased. In stallions, unless it was whittled down, say, against a block of diamantine, the major horn looped back eventually to split the skull from behind. Death's-head had been very young when his mother had died. Did he know to trim his?

The stone mouths echoed the scuff of their feet through leaves so that they seemed to be surrounded by stealthy lurkers.

Then came a flurry of pinions.

A gray bird fluttered down on top of a stone and spread its wings. On each, picked out in shaded feathers, was an eye, the only ones that it possessed. These fanned, then turned to follow them as Chirp led the way out of the circle into the city.

Things there were much as Jame remembered. The streets were lined with low white buildings, no more than fifteen feet high, encompassing two or three stories. Oval, opaque windows glimmered. A decorative band marched above them composed of *imus* alternating with rathorn masks. Open doorways led to diamantine-lit interiors. One had to look closely to see that the walls were laced with cracks. It seemed that a breath of wind would crumble them, but the air was motionless. Time here appeared simply to have stopped, oh, so many years ago.

With a whir, another gray bird landed on a rooftop, then another, and another. Wings spread. Feathered eyes blinked down on them as they passed. Like the stones, like the rathorn, such birds were part of the Anarchies' deeper nature, never tamed by the usurping Builders. This orderly, alien city sat in a wilderness where the native powers of Rathillien now held unchallenged sway.

Jame wondered where they were going. Chirp kept glancing anxiously at her. For Trinity's sake, what did he expect her to do?

The clouded sky seemed to dim, but that might have been a trick of the light. The city continued to bask in its cool diamantine glow, reflected back by the mist. Then the moment passed, like the retreating shadow of an eclipse.

From somewhere, distorted by echoes, came something that sounded like breathy, snickering laughter.

"Heh, heh, heh . . ."

The birds blinked their wings at each other and flew off.

"Look," said Darinby.

On the threshold of a nearby doorway lay a pathetic sprawl of feathers. Jame stirred it with the toe of her boot. The bird's head flopped to one side, its neck broken.

"Maybe it collided with the wall," Rue said.

"I don't think so. Its breast has been ripped open and apparently gnawed. Ugh."

Woodlice spilled out of the wound.

"Heh, heh, heh . . ."

A nasty thought occurred to Jame in regard to that flicker of light.

"Chirp, I know your people can play with space—the step-ward tunnels, for one thing, and inside these buildings are rooms where walls become floors or open into other worlds. Can you also manipulate time?"

The little Builder looked abashed. "We could, yes, if all of us put our minds to it. Some parties are too good to leave. More importantly, when we finish the temples on any given world, it may be years, centuries, millennia until we are needed again."

"What do you do?" asked Jame, fascinated despite her sudden apprehension.

"We sleep. We play. Time passes rapidly in such states. So we would have done here, but the land itself cast us out. How, I do not know. It may be that the city is responding to my impatience, making time pass more quickly than it should. One of my kind alone can not hope to control such a thing. Then again, day and night were always hard to tell apart here."

"You knew that this would happen?"

"No, but I feared it might."

"And didn't tell me." Jame's fingers curled into fists, extended claws pricking her palms. *Be calm*, she told herself, but rising anger threatened to choke her and so did guilt.

A fool's errand . . .

"Dammit, Chirp, you knew I didn't have much time and now, perhaps, I have less of it. You asked for my help knowing that."

He held out his hands to her, his desperation palpable. "Please. For my wife. For my mate."

She backed away. "No. I'm leaving. Be waiting when I return, or go home. Your choice."

She turned and stalked off, Rue and Darinby hurrying to keep up.

"He's a Builder!" the cadet protested, trotting at her heels. "How can you talk to him that way?"

"Easily," Jame said through her teeth, "if I get mad enough."

"Are we going back to Tagmeth?"

That made her pause. Should she? Could she, even, without the little Builder's help? Yes, but what if the way forward was as treacherous as the way back?

Jame thought of the Res aB'tyrr and shook herself.

"I think I can guess the right doorway to Tai-tastigon, if the nexus here is like the ring of gates at the keep. Wait a minute, though."

Here was a threshold opening into a dimly lit interior. Jame stepped cautiously inside. A small panel of diamantine glowed next to the door, its stone frame crazed with fractures. She pried it out with her nails. The cracks spread, then the wall started to crumble. She dodged back into the street as the house's facade disintegrated behind her in a choking cloud of dust. Echoes of its collapse hissed through the city, followed after the last rattle of debris by renewed silence.

"Light," said Jame, holding up the stone. For

something so small, barely the size of two clenched fists, it was surprisingly heavy and bright.

Here was the circle of *imus* and the way down. Once again in the subterranean chamber, Jame chose the door that opened almost due east.

"This one. I hope."

Darinby wasn't eager to enter, but what choice did he have? After a moment dithering on the threshold, he plunged into the dark to follow the diamantine glow.

⚜️ Chapter III ⚜️
Meanwhile
Tagmeth: Spring 54

IT TOOK BRIER IRON-THORN well into the morning to admit that her lady was missing. Rue should have alerted her, but it seemed that the cadet had also disappeared.

The Kendar marshal paused in the courtyard, surrounded by the bustle of chores. Even after all this time, it occasionally surprised her to see so many pale faces. She herself was a native Kothifiran Southron, her own features a permanent bronze and, she had been told, quite unreadable. Trinity knew, she didn't care to betray her current feelings.

Think, she told herself. *Have I forgotten some obscure Merikit ritual?*

In the past, Jame had tended to vanish into the hills to conduct her odd relationship with the local tribe. Brier's experiences during and after the yackcarn hunt outside Tagmeth the previous autumn had only made her more mistrustful of that connection. For one thing, the Merikit had driven those monstrous cattle down on Tagmeth, nearly getting Jame killed in the process. Yes, the keep's larder had also benefitted. That wasn't the point.

She also gathered that—somehow—her lady had a native wife up yonder, and a child that the Merikit queen Gran Cyd claimed Jame had sired, which was absurd. Logic aside, was that any role for a respectable Highborn lady?

But then Jame wasn't respectable, and never had been. To admit that came hard, especially now, when so much was at stake.

"You have to take the lass as you find her," said Steward Marcarn Long-shanks shortly thereafter. Everyone took their woes to him. Now Brier had, too.

He was in the kitchen, following Cook Rackny's instructions as to the making of haslet, otherwise known as mock entrails. Pale green parsley bread for trenchers had been rising most of the morning. Now he brushed the loaves with egg whites and set them in the oven. Then he turned to a bowl of prunes, dates, figs, and almonds that he began to thread together on a coarse string. Truly, without the bounty of the gates, Tagmeth would have been on a much stricter diet. As it was, Marc could exercise his creative urge on a variety of materials.

Brier admired him. While not that way inclined herself, she saw the enthusiasm that drove him, after a lifetime relegated by his size to the role of a warrior. For a long time he had pretended to be a berserker so as not, actually, to have to fight. Foaming at the mouth and chewing one's shield tended to discourage opponents, although he admitted that the splinters had been a nuisance. More recently, he had worked off his creative urge at Gothregor by recreating the huge stained glass window that Jame had accidentally shattered. That project had been left unfinished, for lack of new raw materials. Now more were flowing in through the gates—sand, lime, and ash, along with various trace minerals specific to each area to add color. The growing result was a map so abstract that one could barely read it. Brier could see him itch as these samples collected to meld them into glowing life. A puzzle, a creation, left unfinished . . .

But then, so was that reckless, brilliant hoyden, Jame. Ancestors only knew whose will had formed her, if any. Rather, she seemed her own creation, in defiance of every influence, of all reason. Even now, to whom did she answer? Her brother? Maybe, but Brier had her doubts. On the other hand, Brier gathered that Jame had responded more to her old friend Marc than to anyone else in her life—as far as one knew what that had been.

"It isn't like her, though," Marc now said, "to be so inconsiderate. She left you no word?"

"None."

"Strange. And so badly timed."

An awareness passed unspoken between them that each had a stake in Jame becoming a randon officer. Brier, though already bound, had a strong, instinctive urge to see her position reconfirmed by others. This was her home now. Jame's failure to turn up for the muster could rip that away from both of them and cast Brier adrift, bound to someone who herself had no real place to go. Marc, she knew, was her lady's oldest friend, homeless since his youth. He could have accepted the Highlord's bond. Instead, he had chosen to wait. He could survive disappointment—he had done so often before over a long lifetime—but at his age it would diminish him.

That thought distressed her. She regarded his bent head as he dipped the threads of fruit one by one into batter. His hair had once been as red as her own, if a shade lighter. Now most of it was white, forming a fringe around a bald, freckled pate. The color that remained seemed to have drained into his beard. The Kendar were matrilineal. Still, it mattered deeply to Brier that he was her great-grandfather.

And how would she feel, what would she do, if thus disappointed? She knew instinctively that Jame wouldn't hold her to their bond against her will, just as she knew that she was valuable merchandise, one of the randon college's elite. People said that, anyway. Did she believe it? Huh. Nonetheless, another lord would gladly take her in. Not that she trusted any of them, or any Highborn. The Caineron had taught her that. Still, something in this strange girl spoke to her. In some odd way beyond her experience or reckoning, against her better judgment, they belonged together.

She would ask Char, the cadet in charge of the herds and thus usually in the field. He would have noticed if the rathorn Death's-head was nearby or if the Whinno-hir Bel-thari was missing. Jame couldn't just have walked away . . . could she?

When Brier emerged again into the courtyard, there was her lady's ounce curled up asleep by the eastern gate. Surely Jame couldn't have gone far, leaving Jorin behind. That was a reassuring thought, at least.

A guard's horn sounded, signaling a visitor, with a quaver at the end that suggested hesitancy: was this a friend or a foe? Brier waited. Through the inner gate rode a man on a dusty post horse, leading another piled high with baggage. What Brier noted first, though, was the rider's gaudy robe, azure silk encrusted with frayed silver thread and a smatter of moonstones. It showed no travel stains, as if he had only donned it when within sight of the keep.

He dismounted, staggering a bit on saddle-sore legs, and turned up his nose at the chickens scrambling across the yard.

"You"—this, to a passing Kendar, who looked surprised to be thus addressed. "Stable my horses and be sure that they are properly rubbed down. You. Put my luggage in the guest quarters. You. Get me something to drink."

Then he saw Brier, and flinched.

She knew that thin young face, that dark hair already going thin at the temples, those anxious eyes. Fear lurked in their depths, but also defiance. He would start as he meant to go on.

"You." His voice wavered, but he steadied it. "Inform our lady that her servant Graykin has arrived."

❦ **Chapter IV** ❧
Night in Tai-tastigon
Spring 55

I

THE WAY FORWARD, mercifully, was less confusing than the way back, although it also took longer than Jame had anticipated.

The tunnel's end this time was a decaying door that opened into a cellar half-choked with debris. Jame doubted that anyone else had been here in a long, long time, which in turn suggested that the gate's entrance had been forgotten. Was it possible that Kencyr priests only knew about the step-forward route between Kothifir and Urakarn? She had wondered at the time what that link might say about the priests and Urakarn's false prophet who, after all, had been unmasked as Master Gerridon himself. Then too, Kencyr priests bound for Tai-tastigon had usually gone overland or, more disastrously, by a sea rotten with patches of dead water where ships sank like stones. There were many questions she would like to ask those people, things that her priestling cousin Kindrie might not know.

After hiding the diamantine panel, hoping that its light would remain banked, she followed Darinby and Rue as they cleared a path through the mess, up a treacherous flight of stairs, to a doorless frame opening into the night.

The gibbous moon shone down on a circle of desolation so complete that buildings and streets crumbled into each other. Everything had decayed—plaster, wood, even, it seemed, stone—into a choppy sea of ruin fretted by stationary waves where walls had once stood. It also stank.

"Phew." Rue looked over Jame's shoulder, snub nose wrinkling. "This is Tai-tastigon the Great?"

"Only the worst part of it," Jame said, feeling oddly defensive. "This is the Lower Town, looking even more nasty than I remember. And there, see? That's what presumably destroyed it."

The temple reared out of the ruins, bone-white, forbidding. In one way, it didn't seem large. In another, it loomed. One felt instinctively that it was much bigger than it appeared, and more dangerous. Jame's senses prickled. How well she remembered her first sight of her god's house on that night nearly five years ago, how upset she had been to feel the same power here that had also greeted her in Tai-tastigon's Temple District. Was there only one deity, as her people believed, or many, as appeared in this teeming city? Once, she had thought she had discovered the answer to that paradox, as expressed in the Anti-God Heresy. Now, she wasn't so sure. Whose fault was it if she had been wrong?

Yours, a breath of rancid north wind seemed to answer

as it rattled dust against her boots. *You were so quick, so glad, to think you knew the truth. When has the truth ever been so simple? Foolish, arrogant child.*

What she did know now, as she cautiously let her senses expand, was that the temple was currently very active, but not quite in the way she had known before. The push, the pull of power ... it was trying to draw her in, rather than to push her away. What did that mean?

A stir in the rubble caught her eye. The people there were so gray with dust that they barely seemed real. Some picked their way mindlessly through the debris by themselves. Others hobbled in small, tattered groups. A woman stooped, rummaged, and retrieved what might have been a piece of bleached wood, or a bone. Then she dropped it and scavenged on for some other worthless trifle.

A murmur rose from the dingy masses, repeating numb words as if in a litany:

"My name was ..." "My name was ..." "My name was ..."

"Who are they?" Jame asked Darinby, her voice sunk to a whisper.

He shrugged. "These days, it happens. People are foolish enough to be caught out late and come back like that, as if they had lost their minds. Their families may try to harbor them, but they escape if they can, to come here. Others are thrown out, and here they drift."

"That's monstrous."

He blinked, as if momentarily startled awake. "I ... suppose that it is."

A veiled figure wandered past, weeping for its lost children. Arms rose and fell as it beat its breasts, tore at its hair. It ripped itself apart, then came back together, still weeping.

"Ngh, ngh, ngh," muttered another, snuffling through a pile of trash. Something like a boar's head rose, blew its nose, and shuffled on.

A scurry of rats stopped, piling on top of each other to form a wavering column. Bright eyes blinked nervously. Whiskers and noses twitched.

Something was coming.

People had frozen, looking up, like so many startled deer. Then they fled with inarticulate cries, tripping over their own ragged clothing. No shadows kept pace with them over the desolate ground.

Jame felt the earth shudder underfoot. Debris flew up one place, then another, then another, in pursuit. Rising dust gave shape to massive, invisible legs. Something like ghostly flames wreathed them, leaped into the sky. Down came a coldly smoking hand. It snatched up a fleeing man. If he screamed, it was only a thin, hollow bleat. Then he was dropped, rejected, and crawled away dragging a broken leg. Dust-wreathed, a blind head reared up against the moon, long hair whipping the stars. Its jaws gaped in what might have been an inaudible roar of frustration.

"That's a dead god," breathed Jame. "So were the weeper, the boar, and the rats."

"I told you that they had come back. Mostly, they stay around that temple of yours. Sometimes, though, they wander. We should leave."

They slipped away, skirting the site of greatest desolation where other shapes moved, barely seen. That was another change: before, the dead gods had been repelled by the area surrounding the temple. Now they were drawn to it as if borne, mindlessly adrift, on its inward current. Some of them also seemed to be hunting. New Pantheon gods drew their essence from the faith of their worshippers and died without it. Demons, on the other hand, required human souls. Most of the dead gods, Jame suspected, were Old Pantheon, caught somewhere in between. It was all very confusing.

Rotten wood, crumbling facades, decaying plaster, the wreck of a child's wagon, a doll with its face smashed in.... Not long ago, this had been a wealthy district apparently immune to the pernicious temple that was its neighbor. Then had come the Lower Town Monster, and children had started to sicken. As they died, more and more people moved out. Houses began to collapse. The poorest of Tai-tastigon's citizens moved into the ruins, and in turn watched their children waste away.

One of them was nearby, crying.

Jame followed the sound, and came upon a little boy crouched in the shadow of a wall. His head was on his knees, his mop of black hair bent to hide his face. For some reason, Jame hesitated to touch him.

"Go home," she said. "This place isn't safe."

He shook his head without raising it and drew a dirty hand across his nose. "My name is . . . my name is . . ." Snort, snuffle. "What is my name? Mother says that I am a prince, but Father is no king. Who—what am I?"

Rue touched Jame's shoulder. "Look."

Jame did, and caught her breath. A shadow was crawling down the street toward them, cast flat against the ground by no visible entity. Long fingers quested before it and seemed to pull it along. Then it paused, as if sensing their presence, and raised its head. The Lower Town's desolation showed through its featureless mask of a face.

"Run," Jame said to the boy, but when she turned back to glance at him, he was gone.

She, Rue, and Darinby retreated as tenebrous fingers fumbled after them. The thing moved slowly, but with a terrible persistence. Now they were among standing structures, most abandoned. Others betrayed their habitation by the rags stuffed around the edges of doors and windows. The thing that followed probed cracks as it came, here and there pausing as if to listen for the whimper of children within.

Jame had once known every street in Tai-tastigon. Nearly five years had advanced the confusion here, though, in ways that she didn't understand. She took a wrong turn, then another, and they were lost.

"This used to be a throughway," Jame said, regarding the dead end into which she had led them. Mounds of debris and crumbling walls rose on all sides, looking too fragile to climb. To be buried alive, in such filth . . . ugh. But here those reaching fingers came, probing out of the shadows, around the corner.

"You look a pack of perfect fools," remarked a voice above them. They looked up to see a scrawny figure perched like a monkey on a windowsill. "There's a way to climb, if you watch your feet and don't mind the dirt," it said. "There, and there, and there."

Jame saw that a path zigzagged up the nearest mound, strategically bolstered with planks.

"Meet you on the other side," said their savior, and vanished inside the building, leaving the sill to crumble silently behind her.

"Who was that?" hissed Rue.

"An old friend," said Jame, with the flicker of a smile. "Let's surprise her, shall we?"

As promised, the other awaited them on the far side of the mound, slapping dust from her patchwork *d'hen* with gloved hands.

"Now, what kind of idiot . . ."

"Hello, Patches."

The girl gaped, then threw herself into Jame's embrace where she made a meager armful.

"Talisman! You've come back! We thought you were dead!"

Just as quickly, she drew away, snuffling, scowling.

"Why did you leave anyway? Didn't think we would miss you, hey?"

Jame fingered the girl's lapel. "Nice work. Your mother's? Remember, the Guild was after me for the Sirdan's death. I thought you would all be safer without me. Anyway, it was time to move on."

"What guild?" demanded Rue.

Patches surveyed her. "Who's the great lunk, then?"

The cadet looked stunned. Probably never in her life had anyone accused her of being large. While she outweighed Jame, though, so Jame did this ragged scrap of a girl.

"Before anything else," she said, "tell me: what's the date?"

Patches looked confused, then counted on her fingertips. "Fifty-three, fifty-four...the fifty-fifth of Spring. Why?"

Damn, thought Jame.

She had indeed lost time in the tunnels and the Anarchies, at least a day and a half that she couldn't spare. She had thought that she understood how the tunnels worked, how Rathillien did. She had been wrong. How many would pay for her arrogance?

"Here it comes," said Darinby.

They turned to see shadows creeping over the top of the mound. Where they went, it could follow.

"This seems to be my night for rescuing Kencyr. First a priest and now you. You'd best shelter with us for awhile." Patches plucked at Jame's sleeve if still trying to convince herself that her former mentor was really there. Then she turned away, hunching her shoulders. "It will lose the scent. Maybe."

They followed her to a hovel somewhat more intact than the surrounding ruins. Patches fiddled with the latch. When it opened with a click, she swung wide the door, shedding the rags that had been stuffed in its cracks. They stepped through into a candlelit room. A woman rose to meet them, tall, thin, expressionless, and neat to a fault. Her hands were tightly clasped in the folds of a spotless apron. A silver wedding ring glimmered on one finger. Seven smaller, wizened faces turned toward the door, so alike that they might have been Patches at different ages, the last no more than a toddler.

"Ma," said Patches, introducing the former. "My sibs." The latter. "But then you"—this, to Jame—"will have met them before."

Jame remembered well. She had first come here with the Peacock Gloves as a guilt offering for having indirectly caused the death of Patches' older brother, Scramp.

Now here was her former protégée, avid once again to link herself and her family with Jame's perilous fate. The weight of that first obligation lingered. Patches added to it every time she gave Jame that hopeful, starveling look. What had she set in motion by returning here? Would it have been better if she had stayed away?

Then she noticed another face, glowering at her from a corner, and remembered Patches' reference to a Kencyr priest. Someone had given the stranger a child's chair in which to sit so that his knobby knees rose almost to the height of his shoulders. Above them, set in a narrow face, was a beaklike nose and black eyes under a thatch of mouse-brown hair tufted with the premature white of a Shanir. He wore a long, black, belted robe and a pair of enormous boots.

"Another stray," said Patches, cocking a thumb at him, "caught wandering the Town by night. Some people have no sense. That goes for you too, Master Darinby."

"'Master'?" Jame repeated. "You didn't tell me that you'd been promoted."

"Two years ago." Since they had reached his home city, Darinby had relaxed somewhat, even in their current surroundings. He now gave Jame the ghost of a smile. "Remember, you made journeyman yourself before your precipitous departure."

Patches jabbed Rue in the side with a sharp elbow. "That's the Thieves' Guild we're talking about, of course," she said helpfully to the bewildered cadet.

Jame braced for the inevitable questions, but just then all within were struck dumb by a fumbling at the door. Something leaned against it to the groan of wooden panels. Did shadows have weight? Had Patches locked the door behind them? The latch jiggled. The little thief darted across the room and shot the inner bolt. Her siblings had pressed back against the far wall, ranged perhaps by chance according to age and height. Patches backed up to join that row, one step ahead of it, the tallest there although that wasn't saying much. The sound trailed off. Then came a slow withdrawal that, contrary to all reason, seemed ponderous.

"Well," said Jame, when she could breathe again.

It had, of course, been the Lower Town Monster, but how? She had given Dalis-sar its true name: Bane. That improbable sun god had brought fire and Gorgo the Lugubrious, rain. Between them, the demon based on Bane's soul should have been destroyed and Bane, stabbed so many times, left on the Mercy Seat, should have been allowed, at last, to die.

There was a chance, though, that he had accidentally bound himself to her with a farewell kiss that had nearly severed her lower lip. She could still feel the scar with the tip of her tongue.

Worth a try, he had said with a laugh.

The biter, bit.

Then his soul had answered her when she had called it, expecting one brother, getting another. A thing of shadow, not unlike the Monster but with a mind, it had followed her to the Riverland. There she had given it a choice: pursue the destructive taint so intrinsic to its nature or wait for the honorable death that Bane craved. Bane had chosen the latter. To the best of her knowledge, he now sat in a pesthole behind Mount Alban guarding the Book Bound in Pale Leather and the Ivory Knife until she called for them.

But the thing was this, and she should have thought of it before: the Kencyrath believed that one's shadow was cast by one's soul. It could be detached, as Bane's had been. However, something, somewhere, continued to throw it. A single bone would be enough to trap it between life and death. That was why Kencyr sought tirelessly for their fallen dead to give them to the pyre and then spread their ashes on the wind.

If the Lower Town Monster had survived, not to mention its dark twin in that verminous cell, then it followed that at least some fragment of Bane still existed, perhaps in endless agony.

"Good," croaked the figure in the corner.

Jame blinked. He was Shanir. Had he just crossed her thoughts?

"How d'you know what it . . . he . . . is suffering, and why does he deserve it?"

"He's a bloody nuisance," said the other, with a clumsy gesture as if to thrust off the question. "And he upsets the novices."

She wondered what exactly they were talking about.

"What were you doing abroad tonight?" she asked, trying a different approach.

He glared at her under tufted brows. "It was the last place I could think of to look for them. I had to see, didn't I?"

"What, all of those wretched, wandering folk?"

He hunched his shoulders nearly to his ears in what might have been either dismissal or a flinch.

"That was something I never expected. How could all of those people just give up their souls like that, or were they robbed? If so, by whom? Why? And the three missing priests ... tonight I thought I saw them in the ruins with the others, but they stumbled away. Have they lost their souls too? How?"

Jame struggled to get a grip on the conversation. It seemed to her that he was thoroughly upset and rattled, but she didn't understand why.

He abruptly rose, a younger man than she had thought, and made for the door. "That's it. I'm off."

"Wait. Who are you?"

On the threshold, he paused. "Call me Titmouse. Expect no other name."

That had to be a joke. Rather than a small songbird, the man resembled an overgrown gore-crow. Either he had a sense of humor or none whatsoever of irony.

"What was that all about?" asked Rue as he blundered out, leaving the door open behind him.

Jame realized that toward the end they had been speaking in High Kens.

"I'm not sure," she said.

"But who was he, to speak to you like that?"

"A Kencyr priest, with questions. Shall we be on our way?"

II

THEY LEFT UNDER THE SWOLLEN MOON, against which stray clouds were starting to press. A breeze puffed fitfully from the north with the hint of something rotten on its breath, countered by fresher gusts from the south.

"*Whoo . . . ?*" said the latter as if in plaintive query as it circled the chimney pots. "*Wha, wha, wha . . . whoo?*"

Patches tagged along. So, of course, she would.

Beyond the Lower Town, the state of the houses that they passed improved, although they still presented darkened visages to the streets. These were sparsely populated, however, which surprised Jame. At this hour of the night the denizens thereof should have been abroad, street vendors hawking crisp almond cakes and venison pastries, night markets opening off side streets, jugglers juggling, pickpockets picking, courtesans (lower class in this quarter) walking two by two in a haze of perfume.

Now, however, there were only scuttling shadows and furtive, urgent knocks on doors as latefarers saw the approaching strangers. Were the windowsills stuffed with rags as in the Lower Town, as on the Feast of Dead Gods? Jame suspected that they were. But then, of course, she and her companions were still within the area cupped between the South Fosse and the River Tone.

Demons can't cross flowing water without a bridge, she thought, and wondered what had stirred that memory.

But then there were scattered bridges all along the fosse and river. No place was safe.

To the north, on the riverbank, was the inn called the Moon in Splendor where apprentice and journeyman thieves congregated, surely tonight as always, risks be damned. She had spent many nights there, drinking little, listening much. How slowly the others had come to accept her. Scramp never had. She remembered his challenge: steal the Cloud King's britches. To be fair, she hadn't really. Prince Dandello's uncle had given her the article in question, with an identifying embroidered patch on the backside. In the end, she had proved her skill to them all.

What fun it would be to burst through that door— *Remember me?*—but how would they receive her now?

Closer still was the dour hulk of the Maze, Penari's stronghold. In a way, he had thumbed his nose at the whole Thieves' Guild as represented by his brother Theocandi who had chosen politics over skill. Had she done something similar by using the most sought-after apprenticeship in the city only to pocket its least valuable objects?

"Steal not from your own kind," the god-voice had said, passing judgment through Ishtier's unwilling lips. *"Do with others what you will, so that it be done with honor, until in your thoughtlessness you destroy them."*

Poor Scramp.

Yes, she wanted to see her old master, if only to be sure that he was all right. More than that, though, the Maze itself might have given him valuable insights into the state of Tai-tastigon's very fabric. She felt adrift here, where she had once felt so much at home. And Penari was so close.

"The Maze?" asked Darinby, bemused, when a few minutes later they stood before that building's seven-story, windowless bulk.

"I'll have to ask you to stay outside," said Jame, regretfully. "This isn't a place that welcomes strangers. Patches . . ."

"Huh." The little Townie flipped away Jame's concern with a snort. "D'you think I've learned nothing since you went away?"

Jame stared at her. "Penari has taken you as his new apprentice?"

"Well, no." The girl's expression became suddenly, comically, dolorous, and her shoulders slumped. "I can't say that. You brought him news, a touch of the outside world. He missed that. I'm the Talisman's Trinket, I am. I slip in where even you couldn't. Face it: a motley scrap like me, who notices? But I listen, and I learn, and I report."

Jame wasn't sure if she felt pride in her protégée's achievement or a twinge of jealousy. That had been her job, after all. She had been good at it and proud of it.

"Then show us the way," she said, with a mock bow.

"And me?" asked Rue.

The cadet looked thoroughly apprehensive at being left behind in this strange city, and well she might. Jame smiled at her, yielding. "Come along, then, if you don't mind tight places."

Close by the door, she discovered one of her old torches and was pleased that it still kindled, although the damp wood sputtered mightily. Patches seemed surprised. If not with the aid of fire, how had she mastered the labyrinth? The answer lay in a gray, almost invisible thread running at shoulder height along the wall, leading inward. Patches pretended to ignore it, but her fingers twitched toward its fragile security.

Inside, firelight flared on dark walls of erratic heights. Blocks did service as buildings, narrow passageways as streets, barely passible slits as alleys. There were pits and water traps too, not always where one might expect them. Many thieves had tried to penetrate this labyrinth to find the reputed treasures at its heart. The lucky ones, in Jame's days as the Talisman, had been escorted out. A breath of corruption down certain corridors suggested that others, since, had been less fortunate.

Rue trod almost on her heels. It occurred to Jame that the cadet hadn't much enjoyed the tunnels to and from the Anarchies either. Did Kendar experience claustrophobia as many of them did a fear of heights? Perhaps she hadn't taken Rue's feelings sufficiently into account. Then again, the cadet was here at her own demand, and she had been warned.

Patches stopped. The end of the thread, snapped off, quivered between her gloved fingertips. Perhaps Penari had pulled up his drawbridges, as it were.

Somewhere, stone fell and a shudder passed through the massive structure. Patches and Rue jumped. Jame found she was holding her breath. The close-set walls gave back muted, grumbling echoes until the darkness swallowed them.

Tick went distant falling dust, like an after-thought. *Tick, tick, tick*.

And somewhere, water dripped.

One tended to consider the Maze as monumentally solid. For any part of it to shift, let alone collapse, was unnerving.

"Here." Patches thrust the broken end of the thread into Jame's hand. "Your turn."

Jame had used a string when she first had attempted the Maze. Soon, however, Penari had begun to teach her how to follow the convoluted ways by memory alone. This had only made sense to her when, suddenly, she had realized that each turn and crossroad corresponded to a similar twist in the city itself. The Maze *was* the city, in more ways than one. What happened to one affected the other. So far, she didn't like the signs.

"Sometimes people get lost in here and die," Patches said, nudging Rue, trying to sound chipper although her voice wobbled. "Talisman, tell her about the Architect of the Maze."

"Really?" Jame shot the little thief a look. *All right*, she thought. *You want to scare Rue. Let's see if I can scare you.*

"Master Rugen built the Maze," she said, dropping the broken thread and starting to follow memory's path with the other two close behind her. "Afterward, he and Penari quarreled over which could claim credit for it—who, in effect, was its mastermind, the planner or the builder. Rugen thought that he had the floor plans, but Penari picked them out of his pocket. Trying to find the way out, he became lost and sent Quezal back for help."

"Who?" asked Rue, trying not to sound breathless. How the walls must be pressing in on her.

"Master Rugen's gargoyle. All master architects have one. Quezal is small but very active, so long as you aren't looking at him. Anyway, Penari thought that he had only come back to retrieve the diagrams, and he imprisoned him. Only later did he find Rugen's body."

She coughed, also remembering.

"I found it too, long after vhors had picked clean its bones. I used them to mark various turnings in the Maze as I learned them. Yes." This to Rue, who looked perturbed. "It was a bad thing to do. I suppose I didn't think of others' remains the way I did of our own people's, yet they do seem to have souls. All right: I was young and arrogant. Now I'm just ignorant."

Rue stumbled. "What in Perimal's name is this?"

Her feet had become entangled in a translucent coil of checkered skin. Patches grabbed her arm as she wobbled on the edge of a water trap.

"Monster must be shedding. Tell her about Monster."

Jame glared at her. Very well, then.

"Monster is Penari's pet, a moon python. He slithers around the Maze and occasionally swings from its main chandelier."

"He must be big," said Rue, trying to kick off the snake's clinging residue without falling over.

"About forty feet long, I think, but essentially friendly, as long as he's been recently fed."

Now I'm doing it too, she thought, disgusted, as the cadet at last freed herself. How did Rue feel about overgrown reptiles lurking in the dark? She herself had gone straight up a wall the first time she had encountered Penari's pet.

"Anyway. The Architect. He came after me, a conglomeration of human and vhor bones wrapped in

Monster's latest shed skin, with Quezal perched on his clavicle. It sounds ridiculous now, but it was downright terrifying then. It took a while to find his skull, though. Penari wanted me to smash it, to destroy Rugen once and for all. Ah."

She had come to a familiar dead-end. Fingering the lintel unlocked the hidden door.

"Penari? Master?"

The heart of the Maze was a wide, circular chamber extending up seven levels. A many-candled chandelier lit it, dripping wax on the table below and the papers that covered it. The walls were full of niches in which were displayed the spoils of a lifetime. Pride of place was given to two stones whose theft had created Penari's legend, the Eyes of Abarraden. One was genuine, an uncut diamond the size of two fists clenched together. The other was mere glass.

"Boy? Is that you?"

Penari scrambled down one of the wall ladders that spiraled up the core, his gray beard flying over his shoulder. Halfway down, his foot fell on a broken step, but he clattered on regardless. In Tai-tastigon, belief goes far to create reality. Penari, nearly blind even in Jame's day, had believed in the city as he had known it when still a youth, to the extent that he could cross roofs or steps that no longer existed.

He pattered across the floor and seized her by the arms. His eyes were now completely filmed over, but he seemed not to notice.

"Where have you been, boy?" he exclaimed, shaking her. She had never gotten him to admit that she was in fact a girl. "I heard such stories about you but knew better than to believe most of them. Was I wrong?"

Jame embraced him, at which he gave a snort of surprise and pleasure. "I had to run, Master. They said that I had killed your brother, the Sirdan, which I hadn't. I couldn't stop to say good-bye."

"Well, well, well." He patted her clumsily on the back. "Here you are now."

Somewhere out in the Maze, something collapsed. The chandelier chimed softly and swayed. Dust drifted down.

"What *is* that?" Jame demanded. She found that Rue and Patches were both clutching her each by an arm. She, in turn, gripped the edge of the table.

"Huh," said Penari, disgusted. "An infestation of stone-mites, among other things. This city is sick, no doubt about that. The worst I've ever seen it."

"Do you know why?"

"Heh. I don't walk abroad these days, or even venture much outside this chamber. My spy tells me stories, though. . . ."

Jame glanced at Patches, who shrugged. What could one say? For that matter, how did Patches' master Galishan feel about her moonlighting, assuming that he knew?

"Something has gone wrong," said Penari, chewing the ends of his beard as he considered. "Tai-tastigon used to be so full of life. The people. The gods. Even the buildings. Now I feel death seething through all three, melting their very bones. Yes, stone crumbles. So does wood. So do lives. G'ah, it's obscene."

"When did it start?"

"That's a good question." He spat out the wet ends of his beard and began to count events on his fingertips. "Let's see: Theocandi died. Dally was murdered. Bane was blamed. You left. Men-dalis became the new Sirdan."

"Do you believe that Bane killed Dally?"

Penari tapped his nose as if to say, "Here is a secret." "A convenient story, and the Sirdan's followers stick to it. Too convenient, if you ask me. Besides, something is wrong with Men-dalis. From the beginning there were hints, but he ruled well enough. The Guild was glad simply to be on its feet again and forgave him his little quirks. Then too, he does have charming manners, and I mean that literally. He makes people want to serve him, to make him happy. Oh, they fall over themselves to do that. It must be the god-blood in him. You know that his father is Dalis-sar the New Pantheon sun god?"

"Yes," said Jame. She didn't add that Dalis-sar was also a Kencyr. Things were complicated enough already.

"Around the last Feast of Dead Gods, though, the word is that he became obsessed with the return of the dead. He also listens too much to that foul spy of his, the Creeper."

Patches glowered. "I didn't tell you that."

"Child, you gave me the clues. Should I share all of my deductions with you? For one thing, the Sirdan has become suspicious of potential rivals, who now tend to disappear—this, years before the next guild election. What has he to fear, eh?"

"Open rebellion," muttered Patches. "Did you also 'deduce' how much people hate what's going on, even if they can't seem to say as much to his face?"

"Ha. We may be thieves, but we are a guild of laws. The one hundred landed master thieves (or most of them anyway) support him. So do the lords of the five guild assessment courts. Most of all among those, there's Lord Abbotir of the Gold Court. Many listen to him, all the more so since he was voted our representative to the Five's Council."

"It's just politics," Jame murmured to Rue, who was looking confused. "I'll explain later."

"And yet . . . and yet . . ." Penari frowned. "Something is wrong. The Creeper's shadow increases, as if he were the darkness that Men-dalis casts. I don't know. It's all too much for me. But I tell you this: since the last Feast of Dead Gods, Men-dalis has gotten more and more peculiar. Something happened then that knocked the whole city off balance."

"I've seen the wandering dead gods," said Jame.

"Oh, them too. With Men-dalis, though, it was something more personal. For one thing, he began to obsess about the general return of the dead. For another, he started wearing his late brother's jacket."

Jame stared. Dally's *d'hen* would be a mess; after all, he had died in it either of blood loss or of shock, unless someone had been so charitable as to strangle him first. What could possess his brother to cling to such an object?

The chamber shook again. More debris, somewhere, fell.

"How long can Tai-tastigon stand?" asked Jame, still clutching the table.

Penari grinned at her, all yellow teeth except for the gaps. "Why, how long can you, or any of us?"

A flicker caught the edge of Jame's eye. When she looked up, the scrolls on the table had been rearranged, and Quezal was crouching on top of them like a stone paperweight.

What Penari couldn't see, he could hear.

"What is he doing now?" he hissed.

"Uh . . . rearranging papers." She craned to read. "These have something to do with Abarraden."

"Rugen keeps on about that. She was his mother's goddess, but he turned from her to worship his craft. Sensible, I call that. What's the use of being dead if you can't have your own opinions? The Eye is mine, though, I tell you. Mine!" He turned to shout this at the walls in general. Dust rattled down. "D'you hear me?"

"He's gone."

Quezal could only move when unobserved. Now he perched motionless on the shelf that held one of Abarraden's eyes. The stone rocked, fell, and shattered on the stone floor. So. The fake.

Penari screeched. "Dammit, Rugen, stop it!"

"Is he here now?"

"What do you think?"

Rue tugged Jame's sleeve. "What happened to the Architect?"

Jame had almost forgotten her story.

"It turned out that Rugen's death had been an accident. I asked him for justice. There was a pause. Then Rugen shoved Penari and me out of the way as the chandelier finally collapsed under Monster's weight. In the end, Penari let the architect's bones lie under the floor, wrapped in the linen shroud that was the building plans."

"And he's still there?"

"Evidently. He and Penari would still seem to be quarreling, though."

She regarded the stone slab under which Rugen's bones lay. The grave seemed undisturbed, never mind than his gargoyle Quezal was currently bouncing off the walls. What determined which of the dead returned? Dead gods, yes, it seemed, or at least some of them, but mortals? Not Rugen, who had forgiven his accidental murderer. Did a general absence of guilt explain why the city wasn't overrun by revenants?

"Master," she called to Penari, who was now plunging back and forth with a broom, swatting at every sound, while Quezal popped up behind him every time he turned. "I have to go."

"You're always leaving." The old thief paused, panting, as the gargoyle leered at her over his shoulder. "Next time, don't stay away so long."

III

WHEN THEY EMERGED FROM THE MAZE, Darinby was waiting for them, looking uncharacteristically anxious. What would he have done, Jame wondered, if she had been unduly delayed? Penari's remark about the Sirdan's "charming manners" came back to mind.

Darinby is a good man, but he is not himself.

What had Men-dalis done to her old friend, and to what lengths might Darinby now go to please his new master?

They soon came to the River Tone and, breasting its current, to Ship Island. Why had the Thieves' Guild chosen such an iconic bastion, Jame wondered, much less a nautical one stranded hundreds of miles inland? She stared across at its prow. On it was a stone figure, a maiden holding aloft two severed heads.

She has your face, Bane had said, with a smile. *One head is that of the Sirdan. The other is mine. Have you noticed that every time we meet, someone ends up bleeding?*

They crossed a stone gangplank and joined the crowd gathered amidships. Like the Moon, here was another tradition that would be among the last to go. Every night, apprentice thieves set up booths for their masters, sometimes on spots claimed for generations. From these they hawked their purloined spoils after the appropriate court had assessed how long each agent was liable for their theft and that period of jeopardy had passed. Here also citizens wandered, stopping to haggle for their lost possessions or for those of their neighbors.

Usually the market was a raucous place, some of it good-natured, some not, but tonight it seemed unusually subdued. This changed when a nearby apprentice, snooping on his neighbor's table, grabbed a particularly gaudy necklace and started screeching.

"Wretch, cheat! I recognize this bauble. The woman who wears it lives in my master's district. You've been poaching!"

The thief in question came around his display and threw himself at his accuser. Both went down in a flurry of punches. Burly guards in royal blue *d'hens* arrived, plowing through onlookers, and pulled the two combatants apart.

"Little fools," one guard growled. "D'you want to end up on the Mercy Seat? Be quiet."

Then they saw Jame, and abandoned the small fry.

"Here, Tush, would you believe it? It's that freak, the Talisman. Come back, have you?"

As they advanced, Darinby pulled her toward the palace that opened off Ship Island's forecastle. Some thieves tried to stop them. Even more fought merely to get out of the way. Rue and Patches were separated from them by a wash of struggling bodies. By the time they had reached the door, the entire market had erupted behind them into a lively brawl that owed more to relief at being able to make an uproar than to enmity.

Darinby shoved Jame inside.

"Dammit!" he said, shutting and barring the door against the outer tumult. "It's all right," he added to a servant who came hurrying up. "The Sirdan wants to see her."

"But Rue, Patches . . . !"

"Patches will see that your young friend comes to no harm."

"Darinby, what in Perimal's name is going on?"

"Well, you know that they're still after you for Theocandi's death . . ."

"I didn't mean that. Since when have apprentices been threatened with the Mercy Seat for quarreling? There used to be fights every night. Other thieves bet on them."

He led her on, through ornate rooms, then through a concealed door into the palace's hidden maze. Spy holes emitted shafts of light that laced the inner corridors. The ways were well swept: Men-dalis must make frequent use of them.

Darinby stopped her. "I should have told you before. The Guild has been . . . unsettled of late. Men-dalis has a vision for us, but people keep working against him. We are the stuff of legends, he says. It behooves us to behave accordingly. Anything less is . . . is an insult. To him. To us. Dissent, confusion, criticism—how can we be great while these flourish?"

"What do people criticize him for?"

"Oh." He gave an embarrassed laugh. "Small things. He has doubled his percentage of each night's take—two, four, no, six times. Well, he needs to present a certain image to the ruling Five. Otherwise how can we compel their respect? Without that, what are we?"

A parasite on society, Jame thought. It had never occurred to her before to ask, but what did the thieves offer beyond a reshuffling of wealth? What had Tubain said about stealing, though?

Nearly everyone in Tai-tastigon does or has or wants to. It's fine work, I hear, if you can get a good master and, of course, don't get caught.

People followed the exploits of famous thieves avidly. Their skill, their daring, the noses that they thumbed at Tai-tastigon's more stolid residents of the day. . . . There was a glamor to such work that far exceeded its true worth. The Guild had made it so.

"Wait a minute," she said. "That can't be the only trouble if the Mercy Seat is involved."

"That's the fault of his spymaster, the Creeper. An evil man, or whatever he is. He's always ferreting out dissent.

Some people go to the brig and are lucky not to rot there. It's in the basement below water level, you know. Their families come to plead for them, but what can the Sirdan do? Then, as you say, there's the Mercy Seat." He gulped. "Well, the original fell into a chasm the night you left, but the Creeper replaced it. Now anyone who displeases him is apt to end up there."

"Flayed alive?" Jame asked, aghast.

"Sometimes. Not often. The threat is enough for most. Others are bound there for a day, or a week, or longer if the Sirdan . . . that is, the Creeper . . . forgets. By then they can dine off the fruit and vegetables thrown at them. But, yes, we have had deaths."

"One would think, after Dally . . ."

"Yes. One would think. Here we are."

He opened a door and gestured her through, following on her heels.

The room in which they found themself was not one that Jame had previously seen. Nonetheless, it felt familiar, furnished richly to the point of suffocation in blue velvet and silver gilt. Chairs, couches, statues, and draperies crowded inward, on top of each other. There were no windows, though, and along the walls hung a gallery of smashed mirrors.

Somewhere a door opened—she could tell by the shift of turgid, scented air—and here was the man himself.

Flowing golden hair, sapphire blue eyes, a smile sweet enough to tempt a goddess . . . Men-dalis was even more handsome than she remembered and his garments more lush. He seemed to float in clouds of royal blue silk shot with mute silver lightning. The room expanded around

him into roiling space as if all horizons had rolled back,
and the air was fresh.

Ahhh . . . it breathed.

Oh, to inhale it forever. . . .

Now the room appeared to be spacious, lined with
columns, canopied with a vaulted ceiling on which were
painted delicate astral figures, male or female, impossible
to tell which, as were their activities. Vistas opened out
between the colonnades onto gardens of blue hyacinth
spangled with bobbing white columbine, cerulean lilacs
and pale lilies.

Hanging between, however, was more shattered glass.

Jame tried to get a grip on herself. After all, she had
experienced Men-dalis' glamour before, a heritage from
his god-sire Dalis-sar. In fact, had she ever seen him when
he had not been clothed with it? What did he really look
like, when not clad in glory? But these were fleeting
thoughts, overwhelmed by his present magnificence.

"Lord," she said, and was furious at herself for the
husky note that had crept into her voice. "Why have you
summoned me?"

"Why, what but to do your duty?"

All the things that might involve rose in her mind.
There were glittering tasks to accomplish, beside which
her former triumphs in the Thieves' Guild seemed mere
dross. She would go arrayed in a rainbow of satin by day,
in the whisper of black silk by night. No one would be safe
from her, nor would any want to be.

"I lost my greatest treasure to the Talisman," one
merchant would brag to another, "and glimpsed her as she
passed."

Princess of the evening—no, queen, the delight of her sovereign lord who would value her as none other could ...

Ugh.

"Duties," she heard herself croak. "D'you mean 'to obey the laws of the Guild, to uphold its institutions, to conduct myself to its credit and to that of my master'? That was what I swore. How have I failed?"

His divinely handsome face twitched, then smoothed.

"There are higher standards for people such as you and I. Would you align yourself with those who seek to diminish our legacy? Think how it has benefitted you. Think how we took you in."

Jame coughed. Her throat was dry and seemed to speak despite her. "My master, Penari, saw to that. Now you threaten him."

Men-dalis appeared delicately to shudder. "Ask my servant the Creeper about that."

"I ask you."

"Don't!"

For a moment he turned peevish, and the grandeur around him faltered. That silk coat he wore—surely now it was shorter and more plainly spun although still royal blue, one sleeve fit tight, the other flared. A button was missing at its breast, and dark stains smudged it.

He wears his dead brother's jacket, Penari had said. Why?

Then Men-dalis regained control.

"Ah, do not question me. I am the Sirdan, the master— no, the servant of my people. I know best. Accept that."

His will beat on her. She was so close to agreeing with him.

Dally, she thought, and her eyes cleared.

A trim, familiar figure stood among the flowers, and with it seemed to come a breath of cool, clean air. It smiled at her.

Glass shattered against weeping stone. The garden vista lay in a broken heap, still reflecting a flower here, half of a rueful smile there.

"No!" a shrill voice cried, almost unrecognizable until it modulated itself. "I mean, no. The dead are gone. They cannot return. Besides, he betrayed me."

"He did not."

Jame had dropped to her knees and was scrambling through the fragments in search of another reminder of Dally's face.

"If not then, he would have later. He was jealous of my success."

"He was not. He idolized you." Sudden suspicion made her sit up. "Did you encourage that with your charms?"

"No!"

The voice that spoke was vehement but strained. He was half-Kencyr. Could he lie?

"Did you order your brother's death?"

The whole fabric of the room rippled like a shaken screen. Jame felt herself thrust back into the claustrophobic room that she had at first entered. Somewhere, a door slammed. The Sirdan was gone.

"This way," said Darinby, his hand on her shoulder. He was panting.

Outside, in the corridor, space returned to normal.

"Darinby . . ."

"He's right, you know." The thief's eyes were fixed and his mouth too, in a desperate smile. "I thought, I doubted . . . I was wrong—wasn't I? Yes. No. The entire city depends on his judgment. You don't know what it's been like here—people destroyed, families torn apart, the Guild facing ruin, haunts prowling the streets, the gods themselves, dead and alive . . . it will all collapse if we don't obey him."

Through his voice, she felt his shifting passions.

What she saw appalled the Darinby of old, who had mistrusted all politics and politicians, whose gods she did not know, but they must have been honorable. Now, as Men-dalis had been Dally's hero, so he had somehow become Darinby's, seen as beset on every side by treacherous foes. Therein lay Darinby's weakness, bred out of his strength. Who would be so false as not to support such a master? At the same time, Darinby was a good man. At heart, surely he couldn't believe what he was saying.

She tried a different approach.

"The Sirdan never said why he summoned me."

"Can't you guess that? Dally was a . . . a splendid boy, but he is gone. What has returned, though . . . what can its purpose be except to destroy?"

"Who?"

"His brother, of course."

"Why?"

"I don't know!"

He slammed his fist against a wall in frustration. His knuckles bled. Jame caught his wrist to stop him from striking again and supported him as he leaned, panting, against the bloody stones.

"Is Men-dalis worth it?"

"Yes." He drew himself unsteadily upright and brushed back tousled hair from a white, sweating brow. "He has to be. Come. See what happens to those who will not listen to reason."

"Darinby! Talk to me."

He looked at her with wide, shocked eyes and grinned again.

Their way led down into the foundations of Ship Island. Here stone walls ran with moisture and sodden moss squished underfoot. This must truly be below river level. Jame smelled mildewed wood and rotten leather. The hallway was lit with sputtering torches. Doors opened off it on either side, each with a small, barred window. Voices within moaned.

"Men-dalis sanctions this?" she asked.

"Not he. The Creeper does as he thinks best to support the Guild. So does Abbotir of the Gold Court, my lord's loyal advisor. Sometimes I . . . I help. There has to be someone with dirty hands to accomplish any task."

"We call that Honor's Paradox. It doesn't work."

"It will in the end, so long as no one tells the Sirdan what the Creeper is doing."

"Don't they even try?"

"Yes but, well, face to face with him, they can't. It would be . . . treason? Blasphemy? He doesn't know. We can't let him know. It would be terrible if he knew and yet . . . and yet . . ."

"Let these things happen anyway?"

"Don't say it! Here we are. See for yourself."

What Jame saw beyond the opened door was a stairway leading down into darkness. She descended cautiously on slimy steps, leaning against walls felted with wet mold. Would Darinby shut the door behind her? It seemed not. He was still of a deeply divided mind. Besides, she hadn't yet done his master's bidding. Talk about divided hearts. . . . Men-dalis hadn't even gotten around to saying what exactly his will was although she suspected that Darinby was right: he wanted her to kill Dally. Again.

"Who's there?" demanded a voice below, and chains clashed. "I demand to see whoever is in charge! We pay our taxes. We have rights!"

Jame's eyes adjusted to the gloom. At the foot of the stair, in a small room, was a bed, and on it sat a lumpy figure, glaring up at her.

"Mistress Abernia, is that you?"

"Yes! Have you come to hear my grievances?"

"In a way."

The lowest steps led down into cold water that came nearly to the tops of Jame's boots. The small, sodden bodies of rats floated in it. She waded to the bed and sat down on its spongy mattress.

The cell's inmate glared at her. Jame in turn saw a figure of confusion. Abernia wore skirts tucked at the top into pants, at the bottom into boots. She also wore a bodice pulled down insecurely over a barrel chest. A cowl overshadowed her face.

"Abernia, may I talk to your husband Tubain?"

The other pouted. "What you say to me, he can hear, as if that coward could keep anything from me."

"Please."

Jame eased back the hood. Tubain's face peered out at her through gummy eyes.

"Oh," said the innkeeper, blinking back tears. "We have been so wretched here. Have you come to take us home?"

"I hope so. Soon."

He gave a quivering smile. "Abernia said I was a fool to take you in. I said, 'It will come right in the end.' Is this the end?"

"Not yet."

His face crinkled and he began to cry. Jame held him, her arms not quite reaching around his fat, hunched shoulders. In her mind's eye, she saw the Res aB'tyrr which this man had turned into a haven for so many, including himself. He was genuinely good, as Cleppetty had claimed. The rest didn't matter.

"There, now," she said, patting him on the back. "Can I speak to your wife again?"

Tubain stifled a sob. "If you wish," he said, and straightened where he sat. "Well?" demanded Abernia through his unkempt beard, impatiently wiping her eyes.

This was going to be hard.

"I can try to take you out now," said Jame, with another glance up at the lit doorway. Had Darinby gone away or was he waiting, just out of sight? By now, who might have joined him? "But I don't think Men-dalis is done with either of us. If you go back to the inn tonight, his people may be watching. That's certainly the first place they will look when they realize that you've escaped. Will he dare attack the Res aB'tyrr openly?"

Abernia considered this, reminding Jame yet again that

she was the brains of the family, likewise all the backbone that it possessed. "The Five might consider it an undeclared war between a guild and a trade, which in itself is virtually unheard-of. The fine placed on the instigator would be ruinous, yes, even for coffers as deep as the Sirdan's. I think Men-dalis will hesitate unless, as some say, he truly has run mad."

"Or unless he finds a way to blame you for any trouble."

Abernia gave a bark of angry laughter. "We have been more or less in this situation before, have we not?"

Yes, when a rival inn, the Skyrrman, had tried to destroy the Res aB'tyrr with an unsanctioned trade war. It was a miracle, partly engineered by the Archiem of Skyrr against his own rival, Harr sen Tenko, that they hadn't succeeded.

"I could take you somewhere else." Patches' house? The Maze?

"No." Abernia's fortitude crumbled under the pressure of Tubain's desperate need. "I w-w-want to go home!"

"Then I will do my best to take you there."

No one waited at the top of the stair. A harsh sound reached her from down the hall. Darinby bent over in a far corner, retching. Damn Men-dalis for putting him through such misery, even more so for whatever the Sirdan had done to his innocent brother. Let Dally haunt him. He deserved it.

Here was the door, the market amidships clearing away with the dawn, the Thieves' Guild melting into shadows. Yes, that was as it should be.

⬅⬅⬅ Chapter V ⟫⟫⟫⟫⟫
The Res aB'tyrr
Spring 56

CRACKS OF DAWN showed though the overhanging rooflines, bringing the first faint light of day to the streets below. Rats scurried into the remaining shadows. Ignoring them, cats sat on doorsteps waiting to be let in after their nocturnal rambles. From within came the stir of waking life—a cough, a clatter of pans, someone calling to sleepy children in a sleepy voice:

"Get up, get up, oh do get up . . ."

Surely the city can't be this complicated, thought Rue as she followed her small guide through yet another tangle of back alleys, which they had entered by crawling through an empty barrel from one apparent dead end to another. Rue had almost gotten stuck. Patches had snickered.

Maybe the little thief was trying to throw off pursuit. The uproar of the island market had long since faded behind them into the murmur of the stirring city. Sometimes Rue thought that she had heard feet padding behind them. She knew something about spies, though, after dealing with Jame's so-called spymaster Graykin, and didn't think much of them.

On the other hand, maybe Patches was just trying to confuse her. If so, she was doing a good job.

The farther they went, the more lost Rue became. As with most Kencyr, her memory was excellent, but not trained to this pitch. Jame, as she understood it, was more of an adept in this bewildering city than most of its inhabitants. What a strange life she must have led here.

But as a thief? That still made Rue uneasy. Once again, she was reminded how little she really knew about her mistress.

Just the same, the farther she got from Jame, the more apprehensive she became. Would it be better or worse if they were formally bound together? Like everyone else at Tagmeth, Rue had considered what would happen if— no, dammit, when Torisen gave his sister the authority to bind more Kendar. Rue would jump for that . . . wouldn't she? Oh, but what would she be joining herself to? Every time she thought that she understood Jame, something else happened.

Should she ask Brier Iron-thorn? Maybe not, if the Southron was now in the temper that Rue suspected she would be. That touched a chord of guilt, but before she could track it down, they entered a larger street lit with glowing spheres.

"Where are we going?" Rue asked, not for the first time.

Overhead, a window opened. Patches leaped to the wall, followed an instant later by Rue. The contents of a chamber pot splashed into the gutter beside them.

"Idiot," remarked Patches, starting out again. "Night soil brings a good price from local farmers."

Randon-trained Rue was aghast. "You've never heard of latrines, or sewers, or dysentery?"

"Sewers we've got, and a god to go with them. Sumph the Indiscriminate. Some people are just lazy."

Ahead of them, a black-robed priest paused under one of the hovering globes.

"Blessed-Ardwyn-day-has-come," he muttered in a bored voice. The light went out.

Rue watched him depart, extinguishing spheres as he went. "Ardwyn is another of your gods, isn't she?"

Patches grinned. "I keep forgetting. You Kennies make do with only one, don't you? How's that working out?"

"Not well," Rue admitted. "We don't like him (or her, or it) and he doesn't seem to care much for us either."

She would have reacted more strongly before Kothifir. That had been Rue's first experience with gods other than her own, although she was beginning to suspect that Tai-tastigon was in a class by itself. Still, if Jame had come to grips with it, so could she. Let the priests fight out the theology.

The sense of being lost, adrift, tugged at her again. What would Jame do without her?

"Where . . ." she began.

The little thief stopped so suddenly that Rue nearly ran over her.

"Here."

They had come to a square with a fountain bubbling at its heart and a handsome girl drawing water from it. To the left were the fire-scarred ruins of a large building, partly if ineptly rebuilt. Ahead stood another, far more interesting structure. Its four-story facade was covered with gamboling infants carved in high relief. As the sun rose and the shadows moved, they seemed to laugh and play. There was also a residual glow about them, like the globes, that faded as day broke.

An obese black cat sat on its doorstep, meowing insistently. The door opened. Tail held high, the feline stiffly brushed past the woman who had obeyed his summons, disappearing within. The woman continued to stand there as if on guard. She was tall, thin, and middle-aged. "Sharp" was the word that came to Rue's mind, as to form, posture, and intent. Also, "wary."

The girl at the fountain straightened.

"Cleppetania," she called. "Will he see me today?"

"No," snapped the other. "He's still indisposed. No visitors."

The girl pouted. "You can't keep me away forever. Tubain is my uncle, after all."

"Only by marriage, Kithra."

"Will he see my husband Rothan, then?"

"No. Leave us alone."

Patches crossed the square, Rue behind her, and saluted the woman on the step.

"Mistress Cleppetty. Good morning."

"You again. Who is this?"

"The Talisman sent her," said Patches, trying to match the insouciance of the black cat but with a cautious eye to her hostess. "There's trouble. Well, there always is, isn't there? By the way, is there any word of Mistress Abernia?"

"She's still the guest of the Thieves' Guild, as far as I

know. And still we get no satisfaction from the Five. We're on our own here."

"You don't trust me because I'm a thief," said Patches, with doleful regret. "You should. You do my mentor."

"You mean Jame. She was just here and said nothing about you or any guest."

"Maybe she forgot."

The woman snorted. "Maybe you lie as easily as breathing. Most people do." She turned to Rue. "But you, girl, you're one of her kind, aren't you?"

"A Kencyr, yes. More like Marcarn Long-shanks, though, a Kendar." Rue gave her a clumsy bow. "Honor be to you and to your halls."

The other's mouth broke into a lop-sided, reluctant smile. "So she said to me, once, and Marc is a dear friend. Well, then, child. Welcome to the Res aB'tyrr."

⊴⊠⊠ Chapter VI ⊠⊠⊵
Many Meetings
Spring 56

I

JAME FOUND HERSELF once again by Ship Island, but this time on the south bank. It had seemed important to lead any pursuit away from the Res aB'tyrr by backtracking, although she hoped that she had avoided the Creeper's agents altogether.

The eastern horizon lightened through a haze of clouds. In the Riverland, it would be hours before the sun rose over the Snowthorns, but here windswept plains stretched to the Eastern Sea, a whole world that she had barely thought about since her abrupt departure years ago.

The thieves' market amidships had dispersed. The Guild's night was the city's day, under most circumstances. In her time, she had usually slept while the sun was up. Now, she felt oddly adrift among the city streets. By night, they seemed to rise forever, up to the stars and an inconstant moon. Now, here at least, a vault of blue sky fretted by gathering clouds capped them. Merchants stirred, opening doors from whose cracks strips of stuffing fell. As people emerged on the streets, yawning, vendors began to cook breakfast. Jame's stomach growled. Trinity, how long was it since she had last eaten? Somehow, the lack of food was harder to bear than the lack of sleep, even for someone who ate as little as she did.

Beside her ran the River Tone, its rippling current catching the dawn glow. Something massive surfaced in it, which Jame only saw out of the corner of her eye. It had dived again when she turned to look, leaving a single, liquid comment:

Bloop.

No. It couldn't be . . . could it?

Anyway, what next?

Tubain, she hoped, was safe, but for how long? Mendalis would realize, soon enough, that he had escaped. Would the Sirdan pursue him? Why had he taken the innkeeper prisoner in the first place if not to force her return to Tai-tastigon? That had succeeded. Here she was. But what he really wanted was to be freed of guilt over his brother's murder, even if he hadn't said so directly, perhaps because he couldn't bring himself to do so. Was he responsible for that death? She had always thought so, but with what proof? Even if she obtained it, what could she do with the Five apparently under his thumb through his minister Abbotir?

It was a puzzle with too many pieces missing.

Something tugged at her collar. Reaching back, she encountered a hook attached to a long line. It twitched again.

"Psst," said a voice above. Jame looked up.

"Sparrow!"

"Climb," said the other and Jame did, hand over hand up the taut rope with her feet braced against the nearest wall.

The rooftops of the city opened out before her, a rugged landscape of steep peaks patched with red tile and green slate, dotted with puffing chimneys. Sparrow embraced her at the top.

"We thought we would never see you again!"

"I've been off scaling cliffs, not walls. One, I swear, was three thousand feet high."

He grinned at her. "Why am I not surprised? You always did climb like a polydactyl cat. Welcome back, Talisman!"

"How are you, and how is your king?"

"It's Prince Dandello now. His uncle died of a chill caught after celebrating last Spring's Eve cloud-clad. We honor the god of wind and weather whenever we can, given that we're so subject to the whim of both up here, and better the south wind than the north, that only brings trouble. Oh, we had a glorious pyre to warm the old man's bones. An entire block went up in flames. Anyway, now that you're back, Dandy is sure to want to see you. Just stay away from the edge."

He set off across the rooftops, between chimneys streaming with the fragrance of morning bread.

"So," Jame said, skidding down a steep, slippery incline to keep pace with him. *I used to do this all the time*, she thought, breathlessly catching her balance. *Never mind. The knack will come back.* "How have things been here?"

Sparrow paused on the eaves above a three-story drop.

"In general, not good. They say that people are being snatched off the streets on dark nights and others wander when they shouldn't. Sometimes we see things pass below, and sometimes they climb. Whatever they are, where they pass rot takes hold after them. More roofs crumble every day. How are we supposed to keep our footing?"

He gathered himself and leaped across the street far below.

"Some Cloudies say," he said when Jame caught up with him, "that we should take shelter below, but I don't hold with that. Born in the clouds, I was, and so I will die, if nothing plucks me off a gable first."

That was the Cloudies' creed. They lived above, drawing sustenance from below with hook and tackle, in touch with the street life but separated from it as an angler is from a fish.

Here was a housetop, higher and broader than most, with a flat roof. Nets surrounded it below the uppermost floor. On top, she found the Cloud King holding court.

Dandello sat on a throne of pillows, all in white, looking like a discontent angel under a halo of fluffy, fair hair. On either side of him, portly courtiers tried to interest him in their accounts, scrawled in chalk on roof slates.

"As your Highness can see . . ." one was saying.

"Or would if he deigned to look," muttered the other.

". . . we have lost another half dozen citizens. Two came back, but hadn't the wits left to climb. I saw them. They just stared upward, like lost souls, then wandered away.

More and more roofs are collapsing. We've sent down messages, but the houseowners ignore us. We might as well be so many pigeons, for all they care."

"It's this plague of returned gods," said the other. "I'm telling you, it isn't good for architecture."

"Talisman!" The prince jumped to his feet, scattering pillows. "You two, go away."

The courtiers withdrew, looking disgruntled, and threw themselves off the roof. Just in time not to embarrass herself, Jame remembered the nets. Dandello's passion, before his rise to the throne, had lain in pushing people off of rooftops to watch them twirl in midair. What happened afterward had never interested him.

"Have you come to dance for me at last?" he asked hopefully.

"Not today, your Highness. Condolences on your uncle's descent. Congratulations on your rise."

His full lips pursed into a dissatisfied moue.

"It's so boring. I can't do anything I like anymore. They won't even let me look over the edge. What is life without grace, without fun?"

"My own people won't let me out of their sight either. Being a leader isn't easy, sire."

Oh, Brier, she thought as she said this, her conscience smiting her. *What are you doing right now? Will you ever forgive me? Only if I return in time, and maybe even not then.*

At least she had left a note: "Away on personal business. Don't worry." On second thought, that message might only annoy Brier more.

Four days until Summer's Eve . . .

Sparrow plucked at her sleeve. "The Archiem of Skyrr is coming down River Street," he hissed. "We think there may be trouble."

"Trinity. He's in town?"

She gave Dandello a hasty salute that he received with an impatient gesture, muttering, "No one lets me do anything," and followed the little Cloudie.

II

SPARROW led her back to the Tone. Down the south bank road came a procession of brightly garbed hill nobles, at their head a dark, thin figure, plainly dressed, on a tall gray mare. Jame would have known those sharp, cynical features anywhere. He had acted once to save the Res aB'tyrr in its trade war, hinging his judgment on her own sense of honor, but she had never doubted that Arribek Thane sen Tenzi served first his country, then his canton, then himself. She had only mattered to him as a means to his end.

The Archiem's kinsmen followed him, their harnesses shining with ornate plaques of gold and silver. They carried banners—a green background and against it a bay horse running. Men on foot came after, holding bows half-cocked. It was odd to think that, like the Merikit, the sen Tenzi were a hill tribe, but in some ways a more sophisticated one. She had heard that they moved about their territory in felt-covered carts, each night creating a new, temporary city. Their wealth lay in their herds and in the precious metals with which their land was rich.

They fought incessantly with neighboring tribes, except when the Archiem could negotiate periods of peace.

"Look," whispered Sparrow, pointing.

From this height, Jame could see figures lurking around corners and on lower rooftops along the Archiem's route.

"Look out!" she shouted down at him.

Arrows flew. The Archiem's guard barely had time to shield him against a storm of wooden shafts that plucked against their defense. Then they charged the shadows. Some attackers fled. Others drew again and brought down several horses, including the Archiem's gray with an arrow through her throat. His followers covered him as he fought clear of her thrashing body. When a clutch of would-be assassins was driven back to him, he was kneeling with the mare's head in his lap, her blood running over his knees. She twitched and was still. He rose.

"I liked that horse. Why are you trying to kill me?"

His guards held a young man with his arms twisted painfully up behind his back. He glared at the Archiem.

"It's all your fault."

"What is?"

"What happened to my father. You drove him to desperation. He was ready to try anything, to break your hold."

"My dear boy. Harr sen Tenko and I have been at war in the hills since before you were born. That was his doing, by the way, not mine, as is his impending defeat. But we currently have a truce. He came here. What happened next, I do not know."

"Liar!"

Arribek's sharp gaze lifted to Jame, who had bidden a hasty goodbye to Sparrow and descended to the ground. Now she hovered on the edge of the crowd. It hadn't been her intention to pitch herself into local politics. "Here is one who would take exception to such a word as, in fact, do I. Talisman, what do you know of this matter?"

"Nothing, my lord. I just got here."

His thin lips quirked. "That explains, then, why we are not yet engaged in a full-blown crisis. Ah, yes, little sister. I remember you. Where is your fine hunting ounce?"

"At home."

"Wherever that is. No doubt he pines for you. Harri, I wish you no harm. Why you should wish it of me escapes my understanding."

Tears ran down the young man's face, making him look little older than a boy. "Then you are either a fool or a monster, just as Father says."

"Harr sen Tenko never had much sense. I hope for better from you. Now go away."

The guards released him. He stood for a moment rubbing his arms, then drew himself up and stalked off, followed by his men.

"Was that wise?" asked Jame.

"To release him? Perhaps not, but diplomacy is made of calculated steps. Why, what would you have done?"

"Probably the same, not that I understand the situation."

"Nor do I. Granted, Harr is on the edge of final defeat, not that I intend to press him beyond endurance. His son is intelligent, but only when he comes out of his father's shadow. I was much the same. So, breakfast?"

Jame blinked. "I don't understand."

"You aren't hungry? I can hear your stomach gurgling. The Five meet within the hour to discuss our current situation. Tell me that you aren't curious."

Of course she was, although her past as a thief gave her pause. No one in the lower ranks of the Guild wanted to attract the Five's attention.

Arribek led the way down the River Road, past Ship Island, toward Gold Ringing District, where the Five held council on an island-spanning mansion set in the middle of the Tone. Jame hung back as the Archiem entered, then followed like a cautious cat, keeping to the edge of rooms to avoid notice. It was a luxurious manse full on the first level of ceremonial spaces. The breakfast room was huge, extending at least a hundred feet back at the nether point of the island with towering windows overlooking the Tone on either side. The clutch of people there was dwarfed by their surroundings, as if by the city itself.

Here was the representative of Metalondar: a stout diplomat with ornate hair piled a foot high, secured with glittering pins. Here, the official from Skyrr, looking nervous. Here three representatives of the Tastigon guilds—on this occasion, a merchant, a thief, and a priest.

Looking out of place, a sulky young man stood to one side, holding a glass of wine. He wore a Kencyr court coat of faded purple, rendered further out-of-date by the fussy ruffles around its cuffs. Hunting leathers would perhaps have suited him better. When he thought no one was looking, he sneered at the Metalondrian noble.

Then Jame's attention was drawn to someone else and she slid over to a plump, balding man in a darned robe.

"Loogan, hello!"

"Didn't expect to see me here, did you?" The little priest took her hands. "Nor did I you. Welcome home!"

"Um, not so much that anymore."

He beamed up at her. "Well, I should have expected that. You were just passing through, after all, weren't you?"

"And you, politics?"

He laughed. "It's a change from the old days, isn't it? I was a joke then—no, don't deny it, and no doubt I deserved to be. But it matters that Gorgo overlaps the Old and New Pantheons. Then too, we priests are important in this city, and this city is important to us. Especially now."

"And Gorgo?"

"You may say hello, if you like."

He flipped open a beaded pouch that hung around his neck. It quivered as delicate green toes crept over its braided lip. Wide, bulbous eyes rose, blinking.

"...quink...?" said a tiny, nervous voice.

"Sweet Trinity. He's..."

"Very, very small. I know. It's been happening throughout the Temple District ever since the dead gods came back, or perhaps that's the other way around. Some have shrunk enough to come untempled, like Gorgo here—rather the reverse of what happened when you were here. Others are trying to take up normal lives outside the district. I never realized how bored they were. I mean, they're gods! Who would think it? Then too, they're frightened."

Servants emerged from an inner door at the western end of the room bearing laden platters. Grilled trout, oatcakes drizzled with honey, eels in cream, porpoise pie, parsnip pastries . . . Jame pressed a hand to her stomach to suppress its noise.

"Eat, eat!" a server urged her out of the corner of his mouth. "It's all fresh from the country this morning, I swear, and none of it your mewling street vegetables."

A fish, although boned, began to twitch on its silver platter.

"We have come here to discuss matters," said the Archiem, addressing the other officials, with a gesture relegating his own representative to insignificance. "Shall we begin? First, my lord, our thanks to you for the loan of your palace."

He spoke with an incline of his head to the master thief.

Jame had been regarding this individual askance, sure that she should know him, but the light was in her eyes and he stood in the shadow between window arches. Just the same, it was clear that he must once have been an imposing man. Now he appeared shrunken into his rich robes like a tortoise into its shell. Loose, patchy skin hung from his jowls and a sickly odor emanated from his clothing. His sunken eyes, however, were still fierce.

"My house is at your command," he said, in a grating voice. "As are my services."

"Well then." The Archiem turned from him to the others. "My concern with the current situation is primarily financial. This city pays me—and Metalondar, of course—handsomely for its freedom from our territorial claims. I need that money to support my war in the hills."

"Which you have now brought to our streets," said the

representative of the merchants. "There is blood on your hands."

"Wars tend to spread," the Archiem replied lightly. "So, hopefully, does peace, for which I strive."

"Then too," said the thief, with a sneer at the merchant, "war is bad for business, is it not?"

The merchant shook out his pearl-encrusted sleeves as if to call attention to them, releasing a haze of perfume from their folds against his colleague's stink.

"If our prosperity suffers, than so does yours. You thieves make a fuss about the glory that your Sirdan says you bring to our city. However, what are you but lice on the body mercantile?"

The thief barred yellow teeth in a death's-head grin at the other's florid face. "Say, rather, that we are leeches. Your blood is too rich. We thin it."

"Oh, please don't squabble!" Loogan burst out. "People are suffering! Their city is dying around them, whether you deign to see it or not, and the gods that they look to for help are failing."

"That no doubt cuts back on temple offerings," said the merchant not quite in a whisper to his assistant.

"No new robes again this year," murmured the latter in reply, with a smirk.

Loogan heard and drew himself up, an oddly dignified little figure amidst all of their finery.

"Whoever our god, we serve as best we can, to the greater good of our people. I see you sneering at my threadbare clothes. These patches are badges of honor, others before myself. You walk the day. By night, no doubt, you sit before roaring hearths in sealed rooms and stick your fingers in your ears. What do you know of the terror after dark? Have your sons and daughters, your wives and mothers, risked the streets in service of their gods, of each other? Have you gone to seek them with the dawn and found them wandering without shadows, without souls? If so, what then? Some let them go, even drive them away. Others take them in, and then they must be confined because that gnawing restlessness is upon them. But if they die while under such constraint . . ."

"Enough."

Talk of death upset the master thief. Others looked relieved at his interruption.

"All right." Loogan seemed to deflate. "I'm just saying that that something is preying on the gods, their people, and this city, just as the Lower Town Monster once did on the children of that district."

"That's still happening," said Jame, and then wanted to kick herself for attracting attention.

Loogan turned to her. "You said once that your temple was responsible for the New Pantheon in the first place. I don't know if I believe that, but less power is coming to us than it used to, and we dwindle. Something terrible is going on. Do you know what?"

"I'm trying to find out."

The young man in the dress coat was frowning at her, perplexed.

The Archiem's thin lips twitched into a smile. "Forgive me," he said smoothly. "You two haven't been introduced, have you? My lord, this is the Talisman, one of Tai-tastigon's most . . . er . . . famous thieves. Talisman, meet Lord Harth of East Kenshold."

The Highborn stared at her. "I thought you were Kencyr the moment I saw you, but here, dressed like that, and a thief?" Outrage suffused his plain, fleshy features. "Blasphemy!"

Jame felt her hands curl into fists, claws pricking her palms.

"I've heard of you, my lord. You drove six aging Kendar out of East Kenshold because they had grown too old in your father's service to suit you. They all died on their way here but one, and that was Marc, my dearest friend."

In the face of her cold rage Harth looked suddenly nervous and drew back a step. "I didn't ... I don't remember ... who are you, anyway, to criticize me? Who were they ... oh, now I recall. It wasn't that they were old ... well, not primarily. They lectured me. Me, their lord! They stood there and said I wasn't the man that my father had been."

"I think I know why." Jame's voice threatened to thicken into a purr. She cleared her throat and fought for control, but still she stalked him into the middle of a room from which all others had retreated. "You abused your father's Whinno-hir mare, Nathwyr."

The Metalondarian looked shocked. "Sir! You molested a horse?"

"I only wanted to ride her!"

"Against her will."

"But she is just an animal!"

"So, my lord, are you. You said it best: blasphemy."

"Here now." The thieves' representative stepped out of the shadows, seeming to grow as he advanced. "You are the Talisman? Then I have a question for you, bitch: what did you do to my son?"

Jame felt as if she had stepped off a cliff unawares. "Er . . . what?"

Now she was the one being stalked. The morning sunlight that streamed through the windows was dazzling. The master thief loomed against it, bearing down on her like a mountain about to fall. Dust seemed to rise off his shoulders, or was that smoke?

"His mother tried to ruin him with her heathen beliefs, but I beat that nonsense out of him. He was mine, to do with as I pleased. Didn't I show him how best to direct his passions? Oh yes, he liked that, my dear late wife be damned. When I set him his final test, he agreed, and so he was apprenticed to Sirdan Theocandi himself. Then along you came. 'Good riddance,' I thought when you disappeared, but so did he, on the same night. Where is he?"

It had by now dawned on Jame that she was confronting Abbotir of the Gold Court, Bane's foster-father and Men-dalis' first advisor.

"I last saw him in the Guild Palace," she said, uncomfortably aware that this was dicing with the truth.

"Ha. That was when you assassinated the Sirdan. A chit like you, to bring down such a man . . . obscene."

Jame had to try. "I didn't kill Theocandi. My word of honor on it."

"You." Abbotir rounded on Harth. "Kencyr aren't supposed to lie. Is she lying?"

The young lord was still regaining control of himself.

"The death of honor, we call it. How can a thief be honorable?"

"You see?" Abbotir panted in Jame's face, spraying her with spittle. His breath stank of whatever was killing him. "Liar."

"I never lied to Bane."

"Ha." He had her by the throat now, bending her over backward. Yes, smoke, and a stench as if of smoldering flesh. How strong he was, given his wasted condition. "Then he lied to you. 'Bane' is only what he chose to call himself. His mother left a note: 'You are the bane of my existence.' I couldn't beat that name out of him."

"But . . . but then who is he?"

He threw her to the floor. "As if I would tell you. Now run, you filthy little whore. The guild is coming after you."

"That went well," said the Archiem, helping her to her feet. Abbotir was already at the door, shouting for his guard. "You had better leave now."

"Thank you for breakfast," said Jame, and fled.

III

OUT ON THE STREET, on the south bank of the river, she again took to the roofs to avoid pursuit, although she didn't expect the brunt of that until the next night. Just the same, it was good that Rue wasn't with her, she thought, clambering up a drainpipe. Like many Kendar, the cadet suffered from severe height-sickness. And she might well agree with Lord Harth's attitude toward thieves.

At the top, Jame swung up over the eave. It had rained while she had been in Abbotir's palace and the tiles were slick. Worse, they started to slide under her weight. The wood beneath groaned. She scrambled up to the peak and perched there, clutching the chimney pot, as the roof below her sloughed off like scaly, dead skin into the void. A moment later, out of sight, slate crashed to earth. The exposed timbers swarmed with woodlice. When sunlight struck them, they curled up and died. Jame gingerly stirred their husks with a gloved fingertip, finding them light, fragile, and quite wooden, like so many tiny, intricate carvings.

Was this a sign of the rot that Sparrow had deplored?

The roof peak sagged a bit, but didn't seem to be going anywhere. Jame paused on it to catch her breath and to think.

Abbotir had said much that puzzled her. Did the guild lord know that Bane in fact was not his son?

"Mother says that I am a prince, but Father is no king."

Bane had come to believe that that honor belonged to the priest Ishtier, which was also false.

"Didn't I show him how best to direct his passions?"

Sweet Trinity, what had that meant?

Most of all, though, what was Bane's true name? If she hadn't given that to Dalis-sar, no wonder the Lower Town Monster had survived to this day, not to mention Bane's other shattered aspects.

Beyond all of that, she was collecting clues, but what did they mean? The dead gods, mostly Old Pantheon, had come back. Tai-tastigon's New Pantheon had simultaneously been diminished. Both had something to do with the Kencyr temple, but what? Then too, those poor folk in the Lower Town had lost their shadows and presumably the souls that cast them. According to Loogan, more of the bereft wandered the streets. And what did happen if they died in such a state?

The dead did seem to be returning, or at least some of them.

Had she really seen Dally's reflection in his brother's quarters? Yes, judging from Men-dalis' reaction, if that was to be trusted. Had Dally really been in the garden, though, or was he reflected as he had stood behind his brother? The latter would have put him also, unobserved, beside her, a thought which made the short hairs on the back of her neck rise. Dally was the adopted son of Dalis-sar. Was that divine connection enough to bring him back, or was his brother's presumed guilt, or were both in combination?

Then too, Men-dalis was adept at casting illusions. Had he fooled even himself this time? Her glimpse of what appeared to be Dally's *d'hen* made her wonder. Was Men-dalis really wearing it or did he only think that he was?

Somehow, though, Dally's return didn't seem to fit in with that of the dead gods. It was more . . . personal, at least to her and to Men-dalis. But there must be some connection.

Eh. She truly had too little information and had guessed wrong before, many times.

So many questions. Where to find answers?

Time to talk to some gods, if she could find any.

IV

THE TEMPLE DISTRICT was built along lines unique in the city. Each structure fitted into its older neighbors any which way, creating a puzzle box approach to architecture. Walls were not shared, unless one cantilevering over another collapsed. More had fallen in this way than Jame remembered, most of them revealing dark, apparently deserted spaces within. Whatever was happening to the New Pantheon gods of Tai-tastigon, it was having a widespread effect.

Somewhere, a wall collapsed. *Tick, tick, tick* went dust in narrow back alleys.

In counterpoint, rainwater dripped from overhangs.

Jame paused outside the closed door of Gorgo's sanctuary. Were his followers inside, keeping vigil for his safety and their own, or had they all fled? Where was Loogan?

Once, she had effectively killed the little deity by destroying his priest's faith in him. At the time, she had been experimenting on the gods of the city under the impression that they were false. Monotheism breeds such cruelty. Then she had helped to resurrect Gorgo by restoring his congregation and, eventually, Loogan's belief in his existence. Trinity, she had been thoughtless in those days. Was she any wiser now?

Loogan clearly didn't know what was going on. Did anyone? Now that she was here, whom could she ask?

As she walked on, she passed other temples that pulsed

with worship. Chants, groans, and the occasional shriek echoed in the streets. Clouds of incense billowed out of open doors. Celebrants sat on the front steps getting a breath of fresh air before plunging back inside. A troop of initiates trotted past, splashing through puddles, whacking their penitent superiors on the back of the head with hymnals as they ran.

Here was a street that looked familiar. Surely Dalissar's temple lay down this way, and so it did. Its doors stood open and light spilled down the steps—not the blinding glare of the sun god that she remembered, but bright enough to make her wince. Serious worship was going on within.

A large figure sat on the curb, looking disconsolate. Jame settled cautiously beside him, noting his clothes— old-fashioned plate armor with an embroidered surcoat slung over it. His long hair was drawn back in an archaic braid. His features were hard to make out in the shimmer of heat that rose between the joints of his panoply, especially from the neck of his breastplate.

"What's going on?" she asked.

"They've desanctified the temple for repairs." He had a deep, hollow voice, as mournful as she had ever heard. The puddles at his feet steamed. "Maybe that will help."

"Help what?"

"The temple is faltering, as so many are at present. What will we do if it fails?"

"Find a different god?"

"Some are already looking."

Jame regarded him askance. From this angle, she could distinguish a big, square face, mature but unlined, like that of an overgrown boy who has not yet lost his innocence.

"What will you do?" she asked, delicately testing the situation.

"I? Stay here as long as I am needed, then . . . go home, I suppose. How long have I been gone? It feels like an age."

"Where did you come from?"

"Oh, from the temple guard to the south, in Tai-than, of course. I was a soldier . . . still am, I suppose, although I am not often called on to fight these days. Heliot was king, then, the last that Tai-tastigon knew. What a cruel man. He wanted to be a god, and not just that: the king of gods. All must worship him, even He of the Three Faces."

"I can't see that going well."

"No. Heliot besieged our temple, here in Tai-tastigon. It called out for help. Tai-than sent its guards, us, although it was having problems of its own. This was a time when the natives first noticed our existence and strength. I sometimes wonder what we would have done if they had all converted. Panicked, maybe. But no: it went the other way.

"Anyway, we met outside the city on the eastern plain. Heliot brought fire to the battle. The earth burned. So did my friends. So did I. Then the rain came. My mates were dead by then, and I was dying. The citizens kept me alive to fight him and I did. Beat him, too. The irony was that the sacrifice of his worshippers had indeed made Heliot a god, but with his defeat they lost faith in him and he died. I don't remember much for a long time after that, until I woke up in this temple. I like these people. I owe them my life. But sometimes I do long to be among my own kind."

Jame had edged away from him as he spoke, as a precaution. "Your name was Sar Dalis, wasn't it?" she said. "You were a randon sergeant."

He gave a rueful snort. "My mates called me 'Salad.' I never understood why."

Something . . . someone, was coming down the street.

The overlapping temples cast afternoon shadows. So did lingering rain clouds, so that the street alternately dimmed and brightened, but never with a direct ray. Then, stabbing through this gloom, came blades of light. At first they emerged from around a corner, striking upward through jagged layers of architecture and downward aslant across wet cobblestones. Celebrants scattered off the road. Temple doors slammed.

Then a figure strolled into sight.

Dalis-sar rose. He was huge, much bigger than Marc, but his outline wavered against the surrounding rooflines.

"Heliot," he said.

The other bared crooked teeth in a grin. Framing it, under the bald dome of a head, was a bushy red beard that stirred in an updraft of hot air. He wore golden armor dimmed by the overcast, yet still intermittently brilliant. The gleam that emerged from its joints showed best against shadows; when the street briefly brightened, it faded like flames in sunlight, although heat still rolled off of it. His figure, thus, seemed to shrink and swell as he advanced, in and out of the steam that erupted from puddles under his feet. Briefly, his form coalesced around that of a haughty man in heavy, rich robes who appeared oddly familiar. Then he swelled again until he had to bend under the overlapping roofs.

Jame drew back. Dalis-sar did not.

"Hello, boy," boomed the former king. "Didn't expect to see me again, did you?"

"My people told me that you had returned. That you can walk by daylight surprises me somewhat."

"Ha, ha, ha. Yet here you are too, while others hide. We are not of the common run, you and I. That comes, I think, of us both having once been mortal. Mind you, I see no other advantage to that state, and escaped it as soon as my followers' sacrifice allowed me to."

"I remember your warriors facing ours in battle. They thought it an honor to die in your name."

"So it was, boy. How else? My councilors thought the same, when I asked for their wives and daughters."

"Did they also expect their kin to die?"

"Now, would it have been a sacrifice if they had not? As to what the dear ladies expected, what does that matter? I will yet find my queen, but not among such paltry cattle. Your people, now, you say. Rather, your little pets. So you still place faith in them."

"They believe in me. That creates an obligation, even an affection."

Heliot loomed. His eyes were hot brown, small in his square face but huge as they bent down. His smile became a sneer.

"After all of this time, you haven't learned. Common folk are what we make of them. They live to serve us. What else are their tiny lives worth? What, for that matter, are you to your vaulted god of the three faces?"

"As faithful as it lies within me to be. I am a simple soldier, not a king."

"Simple you are, at least. Oh, sit back down, boy. Let's be comfortable. You too, girl." He peered at Jame, his eyes descending to a foot or so above her head as he shrank. He must have been a bantam of a man in mortal life, she thought, given his attitude, but no doubt he had worn stilted boots if he had felt that he needed a boost. "I can smell one of his precious kind a league away. By courtesy, you are safe from me. Unless I change my mind."

He and Dalis-sar sat on the curb, the latter warily. Jame was trapped between them. The heat radiating off both made her feel parboiled almost at once.

"Why fight me at all, boy?" Heliot wheedled, leaning over Jame's head. Her damp jacket steamed. "We have so much in common, and you have so much to gain."

"What are your plans here?"

"Why, to take over this city, of course, and then this world. The night is already ours, or will be soon."

"But most of your kind can't walk by day."

Heliot grinned. "He who rules the dark also rules the light. Think about it. Day will pay tribute to us because we hold sway when the sun has set. What are sealed doors and hearth fires to us? Oh, so much less than they now, in their arrogance, suppose. Dark is stronger, if only because it rules the imagination. Willing sacrifices are always the sweetest. Harness that and all falls before it. I saw the truth of that, in this city of ancient days. It was mine. More would have been except . . . except . . ."

"Except that people stood up to you."

"Except that they found such misguided champions as you, a traitor to your own divinity."

The tips of his beard burnt into indignant fire. Jame swatted at sparks as they fell.

"No matter! Our time has come again. You are already diminished. Soon you will all be gone. Oh, I foresee a time when the temples will be ours again. Then worshippers will swarm to us, some drawn by fear, others by greed or vengeance or grievance. Believe me, those are the levers that move mere mortals. Our people will have the best of everything and power over all except us. To please us will become their pleasure. Sons and daughters, husbands and wives . . . we will be dearer to them than all such mortal chattel. They will come to see sacrifice to us for the honor that it is. What do you think of that, eh?"

Dalis-sar shivered. "I would rather die first."

Heliot had been leaning on Jame's shoulder until she thought that she felt blisters rise at his touch under her *d'hen*. Now to her relief, he reared back and clapped his big, square hands on his knees. With veiled satisfaction? While he didn't want to fight Dalis-sar, neither did he apparently relish an equal.

"'Simple,' I said, and 'simple' you are. So be it. Lady, come here."

He spoke to a woman hovering within the temple's door, holding a spangled veil across her face.

How much had she heard, Jame wondered. How much could this demon-god sweeten with the sudden honey in his voice?

"I am what you seek. This clod is no longer worthy of your worship, if he ever was."

Dalis-sar rose and turned, pain cracking his expression. "Aden. Please don't."

"I-I have to go. He says that he can resurrect my beloved foster son Dally, who may yet save his half brother, Men-dalis. Can you do as much?"

"No. Nor, I suspect, can Heliot, or not in any way that would please you."

"But people say that the dead are returning." She held out her hands to him, pleading. The veil dropped. She was middle-aged, with the remnants of a great, if simple, beauty. "Lord, can't you . . . ?"

He turned aside. "I have always told you: I am no lord. Only your humble servant."

"Then good-bye, for the sake of our sons. Once I was young, and loved you. I always will."

She departed. Heliot went with her, stooping to drape an arm possessively around her shoulders. At the corner, he turned to leer back at Dalis-sar. Then they were gone.

Dalis-sar sank onto the curb and held his head in his hands.

"Was that . . ."

"Yes. The mother of both Men-dalis and Dallen, once a temple concubine and my love. It was so lonely before I met her, and again after she left to marry Dally's father. When her husband died, she came back, bringing her little son. Dally grew up in this sanctuary. I miss that boy, more than my own blood. Even after he moved on to live with his brother, he used to visit me. He brought you once, did he not? His half-brother never comes. He is jealous, I think. Perhaps I and his mother did favor little

Dally, but Men-dalis was still our true-born son. It broke Aden's heart when they became estranged. Ah well."

He drew himself up, a soldier facing hard facts as he understood them.

"People and times change. I never quite got the knack of that. It comes, I suppose, of always being a stranger here. But I can't go home while these people depend on me, as unworthy as I am."

Jame left him still sitting on the curb, waiting for his temple to be resanctified. There were worse things, she supposed, than simplehearted faith in one's followers.

V

IT WAS LATE AFTERNOON by now, with the sun sliding down behind the Ebonbane. More clouds had gathered to the north, a slow churn of them stirred by fidgeting winds. Perhaps rain was coming again. That smell she had noticed last night was growing almost strong enough to identify. Something about it made her uneasy.

Here was a stand selling spits of roast lamb and pearl onions, dusted with almonds. Had she thought to bring any money with her? Yes, a few coins scooped up from her unspent allowance.

"What's this?" demanded the vendor, turning over a small piece.

"A fungit, from the Central Lands."

"We have little to do with such foreign parts, less each year. How did it get here, then, eh?"

"Does that matter? It's silver." No need to mention that it had probably been minted with a curse in the Poison Court.

"If you say." He bit it. "Doesn't taste like lead, anyway. Here."

He handed her a spit. What she had given him was worth a lot more, but she didn't complain. Bad enough that word of Central Lands' silver was about to hit the streets.

"Fresh," said the vendor, watching her. "I got it from my cousin's sister's son come in from the countryside yesterday. None of your get-up-and-walk-away sort."

"Is that happening?" Jame asked.

"There are rumors," he said darkly. "I hear that beef hearts in Fleshshambles Street keep beating even out of the chest and have to be chased with spits. Beheaded fowl try to fly away. Fish won't stop twitching. Eels slither. There's even talk of the yeast in ale climbing back up the drinkers' throats to choke them."

Jame nibbled an onion, and spat it out.

"That's nothing," said the vendor. "When I trimmed off their roots this morning, they wept. My brother over on River Street says the eyes of the potatoes in his stew keep blinking at him."

Jame remembered the server at the Ringing Gold mansion: mewling street vegetables.

"Let me guess," she said. "You don't want to know what was in the cabbage heads."

He glared at her. "If you knew already, why did you ask? Here, you're one of the night-timers, aren't you? I recognize the cut of your coat."

As Jame walked away, she heard the coin ring in the gutter.

"Filthy nightie!" the vendor shouted after her. "Stay in the shadows where you belong!"

It seemed to Jame, now that she thought about it, that she had been getting hostile glances all day. Day and night in Tai-tastigon must be more at odds than she had realized, as if one saw contagion seeping from the other.

Mewling vegetables, naked beating hearts, roofs infested with woodlice, stone-mites (whatever those were) . . .

The clouds to the north appeared to form wispy, towering shapes as the north wind collided with the south. A shape was forming there that she felt she ought to recognize.

And what was that smell of death borne out of the Haunted Lands? Did the north gate stand open?

Huh.

Sleep, she supposed, would also be good, but she was used to going days at a time without it. Besides, she sensed that if indulged in now, it would bring bad dreams.

Ahead, a crowd of citizens swarmed around the shadow of a stairwell, leading down to a basement door.

"Kill it!" shouted some.

"Filthy abomination!" howled others.

Jame edged in between them. She noted that they held rocks and the fragments of cobbles, but despite their cries they hesitated.

A figure huddled at the bottom of the stairs. Its clothes were fine, but stained and torn. Judging from the wild mop of dirty blonde hair, it was a young woman.

"What are you doing?" she asked a pudgy man near the front clutching a large rock in both hands. "Surely this is one of your neighbors."

He glanced at her, his eyes glassy, his face slack with horror. "No. This was my sister. We cared for her, Mother and I, after she lost her mind. She had gone out to hold vigil for our god. I found her the next day wandering the streets and brought her home. At first she pleaded with us to let her go. Then she fell silent. Then she died. I went to fetch a priest. When we came back, Mother had gone in to make her presentable."

He laughed, his voice shrill with hysteria. Tears ran unheeded down his plump cheeks.

"I found her like that, crouching over Mother's body, gnawing on what was left of her face. Monster!"

He turned and heaved up his rock. Jame put a hand on his arm. He wheeled at her touch, nearly bringing the stone down on her head.

"Why?" he cried, more in bewilderment than anger. "They say that you nightwalkers have cursed us. What did we ever do except provide you with things to steal?"

"I'm sorry. Let me talk to her."

"Talk! Just try!"

Jame edged down the stairs. The girl flinched back into the shadows, hiding her face. Then she raised her head and bared her teeth. They were bloodstained, with strings of flesh caught between them. Her features were swollen, her eyes blank. She hissed. Jame retreated.

"That's a haunt," she said to the young man, "No, wait. Stoning won't help. You have to give it to the pyre."

She left as some of the crowd scattered, looking for fire.

Others stayed. Stone thudded on flesh. Bones broke. As a thin, piping scream rose behind her, Jame remembered the revenant return of Winter, the Kendar who had been her childhood nurse. She hadn't yet asked Singer Ashe if haunts felt pain. All that really mattered, though, was that their case was hopeless—yes, even that of Ashe.

She wandered on for a time, trying not to think, until someone brushed against her.

"Sorry," said a familiar voice.

Jame turned sharply. A blond head bobbed away from her among the throng of shoppers. She plowed after it, against the stream, and clutched a patched sleeve. Startled, the other swung around to face her.

"Canden!"

"Talisman?" He looked at first delighted, then wary. "You killed my grandfather."

"How many times do I have to say this? I didn't. He tampered with the Book Bound in Pale Leather and the master runes in it burned out his brains."

Canden regarded her dubiously. "Coming from you, that almost sounds reasonable."

"Look, where can we talk? The middle of the street somehow doesn't seem appropriate."

"My lodgings are nearby. Come along."

He led her off the main street, whose merchants specialized in hats, into an alley festooned with ribbons—cheap cotton ones, Jame noted, some no more than hanks of colored thread. One had to go elsewhere for silk or satin. Canden's room was over a particularly tawdry shop, with the stench of raw dye seeping up through the floorboards. The door was unlocked.

"Aren't you afraid of thieves?" Jame asked.

She noted that the small space was scrupulously neat except for a table piled high with maps. When she had last seen the late Sirdan's grandson, he had been southward bound with the renowned explorer Quipun to chart lost Tai-than.

Canden opened several cabinets, finding nothing, until one yielded a loaf of bread, a wedge of cheese, and a bottle of wine.

"Ah," he said. "If not for the thieves, leaving things, I would long since have starved. This city isn't kind to cartographers. However, Grandfather still has supporters, although these days none dare say that openly."

Jame accepted a cup of wine—a good vintage, she noted. Her opinion of the current Thieves' Guild changed, marginally.

She regarded her host. Canden was still a young man but much too thin, with a prematurely lined face and straw-colored hair that had begun to recede at the temples. The intervening years had not been kind to him.

"When did you come back?" she asked.

He sipped and shivered. She could see, as he clutched his glass with both bony hands, that he was trying hard not to gulp down its contents.

"Some three years ago. We were on site for almost two years before that, coming and going. It...unnerved me. The city perched on a steep slope below a mountain peak. Far below that was a river, then sheer cliffs, then a cloud forest with mist tangled in its upper branches. The top was so high up that the air was hard to breathe. That caused a curious sickness, a dizziness during which we almost thought we could see the city as it had been. Drinking the fermented juice of certain local berries helped."

He sank down onto his narrow bed and took another swallow from his cup as if not noticing it. His eyes lost focus.

"It had been a wonderful place. The buildings were constructed of cyclopean white granite blocks laid without mortar, following the curves of deep terraces. Workers and priests lived in square houses on streets winding upward. The temples were round, set in green, sloping lawns. There were so many of them that Quipun guessed this was a holy site, set apart by height and location from some lowland capital city long since lost. On the crest of the ridge, at the top of the town, was something different. Taller. Windowless. Alone. It stood in the shadow of the highest peak but seemed, somehow, to dwarf it. I can't explain. It was strange, and ominous."

Jame stirred. "That sounds remarkably like a Kencyr temple. I've heard that one was there."

Canden drank again and shuddered.

"Then there was the city as we actually found it, in ruins. Roofs gone. Trees growing up within shattered walls. It looked as if there had been a great earthquake, except that all of the fallen stone blocks had been pushed in one direction—downhill. Then there were the bones. Lots of them. The ones under the blocks were crushed, but those caught on the exposed side had been smashed to dust. Whatever happened, it seemed that everyone had been caught in it. There were no signs of more recent life."

"How long ago?" asked Jame.

"Quipun thought some two thousand years, on the basis of an uncompleted victory stele. It was in pieces when we found it, but if he got very, very drunk he could read it. It commemorated a united hieratic victory over a common enemy, a blasphemous cult who had set itself on high and proclaimed its truth to be preeminent. All of these people they had put to the sword."

That sounded very like another version of the Anti-God Heresy, Jame thought. She remembered what Dalis-sar had said about his temple having troubles of its own when he and his fellow guards had been sent north to help Tai-tastigon. If all the Tai-than priests had been killed, their unmanned temple might well have eventually exploded.

Yes, if the timing was right. Dalis-sar seemed to have no idea how long he had been in Tai-tastigon, but his followers should know. For that matter . . .

"Canden, when did this city last have a king?"

He blinked at her, confused. "You mean Heliot? That was nearly two millennia ago. Why?"

"I'll explain later. Maybe. What happened in the end to your expedition?"

He raised his glass again to drink, and was bewildered to find it empty. Jame restrained herself from pouring him more.

"We didn't last much longer," he said, his words beginning to slur. "Quipun wanted to see more. We all did. So one night we got very, very, very drunk. The bones rose. The people came back. They were celebrating. 'Our enemy no longer looks down on us,' they said. 'Come, dance with us.' Quipun and the rest went with them in their long lines, weaving around the white houses, the temples, up the linked, sloping lawns to that monstrosity on the crest, around it . . .

"I fell asleep. In the morning I was alone, surrounded by ruins and bones. Now here I am, home again, and oh, so tired."

Jame rose quickly to help him lie down. He was asleep before his head touched the gray pillow. She swung his feet up onto the bed, covered him with a thin blanket, and stood for a moment, looking down at him.

He began to snore.

Little lost boy. Unhappy young man. Good night.

∞∞∞ Chapter VII ∞∞∞
The House of Luck-bringers
Spring 56

I

RUE WOKE NEAR DUSK, confused. Where was she? What had happened?

Oh yes. As she relaxed, still half asleep, memory returned.

"Welcome to the Res aB'tyrr." That was where she was. Mistress Cleppetania, no, call-me-Cleppetty had welcomed her in Jame's name. This was where her lady had lived when she had stayed in this strange city. They had given her and Marc shelter and she had given them her loyalty.

Therefore, Rue was among friends. Reassured, her thoughts drifted again.

Breakfast at the kitchen table. Porridge with a dollop of honey.

Patches fidgeted with her bowl. Given her scant frame, she must not eat much, but Cleppetty still plunked it down in front of her. In this house, even an apprentice thief, it seemed, must be promptly fed.

On entering, Patches had presented Rue with a

flourish, saying, "The Talisman has sent this great moon-calf to help defend the inn."

Rue had choked back a protest. Jame had told her no such thing. What might she have said, though, to the little thief, in case they were separated? Rue knew in theory that some people told lies, but she still found the concept hard to believe.

"Well," Cleppetty said, standing over them, vigorously wiping her hands on her apron. "What has our Talisman been up to, all this time?"

How to answer that?

"Er . . . I didn't meet her until about four years ago, when she snatched up my ten-command and tried to storm Lord Caineron's fortress with us."

"Woo," said Patches, staring. "Start in the middle, will you?"

"I don't know a lot before then," Rue protested. "She came from here, apparently; she and Marc crossed the Ebonbane; she meet her brother at the Cataracts in the middle of a battle; he sent her to the Women's Halls at Gothregor; she escaped."

"My head is spinning," said Patches. "What brother?"

"Torisen, Highlord of the Kencyrath."

"She's nobility?"

"What we call Highborn, yes. And his lordan—that is, his heir."

"Two of them," mused Cleppetty. "And you're all still alive?"

"Well, not all of us," said Rue, with a thought to the late Killy, Vant, and several others. "She does tend to leave her mark, my lady."

Cleppetty snorted. "More like a scar. No, I do her an injustice there. She did us much good as well, here at the House of Luck-bringers. Wait a minute: you said that she escaped these Women's Halls. Did her own people imprison her?"

"That was at first," said Rue, spooning up porridge. "I don't know much about the Highborn, except that they keep their women in seclusion, bind their legs, make them wear masks without eyeholes, and farm them out like broodmares. Jame must have surprised them. She certainly did us."

"I dare say," said Cleppetty dryly. "Bloodstock, eh? No, I wouldn't see the appeal either, were I in her boots. We didn't know what to expect from her either then—still don't now, come to that. She says that the Sirdan has summoned her back. Something to do with his poor dead brother Dally. Now, there was a sweet boy. What happened to him would make the gods weep."

"What did happen?" asked Rue, who hadn't yet caught up with events.

Cleppetty told her.

Rue forgot her breakfast. "Her friend? They did that to him?"

"Someone did. People say that it was Bane who also, in a strange way, was her friend. The gossip on the street is that Bane was jealous of his rival."

Rue grappled with this. "My lady had two lovers?"

"Rather, none that I know of. I don't think she could make up her mind between them. And she's fastidious, is our Talisman. Now, there's a filly who would bolt any stable with a breeding box built into it."

The matter had never been put quite this way to Rue before. She regarded it solemnly. It might also explain, in part, why Jame had fled the Women's Halls.

Cleppetty folded her arms under her apron and hugged her sharp elbows.

"I don't know what's going to happen next," she said, frowning. "Now the Res aB'tyrr is mixed up with the Thieves' Guild or, more specifically, with its Sirdan. And to my mind, Men-dalis has not been right in the head since the last Feast of Dead Gods. For that matter, the whole city has seemed to go insane. The stories I could tell you . . . ! But now things may get worse, fast. The Talisman has picked a perilous time to return, much less to put you under our protection."

Choking back a protest that she didn't need protecting, Rue turned to ask Patches for her opinion on the leader of her guild, only to find that the little thief had snuck off, unobserved, as she and Cleppetty had talked.

Rue jumped to her feet. She hadn't meant to let Patches out of her sight as her last link to Jame. Cleppetty grabbed at her, but Rue shook her off, as gently as her agitation allowed, and charged out the door.

"Wait, wait!" Cleppetty cried after her.

However, Rue had caught a glimpse of Patches turning the corner by the ruined Skyrrman with a mocking glance back over her shoulder. Rue ran after her.

Within a turning, she lost sight of the thief. Within several more she halted at a crossroads, then took off to the right. The multicolored patch she followed turned out to belong to a countrywoman's skirt.

"Sorry," panted Rue, letting go of her captive.

"I should hope so!" the latter retorted and flounced off.

Houses leaned over Rue from both sides, three or four stories high, their upper levels jutting out over the narrow road. It was hard to trace the sun, although she knew that it had risen. People were everywhere, the morning being by now much advanced.

"Sorry," muttered Rue, pushing through them. "Sorry. Sorry."

Most were shorter than she was. It was like being back in Kothifir, although she had spent most of her time there in the barracks of the Southern Host among peers who had dwarfed her.

A "great lunk," Patches had called her. She hadn't noticed her comparative size so much before. Here among the morning crowd, it made her feel hulking and clumsy, an unaccustomed monster among midgets.

Otherwise, Tai-tastigon by day was a much more normal city than she had expected.

People went about their business, buying, selling, trading, as if they hadn't spent the previous night huddled within doors, almost afraid to breathe. Here from a doorway, a merchant extoled the virtues of his wares.

("Pots! Pans! An oven for your bun, madam?")

There another offered samples of his spices.

("All fresh! No city taint! You won't sneeze your nose off!")

If anything, their chatter was more pronounced than she would have expected, as if in defiance of the dark. There was even a street juggler at one corner, although his audience was all adults. Rue saw no children except at windows, fearfully peering out.

Not so normal, perhaps, after all.

She wandered on, lost. Notwithstanding her experiences in Kothifir, she was at heart the child of a small, isolated border keep. How could people live in such a maze without going mad? Maybe they all were. That would explain a lot.

She came to the ruins of an old city wall and turned right again.

If she were bound to Jame, could she find her? It seemed to work that way for Highborn: after all, Jame had found Brier in the chaos of the Western Lands, through one of Tagmeth's gates. But could Brier have found her?

I must ask, thought Rue.

All the Kendar at Tagmeth would be asking themselves such questions as the Randon Council drew near, but could any of them pass muster if Jame wasn't there?

Instead, for some reason, she was here.

At least Brier knew where she had gone, sort of. Jame had left a note.

Rue stopped short. Passersby bounced off her, cursing, but she didn't notice. Her hand dived into her coat and pulled out the scrap of parchment that she had found in Jame's quarters, the one that had sent her pelting after her mistress in the first place:

"Away on personal business. Don't worry."

She didn't remember stuffing the note into her pocket. At the time, she had barely been thinking at all. Sweet Trinity. The people back at the keep had no idea where they had gone. Brier was going to kill her. Maybe Jame would too.

After that, the day was a nightmare. Hot, tired, and

thirsty, Rue wandered on. More often than not, she turned right and so, not surprisingly, began to feel that she was going in circles.

Here was a market in a small shady square with a fountain playing at its heart. Rue drank from cupped hands and sat down on the rim to rest her feet. Potatoes, onions, green peppers, tomatoes . . . most looked good, but few customers were buying.

"Fresh from the country!" one vendor called over and over again in an exhausted voice, as if lamenting the end of the world. "Get 'em before they walk away. You, young lady, have a sample."

He handed Rue a tomato. It was big and red, but oddly shaped with bulges in unexpected places. She accepted it gingerly. Yes, she was hungry—breakfast seemed a long time ago—but the thing gave her pause. Drawing her knife, she sliced into it. As the skin split, little red seed packets spilled out over her hand along with gout of watery juice. Some of the bundles were pulsing.

"Overripe," muttered the vendor, hastily taking it from her and dropping its soggy remains into a box under his cart.

"I think it was pregnant," said Rue, feeling queasy.

Voices rose from the other side of the market, one of them sharp and familiar.

"This is a public place," Cleppetty was saying belligerently to the three men who loomed over her. "We pay our taxes. We've a right to be here."

"Yeah," said her young, gangly escort, trying to sound tough but swallowing hard. "Leave us alone or we'll set the guards on you."

"What guards?" said one, looking around with raised eyebrows. "If you mean Sart Nine-toes, he's on duty across town."

"Ha." Cleppetty jammed her fists on her hips. A market basket hung from the crook of one angular arm. "You made sure of that, didn't you, before accosting us. Brave puppies, to show your teeth when the big dog is away."

Rue rose and quietly pulled out the box of discarded vegetables. The vendor had retreated to the edge of the square where most of his peers stood warily watching the confrontation.

Cleppetty's opponents were large, rough-looking men, not Rue's idea at all of thieves, and they carried themselves like street fighters.

"Old woman, old woman," one said with a contemptuous laugh. "Who's that toothless bitch snarling now? Just tell us where your precious Mistress Abernia is, and your sweet Talisman. Then you can be on your way."

"You leave her alone!"

The young escort lunged forward, and met a fist to the jaw. He fell over backward with a crash and lay still.

"Ghillie!" cried Cleppetty, bending over him.

The other men laughed, until one was hit in the mouth with a disintegrating tomato. He backed up, sputtering, clawing at his face.

"It burns! G'ah, I swallowed some of it!"

Rue changed positions and pelted another man with a cucumber on the ear. It split, raining maggots down his collar. A rutabaga followed it. That made a satisfying thud but it only wobbled off afterward, bruised and whimpering. An eggplant . . .

I didn't throw that, thought Rue, and glanced aside to see the merchants also picking up missiles.

A green pepper. When it split, its seeds unfolded like so many baby spiders and swarmed over the third man.

The first bent over retching. The third frantically swatted at his head. The second recovered himself, spotted Rue, and charged at her. She evaded him with water-flowing Senethar, tripped him as he passed, and sent him sprawling into the fountain where he fell with a great splash and knocked himself out against its opposite rim.

The vendors cheered.

Under cover of a continued barrage of vegetables, Rue helped Cleppetty get Ghillie to his feet and the three of them staggered off into the labyrinth.

"Which way?" Rue panted.

"Follow me. It isn't far."

Nor was it. Here was the scorched side of the Skyrrman. Kithra popped out of the front door, staring, followed by a thick-set fellow who presumably was her husband, Rothan.

"Not now," Cleppetty wheezed.

Here was the fountain court and, at last, there was the Res aB'tyrr with the cat Boo a dark blot on its doorstep, meowing, as if he had never left.

They helped Ghillie stagger up to his second-floor room and then retreated to the kitchen, where Cleppetty at once put on a kettle.

"Mistress, you have problems," said Rue, and yawned. It had been a long day, and it was only half over. Then again, she hadn't slept since . . . when? Time had passed in the tunnels and the Anarchies—how much, she wasn't sure.

"Who were those men? What did they want?"

"You heard them." Cleppetty thumped mugs on the table and rummaged in a drawer for tea. "Mistress Abernia was Sirdan Men-dalis' 'guest.' Ha! Now he seems to have misplaced her, and with her his hold over the Talisman. He tends to lose people, that man, but someone else is always to blame, or so he says. As to those men at the market, they're brigands. Used to belong to Blind Bortis' gang until he disappeared into something called the Anarchies. Instead of haunting the mountain passes, now they hire themselves out as thugs to whomever will pay them. That looks a lot like Men-dalis, these days." She leaned on the sideboard, for a moment looking unnervingly tired. "I wish Sart were here. He could whip these curs into shape, or so he says. Heh, men. In the end, it always comes down on us women."

Rue yawned again.

"You're worn out," said Cleppetty, regarding her critically. "And you're just a child at that."

"Am not!"

"Are so, whatever your age. I'll show you where you can put your boots up for a while. Nothing should happen for hours yet. Then you'll need to be sharp, won't you? And you aren't about to chase after our Talisman again, are you?"

"I suppose not," said Rue, thinking of the day's frustrations, how helpless they had made her feel.

"Good. Come along."

II

AND THAT WAS WHERE RUE found herself now, in a cheery little room with blue flowers painted on the ceiling.

"Wake, oh wake," she thought she had heard a voice calling. The room had been full of a sweet presence and melting light. Now only shafts of the latter slanted in the western facing window. Day was fading.

She hadn't meant to sleep so long, nor did she have much of an excuse except that she had been tired and, well, overwhelmed by recent events.

A child? Ha. Still . . .

Highborn were better at keeping vigils than Kendar. Look at Torisen, who once had spent nearly two weeks awake although, granted, it had driven him almost mad. The whisper was that he had feared bad dreams. One didn't hear as much about such behavior on his part these days, since his sister had returned. Hope, there. Like most Kendar, Rue wasn't entirely sure where her loyalties lay. She was Jame's, bound or not. But Torisen was the Highlord. The health of her home, of her people, depended on the ability of those two to accept each other.

Weighty thoughts. No wonder Rue was finding it hard to breathe. Her eyes had drifted shut again. She opened them. What she had at first supposed to be the heft of anxiety was in fact Boo sitting on her chest, toes tucked in, purring loud enough to rattle her ribcage.

"Hello, cat," she said, freeing a hand from the blanket

to scratch his nocked ears. "We were introduced, oh, sometime much earlier today."

Someone rushed into the room. A girl. Wearing very little.

"You're awake!" she exclaimed. "Good! No one will scold me for disturbing you!"

Rue watched as she threw open the chest at the foot of an opposite bed and began to rummage through it. Clothes flew.

"What to wear, what to wear . . ."

"To do what?"

The girl shot a simpering smirk over her shoulder. "I'm the new dancer, aren't I? Oh, they'll see something tonight!"

They would see a lot, thought Rue, regarding the tumble of diaphanous clothing.

"The trouble is," the girl said, holding up a sheer— scarf? bodice? pair of drawers?—"the B'tyrr set such a high standard, and yet no one I've asked can really describe what she wore. Or didn't wear. Is this fetching enough?"

Rue stared through the transparent garment, whatever it was. "The B'tyrr?"

"Or the Bat-ears, some say. Anyhow, this was years ago—oh, she must be so old now—but her legend lingers, damn her. You should know. After all, she was one of you."

"One of my what?"

The girl rushed out of the room without bothering to answer, trailing filmy snatches of cloth.

Rue pushed off Boo, who complained, and rose.

Her coat and boots were alternately on and under a nearby chair. Had she put them there? How sleepy had she been? No matter.

The bedroom was one of several lining the second-floor balcony that linked the front and back halves of the inn. Below were the stable and its attendant yard. At the north end was a square stairwell that led down to the inn's kitchen, from which delightful smells arose.

Rue descended.

Three kettles boiled over the flames, one for stew, one for soup, and one, tucked under the stair, with a scullery behind it, for wash water. Besides, between the kitchen and the main room spits turned over flames on which were skewered fowl and a dripping haunch of beef.

Rue's stomach grumbled.

"Sit down and eat," said Cleppetty, thrusting a bowl into her hands.

Rue was hungry, but memory of the market made her hesitate.

"Are there . . . vegetables in this?"

"Yes. This nonsense has been going on long enough for us to have learned a few tricks. At first it was enough to buy only from the country or from the gardens in the outer ring of the city. Since then, the blight has spread. Now, we try to catch vegetables and fruits just before they ripen. Their innards may look strange, but they taste all right, if not quite up to their full savor."

Cleppetty sighed, the thwarted professional. "A real trial it's been for us cooks. Still, trial and error. Oh, but such errors . . . !"

She shook herself. "Dried beans have always been safe,

though. That's what you have there, with lentils, basil, and a touch of saffron. As for meat . . . "

Boo had followed Rue into the kitchen and sat up begging for dinner. Cleppetty slapped out raw chicken livers on the kitchen table. They quivered. She flailed away at them with a hand mace until they were flat, bloodless, and still.

Boo protested.

"He prefers them still a-twitch," Cleppetty explained, serving the cat, "like the mice he's gotten too fat to hunt. I found that out when I left the kitchen unattended for a moment and came back to catch him playing with his dinner. But why take chances?"

"And that?" Rue glanced at the beef roast.

"Cook anything long enough and it gives in."

Rue tasted her soup warily. It was delicious.

Cleppetty crumbled something onto a plate and touched a flame to it. Incense spiraled up.

Ahh . . . ! the room seemed to breathe, and for a moment a flush of light washed over it.

"There," said Cleppetty to the air, with a note of huffy indulgence. "Happy?"

"What?"

"Oh, we have a resident goddess, thanks to our Talisman. We don't know her name. She followed Jame home on the Feast of Dead Gods, dying herself, as I understand it. That happens to gods who outlive their believers. Jame may be a monotheist—you all are, poor things—but she'd seen enough to believe that our gods, on some level, are real. She offered that to our lady. She's been here ever since."

Rue wrestled with this. "Jame said that she believed in this goddess on those terms? And you make her offerings?"

"Well, yes, for encouragement. Why not?"

"Have you ever seen her?"

Cleppetty shrugged. "A glimpse, now and then, out of the corner of my eye. Leave something to faith, I say. The Talisman did."

From the dining hall came the sound of the front door stealthily opening.

Cleppetty darted out. Peering past the meat spits, Rue saw that she had collared Kithra as she had tried to sneak in.

"Let me go!" the girl cried, struggling to free herself from the cook's grip. "You're keeping him a prisoner! I just know it!"

Cleppetty shook her. "You know no such thing, you little fool. Master Tubain has taken to his bed, upset over misplacing his wife. That's all."

"For two whole months?"

"He's very upset. I'll not have you disturbing him. Go home."

"*This* is my home, not that horrid wreck! Why can't Rothy and I live here in comfort while it's being rebuilt? Uncle Tuby will agree, I know he will, if only I can talk to him!"

Cleppetty shoved her out the door, slammed it behind her, and stalked back to the kitchen.

Rue hastily resumed her seat.

Her hostess snatched up any stray dish she could lay hands on and dumped it into the streaming wash water.

When this didn't adequately express her feelings, she set about clattering pots and pans as if they had mortally offended her.

Rue ate her soup, trying to look tactful but flushed with curiosity.

"Oh, that girl!" Cleppetty paused, hugging herself fiercely as if afraid that she would fly apart. "It's her own silly fault that she's living under half of a roof. She was a maid there, back when Marplet sen Tenko owned it, but he threw her out. We took her in and Tubain's nephew Rothan married her. That gave her ideas. Rothan is Tubain's heir, y'see. Some day the Res aB'tyrr will belong to him. Well, Kithra decided that it belonged to her now. Mistress Abernia and I were to step aside, if you please. To get some peace, Tubain bought the ruins of the Skyrrman and gave them to his nephew to rebuild on condition that he take his bride to live there in the meantime. He's not been very handy at it so far, even with Tuby paying most of the bills. And so we rub along from day to day as neighbors. Of all times, though, for her to start raising a fuss . . . !"

The front door opened again, flung wide this time. Heavy footsteps stomped across the hall floor. Rue jumped up in alarm as a man nearly as big as a Kendar burst into the kitchen.

"Sweet-tart!" he shouted, and swung Cleppetty off her feet into a smacking kiss. "The captain has given me the night off. I'm yours until dawn! Who is this?"

He turned, smiling, to regard Rue.

She stared at him—wide mouth, small eyes, scrunched features that might have been described as pleasantly ugly—and couldn't decide what to make of him.

Cleppetty straightened her clothing, unaccountably blushed, and introduced her guest.

"Well now," he said. "So the Talisman sent you. I've been told to keep an eye out for that little lady."

"Why?" demanded Rue and Cleppetty, simultaneously.

"Nothing to worry your pretty heads about." He grinned, giving the impression of being entirely trustworthy.

Cleppetty glowered. "You swear?"

"Trust me, love."

She relaxed. "Well then. This is Sart Nine-toes, Rue. My husband."

⚜ Chapter VIII ⚜
Meanwhile
Spring 55

I

IN THE STABLE beneath Tagmeth's courtyard, Brier picked up the chestnut's rear hoof and examined it. The horse shifted uneasily, ready to flinch away or to kick. She gave him a slap on the rump to settle him.

"You thought he might be developing a crack," she said to Cheva.

The horse-mistress leaned down to look. Perhaps it was true that one came to resemble one's partner, or charges, or pets: Cheva's face was distinctly long, bony, and equine, proof if any was needed of her many years among the remount herd.

"That's always a danger with a flared hoof wall," she said, "as I've warned you before. I thought this morning that it felt warm. And he's obviously sensitive to the touch. You'd do better with a different mount, especially for such a demanding ride."

One hundred and fifty miles to Gothregor, starting two

days from now, the longest she dared to wait, with three days on the road. Yes, if they started with sound mounts, pressed it, and didn't depend on the post-stations. After all, it would seem as if half the Riverland were on the road south to attend the Randon Council.

Was she spooking at shadows, Brier wondered, to mistrust the way-stables at Restormir and Wilden? They were manned by Caineron and Randir, though, the houses least likely to want an additional Knorth presence at the Highlord's keep. It would also be in their best interest, as they saw it, to keep Torisen's sister and heir away.

But Jame was already absent, with no sign where she had gone. This was the second day.

Brier released the gelding's hoof, resigned to finding a different mount.

They had to leave, whether Jame returned in time to go with them or not. After all, she wasn't the only one upon whom the Randon Council was about to pass its verdict. All of Jame's original ten-command faced the same trial except for Killy, who was dead. Char, too, must present himself to see if his repeated senior year qualified him to become a full-collared randon. There were several other cadets, too, from different ten-commands. With a jolt, Brier remembered that she was also up for judgment, despite a year as Tagmeth's marshal.

So much had happened. The trip north, the ruins needing to be rebuilt, the isolation, the threat of starvation, the yackcarn stampede, the discovery of the gates, the Caineron attack . . . they had survived it all. Brier had played her part, but so had Jame, despite early fears about her ability to lead—and yes, Brier had also harbored those. Her involvement with perfidious Caineron Highborn made her a skeptic. Her previous experience with Highborn ladies was nonexistent. Judging by Jame, who knew what horrors the reclusive Women's Halls might conceal?

But that wasn't her business. She was bound to her lady. This was her home. These were her people. Those were her loyalties. Belatedly she thought of Torisen, the Highlord. Well, yes. She owed tribute to him too, but Jame (usually) was so much closer.

A cadet ran down the steps from the courtyard.

"It's that Southron," she reported. "He slipped through the savannah gate and got chased by a pride of spotted cats."

Brier swore. Graykin had been a nuisance ever since his arrival, and not just for his Highborn pretensions when everyone knew that he was only Caldane's illegitimate son by a Karkinoran serving wench. Jame apparently found him useful. Brier, however, didn't approve of spies. Neither did Torisen, she reminded herself, having been watched by the Ardeth throughout his early years with the Southern Host. Kothifir was one thing, though. What good did Jame think her peculiar servant could do here in the Riverland?

Perhaps Graykin wondered about that too. Ever since his arrival, he had bedeviled Brier with his suspicions that she wasn't telling the truth about Jame's disappearance, as if she knew what that was. He lurked and listened, all the time in the bright coats that he couldn't seem to put aside. Brier understood his insecurity. Admit it: she was insecure too. But that didn't make her more sympathetic to a half-breed Caineron.

Grow up, boy, she thought. *We all have to*.

He had been fetched back to the courtyard where he drooped next to the well, panting. His hair hung in sweaty tangles, his ornate coat in limp folds of crimson and gold. It was hot on the savannah.

"They only chased him because he kept popping up behind clumps of grass to see where they were," the cadet said in her ear. "They're mischievous little things, best at pulling down rabbits and small fowl. Maybe they thought that he wanted to play."

Graykin glared at Brier. "You're trying to kill me!"

Brier frowned. "What?"

"Why didn't you tell me that the gates were portals to dangerous places? Where was I? What were those creatures? In Perimal's name, what's going on around here?"

"True, I didn't tell you about the gates, but I didn't hide them either."

Had it been in the back of her mind that he might stumble through one and not come back? If so, why not?

"Now you know," she said. "The question is this: can you be trusted to keep your lady's secrets?"

"She thinks so. Who are you, to question that?"

"In her absence, I command here."

He sneered at her, an effect somewhat marred by the hair flopping limply into his eyes, getting into his mouth. He spat it out. "Well, I know more than you can dream about the doings of Jamethiel Priest's-bane, past and current. After all, she bound me first."

Had Brier known that? If so, she had deliberately pushed it out of her mind. Moreover, giving Jame her full title felt like a slap in Brier's face. Who was this little snot to know that? It was in her mind, on the tip of her tongue, to call him a liar. Jame's current doings? What were they? Where was she? Not for the first time, Brier felt as if she were falling.

She didn't trust me. Can I trust her?

"For that matter," Brier said, pulling herself together, "she bound her ounce before either of us." And her gaze shifted briefly to Jorin, once again napping beside one of the closed gates, not even in the sun. Why always there?

"Clean up," she told the spy. "There's a bath chamber below the keep." *Yes, which will take the hide off of you, soft thing.* "We'll talk later. Maybe."

II

IT DIDN'T COME TO THAT. Graykin avoided both the subterranean room with its channels directly to the icy river and dinner, which he ate in his tower room.

That night, the skies broke loose. Lightning glared across the courtyard. Thunder rumbled down the throat of the Silver. Brier woke repeatedly, and cursed herself for her nerves. It was only a storm.

But here was a guard, bursting into her room.

"Marshal, come quick!"

From the barracks' doorway, she saw a figure standing in the middle of the courtyard next to the well. It seemed at first to be bulky, although its face was skeletal and its outline flinched with each crack of light and sound. Rain bounced around it on the stone flags. More coursed down the deep seams of a cloak that appeared to be struggling to escape.

Flash. Boom.

The cloak slipped off to fall with a meaty thud and a splash. At its hem, serpentine heads rose, questing. Then they slithered off in an undulating wave, their tails twitching behind them. Graykin yelped and leaped back as the thing coursed past him into the shelter of the tower.

Left standing in the courtyard was a painfully thin figure, beginning to shiver in the cold rain.

III

"THE LASS DREAMED ABOUT THIS," said Marc. "Over and over again, coming closer each night."

They had met in Graykin's first-story quarters. The stranger had been installed one flight above them, under Jame's room. He still hadn't spoken and was sitting motionless before a newly kindled fire, ignoring the cup of mulled wine placed at his elbow and the dry clothes laid out on the nearby bed. No one had felt like touching him. Drip, drip, went his clothes, somehow audible on the floor below. Outside the rain had stopped.

"Did she say who he is?" asked Graykin. For once, he was dressed in what was probably close to his usual attire—a patched, shabby dressing gown. As if aware of this informality, he kept his arms crossed tight over his narrow chest.

"Someone out of the past," Marc said with a shrug.

"And you mean to keep him? What if he's an assassin?"

"Oh yes?" said Brier. "So weak that he can barely stand? You know her so well. You tell us who he is."

"Not who but what: danger!" Water gathered between the ceiling boards. Graykin flinched from the falling drops. "At least keep him confined!"

"These are your assigned quarters, at the foot of his stairs. Shall we make you his warden?"

"I'll tell you this," said Marc, leaning forward, elbows on his knees. "He's Highborn—mostly Knorth. I've been around the lass long enough to know that. Each house has its own savor. We've been hard on that family in the current age. There aren't many left."

Graykin gave a bark of scornful laughter. "Are you saying that this is some long-lost relation? A thrice-removed cousin? A maiden uncle? Then what was that thing he was wearing, a family friend? Where has it got to, anyway?"

"Upstairs?" said Brier. "It looked suspiciously like a set of matched, living snakes stitched together with silver thread." Now, why did that sound familiar? "Check your bed before you get back into it."

"Tell Jame that when she returns. Where is she anyway?"

Did he think that he could surprise the answer out of her? Would that he could. Brier rose, her fire-cast shadow falling over the Southron. It pleased her to see him flinch.

"Until our lady reappears, we keep him as an honored guest, just as we do you."

With that, Brier left, feeling once again in command but at the same time uneasy. What if she had just made a terrible mistake?

ᕈᕈᕈ Chapter IX ᕈᕈᕈ
Gods and Demons
Spring 56

I

THE SUN HAD SET. Pink-ribbed clouds still crowned the jagged heights of the Ebonbane, but already their edges were fading. Below in Tai-tastigon, twilight lingered in glowing store windows, in the anxious faces of shoppers hurrying for the shelter of home against the swiftly falling night. Soon the thieves would be on the hunt. There wasn't much Jame could do about that, though, except take to the rooftops again, and so she did.

Now what? she wondered.

Usually, life presented her with a series of evolving events, punctuated with disasters. One saw some shape to it, if sometimes only after the fact. So far, today had seemed almost random. Well, then, the pieces couldn't be fit together until they were all found, and several were still missing.

At the moment, though, the stray piece that worried her the most was Rue. She had brought the cadet to

Tai-tastigon and was responsible for her. How was she faring in this strange city? Where was Patches likely to have taken her? Back, perhaps, to her home in the Lower Town?

Therefore, Jame soon found herself in that desolate district. Night hadn't quite fallen there, the ruins seeming more wretched as a result. Doors stood half-open, scruffy children loitering on their thresholds, reluctant to leave their play in the streets, but voices began to call them in.

Here was Patches' house. One of her siblings stood on the step, holding open the door for the wobbling toddler. Both were so wizened that it was hard to tell if they were boy or girl. One of each, Jame thought.

"Is Patches here?" she asked the older. A girl, surely. "Or my friend Rue?"

The girl shook her head. Then, almost stealthily, she closed the door in Jame's face.

Jame was left on an empty street, the last soft thuds of doors sounding down it, farther and farther away. Light showed through cracks, then disappeared inch by inch as each in turn was stuffed from inside with rags. A thin wind rattled dust down the road. Some stars were coming out, but the moon, shrunken by now to its last quarter, would not rise for hours yet. Besides, there were the massing clouds to the north, through which silent lightning stitched. It was becoming very dark.

Opposite her, someone stood in deepening shadows, leaning against the wall. Did he even breathe? She couldn't tell. His folded arms crossed his chest tightly, as if to hold himself together. His black hair hung in shaggy locks over his downcast eyes, from which came the sliver of a silvery glint. He didn't cry, but she was reminded of the little boy she had seen before. This stranger, however, was several years older, almost a young man.

"Are you still here?" she asked him, tentative in her approach, unsure of her instincts.

"Still."

His voice seemed to come from a great distance, and it was as bitter as the dust banked at his feet.

"Did your father turn out to be a king?"

His thin lips twisted in a smile, the gleam of white, bared teeth between them. "No. Nor even my true father."

"Then who are you? What is your name?"

He laughed, and told her.

"Oh," said Jame, blankly. "I . . . see. I think."

"I have . . . urges. Look."

He shoved back a sleeve. His bare forearm was crisscrossed with cuts. The skin hung down from it in looped ribbons.

"The man who called himself my father told me what to do when I hurt, to ease the pain. And so I do. If I can't hurt others, I hurt myself . . . or is it the other way around? Either way, it . . . calms me. I must have done something wrong, to be the way that I am. Father—Abbotir—says so, anyway. But the priest says that I needn't be damned. I have been cut adrift by circumstances, but my true people have rites, rituals. That man who calls himself my father . . . he wants, he orders, he demands. . . . Skin is nothing."

He tore away a strip and grimaced. Blood spiraled, black, down his wrist, dripping off his fingertips to smoke on the ground. He grinned. More teeth.

"See? It comes off. However, honor runs beneath, to the core, if one cuts deep enough. If I am forced to compromise, I will never stop. Then I am damned indeed."

Jame took an impetuous step forward. "Don't trust that filthy priest with your soul. He will only betray you."

However, the other was already drifting back into the shadows.

"Bane!"

She tried to grab him, but her hand scraped against the flaking paint of an empty wall on which someone had drawn the stick figure of a hanged man.

"I will do what I must," breathed the wind. "Honor is all."

II

THE KENCYR TEMPLE stood close by. Jame felt drawn to see it although she expected no comfort thereby. It rose into the night sky, white, cold, unfeeling. Here was a god who gave no hope but the oblivion of fire and ash. And honor? What was that to the dead? Bane, perhaps, could answer—if he was truly gone, which she now doubted.

That thought haunted her. She had her people's horror of the unburnt dead, trapped between life and death. Things should be one way or the other. This in-between state was like the taste of vegetables in the Haunted Lands that shrieked in boiling water and screamed when pierced with fork or knife, but whose savor was only that of watered blood. Tai-tastigon seemed to be experiencing something similar. Was that what she had tasted in her dinner's onions? What did it all mean?

The Lower Town's wasteland opened up before her. A cloud of dust hung over it, raised by the feet of those who stumbled, lost, across its expanse. How many there were. Why were they here, and where were their shadows?

Two figures walked toward the temple, a man holding the arm of a woman. The latter wore a glittering veil that she held with a trembling hand across her face as if to shield herself. When she tripped over debris, the man jerked her back to her feet. That, surely, was Heliot. In the gathering dark, his armor gleamed crimson at the cracks as if it floated on a volcanic lake, and his red beard fluttered up against ruddy cheeks.

"Onward, my dear," he was saying, with a savage grin. "Just a few steps more . . ."

The dust before them stirred. Something rose out of it, to a knee, to its feet. The stars dimmed above it, tangled in its hair. It swayed over their heads like a column of smoke fretted with fire. Aden drew back, but her guide still gripped her arm.

"I want you to meet someone," he said.

"Will he help my sons?"

"Not 'he.' She. Did you think you were the first to catch the eye of a sun god?"

"Let me go!" She twisted helplessly in his clutch. "I came here for Dally and Men-dalis!"

"That doesn't matter now. Your lover is weak. He can't lie. I can. What is the truth but a bright bubble upon the air? Prick it and poof: it is gone. My darling Kalissan, I have brought someone to meet you."

The shape of the dead goddess bent over them. Aden screamed. It seemed to swoop down on top of her, rapidly condensing and gaining substance as it descended, knocking her off her feet. When she tried to rise, it batted her with the huge, smoky paw of a hand and tilted its head to watch her stagger as a cat might its prey. Even Heliot fell back a step, but then steadied himself.

This, Jame supposed, was his chosen consort, undoubtedly of the Old Pantheon with more than a touch of the demonic, accustomed to human sacrifice. Her lineage must be far more ancient than his own, compared to which he was but newly come to divinity. Could Heliot possibly feel . . . insecure?

"Oh yes," he said softly, regarding the fallen woman. "This one is not another empty husk. Observe her shadow, which you have made dance, oh, so charmingly. Hush, lady. Is this not your proper fate?"

"Dalis-sar, save me!" Aden cried, and tried to run.

Another tap. She fell again and cowered, weeping, as Kalissan crouched over her. With the tips of long nails and surprising delicacy, the goddess drew aside Aden's veil. A third eye opened in Kalissan's forehead, clearer than her other two that were so blood-shot they glowed like monstrous carbuncles.

"Yes," said Heliot as Kalissan bent to peer down and to sniff. "She has borne a god's son. So pretty once, now so old . . . ah, mortals. You and I, my love, have seen millennia pass, yet we are coming once again into our prime. Is she acceptable?"

The goddess gathered the mortal woman, rigid with terror, into her arms. Aden gasped. Kalissan held her, crooning into her ear, and licked her eyelids with a barbed tongue that drew blood. Aden's shadow tore loose and was dragged, struggling, to pool at Kalissan's feet. With a sigh, Aden went limp. The goddess let her slide to the ground.

Heliot offered Kalissan his hands and drew her up. She rose in the shape of a woman, if with preternaturally sharp features, pointed teeth, and a belt from which hung the flayed skins of babies. Her nostrils flared. Her third eye quested—for the living, Jame thought. She felt it lock on the ruins of a wall behind which she crouched. Such hunger. . . .

Heliot reclaimed the newborn demon's attention with a chuck under her chin, to which she responded reluctantly, her eye straying back to the spot where Jame hid.

"You are my queen now," he told her, "and thus I am at last a true king. That creature's soul will support you in your new state, but you must still feed to gain strength. Come. Let us hunt."

They walked off, she stumbling a bit in his supporting grip, still looking back over her shoulder, but growing steadier with each step.

Jame emerged from hiding and ran to Aden's side. Dalis-sar's consort wasn't dead as she had feared, but when she opened her eyes they were blank in a ravaged face, and her shadow was gone.

"My name was . . ." she murmured, floundering to her feet. "My name was . . ."

Should Jame take her to Patches' house? Would she even go? The urge to wander had already seized her and she tugged fretfully at Jame's grip.

"My name . . . my name . . ."

Dammit, Jame had stood there, transfixed, and watched it happen. She could have . . . what? Rushed out? Demanded that they stop? Here, next to the temple, she might even have danced that witch and her consort down, never mind that they were gods and she was only the third of one in nascent form. But she hadn't. Thus, Aden had been lost.

Figures rose about her. In the dim light, it was hard to see if their robes were brown or black, but she recognized them as Kencyr hieratic garb.

Aden twisted free and fled. Jame took a step after her, but her way was blocked.

"Child of darkness, we know who you are."

The priests wove around her, arms outstretched.

"We also know your friends. Defy us, and we will hunt them down—yes, even that pathetic little thief and all of her scrofulous family. Will you risk that?"

She didn't dare.

They escorted her to the temple, keeping their distance as if from something unclean. The doors swung open. Inside were the familiar curving corridors, their floors laid out with triangles of serpentine, lapis lazuli, and ivory. Power flowed inward like swift water over that tessellated bed. Jame staggered, then caught her balance. It felt as if the pavement were rippling underfoot. So, perhaps, it was. She had seen that happen before when the current was particularly strong. In the past, however, it had flowed mostly outward to the hungry gods of the city—spectacularly so on that last night when they had gorged to the point of bursting out of their temples.

"Well, go on," said one of her conductors—an acolyte, she now saw, by his brown robe. He gave her a push, then stepped back hastily as she turned on him. Hah. This kitten had claws.

Why not continue, though? She had questions to ask, more and more by the minute. Jame let her feet take her away from her guards, barely in touch with the floor, inward with the flow.

The halls boomed with power. Walls seemed to swell, in and out, out and in, like passing through the guts of some monstrous creature. She floated above her feet, toes scrabbling for contact.

Dust shaken out of paving cracks jittered on the floor and spiraled up in corners. A figure formed there, watching her. When she turned to look, however, it was gone, except for the lingering hint of a smile.

Ah-ha-ha-ha . . .

"Stop it!"

Her shout surprised even herself. The temple had always been alarming, but not like this.

. . . ha-ha-ha . . .

The laugh chuckled away. She was alone again and, strangely, regretting it.

Here was the central chamber, where she had first met that noxious hierophant, Ishtier. The door closed behind her. The room grew still, the floor quiet underfoot except for a slight, nervous tremor as the outer temple pressed in on it. Jame could feel that same pressure in her head, but tried to ignore it. This was no time for clouded wits.

To one side was a well-defined whorl in the tessellated paving where she had danced down the power set loose by Ishtier in his ill-conceived experiment with divinity. The major pattern, however, still spiraled around the black granite figure of her god. Torrigion, That-Which-Creates; Argentiel, That-Which-Preserves; Regonereth, That-Which-Destroys, fused back to back to back, facing outward. Odd, she hadn't seen anything like it in the Kencyr temples she had visited since, but then Tai-tastigon was an odd place.

Someone stood beside the statue, in a belted robe as black as the stony folds above it, in outsized boots.

"I want to talk to you," said the young priest in his abrupt manner, unfolding from the shadows. "Especially after learning who you are. The legendary Talisman. A thief, of all things and, worse, a rogue Kencyr. You also had something to do with this temple's near collapse five years ago. I was one of the priests sent to pick up the pieces."

"Sorry about the mess," said Jame. She had wondered what that rescue mission had found. "You've been here ever since? What have you heard from the Riverland?"

"Precious little. The high priest told us virtually nothing when he returned with his followers. I only just learned about you."

Jame braced for outrage similar to Lord Harth's. Instead, this peculiar priest regarded her more with skepticism than animosity. *Really?* his arched eyebrows seemed to say. *You caused all that trouble?*

"What were you doing in Tai-tastigon in the first place?" he asked instead. "This is hardly a Kencyr enclave."

"Oh, I was just passing through, but ended up staying longer than I intended."

"Didn't you find it strange here? All these temples, these so-called gods . . ."

Jame gathered her thoughts. Something about this man made her want to talk. *Shanir*, she thought again. *Be careful.* But still, how often did she have a chance to compare notes with one of her own priests?

"When I first arrived," she said, beginning to pace, "all the supernatural entities in this city panicked me. We are taught that there is only one god. Here there are many. We also value truth as much as we do honor. So. Is our long, painful history based on a lie?"

Now he was pacing with her, hands clasped behind his back. Five steps one way, turn away from each other, five steps back. Turn. *Clump, clump, clump* went his heavy boots as their god's image seemed to sway above them.

"I did eventually realize," she said, turning again, "that Tai-tastigon's New Pantheon came into existence at the same time that our temples started up, immediately after the Fall and just before our arrival here on Rathillien. Then I saw the gods of Tai-tastigon flare and come untempled when Ishtier let the power of this temple run amok. Between, I realized that the New Pantheon draws its power from our temple, but its shape from the beliefs of its worshippers."

Titmouse grimaced at Ishtier's name, but otherwise his pace remained steady.

"That was when I first heard of the Anti-God Heresy— the belief that 'all the beings we know to be divine are in fact but the shadows of some greater power that regards them not.'"

"Wait. The local priests say that?"

"They aren't all fools, and this city's gods aren't just parasites. It's more complicated than that."

He glowered at her. "I don't see why it has to be, but go on, tell me: how?"

"The thing is, there was native power here before we arrived, before the New Pantheon arose. The first I knew of it was when I met the Four."

"Who?"

"Earth Wife, Falling Man, Burnt Man, Eaten One, the elementals of Rathillien. They also came into being when our temples started up, but before that they were mortals who worshipped gods even older than they. That would be the Old Pantheon, which owes nothing to us. And before that, there were what Granny Sits-by-the-fire calls the 'Big Truths' wholly native to this world. In the desert, they were such as Stone, which tells truths hard to bear. Dune, which reveals with one hand and covers with the other. Mirage, which always lies and lies without purpose. And Salt the Soulless. Mountain and Ocean presumably had others. Field, cliff, and hedgerow too, as far as I know. Perhaps they all still do. The Arrin-ken might know."

"You make my head spin."

"So did mine. To summarize . . ."

"Must you?"

"You will thank me. The point is that while our temples have had a tremendous impact on the nature of this world, there was native power here before us that lingers to this day in the Old Pantheon and especially in the Four. It seems to me now that divinity isn't one thing, nailed down forever. It changes as people change, and people are changed by it. Did that make it untrue for Rathillien? Does it for us?"

"Are you saying that we should no longer believe in the Three-faced God? Because of your . . . researches?"

"Oh, our god is real, whatever that is."

Ancestors knew, she felt at least one aspect of him (or her, or it) thrumming through her even as she spoke. What was such power good for, though, if not to break down outworn concepts, old ideas? If she overstepped, it was in recklessly creating new ones, or in clinging to what she only wished to believe.

"Here's a thought," she said slowly, considering it outloud. "In the beginning, say that the Three-faced God existed alone on our three home worlds, monotheism incarnate. We accepted that destiny, were proud of it. Too proud, perhaps. We lost. Fleeing down the Chain of Creation, we shattered our direct link to our god. He didn't abandon us. We left him behind, except for fragments embedded in the Shanir, waiting to reemerge as the Tyr-ridan."

"You're guessing."

"Yes. There could be any number of explanations. For example, here's another one: Perimal Darkling invades the Chain of Creation. The Arrin-ken bring together the Kencyrath. Looking for a reason, we create our deity with our faith out of the god-stuff present on all of the worlds. In our pride, we have to be unique, so that's how we see our god: monotheistic. See? I can spin you ideas all night long."

"Next you'll say that the Builders were to blame by

undermining worlds with their god-engines, otherwise known as our temples."

Jame shot him a sidelong glance. "Oh, you're good. I hadn't thought of that. Go on. What else?"

"Maybe the first three Arrin-ken were called Torrigion, Argentiel, and Regonereth."

"Now you're scaring me. This isn't the first time you've thought about this, is it?"

"Nights in the Priests' College are long and not always quiet. Sometimes one can't sleep."

Yes, he had endured that pesthole at Wilden where the strong preyed on the weak. Titmouse had undoubtedly been one of the former, although even based on this brief acquaintance she didn't think he was a predator. How, then, had he felt, hearing those cries in the dark? Had he known her cousin Kindrie?

Jame wrenched her mind back to the present.

"I think," she said, "that all of this makes my point. Why have we let one interpretation shape our entire society? What do we really know about what happened thirty millennia ago? Oh, perhaps the Arrin-ken do, but they haven't talked freely to us about such things in a long, long time, if ever. In a sense, maybe it doesn't matter except in how it helps us to move forward. And the last days are coming. I can feel it."

She cleared her throat. Some thoughts choked her with horror. So much was coming, so much depending on her and upon those whom she loved.

"At least you haven't yet accused me of blasphemy," she said with a shaky laugh. "I'm trying to figure out how our past became our present, without invalidating either."

"You're forgetting the God-voice."

"So-called. On rare occasions since we came here, the voice has spoken through rare individuals, Ishtier for one. I've come to believe, though, that that was the Arrin-ken."

Titmouse blinked. "What conceivable reason can you give for that?"

"Think about it: There's the Fall, with Gerridon trying to create his own future at the cost of everyone else. After it, the Arrin-ken support Glendar as the new Highlord on Rathillien, but the priests try to turn us into a hierocracy. For the first time, the God-voice speaks through the high priest to smash their pretensions. Sorry. I forgot for a moment that I'm talking to a priest. Say, though, that that was actually the Arrin-ken again."

"Then they lied?"

"They didn't actually call themselves God's Voice; they let the priests assume it."

"A lie, then, by omission."

They had still been pacing but now stopped, facing each other.

"I don't know the mind of an Arrin-ken," said Jame. "I don't think one would deliberately lie, but their morality is . . . different."

He snorted. "And these are our judges."

"They would be, if they deigned. We aren't what we should be either. There is this too: since I was last in Tai-tastigon, I've met two of them face-to-face, Immalai the Silent whose territory is the Ebonbane, and the one we call the Dark Judge, from the Riverland. After the fact, I recognized their undertones in what spoke to me out of

Ishtier's mouth. What game are they playing? I'm still not sure."

"Huh. At least you admit some ignorance."

"About a great deal. Life has been very confusing over the past few years. Think about it, though: what good have the temples done us since we first came here, perhaps even before? Yes, up until now they've allowed us to flee from world to world, but what world have we managed to hold except, so far, Rathillien? And the temples here are crippled. The one in Kothifir was never even completed. Since then, several others have been destroyed. Where are we today? What's going on here in Tai-tastigon? You have a host of dead gods on your doorstep. Some of them are preying on the souls of mortals and, I think, becoming demons in the process. I refuse to believe all of that is coincidence. What does it have to do with this temple?"

"As to that . . ." he began, but was interrupted.

The door opened and a novice thrust in his head, eyes showing their whites.

"M'lord," he said. "Dinner has been carried away by a seething of maggots, and a headless chicken is wandering the halls."

"I say nothing about the chicken, after the escape of last night's bustard. Cook can't deal with a few ambulatory sausages, though?"

"Cloth weevils are eating his hat. Just the same, he refuses to take it off."

"Oh, go away," said Titmouse.

The door closed, reluctantly.

"Problems?" said Jame.

"First it was a shadow. Don't ask me what cast it. Those

it touched had nightmares of being wrapped in darkness and afterward couldn't stop shivering. Our novices were most affected, although I have felt it too, watching me as I slept. Then it was bloody footprints, starting at one wall, ending at another or in the middle of a room. Then it was a figure lurking in the corner, sometimes composed of dust or old clothes, sometimes of insect wings. How in Perimal's name do we get flies inside with only one door and that usually shut? But the thing always falls apart if anyone touches it."

Jame wondered who would be bold enough to try.

"It's a bloody nuisance," the priest concluded in exasperation.

"You said that before. Are we talking about Bane?"

The door opened again, a crack.

"M'lord," hissed the novice. "It's in the pantry now. The floor is crawling with black beetles, making obscene patterns. The novices are hysterical. And the high priest is coming."

"I said go away. You too." Titmouse flapped a big hand at Jame as he turned aside. "I want to think."

III

OUT IN THE NIGHT AIR, Jame paused to consider. She had gone to ask questions and ended up instead mostly answering them. Obviously more was going on than she knew. That, however, was hardly unusual. If only time wasn't so short and her way so confused.

The gibbous moon had yielded to its last quarter, rising

over the eastern plains to under-light the clouds that continued to gather over the city. The north wind seemed to be banking them there, almost into a recognizable shape, while stray huffs of the south wind teased its edges. It must be around midnight.

Debris crunched.

Jame turned to face those sad figures shambling through the ruins. One of them must be poor Aden, although from here Jame couldn't discern the woman's hunched form or shimmering veil, if she still had the wits to wear it.

From her fate, though, Jame had realized that the dead gods were feeding on mortal souls, and that was turning those who already had the proclivity into demons. Kalissan appeared to fit that description. So, from what she had heard, did Heliot, with his dependence on his followers' sacrifice. Ironic, but not surprising, that he should aim for godhood and end up a demonic predator instead.

For that matter, Ishtier had never understood the distinction. To him, it had only been important that his experiment, the Lower Town Monster, supposedly disproved his god's monotheism and therefore severed Ishtier's loyalty to that divinity even while he continued to make use of its power. Also, he had seen the Monster as under his control, but had that been true? It was hard to tell, since he had let it wander freely, feeding on the souls of children as it went. His control over Bane had been intermittent at best.

A dead god plus a human soul equaled a demon. She remembered her glimpse of that haughty man at Heliot's core. Who was he? Did Aden now reside, aghast, in the monstrosity that was Kalissan? One soul might act as an anchor, but more apparently were food, to give strength.

G'ah. There were so many pieces to this puzzle. What a mess she had unwittingly left behind when she had fled this city. What an irony, if it turned out that she had had to return to sort it all out in order to secure the future of her own people. Tai-tastigon was important. She had always sensed that, even when she had sought to discredit it.

Three shambling figures approached, hooded like lepers. For a moment, Jame thought that the temple acolytes had returned. These robes, however, were black, if dusty and tattered. A stench wafted toward her, part stagnant water, part rotting flowers, part something indefinable that made her sneeze. Bone-thin hands reached in supplication.

"Name, name, name," stuttered voices, and one, the foremost, croaked, "Help us. Please!"

They spoke in Kens.

Jame backed away. Were these the missing priests whom Titmouse had mentioned so disjointedly in Patches' house? What had happened, to bring them here, in such a state? Help them? Sweet Trinity, how?

A pebble skipped between them. They turned and stumbled off, another flung stone kicking up dust at their heels.

"I thought they would never leave," said someone perched on a nearby pile of rubble. "Really, the company that you keep!"

Jame regarded the stranger with a sense that she knew him. Her second intuition was one of dislike. Who . . . ah. Men-dalis.

The Sirdan rose and shook out his robes. There was little glamour in them tonight. His face, even, wavered between the semi-divine and the thoroughly mundane.

"This is you, incognito?" Jame asked.

"May not a king go masked among his humble subjects?"

No one seemed to be with him, although shadows lurked in nearby doorways. One, closer, smiled at her over the Sirdan's shoulder. Dally. She had thought on Ship Island that he had been literally in the mirror. Perhaps, though, he had only been reflected there, standing behind his brother who had cast no reflection himself. Neither had she, for that matter. Men-dalis' glamour did seem to be turning on him.

For a moment, the coat that he wore took on the lopsided dimensions of a *d'hen*, impossible to tell in this faint light of what color. He turned quickly, but not fast enough to catch that fleeting image. The illusion faded.

"Sneaky little brat," he muttered. "I'll get the best of him yet, you wait and see. Ahem." He cocked his head at Jame with a winsome smile. "Shouldn't you be doing something?"

"What?"

"You were summoned, you know. I did that because, because . . ."

"Why?"

She wanted him to confess—to what, she wasn't entirely sure and almost feared to know. He had drawn her all the way from the Riverland, at a perilous time, with a threat against her friends. What could justify that?

"I know that my . . . er . . . guest, the innkeeper's wife,

has been removed. Such a gross betrayal of my hospitality. Darinby should not have helped you there."

"He didn't, deliberately." Sudden apprehension struck her. "Is he all right?"

"I spoke to him. He admitted his lapse in loyalty. Is he 'all right'? Well, he drooled for a while but that, I think, cleansed his spirit. Sometimes one needs to be reminded whom one's master is. As for you, if you will not do this little thing for me, what good are you?"

"What 'little thing'?"

"Ah, you know." His voice sank momentarily to a rapid whisper, as if he was afraid of being overheard. "You have seen it. The dead have returned, but I will not have it so. It's so unfair! This regards that which stands behind me and will not go away. Hush. Do not name it."

Then his voice rose again and his smile returned.

"Abbotir would like to see you dead, to pay for the death of his precious Theocandi. I tell him that I am his Sirdan now. He needs no other. But he will not listen, nor will certain others. Perhaps, instead, I should listen to them."

"Dead, how can I serve your purpose?"

He laughed lightly. "Oh, you will serve me, one way or the other. Everyone does, eventually. They should know that by now, yet I am not always given the love and respect that I deserve. If I were to avenge my predecessor, though. . . . Now there is a thought."

With that, he turned and drifted away, drawing shadows after him. One stayed. Small, dark, crooked . . . Men-dalis' spymaster, the Creeper, lurked on the edge of the town's desolation. Faint moonlight glimmered on pale eyes within the recess of a hood, on the slight, mocking curve of a smile. Then he turned and fled.

Jame ran after him, hardly knowing why. His master wouldn't answer questions. Maybe he would, if caught.

Did someone chase after her? Her instinct said yes, but she shrugged it off even as she heard a familiar voice call out for her to stop. First things first.

They were out of the Lower Town into the south bank districts when Jame realized that the Creeper paused at each crossroad, deliberately remaining in sight. Had it been wise after all to follow? She slowed just in time to avoid running into a figure that stepped out of an alley to block her path. Others emerged to surround her.

This is ridiculous, she thought, backing up. *Twice in one night . . . ?*

Before she could turn, she was grabbed from behind and her arm jerked up behind her, throwing her off-balance with a jolt of pain. Her cap was snatched off, her head jerked back by its loosened hair. Moonlight shone on the blade held under her chin, on the keen edge. She recognized by the other's full, reinforced sleeve across her throat that one at least of her assailants was a thief, dressed to commit a flash-blade's violence. In the dim light, however, it was hard to distinguish the color of his *d'hen*—royal blue for Men-dalis, black for dead Theocandi, or something else altogether.

The Creeper crouched in a doorway, watching. "Cut her throat," he said in a hoarse whisper, and licked his lips with the pale worm of a tongue.

"Wait."

Darinby stepped out of the shadows, hands raised in

protest. He was breathing fast, as if from hard pursuit. Patches' goblin face, twisted with alarm, peered out behind him, then ducked back out of sight. They must be the ones that she had heard following her.

"Our master forbids it."

"Men-dalis does not know, nor will he ever."

"Then I will tell his advisor, Abbotir. You and he are rivals for the Sirdan's favor. Everyone knows that."

The Creeper hissed and jerked his head. Darinby was also seized, also threatened with steel. The blade nicked him through his *d'hen* and he bled.

The goblin spy sneered. "Pretty boy, I do for my master what he cannot do for himself, no, nor yet his precious lord of the Gold Court. Abbotir is dying, and he has made a fool's desperate bargain with death. Ask him if you dare: where is his shadow? As for this girl, do you think that she can save Men-dalis? If so, you and he are greatly mistaken."

"Darinby, I'm about to be decapitated. Do something."

"This one's blade is a bit lower."

He held very still, with only a hint of tremor in his voice.

"Creeper, why are you doing this? The Sirdan's brother has come back to haunt him. Only he, or perhaps you, knows if that is justified. But this was Dally's friend. He loved her. Surely he will listen."

"What will she tell him?"

"The truth!"

"What good has that ever done anybody? My lord only needs one agent. Do you plot to take my place? Damn Abbotir. Damn that pampered brat Dallen. Damn you.

I." He thumped his shallow chest with a scraggly fist. "Me. Mine. Daughter, show yourself."

Patches edged out of the alley, looking wary. "Don't call me that," she said.

"My name holds power. So should yours. What are we, if not the shadows of greatness?"

Patches drew herself up with a jerk. "I'm the Talisman's Trinket, I am, and proud to be so. That's honor enough for me."

"Foolish girl, to settle for so trifling a thing. If not you, then one of your siblings. The baby, perhaps? Oh, I could raise him to suit me, if you should fail."

Jame felt the knife's edge under her chin and held her breath. Then she felt something else through the soles of her feet: the cobbles had just lurched.

Whump . . . whump . . . whump . . .

Something very large was approaching, or at least something very heavy. Stone juddered again. The thieves holding Jame and Darinby released them and backed away, looking frightened.

"No, no, no!" hissed the Creeper. "Kill them! Kill them all!"

Instead, his minions ran.

The thing, whatever it was, was coming down the street. Moonlight traced a dim, gigantic, lurching form, defined mostly by the dust that it raised even on a street still wet from the day's rain. Broad, circular depressions marked its advance. Fissures radiated out from these to zigzag up the neighboring walls. Furniture crashed over within darkened rooms. People screamed.

The thing seemed to hear. It reared up and slammed

against the nearest second-story window, which exploded inward. A confusion of near-invisible tentacles—or were those proboscides?—fumbled through the opening, drew out a shrieking woman, and dropped her on the street.

Whump.

In the center of a new depression, her body flattened and spread in a jumble of flesh and blood and broken bone. The monstrous head bowed. Blood briefly traced a round mouth set with a ring of teeth.

Jame and Darinby had backed up against a wall. Across the street, they saw the Creeper hesitate a moment, then bolt.

The head turned. A foot came down again.

Patches grabbed the fleeing figure and swung it out of the way, nearly getting crushed herself in the process. She tried to hang on, but the master spy twisted out of her grip and darted away.

The apparition stomped past through puddles, leaving rubble in its wake.

"What the high, holy hell was that?" asked Darinby as he and Jame joined Patches in the middle of the ruined street, staring down the path of destruction.

"Once a dead god, now a demon," said Jame. "It took that poor woman's soul through her blood, and no doubt walks all the more heavily as a result. Oh, schist. Here it comes again."

Perhaps it had heard them. The gigantic footsteps were coming back, picking up speed.

Whump! Whump! Whump! Splash!

They had come down in a broad puddle. The demon sank into it amidst a seethe of thick limbs. Its head reared up, appendages flailing, and it clawed at the rim, but something gripped its nether limbs and jerked it down. For a moment, ripples slapped the edges. Then something rose. Eyes the size of bucklers, fiddling whiskers . . .

Bloop, it said, and submerged.

Water drained out of the puddle through the surrounding cracks. The bottom was barely an inch down.

"Really?" said Jame, staring after it. "Again?"

"What?" demanded Patches, clinging to her sleeve.

"An old friend, I think, although I never expected to see her here."

"Her?"

That was a good question. Did one differentiate between the inner and outer fish? Then there was the question of Drie. Maybe she should have said "them." Time to change the subject.

"By the way, what did you do with Rue?"

Patches let go of her, glowering. She knew when she was being put off.

"Took her to the Res aB'tyrr, of course."

That would have been the safest place for her, once, but now?

They were walking now as they talked, none quite sure where they were going, but with an unspoken consensus that it would be best to leave this particular part of town.

Perhaps because she was on the ground, Jame saw more than she had the previous night. On one street, phantom flames licked houses, kindling any wood that they touched, especially around window frames. Glass fell in molten drops. On another road, ladies in white swirled past, whispering, "Dance with me, dance with me," all in the same plaintive tone. On a third, long tresses of hair floated out of alley mouths.

"We offer you wealth, fame, love," breathed seductive voices in the shadows, and the hair became clutching brambles that scrabbled after them as they passed.

Dead gods, all.

"Patches," said Jame, picking burrs off her sleeve despite piping protests, "why did you risk your life to prevent the Creeper from getting squashed? I would have said, 'Good riddance.'"

"Would you?" the little thief replied vaguely, refusing to meet her eyes. "Doesn't the Talisman usually save her enemies?"

"Not all the time. Not that one. I would like to ask him some questions, though."

"Well, then."

"Not so well. You're hiding something from me."

The girl wriggled as if to free herself, then gave in with a sigh.

"It's a long story, and you're partly to blame."

"Me?"

Patches scowled at her. "You left, didn't you? You don't know what that last night was like and I don't know for sure what your part in it was, but I bet it was plenty. Anyway. . . ." Here she gulped. Jame felt sure that she bridged a gap in the story. "Most people survived. I did. Then I went home to see if anyone else had."

All three ducked as a swarm of rats burst out of a side street and took flight over them in a whir of leathery wings. Dead gods come in many strange shapes. These, at least, didn't appear to be demons.

When Jame glanced at Darinby, once so elegant, now so disheveled, he wouldn't meet her eyes. Perhaps he was again wrestling with his faith in the Sirdan. How strong was the grip of Men-dalis' glamour on him?

...enough to make him drool...

"Go on," she said to Patches.

"Oh. Well, that involves guesswork, and I don't like what I'm guessing. The night you left, after all the rest, Men-dalis sent his thugs to our house in the Lower Town, to hold my family hostage, to make me tell them where you had gone. I didn't know, of course, not until later. The Creeper scared them away before they could hurt anyone. I was mad at him, though, for using Dally's death to start the guild war that put Men-dalis in the Sirdan's seat. 'All wars have casualties,' he says. Just like that, as if it didn't matter. I tried to punch him in the nose. When my fist got tangled up in his hood, I sort of groped around inside and pulled out this."

Looking defiant, she stripped off a glove and presented a plain, silver wedding ring, loose on her knobby finger.

"Mother wears one just like it."

"Are you saying that the Creeper is her husband, your father?"

Patches' expression crumpled. "He even called me 'daughter.' You heard him again, just now."

Jame had to admit that there was a family resemblance, not just with Patches but with all her siblings, so preternaturally alike.

"You've never met your father?"

"Some nights we sleep so deep we might as well have been drugged. Some nine months later, usually less, there's another of us—one since you left, as you may have noticed. Oh, you don't know what it's like to have a monster for a father!"

"I thought I did," said Jame. Her new experience of Ganth was still sinking in. She wondered how Tori was coping. After all, he had harbored that malignant shard of their father in his soul-image most of his life. They still had so much to discuss.

But Patches, the Creeper's daughter? Sweet Trinity, what did that mean, and who or what was the Creeper himself, come to that?

Ahead, the street curved. Light and shadows moved, gigantic, against the opposite wall. Voices murmured.

Patches caught Jame's arm. "Now what?" she hissed.

A small group of people came into sight, their leader carrying a candle hooded in a lantern. In his other hand was a ball of twine that he wound up with deft flicks of his wrist as he advanced. Although he was coming straight toward her, Jame saw no sign of the extended string beyond the flickering halo of light.

He stopped. "Who calls?"

"Two who wander," Jame answered. She thought that she recognized this pudgy, strangely dignified figure in his loose white robe. His shock of hair was also white and his blind eyes, without pupils.

"Are you lost?" he asked.

Jame glanced around. She hadn't been paying attention, but she recognized this crossroads from her training, also by the banners of an obscure lay brotherhood that hung from balconies above, notable for their priapic designs.

"This is the corner of Leek Lane and Oyster Street. We're three blocks from the River Tone and the Moon in Splendor."

"I thought so. See?" He turned to his clustered followers. "The way is clear."

"Pardon me," said Jame, approaching him, "but aren't you Pathfinder, sometimes called the God of the Lost?"

He smiled. "I was. Now I merely wander. These are my friends, who wander with me."

A dozen pairs of anxious eyes regarded her. These must be the loyal remains of his congregation. She remembered Loogan saying that some gods had come untempled and fled the district to start a new life among mortals. This would appear to be one of them. What better home for him than the labyrinth, given his nature? Among other things, she remembered, he was patron of the Guides' Guild, so vital to strangers and even to many residents seeking to navigate the city's maze district by district. Nonetheless...

"These streets aren't safe," she said. "Especially at night. You should find shelter."

"My house is close by," said one of his followers, a prosperous but nervous-looking man. "With room for us all."

"You are generous, Nathe."

"I have cause to be. When my wife died, I was truly lost—until you showed me the way."

"Listen," said a woman, catching Nathe's sleeve.

Little huffs of air disturbed grit in the gutters.

Forward it rattled, then back. Above first one banner stirred, then another and another, swaying back and forth. The sound came again like a monstrous snuffling, in and out, out and in.

Something big and dark came prowling down the street, a black node from which shadows writhed.

Sniff, sniff...ah, it went, and settled on its haunches with a satisfied grunt, obscuring several houses.

"I won't be lost again," cried the woman, on the edge of panic. "I won't!"

"Then stand behind me," said Pathfinder.

Patches nudged Jame, "Maybe we should too."

But Jame stood rooted, continuing to stare at the approaching shadows. When they fell over walls or cobblestones, they seemed to be totally opaque, and they writhed as if trying to escape. Whatever cast them now crouched in the middle of the street, somehow even denser than they. Huge yellow eyes opened level with the balconies. The gash of a mouth gaped, fringed with a double row of white teeth. A red tongue lolled out over them, licking chops.

"So, Pathfinder," it growled, a cavernous, hungry sound hoarse with echoes. "I have tracked you down at last."

"So, Pathless, you old black dog. Come back from the dead, have you, and in what form this time? No matter. Those who worshipped you are long since gone."

The other snarled. Paint peeled off windowsills at the sound. Ice spread around the shadows' edges in torturous forms. "As if I ever really needed them. Now, as in olden days, I hunt and feast on souls. One was even given freely to me, to wake me to this new life. Besides, my old followers left me for you—me, who gave them the freedom of the night!"

"You gave them terror and confusion. Their worship was appeasement and blood sacrifice."

Listening, Jame experienced a creeping horror. She no longer knew where she was. The street names hovered, meaningless, in her mind. The city dissolved around her, all of its ways swirling into chaos as if she had never known them. Worse, she felt empty at the core. Why had she thought that she mattered in this world where demons lurked?

I am nothing. I am nobody. I am alone.

The fiend crouched and licked its lips. "All ways are futile," it crooned through ropes of steaming slobber. "All ends are meaningless. What is life but a mindless scramble in the dark? But I can be kind. One snap of these jaws and all is settled. You curs who follow this old man. Give me your failed god."

Patches' nails dug into Jame's arm. "Do something!" the Townie hissed.

Jame shook herself. Dammit, she hadn't come this far to fail now. But it still took all of her willpower to step between the demon and the god.

"It can't take you against your will," she said to Pathfinder, hoping that she spoke true. "Only your followers can betray you."

"I don't want to die!" screamed the woman, and fled.

Shadows lashed out after her, cast like a net. They entangled her. She fell. The web cut into her flesh like string through moldy cheese. As the shades withdrew, darker than before, it was unnerving how inert her body lay, as if it had never lived at all. Then it sank into the cracks of the road.

"This is obscene," said Jame. "Your pardon."

She took the lantern from the god's hand and threw it into the crouching presence. Glass shattered. A single flame spread with a whoosh, kindling invisible veins. The creature lurched away. Shadows burned back to the body in a rush and freed souls fled, gibbering. The black dog's body writhed and shrank with the heat. Now it was a cruelly misshapen canine, now a hunched man with wild eyes and frantically moving lips.

Save me! he mouthed, without sound.

Jame went forward a step. She almost knew that face. "Who are you?"

But he was gone. On cobblestones a-drip with stinking ichor, the demon Pathless huddled and slavered.

"Go," said Pathfinder.

It went, whining.

The light remained, emanating even more brightly than before from the god's body through the white folds of his robe.

"I'm sorry that I put out your candle," said Jame.

He smiled at her, or rather in her general direction. "That was only a prop. Look. I still have my ball of twine."

IV

HIS LIGHT dwindled down the road as he and his followers withdrew. As many as could clutched his robe. Jame wished, briefly, that she could join them. Pathfinder seemed so clear, so benevolent, so reassuring. It must be wonderful to have such certainty, but dangerous too, if one stopped asking questions.

"Psst."

Jame looked up. A gable moved, resolving itself into Sparrow, hunched far out over the eaves with unnerving insouciance.

"You took some finding," the Cloudie said. "Cavorting all over town, aren't you?"

"Why were you looking?"

"Well, I have a cousin, name of Robin, who likes to hang out around the Temple District. No accounting for taste. The roofline there is a nightmare, which may be the attraction for a daredevil like him. Anyway, he says that there's trouble. All else aside, your friend Loogan is frantic. He sees Robin and shouts up at him to find you. 'Come,' he says. 'Come quick.'"

"Why?"

"My daft cousin didn't wait to hear. To be fair, the roof he was on had started to crumble. Woodlice and stone-mites are getting to be something fierce. I'm for home before this roof collapses too. Bye."

"You aren't going there," said Patches as the Cloudie vanished.

"Loogan needs me."

"Huh. Everyone needs you, or haven't you noticed? What about me?"

Jame considered. By now, Men-dalis would have a new target: the Res aB'tyrr. Did he know yet that Tubain, or rather Abernia, had returned home? He saw the latter as his hold on her, not that she had done much for him yet

even under that threat. When in doubt, he would think,
apply force. Could he attack without the surety that
Abernia was there? Anyway, what were the rules about
abducting an innkeeper's wife? Such things in Tai-tastigon
were complicated, hinging on the judgment of the Five,
but they were currently preoccupied. She should have
spoken to the Archiem about this situation. After all, he
owed his edge over his rival Harr sen Tenko to the
destruction of the Skyrrman that she, in part, had caused.

"You drove him to desperation," Harri had said of his
father. "He was ready to try anything, to break your hold."

Save me!

G'ah, everyone wanted help.

"I need you to check on the Res aB'tyrr," she said to
Patches. "I value those people above my life, above my
honor. It shames me that so far I've only put them in more
danger. Patches, please. Who else can I trust?"

The Townie squinted at her sideways, jealousy and
pride in the balance. "Well, if you put it like that . . ."

Jame watched her go, a slight, crooked form twitching
patchwork *d'hen* and shoulders nearly straight as she
went. Should Jame have gone herself? If the Sirdan
moved against the inn tonight, what good could the little
thief do, and at what risk of getting herself killed?
However, some instinct warned Jame to keep her distance
until she had achieved some results. Her role was still out
in the city.

Follow the smell of trouble, she told herself. *Sooner or
later, the pieces will fall into place.*

When she at length approached it, the Temple District
was dark, but with light blooming in bursts through the

cracks of its improbable roofline. Yells and shrieks echoed within, also booms that shook the ground. Jame entered cautiously.

The first street she came to, two monstrous half-seen figures thrashed back and forth across it. Walls fell as tails lashed. Jaws yawned silently and tore. The apparitions seemed mostly saurian. Intermittently, as if lit by strokes of lightning, two bewildered men fumbled at each other. One, glimpsing her, mouthed, *Help us!* and then was gone.

Jame edged past.

The district seethed with scrambling, indistinct forms. Here a figure with the head of a bull rutted around the door of a New Pantheon god dedicated to masculinity. Here something crawled, snuffling, before a temple to avarice. Here a filmy woman murmured seduction on the threshold of yet another sanctuary.

That door cracked open. A man leaned out, glassy-eyed. Hairy black legs emerged from under the woman's skirts and snatched him. As the spinneret between her nether limbs began to wrap him in silk and she eagerly locked him lip to lip, hidden hands stealthily closed the door in his wake.

Packs of other dead gods roamed the streets, except that by the behavior of most, they had been transformed by human souls into demons. The air throbbed with raw hunger. Jame remembered Heliot's consort, Kalissan, who had needed to hunt to gain strength even after her transformation. These creatures appeared to be only single-souled. Thus they were much weaker than the more successful hunters of their kind, and more desperate.

She saw that they were attracted in particular to the temples of the New Pantheon rivals who had supplanted them. Some of the latter stood defended by their worshippers, the diminished gods themselves presumably huddling inside. Others were abandoned. When the demons found such a temple, they swarmed into it in a froth of phantom limbs until its very emptiness drove them out again. There were no souls to prey on here.

Other ragged figures hunted in their wake, avid for scraps. These looked like townfolk except for their tattered clothes and scuttling, disjointed movements. No demon bothered them, because they cast no shadows.

One paused, sniffing with what was left of its nose. Jame saw that it was a haunt. And it had caught her scent. The whole pack swarmed after her. She fled.

Turn one corner, skid around another . . . where could she find shelter?

Ahead was a temple that Jame remembered well, a boxlike affair in the section dedicated to those of the Old Pantheon who had survived the change to newer times, if just barely. The one who had dwelt here five years ago had been all but dead. As she approached, a clot of demons was expelled from the temple's door and bolted, silently shrieking, into the night.

The haunts were right behind her. She ducked inside.

Snuffle. Scrape. Whine.

They were on the threshold, but none dared to enter. Hunger soon drew them back into the night, onto their never-ending hunt. It wouldn't have helped them if they had caught her, Jame thought, leaning back against a wall to catch her breath. Like the demons, these haunts craved the souls that they had lost and now smelled through the flesh of the living. Unlike the demons, they could never reach that deep, gnaw as they might.

Now, what had made them flee this place?

The structure had grown several times since its founding, each shell encasing its predecessor. All of them seemed to be abandoned, until she came to their heart. This should have been dominated by the looming statue of an Old Pantheon fertility goddess named Abarraden, she whose eyes Penari had stolen. The last time Jame had been here, with her old master, the inner sanctum had consisted of said statue on a small island, enclosed by a moat, and nothing else.

It was dark within, the only light coming from the embers of an enormous fireplace set against the far wall. That hadn't been here before. Neither had the figure silhouetted by its glow.

"I said," boomed a familiar voice across the room, "GO AWAY."

Jame fell back a step, then checked herself. Cautiously, she advanced. Underfoot was an earthen floor. The ceiling loomed as high as she remembered, but now it was crossed with blackened rafters from which hung many bundles of leather and fur.

"*Quip?*" said a sleepy voice, and wings stirred.

The figure before the fire seemed to grow as she approached until it might have been the missing statue of Abarraden itself, stepped down from its plinth. Its back was turned to her, she saw, nearly as broad as it was high. She touched it gingerly at the level of its hip, shoulder height for her.

"I said . . . oh. It's you."

"Mother Ragga? What are you doing here?"

"Where is 'here'?"

"Rathillien. Tai-tastigon. The Old Pantheon District. Abarraden's temple. You really don't know?"

"Huh. I might have guessed. This must be my punishment."

Jame settled cross-legged beside her and glanced up. The fire's glow touched the Earth Wife's dumpy, mashed together features—dough-like cheeks, pursed mouth turned downward in a frown, furrowed brow . . . but what was wrong with her eyes?

"Why should you be punished?"

"I worshipped the old biddy, didn't I? Long, long ago. She was comfortable, and good for getting babies. Farmers were in and out all day long, come about their herds, bringing offerings. Only grain, vegetables, and fruit, mind you. No blood for her, not that farm wives don't know the taste of sausage. That made me wonder, early on. The Old Pantheon liked their sacrifices, though. Not so much these new folk. Abarraden was before her time there. Thin blooded, I call her, and them. Still, they prevailed. Abarraden was one of the few to span both orders, Gorgo another. But I was a child of the old order. Maybe I never believed as much as I should have. In those days, you did as you were taught and didn't ask questions. I prayed for a son. Abarraden gave me one."

"'There was an old woman,'" murmured Jame, "'who dug her son's grave. And when it was done, he buried her in it.'"

"My mother's goddess didn't save me then, oh no. I did that myself. Afterward, things were different."

They would be, Jame thought, when Mother Ragga found herself apotheosized into one of the Four. It had occurred to her before that not only had Rathillien's elementals once been mortal, but that they had probably been raised to believe in their people's gods among the Old Pantheon.

"You think that she's punishing you for being an apostate?"

The Earth Wife snorted, a volcanic sound that shook the floor and caused logs to topple in the fireplace. A spurt of flame revealed her feet—cloven, like Abarraden's. "A fancy word for a child's fault. That's all I was then, compared to what I am now."

Jame shuddered, remembering her own cry: *"I was only a child! What did I know of consequences, of right and wrong?"*

Enough, sense had told her, *to know better*.

Mother Ragga subsided, rumbling morosely, gumming jaws large enough to munch a full-grown pig whole.

"You grew up here?" Jame asked, to keep her talking.

"It was a big city even then, although less complicated. The change was yet to come, from old to new. These days, I stay away. Too many of these newfangled gods running around. Too much noise. Too much . . . guilt. She's dead, you know. Poor old Abarraden. Ran out of worshippers. Lost her eyes. Look."

She twisted about and bent over Jame. Her sockets were pits, crossed with scars in their depths. Whole galaxies could have fallen into them and disappeared without a trace. Solar wind keened silently between dead stars. She turned back to the fire, grumbling.

"I don't know what happened to the second eye. The first . . . ah, that was a long time ago. I loved a boy, you see, much younger than I was then, but the father of my only son. Doted on him, like a fool. Then one night I caught him stealing the orb, a gift for that nasty goddess he worshipped. Now, what was her name? Kal-something. He sweet-talked me into keeping quiet. Many a time I've regretted that."

Jame remembered asking Penari how Abarraden had come to have the glass eye that he had stolen on a dare. He had guessed that a rogue priest had made off with the real one, just as he had with its mate some fifty years ago.

"It doesn't look as if the sect survived losing them both," he had said.

There, he had been right.

How odd that Mother Ragga had also played a part in this old tragedy. As to more recent events . . .

"So you were drawn back to Tai-tastigon," Jame said, thinking out-loud. "Curiously enough, the Eaten One is here too. I've encountered him—her? them?—twice since my arrival, once in the Tone, once in a puddle."

Enormous shoulders stirred up near the ceiling. Jame was uncomfortably aware of the other's attention shifting from its own misery to focus on her.

"I think the Tishooo, the Falling Man, is also here," she continued, now with the sense of reporting unwelcome but important news. "At least people keep mentioning the south wind as opposed to the north, which they fear.

The Cloudies even worship it. I've felt it hunting around the rooftops, as if it doesn't quite know what it's doing here."

"Nor, perhaps, does it. Do I, for that matter? And the Burnt Man?"

Ah, there was another fraught point.

"Nothing. Yet. What is he likely to do?"

"Whatever is least obliging. You know Burny. He doesn't think with that cinder of a brain. He feels. Anger, mostly. Blind, insane rage. That's what drew him to that precious cat you call the Dark Judge. Of course, it also counts that they both have had a taste of fire."

"It sounds to me," said Jame, "that whatever is going on here is more important than I thought. This city isn't just a mess; it's on the edge of a catastrophe big enough to have drawn you four. But what is it?"

"Huh. You find out, you tell me."

There was nothing more to say, and it was time that Jame found Loogan. She rose and slipped out of the room, out of the temple, leaving Mother Ragga to glower blindly at the fire.

Remember those whom you left behind, the dead had said in her dream. It appeared that Mother Ragga was haunted as well.

By now, it was nearly dawn and the streets of the district had emptied. Most demons, it seemed, didn't like daylight.

Doors cautiously opened as she passed.

"Is it clear?" ran murmurs from threshold to threshold, from priest to priest. "Are we safe?"

For the moment.

Or maybe not.

Here was Loogan's temple and here came the little priest himself, tumbling down its steps in his haste to meet her.

"He's gone!" he babbled, seizing her. "Gorgo has disappeared!"

⟪⟪ Chapter X ⟫⟫
Haunts by Daylight
Spring 57

I

"IT'S ALL MY FAULT," Loogan wailed, pacing the inner chamber of his god's temple, tearing at his scanty hair. "I knew he was afraid. I tried to protect him but I failed—again!—and now he's g-g-gone!"

"When did you last see him?" Jame asked.

Loogan clutched the bag hanging from his neck as if even now hoping to find a small, green lump in it. "He was here—safe, I thought—but then things got... confusing. This was last night. There were demons at the door. I put the pouch in the hands of the idol, thinking his own image might protect him better than I could if they broke in. Then these people came swarming up out of the ground and drove the demons away. When I retrieved the pouch, I didn't think at first to make sure he was still inside. When I did, he wasn't!"

"Stop that," said Jame, and captured his hands before they could inflict further damage on his beleaguered, rapidly balding head.

193

The room in which they stood was dark, dank, and high, dominated by the statue of the god, or rather of the grotesque thing that Loogan's many-times-great grandfather Bilgore had made of him by turning a simple rain deity named Gorgiryl into Gorgo the Lugubrious, Lord of Tears. The god was represented as an obese, crouching figure, with a sorrow-stricken face and unusually long legs, the bent knees of which rose a good two feet above its head. Its green glass eyes had been smashed, then fitted back together with love, but little skill, into an even more bulging configuration. Lachrymose water trickled through the cracks, channeled into the statue from a reservoir on the roof. No wonder, when Jame had taunted Loogan into causing Gorgo to manifest and he had appeared half this image, half that of a clumsily bedizened priest, the mirror of Loogan as he had then been, Loogan had suffered a cataclysmic loss of faith that effectively killed his god. Between them, with the help of his congregation, they had resurrected Gorgo in his older form, green and froglike. It would have been better, Jame now thought, if Loogan had also changed the statue.

In its cupped hands was a scroll, one of the elder archive concealed beneath the temple's courtyard, brought up for resanctification. That was another story. Connected to it, however, were the figures in shabby, funereal finery now dismantling the plumbing in search of their god.

They had apparently burst forth from their burial slots when the temple above was threatened: the novices who had moved the archive to beneath Gorgo's temple for safekeeping; the hierarchs who had ordered them to do so, and then had given each a fine funeral as a reward.

Bilgore himself was among the latter, noticeable by virtue of his ornate if tattered robes and his manner. He kept stomping back and forth, haranguing anyone he could catch, although the ruin of his face turned his words into gibberish. Things had plainly not gone as he had intended. Sorrow was no longer enshrined instead of life-giving hope, tears instead of rain. He tugged irritably at fellow high priests and at novices, breaking brittle limbs off from some of them. To one side, novices fumbled after a fellow's eyeball dislodged by his superior's impatient poke.

Cry, damn you, Bilgore might well have been demanding. *Here: I give you cause.*

"He went too far," said Loogan, sadly regarding his agitated predecessor. "First changing his god so drastically, then trying to offer him sacrifices literally drowned in their own tears. Think how long it must have taken to collect them! Now, there's dedicated grief. But Gorgo wouldn't accept. A lot of the old gods did, you know. Not so many in the New Pantheon."

"I wondered if our current crop of demons might once have had that habit."

Loogan shrugged. "Likely enough, for accustomed predators. It's a nasty practice, but at least only fatal to its victims. When you start taking souls, now, that's serious."

"Why?"

"They say in the Priests' Guild that souls hold together the world. To tamper with them is . . . obscene. Unnatural. The forms of worship in Tai-tastigon are very diverse. I can't think of many taboos. This is definitely one of them, though, and the main reason why we see demons as abominations in a way that mere dead gods never have been."

Tick, tick, tick went the novices' overgrown nails against the floor, against the pipes.

"Nah," said another one across the room, turning to Loogan and shaking a deformed head at him.

"Good chaps at heart," Loogan had remarked earlier. "They were a bit much for the regular congregants, though. I sent those folk home. Anyway, it's too dangerous to be abroad these nights if you aren't already dead. Well, maybe even if you are."

The deceased novices at least seemed respectful, the former high priests less so. Everyone had an opinion, however unclearly expressed.

"I suppose," said Jame, fending off a particularly insistent tiny elder driveling dirt and mutilated words, "that you could call these holy haunts. They still seem to have their souls, though."

To her, that was a horrifying thought. Who would choose to spend eternity in a crumbling body? Still, they had apparently sacrificed themselves willingly, assuming that they had known what lay in store.

"I never noticed if the haunts that I met in the wastes had shadows or not. Some were more aware than others." Ashe. Winter. The thought of the beloved dead, especially the latter, threatened to choke her. She swallowed. "Then too, they contracted the disease from the land itself or from the bite of someone already infected. Things seem a bit different here. Except for your initiates, most of these haunts have had their souls reaped by demons and then have died bereft, if you can call it truly being dead."

On the other hand, in regard to demons, Theocandi hadn't been able to die at all until his soul had returned to him in the form of the Shadow Thief. She had assumed much the same about Bane and the Lower Town Monster, but without Bane's true name, that hadn't been put to the test. He and Theocandi had been different from this new demonic breed, however, in that no dead gods had been involved.

"Maybe the living can still be saved." Aden, she thought. Those whose souls now enabled Heliot, Pathless, the Kencyr priests, and so many others.

"If Gorgo's people can also come back, though, why not all of Tai-tastigon's dead?"

"Perhaps because the city requires cremation," said Loogan.

The persistent haunt was now tugging at his sleeve and standing on tiptoe, trying to mumble in his ear. Jame didn't envy him the stink of his dead colleague's breath.

Loogan shrugged, attempting to free himself without being impolite. "Can you imagine burial grounds within such tightly packed quarters? You may have seen the smoke rising from pyres outside the walls. These were buried below on the sly—another reason for not telling the Five."

"You know," said Jame, regarding the tiny priest, "I think he's trying to tell us something."

The haunt nodded as vigorously as his desiccated muscles allowed, and his jaw fell off. Loogan handed it back to him. He tried to reattach it, failed, and threw it aside in frustration. Then he pointed at the image towering over them.

"Statue?" asked Jame. "Idol?"

"No," said Loogan, beginning to look excited. "He means Gorgo."

The little haunt nodded again. Dust rattled out of his ears. He lowered himself stiffly and tried to hop toward the outer door. His knees exploded. Between them, Jame and Loogan picked him up and seated him on a nearby bench. He was as light as a dead bird. His friends flocked around him, fussing.

"That's clear enough, anyway," said Jame. "Gorgo has left the temple."

Loogan was horrified. "He's outside?"

He made a rush to the outer door. When he jerked it open, a folded paper fell from its crack.

"That wasn't there before," Jame said. "Someone has been watching the building."

Loogan picked up the note with shaking hands. "I've thought before now that we were a target of the Thieves' Guild," he said, distracted, fumbling with the paper's folds. "Scrolls have gone missing from the idol's hands— the strangest things: a collection of very bad poetry, an old innkeepers' manual, someone's laundry list. It's as if some thief thought that anything that old must be valuable."

The folds yielded. Loogan stared at the contents, then, speechless, handed the paper to Jame.

"If you want to see your false god again," she read, "come to the one true temple."

It was written in Kens.

II

BY NOW, IT WAS NOON, hot and hazy even in the shaded Temple District. More rain had fallen. Roofs dripped. Walls sweated. In some places, whole facades had collapsed. This seemed most prevalent where the demons had swarmed the night before. The steps where Jame had seen the spider woman had completely disintegrated, and the street where the giant saurians had fought was pitted with water-filled holes into which Jame dared not step. It reminded her of the damage in the Maze. How much worse might things be there today, and how was Penari faring? She couldn't stop to examine the destruction, though, not with an anxious Loogan urging her to hurry, hurry, hurry.

Out of the district, streets steamed and puddles smoked. By contrast, shadowed side alleys exhaled cool air to form miniature fog banks at crossroads. The sky was overcast, with a sulfurous tinge. One felt, instinctively, that something vast was happening out of sight, above the clouds. An intermittent hollow grumble came from above like muted thunder or the grinding of teeth. There was also a smell, stronger than the day before.

Fewer citizens were out than usual for a working midday. They scuttled about their errands or collected in huddles on street corners, flinching whenever the sky growled. More than one fell silent and shot an angry glance at Jame and Loogan as they passed. Well, Jame thought, it was uncommon to see a thief and a priest in company by daylight, or any other time, for that matter. One consolation was that Abbotir's hunters were unlikely also to be abroad.

They crossed the Tone but couldn't see it due to the mist rising off its surface. No one said *Bloop*, but Jame had the sense of being watched.

Whoo? breathed a stray gust of the south wind, as if in confusion, rattling papers at their feet. *Wha, wha, whoo?*

Jame picked up one of the scattered notes. "Beware . . ." it said, as if on the Feast of Dead Gods, but then it trailed off. "Beware . . ."

On the south bank, somewhere to the left, someone was shouting. The words were unclear, but the tone was angry. Curious, Jame steered Loogan that way, without telling him that they had gone off the direct path to the Lower Town. Here was the residential district that she had visited with Rue and Darinby on her first night in the city. Here was the street where they had met the whumping demon.

A crowd had gathered, more people than she had seen together before, listening to a speaker. Jame recognized the vendor who had spurned her coin and called her a filthy nightie.

"What's going on, hey?" he shouted to his audience. "This is our city! Who's trying to take it away from us? The poor woman who lived here, d'you think she deserved what she got?" He gestured wildly upward, then, with a plunge of his hand, down. The shattered second-story window above him gaped inward as it had before, its interior a deserted void. Below, in a circle of crushed cobbles, was a red puddle.

"Who's going to be next?" he howled.

The listeners muttered and shifted.

His voice dropped to a wheedling note. "I'm telling you, friends, dear friends, night is on the rise. We've put up with it all of these years. Thieves, prostitutes, deviants, the unnatural of every stripe, now dead gods gone rogue! Once a year for the Feast was all right. We stuffed the cracks and waited that out. Families got together. Many a noggin I've drunk while the dark crawled outside, but in the morning, it was gone. Now where is it? Among us! You, thief, what have you to say for your master, night?"

Angry faces turned toward Jame. Hands twitched.

What was day without night, light without dark, she wanted to ask, but that wasn't a true analogy. What had come upon these people had little to do with their fellow citizens, however nocturnal. Heliot had spoken of day paying tribute to night, of sacrifices voluntary and not. This merchant had caught the scent, if not the essence, of oncoming nightmare.

Grit rattled down the wall. Cracks spread. Part of the structure, where the demon had reared up against it, was giving way.

"Look out!" she cried.

The vendor sneered at her, until he heard the grind of stone above him. Blocks shifted, spitting mortar, and fell. The street shook with their impact. People lurched backward, some stepping into the puddle where the Eaten One had surfaced and there they sank. Jame pulled Loogan clear. Dank, choking dirt clotted the air.

Amid the coughing and sobs of the stricken, she edged forward. Nothing could be done for the vendor, smashed and running red between blocks. The stones themselves, though . . .

In the filtered sunlight, they appeared mere rubble. Where the shadows fell, however, they teemed. Tiny bodies burrowed through them like maggots but were made themselves of stone like tiny gargoyles. They spat acid and chewed the damaged rock. Their excrement fractured passageways behind them. More blocks crumbled. Above, the roofline sagged.

"Ugh," said Loogan, looking over Jame's shoulder. "Stone-mites. I haven't seen them since that bad storm out of the north when I was a child. The damage there was awful."

Stone-mites, petrified woodlice, hearts out of the body that wouldn't stop beating, haunts, the living that died and then came back . . .

Jame didn't like the way this was shaping up.

People in the street were sorting themselves out, and realizing that many of them were missing.

"Demon!" one shrieked. "What have you done with my sister?"

"My aunt?"

"My second cousin?"

"Run," Jame said to Loogan.

They ran. The mob followed.

Here was the dead-end of an alley out of which Jame could easily have clambered, but Loogan was wheezing and clutching his side, already all but spent. He could run no farther, much less climb.

Voices cried behind them: "This way! This way! Here!"

People emerged from the haze, panting, carrying

stones. Jame thrust the little priest behind her. She didn't want to hurt anyone; much less, though, did she want Loogan injured, or herself. The townfolk advanced cautiously. Similar thoughts were no doubt occurring to them.

"Boo!" said Jame.

They jumped backward, then edged forward again.

"We need fire," said one nervously. Jame recognized the pudgy brother of the haunt girl.

"In this weather?" someone else asked. "Good luck with that. I heard that not even the pyres are catching properly."

A broad figure loomed behind them at the alley's mouth.

"Here, now. What's all this?" asked a familiar voice, suffused with genial cheer.

Rocks dropped from suddenly shy hands. "Her, her, her!" voices clamored as the bloodthirsty pack turned into a parcel of self-righteous accusers. "It's all her fault!"

"What is?"

"Everything!"

"Be that as it may—and I've no doubt that it is—go home, the lot of you. I'll see to this."

They slunk around him, out of the alley, into the mist, gone.

"Sart Nine-toes," said Jame, advancing on the big city guard. "I'm very glad to see you."

"Huh. I thought it was you, girl. Who else attracts lynch mobs as honey does flies?"

He emerged from the haze, nearly as large as Marc but broader, with a wide mouth upturned in a grin.

"How is the Res aB'tyrr?" Jame demanded.

The corners of his smile turned down like those of a dolorous clown. "Well you might ask. How else in these times? We had no customers last night, even with a new dancer as a draw—not that she was very good. She blames the B'tyrr for that, by the way. Seems that you set an unfair standard. Then too, more and more of the Sirdan's hired brigands are hanging around the square, day and night. I hear that we have you to thank for that too."

"Sart, you know that I would never wittingly harm the House of Luck-bringers."

He looked at her sideways. "I've noticed that what you mean and what happens are often very different things. You're a perilous friend, you are."

"Er . . . yes. What does the Widow Cleppetania say?"

He snorted. "I've been that good woman's husband for nearly five years now, off and on. You'd think that some people would remember by now."

"Sorry. But still . . ."

"Does she blame you? I won't say yes or no. Should any of us? But Master Tubain won't come out of his quarters until his wife returns home. We miss him. He's our luck-bringer, and well you know it."

Yes, Jame supposed that she did.

They were walking now, with Loogan tagging diffidently along behind. The streets were empty, the sky louring. *Grumble, rumble, growl*. If that was thunder, it was closer than before, as if it had run aground on top of the clouds. Jame wondered what was going on.

"I stand guard when I can," Sart continued, "and try to get my mates to spell me when I'm on duty, but the word is out that the inn is off-bounds. Some business with the Five, the Skyrr Archiem versus Abbotir of the Gold Court. Politics, damn it. It's like a siege. Your cub Rue helps. So does little Miss Patches, now that you've sent her back to us, although her ideas are more fanciful."

"Is it serious?"

"Only once, so far. Four of the Bortis boys caught the cat Boo on his way out for a prowl last night. They were pulling one each at his legs, laughing, as if they meant to tear him apart. He certainly screamed as if they were. Rue was out the door in a flash. They just stared, as if they couldn't believe their eyes, until she hit them. I've seen you fight. She isn't as good, but by the gods she tore into them while their mouths were still hanging open, and she left her mark. At least one of those lads will be walking at a crouch for the foreseeable future. Walked right up him, she did, stomping all the way, then whoop, a flip over his head, and down the other side. I don't think he'll be sitting much either."

Sart laughed, half appreciative, half condescending. Oh, the ladies, bless their little boots. Then he sobered.

"Boo huffed for an hour after that, but he wasn't badly hurt. So now you ask, is it serious yet? My sense is that they want to know where you and Mistress Abernia are before they make their move. Master Men-dalis has put himself in a tricky situation there. Guild lords do not abduct merchant's wives without even holding them for ransom. Sanctioned—that is, taxable—civil wars are not conducted on those terms. The fines would be ruinous. The Archiem would see to that, given how he feels about Abbotir. Dammed if I can see, though, what Men-dalis is up to."

"You make me very nervous."

He regarded her askance. "Glad to see that something does."

"You have no idea."

She noticed that they were moving northeast, back toward the Tone. Loogan apparently hadn't realized this, but then he rarely left the Temple District. "Where are we going?"

The river came into view, smoking in its bed. Rising out of the mist was the mansion where Jame had almost had breakfast.

"Oh no," she said, stopping. "Abbotir."

Sart took her arm in a light but firm grip.

"The word was out for your apprehension. Sorry, Talisman."

III

THE MANSION seemed at first to be deserted. At least, no servant met them at the door, which proved to be unlocked.

"Hello?" Sart called, but in a wary, hoarse whisper as if afraid of being heard.

The halls within echoed hollowly.

"Maybe no one is home," said Jame. She tried Sart's grip, but found it unrelenting despite his hesitation. It should have occurred to her that as a member of the Five, Abbotir had the city guards at his command as well the Guild's. She had been watching for the wrong hunters.

"We have to go," hissed Loogan, tugging at her sleeve.

"Tell him that."

Sart ventured in, pulling her with him almost as an afterthought. Part of his training, as Jame remembered from Marc's tales of guard duty, was to investigate any unexpectedly open door, especially of the rich, and the master of the thieves' Gold Court was indeed wealthy. Gold must be one of his ruling passions. Statues, gilt furniture, golden brocade, tapestries of spun bullion glimmering in the shadows. . . . Jame could imagine him holding back the finest of everything that came through his hands as a guild official.

Odd, though, how tarnished everything seemed. Yesterday, she had been dazzled. Today, what was this bloom of dust, this dank miasma of decay? Even the air had turned stale, although that might have been because of the makeshift curtains that veiled every window.

Here was the breakfast room. Here too, the towering windows on either side were draped with everything from ornately embroidered arras to what appeared to be freshly dyed bed sheets, the servants' last act, perhaps, before they had fled. The effect was half stained glass, half patchwork quilt. It was also stiflingly hot. Flies bumbled on either side of the cloth, in the room, against the closed windows. More swarmed by the chamber's high table, which itself was withdrawn into the western shadows of the room.

Someone sat there, a dark, glowering presence. The table spread before him was that of yesterday's feast but strangely animate. The trout flopped. The eels seethed. The oatcakes bloomed in many-hued mold except where incorruptible honey touched them. Maggots bred in the porpoise pie, white and wriggling among the blood-red currants. The man at the table helped himself to the latter, scooping up writhing handfuls with clumsy fingers.

Jame recognized him, barely, as Abbotir.

"Lord," said Sart, staring, "what's happened to you?"

"What should have happened, you dolt? I am as I always have been, if not more. Should that coward Death take me? I am much stronger than he, and have better allies."

Silk rustled. A slender figure clad in fine robes stepped out of the gloom.

"You are too kind," said Men-dalis smoothly. "You again." This, to Jame. "And not yet about my business."

"Things keep happening," said Jame, thinking, *That could be my motto*. "You still haven't told me exactly what you want me to do."

She thought that, behind him, she caught a glimpse of a fair face and a smile in the weave of shadows. Dally again, waiting. For what?

Say what you want me to do! she almost cried.

He was there, so close. What an ache, where she had lost him. Had it been her fault?

The Sirdan waved a ring-bedecked hand, relegating responsibility yet again. "Oh, I leave the details to you. But, mind you, my other option looks more and more appealing. I will not be disobliged forever. Then too, there is that inn that you love so much. Don't leave it too late for them, eh?"

"Speaking of that infernal inn." Abbotir picked up a dingy scroll from among the dirty dishes and thrust it at Men-dalis. "Here. Do with it what you will."

"I thank you." Men-dalis slid the parchment into a full sleeve. "For this and for all of your other kind attentions."

The lord of the Gold Court waved him away. "You keep me from my food. Begone . . . my lord."

Men-dalis raised an eyebrow, but retreated with an ironic bow. His eyes lifted to Jame's. *Remember*, he mouthed with a smile. Somewhere in the recesses of the chamber, a door softly opened and closed.

Abbotir started to reach for a distant bowl, but his arm refused to bend. Gripping the afflicted wrist, he jerked it toward his chest. The locked elbow popped and moved—sideways. He reached again, hooked the bowl's rim, and dragged it to him. Curdled cream and moldy berries sloshed on the tabletop.

"Ah. I had no appetite before. Now I am ravenous." He glared at Jame. "You, girl. I said I would have you. Now here you are."

Jame pulled out of Sart's loosened grip. "What did you mean when you said that you had taught Bane how to direct his passions?"

The master thief leered at her. "You would remember that. Tell me, chit, do you still dream about him? I see in your eyes that you do. True, he was a very handsome boy. He got that from his mother. Would she have liked you? Perhaps. Both of you, after all, are Kencyr, and therefore unnatural women."

"I know I am, by the standards of several societies, but why was she?"

"Ha. I took her in. I gave her a position, wealth, and, I thought, a son. Then she let slip that he was not mine.

This happened at the height of an argument between us over how the boy was to be raised. As if there could be any question. I had publicly accepted him as my own. I would not be shamed by admitting that he was not, so he must do as I said. Before that, though, she had wormed her way into his mind. He must follow that ridiculous code of yours, she said. Honor. Discipline. Self-sacrifice. I saw how ill it suited him."

Abbotir thrust back his chair and lurched to his feet. Murky shadows seemed to rise with him as if clinging to his full sleeves. He began to pace behind the table, never in the light, back and forth.

"I tried to beat it out of him. He never cried. Then I knew: he liked pain, both to inflict and to suffer. Before, he had lashed out at every playmate, every servant, even at himself. I showed him, though. How to cut without killing too soon, even without leaving scars if he so chose. How to savor the kiss of the blade. How to turn pain into art. It calmed him."

Back and forth he went, his broken arm dangling, his face anything but calm. A snarl of shadows went with him. One over his shoulder showed the glimmer of yellow eyes and white teeth. Was Pathless the guardian of his soul? Others hinted at demons Jame had seen who had lost or devoured all the secondary souls on whom they depended for strength, if not the prime soul that made them what they were. These clustered, it seemed, where they found power, like flies around rot.

Jame kept pace with the guild master on the other side of the table, with Sart and Loogan backing nervously out of her way. So far, Abbotir had talked with unusual abandon, as if half to himself. Perhaps he would continue if she kept him going.

"And his mother?"

"She saw. She wept. I was avenged on her for deceiving me . . . or so I thought. Yes, he joined the Guild when I insisted, but would he steal? No. Unlike you, I hear. So much for Kencyr honor. Nonetheless, she could not endure the shame. I came to her, but she was cold and still. So much blood. The White Knife, you Kencyr call it, do you not? Rather, a thumb in the eye. Spiteful, selfish woman . . . she couldn't stand to lose, nor to give me the respect due a winner."

He was beginning to stumble and flag. Poke him again.

"'You are the bane of my existence.' She was talking about you, wasn't she? Not about her son. But you told him otherwise."

"It was true enough!"

"Oh, devious, to play such games with a child's mind. Nonetheless, I begin to see where Theocandi learned his taste for all things Kencyr. From you. From Bane. Perhaps, even, from Bane's mother."

He whipped about, with a glare wild enough to drive her back a step. "That I deny! It was that bastard Ishtier. He got his claws into all three of them. A little knowledge, a little mystery . . ."

"You were drawn too."

"Argh. What is it that you people know? Why do I feel as if we all dangle on your strings? What you believe is nonsense and yet . . . and yet . . . there is some deep truth in it. This world makes no sense. The worthy wither. The worthless thrive. I . . . I am not where or what I should be. Why? *Why*?"

"You have position and wealth. What do you lack?"

"Power. Love. Ah, forget that last. Love is only a lure for the weak. Respect, though. . . . I respected Theocandi. Now there was a master politician and thief."

Who could never match his older brother, Penari, thought Jame. Therein lay his weakness, which he tried to overcome by turning to the Book Bound in Pale Leather, that dire Kencyr artifact.

What are we, the pot of gold at the end of the rainbow sought by every fool? The yearned for but mistrusted truth beyond all reality?

So Ishtier would say, but he also had his weaknesses. So did she, of course, however much she learned, whatever her intentions.

"But I will have my revenge." Abbotir drove a fist into the table, splitting knuckles, unsetting a dish of fried crickets that tried to crawl away on brittle, snapping legs. "You, little man"—this, to Loogan, who was staring at him aghast. "Didn't I tell the Kencyr priests that you and this witch were friends? Haven't they taken your petty godling to lure her out of hiding? And it has worked, hasn't it?"

Loogan goggled at him. His round face suffused with color. "How d-dare you endanger my god to bait your obscene trap?"

Abbotir laughed at him, choked, and spat among the platters laid out before him. "What is he, who are you, that it should matter?"

Gorgo's hierophant drew himself up. "Besides being a

priest, I am currently one of the Five. That makes us equals."

"Ha. You make me laugh."

Loogan turned to Sart Nine-toes. "Wasn't that why you brought us here? Because he sits on the Council? Then, as his peer, I demand that you take us away."

Sart shifted where he stood, uneasy. "That was it, sure enough." Clearly, he was unnerved by the guild lord's current state, which he didn't understand, but he still held him in awe. Loogan, by contrast, didn't look very impressive.

Abbotir leaned forward, glaring. The shadows behind him mimicked his move like so many animate, misty gargoyles emerging into the hall's multicolored gloom. Each had at least one soul to give it substance. Did Abbotir? Where he touched the light, however dim, his flesh smoked.

"Then hear me now, guard," he wheezed. "Take this assassin to the Mercy Seat. There she is to be held until night falls and her executioner comes."

"Now see here," Sart began, clearly upset. "We had justice in this city, once. You say that the Talisman is a killer. She says that she isn't. Who judges her?"

Abbotir slammed down a fist. "I do! Take her, guard, or be taken yourself."

Sart shoved Jame behind him. "I don't understand this business at all, but it isn't right."

The demons seethed out of the shadows. They descended on Sart in a gray tide and tore at him, each ripping off an element of his being as they reached down for his soul. Thoughts, memories, flesh . . . He bellowed and flailed at them.

Sudden light flooded the hall. Loogan had ripped down a swathe of curtains. Demons retreated, keening, as even the overcast sun tore strips off of them. Abbotir didn't move, although smoke continued to rise from his shoulders as if from a pyre.

"You are marked, guard," he grated, "no less than those whom you have so foolishly tried to protect."

Sart staggered to his feet. "Well," he said, swaying. Jame and Loogan made a dive to support him. "We'll just see about that, shall we?"

They got him out of the palace, one under each arm and no easy load he was to carry. Shadows followed them through the gilded rooms, gibbering, but none dared to attack.

"That," said Sart, when at last they emerged into the steaming day, "was unpleasant. What was wrong with m'lord, anyway?"

"I think he died sometime during the night," said Loogan. Then, to Jame, "You guessed it too, didn't you?"

"Yes. When he shattered the death-lock in his arm. If he had waited for it to release naturally, he needn't have broken his elbow. I don't think, though, that Master Abbotir would admit any such weakness. Death is for losers."

Sart looked confused. "But haunts don't have minds."

"Some do," said Jame grimly. "Someday, let me introduce you to Singer Ashe."

"That I can well do without. What next?"

"What else?" said Loogan, straightening, resolute. "We rescue Gorgo."

IV

"HERE I LEAVE YOU," said Sart Nine-toes.

They stood in the Lower Town on the edge of the desolation that circled the Kencyr temple.

"I know when I'm outmatched. Dead gods, haunts, and demons are one thing. Your god, though . . . ugh. And I'm on duty tonight. I'd quit to stand by my love, but we need the money, in case Kithra gets her way and throws us out of the Res aB'tyrr."

"She would do that?"

"So she says, when she loses her temper—which, with Cleppetty, is often enough."

"Truly, a marriage off and on?"

"Mostly on. She's a strong woman, my Cleppetania, with strong opinions. When those arise, a wise man stands back."

They watched him walk off, still rather unsteady but gaining certainty with each stride. A strong man, that, not greatly injured by his recent trial.

By now it was late afternoon under a brazen sky, the air murky with dust and thick with heat. Grinding sounds still came from above, muffled by clouds. A weight seemed to press down. Jame and Loogan crossed the expanse. Ragged figures rose from the ruins to shamble after them and to line their way. Jame thought that she saw Aden, although so disfigured with dirt as to be barely recognizable. Another figure caught her eye—stout, clothed in rich if tattered finery. She had seen him somewhere before. Yes. In the square before the Skyrrman five years ago as it had gone up in flames. Harr sen Tenko: Harri's father, the Archiem's rival. There, too, were the three soulless Kencyr priests huddled together, one drooping—dripping?—between the other two. Again, there was that stench of fetid water and rotting vegetation, again that sharp odor that made Jame sneeze. What did they all want? What, if anything, could she give them?

Here was the temple door, shut. Jame knocked. No answer. No keyhole, either, with a convenient lock to pick.

See, little thief? What good are your tricks now?

"Try again," said Loogan, anxiously shifting from foot to foot.

This was no time for subtlety. Jame hefted half a brick and slammed it against the door. The brick crumbled. The door remained unscathed. After a moment, though, a crack opened in the apparently seamless wall and swung wide. There stood Titmouse. He had shed his black coat. The white shirt beneath drooped with sweat and his tufted hair stood more wildly on end than usual, moving in an unfelt breeze. At first he seemed glassy-eyed, barely able to focus on his visitors. Then he blinked.

"You."

"We've come for the frog," Jame said, glowering up at him, and thrust the note into his hands.

He peered at it, lips moving as he read. Blink, blink. "Oh. Good."

They followed him into the temple. The halls thrummed with power, much more fiercely than they had on Jame's last visit. Her feet didn't touch the floor at all. This was more like trying to stay afloat in savage rapids.

She grabbed Loogan as the current threatened to upend him. Force keened. Hair bristled.

This time, she saw nothing reminiscent of Bane, unless it was the tangled clots of spider web that twisted in corners.

"How in Perimal's name do we get flies inside with only one door and that usually shut?" Titmouse had asked.

Now spiders? Bane had liked them. Perhaps he was here, in some form, but how? And why?

From somewhere ahead came a sound: shuffle, shuffle, stomp; shuffle, shuffle, stomp. It reminded Jame of her descent years ago into the Priests' College at Wilden when the earth had seemed to move around her with ponderous effort.

The door to the main hall stood open. She and Loogan clutched the posts, left and right, to avoid being swept inside, where the priests danced. There were more of them than she had expected. Outermost were the brown-clad novices stamping and turning in the kantirs of earth-moving Senetha. Within was a ring of grey acolytes, some flowing as if in swift water, others leaping like flames. Where they crossed paths, the air hissed with steam. Inner still, priests channeled the current into the swift, airborne subtleties of wind-blowing Senetha that fretted the uncertain air into eddies and spirals. All moved independently yet together, the kantirs of one form reflecting its counterparts among the other three, circle rotating within circle. It was the Great Dance, which gathers power and molds it to the dancer's will.

One black-robed figure stood at the maelstrom's still heart, where Jame had once left a whorl in the stones of the tessellated floor. To his right was Titmouse, swaying slightly. To his left, suspended over an unlit fire-pit, was a glass bowl in which floated a green, straddle-legged form.

" . . . quink . . . " piped tiny Gorgo piteously, scrabbling at the glass with webbed toes.

The high priest raised his head. The slit of a mouth appeared, then the tip of a long, thin nose. The hood slid back entirely to reveal a skull-like face, the waxy yellow of its brow.

"We meet again," said Ishtier, smiling.

He raised his claw of a hand. It only had three fingers. Jame remembered when the priest had chewed off the fourth, in this very room, after he had been so ill advised as to touch the Book Bound in Pale Leather. As he brought his maimed hand down now, the circle of dancers parted into eddies but never stopped moving.

"I thought you were dead," said Jame.

"You hoped it, certainly. Before I left to reclaim my rightful place here, I heard much about you, little to your credit. The Women's Halls cast you out, did they not? Then you went to Tentir, of all places. Truly, randon standards have become lax in this degenerate age. Have they found you out yet? If not, rest assured: they soon will. But before all such misadventures, there was Tai-tastigon. Have you told your brother about your sojourn here?"

Jame had shared much with Torisen in these latter days, but not everything. "He knows what he needs to know."

"Ha. Then you have lied by omission."

"And you, about me, on purpose."

His sunken eyes glittered. With anger? With amusement? "Priests trust priests." He spread both hands. His mouth lifted in a sneer. "Behold my faithful followers."

Titmouse twitched.

"Now that we are here," said Jame, to distract the high priest, "what do you want with us?"

"Not with him." Ishtier indicated Loogan with a contemptuous jerk of his pointed chin. "With you. Why, as a gift for Master Gerridon, of course."

Sweet Trinity.

"He's here?"

"Not yet, but he will come, soon, when he sees what I have to offer him."

Through a haze of panic, Jame began to work this out. Here, perhaps, at last were the reasons for the city's plight that had so far eluded her.

"You changed the flow of the temple's power inward, rather than out. Why?"

"This is how it always should have been, how it was on all previous worlds. An old song told me that and an old singer, when he had been induced to perform. The Priests' College at Wilden is set up properly. Our temples here, for some reason, are not. Think about it: why should we feed power to such jokes as this amphibious godling and his pathetic priest?"

Here he paused to strike a spark in the fire-pit. Loogan squeaked as flames rose to lick the rounded bottom of the glass. Gorgo goggled.

"The Chain of Creation was meant to serve us, not the other way around," said Ishtier, ignoring the growing conflagration at his elbow even though it threatened his sleeve. "We in turn were meant to do what we thought best with it. But that was before our god failed us, oh, so long ago. To whom should we turn now if not to the shadows?"

Titmouse moved sideways, stumbling a bit over his big boots. He tapped the shoulder of a fellow priest as if to wake him from a trance. "Listen."

"The Arrin-ken, those filthy cats, betrayed us in disowning Gerridon and naming his kinsman Glendar as our leader when we first arrived on this world. I realized that when his descendent, Ganth Graylord, was driven into exile some thirty years ago. Surely that could not have happened to a true Highlord; therefore, he was not one."

"You only say that to justify abandoning him in the Haunted Lands."

"He was not my lord!"

It came out almost in a shriek. More dancers faltered, as did the current in the room. Ishtier caught himself with a gasp and resumed with a sickly smile meant to show how reasonable this all was, how dimwitted—nay, insane—anyone who questioned it.

He's mad, thought Jame.

"That honor belongs to Gerridon, who saw the truth about our so-called god and led the way to freedom, to immortality. Our ancestors were fools not to follow him."

The water in the bowl began to steam. Gorgo paddled in it anxiously. Enough of the past.

"What are you trying to do here?"

Ishtier snorted. A drop of snot gathered on the tip of his long nose and fell, unnoticed.

"Trying? What can I do but succeed? Why do you think all the other worlds fell?"

Jame felt suddenly sick. "Oh god. We drained them. They had native powers, native gods. Like Mother Ragga. Like the Falling Man and the rest of the Four, not to mention the Old Pantheon and the Ancient Ones. We bled them until they couldn't protect themselves or their worlds, just as you're trying to do here in Tai-tastigon, now. Wait. All of that was long before Master Gerridon betrayed us."

"Heh. Did I say that this was a new thing? The priests have always known that ours was the power to take, to use."

"But not wisely. World after world has fallen."

"Was that our fault? Our god betrayed us. Therefore he . . . she . . . it was never meant to win."

This was more than Jame had expected, more than she could accept. Tai-tastigon had tried her faith before and nearly broken her. Was it about to do so again?

"Never meant by whom?"

"Ah." He threw up his hands dismissively, as if scattering birds of bone upon the air. "Questions, questions."

By now, Titmouse had tapped perhaps a dozen of his colleagues and they had stumbled out of step, looking dazed. Jame noted in passing that none of them belonged to the group who had taken her prisoner before. Were those Ishtier's supporters, who had followed him on his return here, and therefore not friends of Titmouse?

"No, no, no!" raged high priest. "Dance, damn you, dance! We are so close!"

To what? Jame was still scrambling to make sense out

of what she had already heard. "But . . . dead gods? Souls? Demons?"

Ishtier sneered. "And some fools call you clever. That was my doing, an extension of my earlier experiments with the Lower Town Monster and the Shadow Thief, both limited, mindless creatures. Incorporating this world's so-called dead godlings has added the power of personality. Of purpose. Besides, as former Old Pantheon gods, these demons have already shown their affinity to human sacrifice. That makes them more deadly to this world than their New Pantheon descendents, who for the most part only seek that weak thing, faith."

"Now I'm confused. Again. What, then, does our own god require?"

The priest laughed, a shrill, jarring sound. "Faith, he says, but does he give us a choice?"

"Well, yes, if you want it."

Ishtier waved this away. "More trickery."

"Loogan tells me that the real danger lies in taking human souls. He says they glue together the world."

Titmouse had circled closer, drawn by their debate. "If here," he said, "what about down the Chain of Creation? Is that why the previous worlds fell?"

A colleague drifted up to them, still mimicking the kantirs if not fully committed to them. "We've never understood quite what Perimal Darkling is. What if it uses the souls that it overwhelms to propel it farther down the Chain?"

"To fresh food?" said Jame. "I can see that. Perhaps when it dissolves the bonds, it creates the energy by which it lives. It's a predator, like the demons, who also break down barriers and feed on souls, and it's always hungry. Like Gerridon, for that matter. Is he now also a demon? What is a demon, anyway? Dead gods needn't be involved. They weren't with the Lower Town Monster. What if feeding on souls is enough in itself to make one demonic?"

Ishtier stomped his foot. "Questions, question, questions! I go by what I see. Demons please the Master. They bring Rathillien closer to the Haunted Lands, to Perimal Darkling itself. Wherever they tread, the shadows rise. Life mixes with death, animate with inanimate. What an army I bring to serve my lord! What we do in one of Rathillien's strongest cities, we can surely accomplish anywhere on this world. What more do you need to know?"

"Oh," said several voices. "A lot."

"Shut up!"

This all had the sickening ring of truth, as far as Ishtier understood it.

"And these demons obey you?"

Ishtier showed the bloodshot whites of his eyes, the yellow of his teeth. "Of course. I created them."

"Heliot says that he means to take over this city, this world, solely to feed his appetite. He's come back as a demon, thanks to you. He preys on human souls. Then too, what about those of Heliot's kind who are breeding freely?"

"What? Impossible."

"I saw it happen when a dead goddess, Kalissan, absorbed a human soul. You didn't sanction that, did you?"

"Of course not. You lie."

Jame felt, at last, a rising twinge of anger. Her fists clenched, nails pricking into palms.

"Those who know me best do not say such things."

He sneered, although one corner of his mouth twitched. More dancers broke stride, looking confused.

"The Master sought immortality," he said, his voice rising in a harangue to reclaim his followers. "Perhaps he did not get exactly what he wanted, but why should we not? Souls are cheap. Everybody has one. Most will sell them for the right price. Look at the people who first volunteered theirs for this great experiment. City lords, hill chieftains, even some from our own temple."

"What?" said Titmouse.

"Oh yes. Your so-called missing priests, from among those who came with me from the Riverland. I told them the truth. They trusted me. Who are you to say that they did not get what they wanted? Part of them will live forever, or at least until they run out of inferior souls on which to feed. What are mere bodies compared to that? The strongest survive. Gerridon taught us that. Do you think yourself wiser than he?"

"I think that he is a selfish moron," said Jame, "trying to bend forces beyond his control who in turn seek to make him their creature, their one voice."

"Blasphemy!"

He raised his hands again and brought them sharply down. The dancing priests converged on the center, except for those who had hesitated.

Jame pushed Loogan to the wall, out of the way.

"But Gorgo . . . !"

"Trust me."

The dancers circled Jame, trying to draw her into their pattern. Turn, cup the air with a hand to gain command of it, slide forward and back with a foot to draw in power, turn again, release . . .

A blast of wind made Jame stagger. It stank of singed power. Oh, where was the Tishooo when she needed him? Not in this enclosed space.

The priests were in motion again, circling, circling, and the room seemed to spin with them.

"Dance, puppet, dance!" cried Ishtier, clapping his hands.

He might have signaled the change in the Sene, from Senetha to Senethar, from dance to fight. An acolyte sprang at Jame—she recognized him as the one who had shoved her when last she had been here. She channeled aside his fire-leaping kick, scooped up his leg and dropped him backward on his head.

"Next?"

The high priest hastily clapped again.

The Great Dance once more gripped the room, commanding body and soul. Jame felt it tug at her senses, but brushed it off with a wind-blowing shrug of the mind. Trinity, but she was tempted to use this game against them as she had once before (oh, so irresponsibly) to enthrall guests at the Res aB'tyrr.

Turn, sway, reap their souls, as the Dream-weaver would have done, as she had been taught to do by golden-eyed wraiths under shadows' eaves . . .

No. That was the role for which the Master had bred her. She was not nor would she ever be his puppet.

The swirl of dancers brought her back face to face with Titmouse.

"I don't understand," he said. They mirrored each

other in the Senetha that in itself mirrors the Great Dance, but on a less potent level. "Why would the Master want you, a thief, a tavern wench?"

"Torisen Highlord is my twin brother and I am his heir." *Speak truth to this man*, her instincts told her, even while caution whispered, *Shanir*! "Gerridon is my uncle. Our mother was Jamethiel Dream-weaver."

Two priests, fighting, parted them. Ishtier's control was breaking down. Jame used water-flowing to pass between the combatants. The high priest was screaming. The room seemed to tilt.

Here, back, was Titmouse.

"Also, I think that I'm one of the Tyr-ridan," she shouted at him over the uproar.

Some of the dissident priests had formed a line, arms linked, and were dancing together. Stomp, stomp, stomp, kick; stomp, stomp, stomp, kick.

"Which one?"

"Regonereth. That-Which-Destroys."

"Oh. Who are the other two?"

"Torisen and our first cousin Kindrie, whose father was Gerridon, but I don't hold that against him. We three are the last pure-blooded Knorth."

Titmouse stopped. Priests bounced off his sudden wall of stillness.

"Why didn't you tell me this before?"

"Would you say such things to just anyone?"

She spoke in a startled lull, louder than she had intended. Priests stared at her.

"*What*?"

Titmouse grabbed Gorgo out of his steaming bowl and

stuffed him, all flailing limbs, into his pocket. "Come on," he said, catching Jame and Loogan each by an arm and hustling them out of the hall.

A shadowy figure leaned against the wall opposite, greeting them with a raised eyebrow.

"Oh, go away," Titmouse snarled at it, and swatted a clot of cobwebs out of his path.

V

WHEN THEY EMERGED from the temple, it was early evening. The air still hung heavy with heat and the dull, molten glow of sunset, but the clouds continued to lift and gather to the north. Distant thunder rumbled there. Pale lightning flickered above and between the mounting banks, behind which darkness reared. For the first time, Jame recognized that vague, towering shape.

"So that's what Ishtier is doing," she said.

"What?" asked Loogan, his attention divided between the cumulous mass, the Lower Town's ominous wasteland, and Titmouse's bulging pocket.

"Look at it. Imagine that those peaks are gables; those holes in the clouds below, windows. There! See how the lightning peers through, as if you were looking from the outside into some vast, vacant interior? It's becoming the Master's House."

Both priests stared at her.

"I don't see it," said Loogan, again watching the other's pocket, out of which green, webbed toes cautiously crept.

"I do," said Titmouse grimly. "But why?"

"The House exists mostly in Perimal Darkling, but its front projects through the Barrier into the Haunted Lands. Sometimes you could see it from the keep where I was born. Ishtier is using the Dance and the demons—in fact, all of this chaos—to bring it closer. He's using it like a ram to batter down the Barrier between our ancient enemy and this world. But do the dancing priests realize that?"

"I didn't," said Titmouse. "Ishtier told us that the power we harnessed would help us to defeat the shadows. It was up to us as priests, he said, to save our people. The Kencyrath had been weakened by internal, petty politics and the Highlord was spineless, he said. He lied?"

Jame bypassed the issue of politics, about which she and Ishtier nearly agreed, if for different reasons.

"His ideas about saving anyone are warped," she said. "He thinks only of himself and his precious Master, and seems to believe that service to Gerridon will somehow redeem his own lost honor for abandoning his lord, my father. Yes, he lies, especially about my brother and me."

"'What we do here,' he said, 'we can surely accomplish anywhere on this world.' He was talking about the ultimate fall of Rathillien, wasn't he? Our last bastion on the Chain of Creation. The end of everything."

"Yes," said Jame. "Sorry."

He turned, looming over her. "You pity me?"

"I would anyone, learning such a thing for the first time."

"But you suspected?"

"If not this exactly, something like it. The Master has tried it before elsewhere, on a lesser scale. Besides, I told you: I have dire bloodlines and a potential fate that I wouldn't wish on anybody, least of all myself."

"Huh. I begin to believe you. Besides, I can feel the power fluctuating around us. The dance draws it in, but the temple itself seems to radiate it outward. Back and forth. In and out." He shivered. "It feels . . . unbalanced."

Jame had sensed this too, as soon as the dance had faltered. With luck, Ishtier's plan might collapse, but Titmouse was right about the current instability. Anything might happen now.

Here came gusts of the bustling south wind to whip up dust around them.

Figures shambled forward through the sudden haze— foremost, two supporting a third. All three wore hieratic robes reduced to rags. Those garments that clothed the third were dripping wet and his half-seen face was grossly bloated. Bubbles burst at the corners of a slack mouth. Dangling tentacles fringed his lips. He must be the one whose soul had been used to create the demon that the Eaten One had dragged beneath the cobblestones, now slowly disintegrating. So the link worked this way, too.

"I know these men," said Titmouse. "They came from the Riverland with m'lord Ishtier to join our ranks, but I deliberately never learned their names. 'Here, you. And you. And you.' I see now that that was my petty act of rebellion against the high priest."

She had been right, then, about the split within the temple. "The rest are your friends?"

"Not all. M'lord Ishtier has seduced some even among them."

"How many does he need?"

"I don't know. Every one will count."

"*Whoo* . . . ?" said the south wind, stirring the dust, obscuring the three tragic figures and those who swayed in the murk behind them. "*Wha, wha, wha, whoo* . . . ?"

"Tishooo, Falling Man, can you help us?"

The dust swirled, almost into the semblance of a bewhiskered, disgruntled face. "*Youuu* . . . ?"

"Me. I'm sorry that I sent you to the Western Lands, or what's left of them. At least I got you out again."

"*Huhhh!*"

"Well, yes. That was by accident, and it was nasty, but do you want to lose this part of Rathillien as well?"

The wind buffeted her, flipping her loosened hair into her eyes so that she had to hold it down with both gloved hands. Titmouse braced himself. Loogan huddled behind him.

"*Ha* . . . !"

"Oh, stop it!" Jame shouted at the vortex of debris whirling above them, slapping her in the face. "I know that you didn't ask for this, but this is your world too, dammit!"

A blast of wind almost knocked her off her feet. She had forgotten that the Four regarded the Kencyrath as intruders here as much as they did the shadows. Convincing them otherwise had so far been hard but oh, so necessary to the survival of both. It didn't help that many of her own people still saw themselves as masters of any world on which they found themselves. Hadn't their Three-Faced God and his priests assured them of that?

Huh, as the wind said.

Above, the outlines of the House shivered, edges sloughing off of its eaves, windows breaching. Was that due to the Tishooo, to Ishtier's faltering dance, or to something else? Muted thunder strummed again on high and the sky darkened with sunset. This was still a gathering storm.

From the north came footsteps heavy enough to shake the ground.

Thud, thud, thud . . .

A shape loomed out of the dust with hot brown eyes and huge fists that opened and closed.

"Priest!"

Heliot's shout boomed against the houses still standing, rattling what windows remained, and against the stark tower of the Kencyr temple.

"Come out, damn you!"

Ishtier had, in fact, already emerged and now stood on the desolate plain before his front door. The wind swirled his black robe about him like a storm cloud. All that was visible of his face under the hood was the thin line of his mouth, turned downward.

"I did not summon you, creature."

"Oh, but you did. You promised me power. Now you renege?"

"Not so. When the time comes, you shall have it in full measure."

Night had fallen, moonless at this hour, and the sky was again obscured with clouds. Heliot brought his own light, the red of fire glowing through the seams of his armor. Another shape rose out of the dust behind him, and another, and another. Foremost stood Kalissan, swaying, her third eye like a lamp that only illuminates the living. It followed the wanderers at her feet who fled but cast no shadows, then closed. The two eyes beneath opened onto smoldering pits within her skull. She smiled, with pointed teeth.

"I gave no orders for this creature's making," snarled Ishtier. "You forget yourself, demon."

"Ha, ha, ha. No, priest. I remember myself. Who I was. What I have become. Did you think to control me?"

"I created you!"

Heliot bent over the priest. With the tip of a finger he seemed about to flick him contemptuously away.

"Little man, little mortal. My first worshippers raised me to godhood, then betrayed me the first time that I lost a battle. True, I was among the ranks of dead gods until you infused me with a voluntary human soul. I was your first such creation, was I not? Since then, you have shown me how to use those traitors' descendants more efficiently, that I grant you. However, there are new sources of power here now."

"Yes! This temple!"

"And the usurping New Pantheon gods that it feeds. Now I feed upon them and upon their followers, but there is something else at work here . . ."

Ishtier all but stamped in frustration. Consumed as he was by his own ambitions, he barely seemed to reckon with the looming form that threatened to annihilate him. "Yes, yes, yes! Whatever you do to weaken this world strengthens my Master and feeds his shadows. When Rathillien falters, there is another reality beyond waiting to flood in on us. That is what I serve and, by extension, so do you."

Heliot straightened, thoughtfully scratching his beard. It crackled with sparks. "No, I don't see that," he said. "Why should I work for someone else's gain? I was going to mash you like a bug, little priestling, but I suppose that I owe you something. Just don't cross me again. Now, thanks to you, I have business to attend to elsewhere."

With that he turned and strode off, leaving Ishtier sputtering behind him in incoherent rage.

Titmouse stifled a yelp. His pocket bulged and split. Gorgo plopped to the ground and grew, and grew, and grew. The stubby remnants of a tadpole tail merged with his body, making his head swell even more and his eyes bug out.

"Quonk!" he said, raising one foot after another to regard his webbed toes.

Loogan held back for a moment, as if shy, then threw himself into his god's arms. They embraced, small priest, not-so-small god in that Loogan's arms only went halfway around Gorgo's mottled bulk.

"So far, so good," said Jame to Titmouse.

Gorgo shuffled around and hopped off, following the impressions left by Heliot's massive feet. Loogan scurried after him.

"Now what?" Titmouse demanded.

"We follow them, of course, probably back to the Temple District. I suspect that Heliot has a bigger problem on his hands than he realizes."

⚜ Chapter XI ⚜
Meanwhile
Spring 56

I

BRIER IRON-THORN drew a bucket from the courtyard's well and scooped up water to dash in her face. It was cold enough, almost, to make her gasp.

Wake up, she told herself. *Wake up. Maybe, then, this nightmare will end.*

That night after they had left their strange guest to his own devices, she had dreamed that she had gone in search of Jame—out into the empty wards, in through the oddly echoing dormitories, up to her tower quarters, and had found the latter torn apart. There she had woken with a start, standing amid strewn clothing, broken furniture, and scattered bedding.

Did I *do this?* she had wondered, aghast. *Am I going mad?*

A dry laugh had answered her, seeming to rise through the floorboards like gouts of dust.

Were the lordan's quarters still like that or had she only

dreamed it? In her mind, reality flickered back and forth. It shamed her to admit that she hadn't dared to go back.

It was two days since Jame had disappeared. Tomorrow, with or without her, Brier and the rest of the third-year cadets would depart for Gothregor.

Here came another one of them, pretty Mint, looking anxious.

"Ten, I hate to ask, but have you thought of the smokehouse? The nights have been so chilly. . . ."

Of course, she seemed to suggest, Jame would crawl into any source of warmth like a stray cat. Someone else had already mentioned the bakery oven.

"I looked," said Brier. "Also on the rooftops, in the cistern, and behind Kells' potting shed. She isn't there."

"Sorry." Mint backed off, turned, and fled.

Brier was aware that everyone had been treating her with great care these past two days, while at the same time fighting the urge to cling to her for reassurance. She had been master ten both at Tentir and Kothifir, as well as marshal of Tagmeth for almost a year, yet this had never happened to her before. Was it because this was now their home, however the Highlord decided to judge it? Were Kendar really so needy? To depend so on the fickle goodwill of a Highborn . . . where was their pride? Where was hers?

Jame had had to prove her ability to lead in adversity. Maybe now it was Brier's turn.

The watch horn sounded, ending on an upward note. This was a friend, coming from the north.

Char rode into the courtyard on a dusty post horse.

If he passed the muster, Brier thought, watching him

approach, and if Jame offered him the bond, would he accept? Once, she would have said, "Never." He had been a scowling enemy at Kothifir, one of the class jumped up from the Cataracts that other cadets thought of as uncouth. A year at Tagmeth seemed to have changed him, though. Now he was someone whom Brier and, apparently, Jame trusted.

Why, though, should he, should anyone, put faith in the lordan? Granted, she was brave—Trinity, foolishly so. To raid Restormir, to ride foremost against the Karnid horde, to stand in the way of a yackcarn stampede. . . . All right, the rathorn colt had given her an advantage at Kothifir. And she was loyal—even, it seemed, to those who should have been her enemies. Char, Shade, Timmon, Gorbel . . . That last was another Caineron, and a potent one.

Life had been much simpler for Brier before the Knorth had crossed it. One obeyed one's lord, in her case, Caldane Lord Caineron. What he did had been distasteful but not crucial, until he had tried to subject her to one of his tests of loyalty. Jame had saved her. There was always that.

Behind Char trailed a vaguely bovine creature that seemed to be all spindly legs, knobby knees, and oversized head, with high withers, a prehensile lip, and virtually no neck. The yack-cow calf Malign was quite possibly the ugliest baby Brier had ever seen, now barely a season old. Worse, every time Brier saw her, she appeared to have grown yet again. Her mother had been a cow named Beneficent who, inexplicably, had followed Char everywhere. Her father was a diminutive yackcarn bull.

Yackcarn females, however, grew to frightening proportions. Malign appeared to have inherited both size and devotion. The Kendar, of course, found the latter adorable.

Soft people, Brier thought with a passing sneer, then checked herself. More than once, she had almost smiled too.

"Blaah!" said Malign, snuffling toward the pail of water.

Char's thirsty horse also had designs on it, but backed away, ears flat, as the calf eagerly pushed past. Their shoulders were nearly the same height.

"Well?" Brier demanded of the cadet as he dismounted.

"She isn't in the Merikit village, nor do they have any news of her." He gave a short laugh. "Gran Cyd says that no doubt she will appear when it suits her."

The Merikit queen could afford to be nonchalant, thought Brier sourly. Her future didn't depend on Jame's presence—or did it?

"Cyd claims that I sired her daughter. Well, who am I to contradict a mother?"

From the storage room came a yelp and near-hysterical swearing with a definite Kothifiran tinge. Something black slithered hastily out of the dark, then paused on the threshold to fight over a mouse that one of its heads had caught.

Snap, snap, tear. Blood sprinkled the flagstones.

By an eastern gate, Jorin raised his head in interest.

Cook Rackny loomed over the node of vipers, wielding a cleaver. His earlier encounter with a parasitic blackhead had clearly put him off anything remotely serpentine.

"No!" Brier cried, involuntarily.

Fragments of mouse disappeared down several gullets, then the cloak surged into the courtyard. All but one snake, still struggling to swallow, moved in unison. The one out of order was jerked back into it by the silver thread that stitched it to its fellows. Together, they lunged past Char's horse, which threw up its head, eyes showing their whites, turned and bolted down the ramp into the subterranean stable. Voices below shouted a warning as its hooves clattered downward.

Startled, the knot of serpents swerved back into the mess hall. Char stared after it.

"What in Perimal's name was that?"

"I forgot. You weren't here when it or its bearer arrived. I think," said Brier carefully, "that may be the Serpent-Skin Cloak."

"As in the Ivory Knife and the Book Bound in Pale Leather?"

His expression changed.

"You aren't joking, are you? What, here? Now? Why?"

Brier threw up her hands. "Do I look like a Tyr-ridan, to answer such questions?"

But Jame had said that she was on the edge of becoming one of that long-awaited, long-despaired-of Three. And a potential nemesis, no less. Sweet Trinity. Did myths and legends again haunt the Kencyrath? What good had they done in the past? Weren't things complicated enough as it was?

Please, not in my age, Brier thought, then shook herself. Whining never helped. That she should even think of doing so appalled her.

"I'll explain later," she said to Char, "as best I can. Go see to your horse."

Char nodded, frowning, and trudged off, followed by a shambling Malign. Brier could almost hear his thoughts:

Leave this place on its own just for a minute and all Perimal breaks loose.

II

GRAYKIN PEERED DOWN out of the tower's second-story window into the courtyard, instinctively keeping to one side in order not to be seen. The cadet Char parted from the Marshal and descended the ramp, followed by that monstrous mooncalf that he called Malign. Oh, she would be welcome below among those close-set stalls where the cadet's mount was probably even now having hysterics.

Brier Iron-thorn stood for a moment, as if taking stock of the surrounding chaos, then went over to soothe the distraught cook who apparently had not seen where the cloak had gone and was looking about wildly, waving his cleaver.

Graykin stealthily withdrew from the window.

The Marshal was hiding something. She must be. As ramshackle as this keep appeared to him, Jame couldn't have simply walked out of it without someone noticing—could she? He remembered what he had just seen, the blind ounce Jorin settling down again before that eastern gate. Had anyone realized that he might be keeping watch, as it were, for the return of his mistress? Had anyone looked for her there? Graykin briefly considered slipping through the door that the ounce appeared to be guarding. His experience with the savannah, though, gave him pause. It wasn't that he was scared, he told himself. It was just that the job of scout belonged to someone more expendable. He was a spy, and proud of it. Moreover, he was the lordan's spy. That reflection stiffened his spine with pride. But what good could he do here in the Riverland, where everyone regarded him with such suspicion?

He turned back into the room, nervously fidgeting with the coral trim of his pink dress coat.

Had it been a mistake to wear such finery? He stuck out here like a gilded hangnail but, dammit, he would not be looked down upon, especially by that ironbound Kendar Iron-thorn. So what if she was on her way to becoming something special among the randon. Everyone thought that she was so wonderful. His agents had at least told him that much. Well, there was brazen glory, all big muscles, hard eyes, and strong jaws, but also there was the more subtle kind, based on intelligence, on wits. What hurt him most was the thought that Jame might turn to Brier rather than to him for counsel.

"Did you see what he wore today?" one might ask the other, and both would laugh. . . .

Graykin shuddered at the thought.

To forestall that, to prove his worth yet again, he must offer the lordan new information, something valuable.

A gaunt, motionless figure sat before the dead fire, staring at nothing. Graykin drew up a chair opposite him.

"So," he said with what was meant to be an engaging

smile. "Have you decided to talk to me yet? I won't go away, you know, until you do."

III

THE DAY WORE ON. More Kendar reported having slept poorly and hinted at bad dreams. Some spoke of falling into an abyss, others of being left behind in the dark. All felt abandoned, and mocked in their abandonment by soft, sly laughter.

Nonetheless, preparations for the third-year cadets' departure the next morning went smoothly, having been started days before. Maybe they could leave early. Brier wished so, devoutly. That alien presence in the second-story quarters of the keep weighed on her. Moreover, she still hadn't gone above that to see what state the lordan's room was in. She had to wait, though . . . didn't she? What if Jame came home today, tonight, tomorrow at dawn?

She is your lady. You owe her that.

When everything about the journey was as well in hand as could be hoped, Brier found herself obsessing over the keep's schedule while she was gone.

"Keep an eye on my horse," she told patient Cheva. "I don't want that hoof to crack any farther."

"Kells, if you go out herb collecting, take a guard with you. Yes, I know that it's always been safe near the keep, but these are troubled times."

"Rackny, I know you mean to prepare a feast for Summer's Day and am sorry I won't be here to enjoy it.

But d'you have enough provisions on hand? I don't want anyone going through the gates while I'm away."

"Swar, your forge needs to be reorganized. It's a mess."

Finally Marc drew her aside. "Be calm," he told her. "Be serene. Fussing only puts them more on edge. They all know their jobs."

"Are you saying that I don't?" she snapped at him, and then felt ashamed of herself. "Sorry. It's just that I overhear them talking among themselves. If your pet were to offer them the bond now, who would take it? A year she spent, winning their trust, and now to risk it with Ancestors-only-know what freak of an escapade . . ."

"The lass understands her duty as well as you do. What you don't know are all of her other responsibilities. Nor do I, come to that."

"Being the commander of this keep isn't enough?"

"She's also her brother's lordan, the Earth Wife's former Favorite, somehow father of Gran Cyd's child, and potentially one of the Tyr-ridan. Her life is . . . complicated."

"Huh!"

Damson dragged a cadet across the courtyard toward them. Brier recognized second-year Wort, who was often too clever for her own good and prone to baiting her humorless ten-commander. So far, she had gotten away with the latter. Now, however, she clutched a blanket over her head and seemed to flinch away from the light.

"This little fool has been hiding under her bed all day," Damson said, without preamble. "Show Ten."

Wort hesitated, then defiantly shook off her covering. She had had long black hair twisted into an elaborate braid of which she was inordinately proud. These days, the randon favored a short cut, meaning less for an enemy to grab. To wear one's hair past the ears was a minor act of rebellion or, at Tagmeth, a declaration of loyalty to Jame whose own hair, when loosed, was notoriously long. The cadet's braid had been crudely lopped off next to her skull, leaving her with a frayed halo.

Brier swore.

"You have no idea who did this?"

"None, Ten," said Wort, fighting tears. "At least, I dreamed that someone sat on the pallet beside me and stroked my hair. 'You think to honor her,' he said. Yes, it was a man, gloating. He made me want to crawl inside my own skin to hide. 'Little girl, witness her weakness.' And he gave me these."

In one hand she held a knife; in the other, the severed braid that she had been clutching to her breast.

"I thought we were past such things," Brier muttered to Marc as the cadet wobbled away. "Killy was the prankster. Killy is dead. This seems more . . . visceral. And it's so petty. Her throat might just as easily have been slit."

"Ah, don't say that. Think what an uproar there would be then. Someone didn't want that. Besides, she may have cut it off herself. In her sleep."

Brier's eyes flickered to the tower's second-story window. Of all the things that had changed recently, the most disturbing one was the arrival of their mysterious guest of the previous night. However, he had neither moved nor spoken since and still, as dank as his clothes were, no one had dared to touch him.

What about the lordan's third-story quarters? Dared she go see what state they were in? No.

Then there was Graykin. Brier didn't trust the spy, but she also didn't see any reason for him to creep around the dormitories by night harvesting hair. It occurred to her that she hadn't seen him all day, though, which was odd.

The watch horn sounded, on a wavering note. The newcomer was suspect but not in force, and coming from the south. Brier gestured to the guard on top of the wall: *let him through, but beware.*

She waited in the courtyard, thinking, *Now what?*

A hunting party rode in, several Caineron Kendar, but also a Highborn. Fash swung down from his horse, grinning.

"Ah, Brier Iron-thorn. And where is your mistress, Jameth Priest's-butt?"

Brier smiled tightly. "We know her as 'Jame,' ran. Or M'lady. Or Lordan."

"You would, as close as you two have always been. We've laughed about that, many a night, over our cups."

"To what do we owe the pleasure of this visit?"

"Oh," he said, with an airy wave of his hand, "I was nearby and just thought I would drop in. I'll take a cup of wine, if you still have any."

Wine was one thing that the gates did not provide, although Kells was experimenting with dandelions. The keep only held a few precious bottles.

"Hard cider or nothing," said Brier firmly. "For your men too."

Fash wandered off, looking around him with a condescending smirk, while his stony-faced servants continued to sit their horses. Brier gestured for the cider, also to indicate that Fash's mount was not to be stabled. With luck, this would be a brief stay.

The Caineron turned into the mess hall. Brier followed. She noted that the Serpent-Skin Cloak had crawled up onto one of the chairs by the fireplace. There it lay coiled, looking innocuous, like a fat, breathing rug, as it slept off its meager meal of mouse. As usual when not needed, the mess tables and benches had been cleared back to the walls. Fash wandered restlessly about the open space between fireplace and kitchen door.

"I'm surprised that you haven't left for Gothregor yet," he said. "All of our class will be there. Gorbel, Higbert, and the rest set out days ago from Restormir. Timmon, Shade, our instructors . . . there will be parties in camp every night until the muster, and then a feast of celebration in the great hall, or what passes for it in the Highlord's keep." He laughed. "I hear that Torisen decks out a space in the abandoned rooms, under the open sky. Quaint. I suppose, though, that it's the best he can do given that most of Gothregor is a ruin either overrun with ghosts or infested by the Women's World. Have you heard any news of him?"

Brier received more or less regular letters from Torisen's steward Rowan, who seemed to think that her lord's sister should be kept informed, judging, rightly, that Torisen himself was an indifferent correspondent.

"I hear that he has recovered his health. Mostly."

"Tsk. Lung-rot is a tricky thing, or so I understand. It never occurred to any of us that an adult Highborn could catch it, much less nearly die of it. There must have been some weakness there. I hear that the Council Meeting was called off because he kept coughing up blood."

Brier felt her lips tighten. She didn't know what exactly had happened—no one did except Jame, Torisen himself, and their cousin Kindrie. It was enough for her that the Highlord was on the mend.

Enough, too, of the offensive. Attack.

"If your lord Gorbel left for Gothregor days ago, why didn't you go with him?"

"Oh," said Fash, attempting to speak lightly although his smile cracked at the edges. "Didn't I tell you? I am no longer a randon cadet."

Brier was shocked. "But you passed into your final year!"

"Things change."

He spoke now as if unable to stop, and continued to pace.

"I went to Tentir because Gorbel did. He was the Caineron lordan—still is, for that matter. He was to be my patron, my lord. But he doesn't like me. Why? I supported him. I opposed his enemies. What else was I supposed to do? Then he met that bitch Jameth and he changed unless . . . unless I was wrong about him all along. Maybe he was always weak and I just didn't want to see it. No. She seduced him, without so much as a touch given or received nor wanted on either side, as far as I could see. You Knorth, what is it about you that changes things?"

He seemed genuinely to be asking, but Brier had no answer. She had been Knorth ever since she had broken with the Caineron and sworn to Torisen, but realized now that she had not at heart considered herself as such.

She thought of her anger against Jame.

What is this wall that I raise between myself and all Highborn? Am I so damaged that I can not truly acknowledge any of them? Do they deserve it, though?

No. What Jame had done...in running away? In choosing other loyalties?...was inexcusable.

A Kendar arrived with a glass of cider. Fash impatiently waved him off. Brier accepted it and sipped. Its bright tang cleared her throat and her head.

"What will you do now?"

He laughed, not with humor. "Lord Tiggeri offered me a position, provided I quit the randon. 'Jumped up bullyboys,' he calls them. What reasonable man would submit to such discipline? I wasn't happy at Tentir, you know. All of those restrictions, those rules...Honor, always honor! Where was the scope for my talents? Tiggeri understood. And Gorbel had as good as shrugged me off. So here I am."

"Yes," said Brier. "I can see that."

One tended to focus on the Kendars' need to be bound. Everyone knew, though, that the Caineron had more Highborn than appropriate positions for them. A stud-barn run amuck, someone had once said, holding too many frustrated stallions.

"Has Tiggeri bound you yet?"

"No. He will, though. He as much as promised."

In the meantime, on that scant reassurance, he had given up his career as a randon cadet. All of his friends had left for the muster. Whatever else their future held, they would at least be randon officers. He wished that he could have gone with them. Brier saw, now, why he had come to Tagmeth, no doubt having heard that the Knorth contingent had not yet passed Restormir southward bound. He had hoped that they, too, were somehow stranded, as they would be if she waited any longer for Jame. It would have been sweet to jeer in a Knorth face. It might have made him feel better.

Brier almost felt sorry for him, but not quite. This, after all, was the hunter who had provided Lord Caineron the Merikit skins with which he furnished his private quarters. Brier's attitude toward Jame's pet hill tribe was ambiguous—after all, they had killed Marc's family, which as his great-granddaughter was also her own—but she preferred to see them wearing their own pelts.

From the distance, muffled by walls, came a wail.

"That sounds like a cat fight," said Fash, looking fretful.

Brier, however, recognized the racket with horror. The baby Benj had a particularly piercing cry, and he didn't stop for days on end. His nurse Girt must be bringing him through the gate from the oases. Benj was Must's son, sired by rape by her half-brother Tiggeri. Jame had sworn that the child wasn't at Tagmeth, which had been true at the time. Tiggeri's servant Fash must not know that he was here now.

"So," said Fash, assuming a smile. "Where is your lady anyway?"

"Out," said Brier brusquely. "About. Should she hang around in case you chose to drop in?"

The noise was getting closer, and louder.

"I'll see if I can find her," Brier said, thinking fast. She had to get rid of this most unwelcome guest. "In the meantime, why don't you have a seat?"

"Courtesy, at last."

Fash looked around with a hint of renewed arrogance. Brier Iron-thorn might be Tentir's darling, but she was, after all, only a Kendar. All that offered itself was the chair by the fire. The "cushion" no doubt looked soft to him, after hours in the saddle. He threw himself down on it with a negligent air.

Instantly, his expression changed. From under his buttocks erupted a great hissing and writhing. He grabbed the chair arms and raised himself on them as if trying to levitate his entire body. Black tails whipped his legs. Indignant heads snaked up between his spread thighs.

Hiss, snap, eek!

Fash launched himself off the chair with a falsetto screech and bolted out the door, clutching at every part of his anatomy that he could reach below the waist to make sure that it was still there. A wild clatter broke out in the courtyard as he threw himself at his startled horse, which plunged out of the keep with Fash clinging to its side.

His servants exchanged looks. Then as one they shrugged and spurred after their master.

Marc looked into the mess hall. "What on earth did you do to that boy? Here now, have you been laughing?"

Brier wiped her eyes and straightened her expression. "Who, me?"

"I think," said Marc profoundly, "that you have a very strange sense of humor, but it's good at least to know that you have one at all. You may need it. Here's Nurse Girt come to see you."

IV

THE KENDAR GIRT stood by the gate to the oasis, trying to hold an infant who seemed to be all flailing limbs and bloated, red face.

She had done Malign an injustice, thought Brier. Benj was a much uglier baby than the yack-calf.

He now paused in his wailing to stare at her. Maybe this would be all right after all. When she took a step closer, however, his mouth opened, seemingly from ear to ear, and cacophony spewed out.

"He won't stop," Girt said, her voice unnaturally shrill, pitched to rise over the uproar. She looked distraught, with bruised, sleepless eyes and loose skin that hung off the bones of her face. "Day and night, on and on and on . . . this will kill him!"

It will certainly kill you, Brier thought, keeping her distance.

"You nursed both his mother Must and her mother before her," she said. "Surely you've handled such a situation before."

"No!" Girt wailed. "They were both such good babies! I thought that other nurses exaggerated their problems. Infants are sweet little things that cuddle and coo. This one, though . . ."

Benj drew a deep breath and screamed. His face turned almost black.

"Even in his sleep he fusses unless I hold him and even then . . ."

Brier was beginning to feel fraught too. She had no experience with babies except for that once. Memory jolted her back to Kothifir, outside the burning tower. His mother had thrown him out a window just before the flames had engulfed her. Brier had caught him. *Oh good*, she had thought, with such a sense of relief, but then she had realized that the child wasn't breathing. The fall and her own arms had broken his neck.

Hold his head just so . . .

Forget that. Forget.

"There are other Caineron refugees," she said. "Can't one of them help you?"

"Most of them are men. What do they know? The others tried. Nothing worked."

Knorth Kendar had begun to gather around them, drawn by the piercing wail—some women, some men.

"Swaddle him," one suggested.

"Burp him."

"Take him for a nice long ride down the valley."

"I've tried!" cried poor Girt, nearly in tears. "My lady's child, my future lord, I've failed him!"

Graykin emerged from the tower, looking frazzled. "Will no one shut up that brat?"

Brier turned on him, almost in relief. Here was someone at whom she could lash out.

"Where in Perimal's name have you been all day? Don't you realize that Tagmeth's very existence is at stake?"

"Oh, bother this precious keep!" He stomped, his overlong, oversized pink court coat flouncing against patched breeches. "I know what I know, which is more than you do. He's talked to me. Finally."

"Our guest? What did he say?"

Graykin sputtered. It was against his nature to give away information, but now, under these circumstances . . .

"He . . . he . . . for a long time, he just huddled there, as if he hurt down to his very core. His eyes were . . . anxious? Haunted? Trinity, I've never seen anyone look so wretched! 'Jamie,' he said once, and gulped. 'Warn . . .'"

"Who? About what?"

"'I am not who I am.' He said that too, whispering, all in a rush as if afraid that someone would stop him. 'I would never hurt . . .' Then his expression changed and he smiled, oh, so slyly. 'Jamethiel,' he said. 'Child, I wait.'"

Brier shivered despite herself. Graykin had conjured up the smirk of a skull with dead eyes.

"I don't know who or what he is," said Graykin, "but he's dangerous."

The boy looked so nakedly earnest that Brier almost believed him. Almost. But he wasn't a boy. He was a spy. And a half-breed. And Caineron's own spawn.

"So you said before. Prove it."

Benj gathered himself together in a knot, then flung wide all of his limbs. His cry was enough to split stone.

"Oh, for Trinity's sake!" Graykin snatched him out of Girt's arms and shook him, hard. "Will . . . you . . . shut . . . up!"

Kendar dived at him. Brier found herself in a kind of scrimmage amidst flailing hands, the baby bobbing above it, across fingertips. He landed in her arms.

"Coo," said Benj. Then his face scrunched up.

"Here." She thrust him back into Girt's anxious embrace. "You"—this, to Graykin—"get out of my sight."

The Southron staggered back, looking stunned. "I'm sorry! I didn't mean . . . I wouldn't hurt . . . but I'll show you yet. This is a trap set for our lady, in the guise of a friend."

"Go," said Brier.

Graykin went.

V

BRIER FOUND HERSELF suddenly frantic to leave. It might already be late afternoon, but the traveling party was ready. Why wait until the next morning? Jame wasn't here now. There was no guarantee that she would arrive before then, curse her.

"Then too," Brier said to Dar when he answered her hasty summons, "who knows what Fash will say about his visit?"

Dar scratched his head. "Maybe he won't say anything. After all, he came off looking like a proper fool, and his followers won't know what happened at all, unless he tells them. Still, if we ride on his heels, we should be able to slip past Restormir before dawn. They won't expect that."

It was also in the back of both their minds that they didn't want to spend another night at Tagmeth given its current guest. Dar had had bad dreams too.

Up in the tower, Graykin screamed.

He wasn't in his first-floor apartment. Her heart pounding, Brier charged up the stairs, Dar and half a dozen other Kendar close behind her. They piled into her back when she stopped abruptly outside the second-story door. It swung open at her touch, creaking. One chair by the fire had been overturned. In the other sat a hunched, gaunt figure, whose raised shoulders quivered. He lifted the face of a skull and laughed silently up at her. That was bad enough but his eyes, oh, they were terrible.

A shape huddled on the hearthstone. It too shook, or maybe that was only the throb of the black cloak that overspread it.

Brier gingerly reached past the serpents' heads. Some hissed. Others wound about her hand in what seemed almost like a scaly caress. Graykin stared up at her with wide, crazed eyes. He drooled. A growl edged through lips bitten raw, then a whimper, then a howl.

"Now what?" asked a shaken Dar as Brier half-closed the door on the scene. Inside, the wail went on and on, interrupted by slobbering as the Southron attacked his own already mangled flesh.

"How can we help either one of them?"

That sounded hollow even to Brier, who had spoken; but, really, what could they do?

"The White Knife," said one of the other Kendar hoarsely. "Kill them both."

"We could at least hack those snakes off of him," said another.

"I don't think so." Brier tried to collect her scattered wits. She didn't know what the Serpent-Skin Cloak was supposed to do, but destroying it didn't feel like the right answer. It was *the* Cloak, for Trinity's sake, one of the Kencyrath's three no-longer-so-lost objects of power. If the Tyr-ridan was finally about to appear, why not them too?

Endgames, she thought, and shivered.

"This is something for our lady to sort out. We are still going."

"But . . ."

"I know. This leaves the garrison in a bad situation. All I can suggest is that those two be separated. Ask Kells about drugging them. Everyone else should sleep as little as possible. Do it in shifts, if necessary. Keep watch on each other. No more sleepwalking."

Her gaze rose despite her to the floor of the third story, to Jame's quarters. No, dammit, she would not climb to see what state they were in. Let Jame deal with that too, when she deigned to return.

⊰⊱ Chapter XII ⊰⊱
By Demons Possessed
Spring 57

I

THE STREETS OF TAI-TASTIGON darkened as night fell. Doors closed, then opened again, just a crack, as rumors ran through the city:

"Have you heard . . ." "Is it true?" "Yes, in the Temple District, all of them coming together!" "But what about our gods? They need us." "They didn't call." "They *need* us."

Doors opened farther. The night folk were already abroad, streaming past. Listen to the swift patter of their feet on the cobblestones, the swish of dark robes. One by one, the day folk emerged. Some were drawn back inside by anxious wives or husbands, mothers or fathers. Some crept back by themselves as their nerve failed them and there they would sit, huddled over banked fires, their ears stuffed with cotton, the rest of that long, long night. Meanwhile, their neighbors took to the streets, men and women, young and old. The patter became a rush.

They need us. They need us. We are coming.

The tide swept up Jame's small party and carried it across the city as if on invisible wings.

Bloop, said something as they hurried across the bridge.

Wha . . . ? asked the wind, but it already knew.

Over the city loomed that monstrous House, building and collapsing and building again out of clouds and ash driven south from the Haunted Lands, from Perimal Darkling itself. Pallid lightning fretted its gables and outlined from inside the vacant eyes of its windows. Muffled thunder growled. Trinity, that smell . . .

Is the Master really coming? Jame wondered as she ran, and her heart pounded at the thought. *Sweet Trinity, what then?*

Her hand was under Loogan's left elbow to help him keep up. On the other side, Titmouse gripping his right arm. As he was borne along between them, the little priest's sandals barely touched the ground. Gorgo surged ahead of them. His size and the distance of each leap varied as the power ebbed and flowed, now feeding the city's gods, now draining them. Everything was in flux.

"Awk!" said Loogan as his god shrank almost under his feet. For a moment, the three of them tottered on the brink of theocide. Then Gorgo was off again, and so were they.

The Eaten One was in the River Tone. The Falling Man was overhead. Where was the Earth Wife? Where (Ancestors preserve them) was the Burnt Man? With whom did their sympathies lie, if anywhere, and what had drawn them here? Tai-tastigon was important. If it could fall to the shadows, so could Rathillien. So, who stood by the gods of the city on this fateful night?

They need us. We are coming.

Others followed. All of the bereft from the Lower Town seemed to be shambling after them, drawn by the congregated demons that possessed their souls. Foremost among them came the three Kencyr priests, the two supporting the stumbling third as if in horrible mockery of those whom they trailed.

"Look out!" shouted someone to the rear.

Stinking bundles of rags coursed through the crowd, snapping right and left to clear the way. Haunts. After them, as if behind a leashed brace of hounds, came something large, heavy, and speckled with luminous warts, so intent on its course that it ignored those upon whom it trod and flattened.

A smaller, single-souled demon with entirely too many legs wheezed past on its heels, its smell making Jame sneeze. What Old Pantheon dead god could possibly have been based on a centipede?

One of the three Kencyr priests dropped the arm of his brother and stumbled after this second demon, his arms and legs in an uncouth windmill that mirrored what scurried before him.

"My name . . . my name . . ." he sobbed as he ran, soon to be lost in the crowd.

Ahead lay the Temple District, fire showing through the angles of its improbable roofline. Booms, crashes, and wails echoed within. Even at this distance, the earth shook.

Once within its gates, Gorgo lurched purposefully toward his temple with Loogan puffing after him.

Worshippers milled around before it. On the steps were the dead novices and the former priests, urging them to seek sanctuary within. Both groups scattered as Gorgo scrambled up the stair and hopped inside.

"Come, come!" Loogan cried, drawing them all in.

The living and the dead came, although still hesitant to mix, the former drawing back in fastidious horror, the latter, fragile, wary of jostling elbows.

"You, too," Loogan called to Jame and Titmouse, who had both hung back.

"I don't think this is right for us," said Titmouse, scowling. He gave a clumsy bob of acknowledgement. "Thank you for your invitation, nonetheless, m'lord."

"Then keep safe. Who knows what will happen next?"

"Not I," muttered Jame, turning away from the closing door.

"Huh," said Titmouse, without looking at her.

Jame hesitated, unsure what to do next. Events were spinning out of control around her like a series of muffled explosions, of which there were also many. If nothing else, it was up to her now to make what sense she could of this mayhem, to deduce what she could.

There, a troupe of the faithful spun in place to evoke their absent god through ecstasy.

There, worshippers of chance cast the bones against a wall, over and over again in desperate search of a winning combination.

Here, at a curtained corner stall, puppets bashed each other with stocking-clad hands to represent the triumph of good over evil.

The latter display, even in this chaos, had attracted a

small, rapt audience. Most were dead gods, dumbly staring. Among them was one still alive, if barely, a huddled, cowled figure holding the hand of her last true believer, a small child.

Bop, bop, bop, went a priest's hidden hands within the socks, belaboring each other with fratricidal fury.

The child crowed as the one in red flopped over, its ribbon of a tongue spilling out down the front of the stall.

"See, lady? The bad people can't win! Or . . . or was Mister Poke supposed to be the hero?"

Here came another god—a belligerent little fellow sacred to a Skyrr hill tribe that had, somehow, wrangled him temple rights in the city. He wore leather armor sown thickly with plaques of silver and gold. His long hair was braided with black and white feathers that fluttered in his self-important wake. One of those who followed him held high a banner depicting a piebald horse running under the stars. That flag-bearer—surely it was Harr sen Tenko's son, Harri.

The current in the street seemed to change, tugging at one's very guts. The Kencyr temple had been radiating force to the city's gods. Now Ishtier had apparently regained control of it, and it was sucking power in.

The sen Tenko deity faltered. With a whine as if of expelled breath, he shrank within his armor. Dislodged plaques rattled on the cobbles like fallen scales. Feathers flew. His followers stumbled, including Harri, who nearly dropped the banner.

Jame felt the others coming up behind her before she saw them and hustled Titmouse back against a wall.

It was a hunting pack of haunts.

The god uttered a shrill squeal, turned, and fled, shedding armor down to bare skin. His people wavered, then plunged after him in a rout. Harri hesitated.

"Go!" Jame hissed at him.

He gave her a wild-eyed stare, then turned and ran, his banner held like a lance before him, charging at nothing.

One of the followers tripped and fell. Judging by her clothes, she was a wealthy matron from the hills on pilgrimage to the house of her displaced god. Others tried to help her but panting, she waved them on. Then she turned with blanched features and trembling lips to await her fate.

The haunts swarmed around her, snarling. Perhaps she recognized some of them, for she cried out with horror. Then again, they were horrifying. But they didn't savage her. Rather, they milled about as if kept on an invisible leash even as they slavered against its restraint.

Snap, snap, hiss.

"Grandma," lisped one, a small girl, smiling through a mouth full of spittle and loose baby teeth.

The woman cried out again and stumbled to her feet. They drove her back the way they had come. Jame and Titmouse followed.

Here was a courtyard and a collapsed temple. On its ruins, as if on a throne, lounged Heliot. The seams in his armor appeared to have widened so that red light glared down on the wet, steaming cobbles at his feet like spilt blood.

The pack played the matron back and forth before him until she stumbled, sobbing, and fell. Her gray-streaked hair had broken loose from its net and tumbled about her face. She pushed it aside with a shaking hand, as if trying to reestablish order in the sudden maelstrom of her life.

Heliot had appeared to ignore the antics of such a trivial offering, but now he deigned to stoop. His clawed fingertips snagged the woman's shadow, ripping it off. She fell. He raised her soul to his lips and licked it as if to determine its taste.

"Ah," he said. "One of the righteous." And he swallowed it.

The cracks in his armor narrowed, slightly, but more opened like bleeding wounds.

"More," he said, leaning forward, radiating hunger. "Bring me more."

The haunts coursed off, baying after fresh prey. Too impatient to wait, Heliot rose and followed them.

"Is she dead?" Titmouse asked in a hoarse whisper.

"Not yet. He will feed on her soul until it is eaten away, which may take a while. Then she will die and come back as a haunt."

"Harsh."

"True. Ancestors preserve us."

That was another question: What happened to a feeder soul if the demon possessing it died? Maybe it escaped. Maybe that depended on how much of it had already been consumed, say, too much for it to survive. G'ah. There were too many variables here.

After a moment, the woman rose. She stood, swaying, blank-eyed, then tottered off after the pack, leaving her shadow behind. Somewhere in the district, her god howled at her loss and subsequently at his own. What, after all, was a god without his followers?

That forlorn cry seemed to call forth another presence. Smoking puddles quivered like gelid blood where Heliot had been. Out of one, a huge, bloated...something... scrabbled at the edge. It was the whumping demon. The sodden priest gasped and fell to his knees, his remaining brother leaning over him. Water leaked around both of them. The thing tried to pull itself up onto solid ground. Were those translucent tentacles clutching at the stones' margin? If so, they oozed and stank and some of them sloughed off. The priest gasped again, clutched his chest, and collapsed. In death, he seemed to melt within his tattered vestments, leaving them vacant and slimy on the ground. The demon sank, wailing, likewise dissolving.

The demon's dire straits had clearly affected the priest whose soul had been his core. The priest's death, conversely, had doomed the demon. It seemed to go both ways.

The remaining priest rose, his brother's empty robes in his hands. He dropped them and looked to Jame as if to ask, what next?

Me, she thought bitterly. *Always me.*

"This is ridiculous," said Titmouse. "These people will all die if they don't pull themselves together."

"I think," Jame said, "that I know someone they might follow, also someone you should meet."

II

SHE LED THE WAY deeper into the district, dodging demons and gods alike while the followers of both clashed on street corners. Yes, some mortals supported these abominations, as Heliot had foretold. "Greed, vengeance, grievance, these are the levers that move mere mortals," he had said, and so here they were. "To please us will become their pleasure. They will come to see sacrifice to us for the honor that it is."

Some people, Jame thought, were stupid.

The remaining Kencyr priest followed them mutely, but died at a crossroads when the demon possessing his soul as its core burst out of a side street and accidentally trampled him. The demon floundered to a stop in chagrin. He appeared to have devolved from an Old Pantheon god of the fields. Numerous festering lilies sprouted from his muddy flesh, their stench appalling. Brown blossoms rained down, melting into slime as they reached the ground, even as he clutched after them.

Perhaps those were the souls he had harvested to feed upon, Jame thought, pressing back into a doorway with a hand to her nose. If he had caught one, could it have become a new core to sustain him? Probably not, given the shape they were in. With a moan, he sank to the pavement, on top of the priest's broken body. Both dissolved into a filthy puddle.

Here at last was Dalis-sar's street and his temple.

A priest caught her by the arm as she entered. "Oh come!" he cried, drawing her inside. "Oh come!"

She could see that he was blind, as were many of Dalis-sar's servants after years of gazing with open-eyed adoration into his radiance.

The temple was sunk in gloom now except for the glow of candles on the altar. Against this flickering light reared the bulk of Dalis-sar, sitting on the steps, holding his head in enormous hands. It was so like her first glimpse of him on the curb that Jame blinked. At least he hadn't shrunken in the continual flux of power. Perhaps he had the faith of his followers to thank for that. Why, though, had he gone dark?

"She is dead, isn't she?" he said, without raising his head, as Jame cautiously approached. His voice seemed to come from the bottom of a very deep well.

Who . . . oh. Aden. Of course. "Not as far as I know."

His eyes lifted, a spark kindling in their depths. "I felt her soul pass. Are you saying . . ."

Trinity. He was a god now, and could blast her where she stood. Moreover, he was essentially an innocent. Such people, when imbued with power, could be very dangerous.

"Kalissan reaped her soul, at Heliot's behest," Jame said carefully. "She was the demon's first victim and now, as far as I know, is the core of that creature's being."

Dalis-sar rose, trailing fire.

"Are you telling me," he boomed, "that she still lives? Then I must rescue her!"

His priests cowered away from him. Jame, with an effort, stood her ground.

"Sar Dalis," she said, swallowing hard. "You also owe a debt to your people, perhaps to all of those who risk their lives tonight for their gods. Think what we have sacrificed over the millennia to our own deity, with precious little return. These gods, at least, give their followers something. Very well. Let them stand or fall according to the faith of their worshippers. I didn't believe, when I first came here, that they were real at all. What happened to you is . . . strange, but not out of keeping with the properties of this city or this world. Please, take control of this battle. You're the only one who can."

Dalis-sar paced back and forth in front of the altar, shaking his head. Sparks snapped at the end of his long braid as if it were a fiery whip. He was rousing, at least, but what next?

"Aden, my friends, you." His lambent gaze fell on Titmouse. "Are you a Kencyr priest?"

Titmouse stepped around Jame, his jaw jutting with defiance, although his eyes were confused. "Yes, I am. What are you?"

Dalis-sar fell to one knee. The temple shook. "A loyal soldier of our god. I am lost here. Tell me what to do."

Titmouse seemed taken aback by this—how not?—and glanced involuntarily toward his fellow priests. They were urging him forward.

"Er . . . do these people have reason to depend on you? If so, as the Talisman says, you have a responsibility to them."

"I have served, oh, so long. When am I entitled to anything for myself?"

"Others come first." Titmouse cleared his throat. "I know that that is hard to hear. I, also, have sacrificed, and asked questions, in the dark, at night. Where does duty lie? As a child, I would have said to our god. Now, I think, to each other."

Dalis-sar seemed to swell like a forge before the bellows.

"You." He loomed over Jame, all but blasting her with his fiery breath. "Do you swear that she still lives?"

Jame flinched, trying not to inhale. "I . . . can't."

"Pray to our god that she does."

His smoldering gaze swept over her, alighting on his priests. They, being blind, only felt the heat, which seemed to brace them.

"I need to know what is going on," he said, a natural commander thinking out loud. "Also, I need links to the other priests and gods in the district. We must act together."

His own high priest stepped forward, a wizened little man with sunken eye sockets beneath lids sewn shut. "We can reach out to our fellow clerics and they will listen to us, such being the respect with which they regard you. Leave that to us. As for being scouts, though . . ."

He tapped regretfully on the dried seal of his lids. *Tick, tick, tick.*

Dalis-sar's face creased with sudden chagrin. "I spoke without thinking. You know how much I regret that."

The priest fumbled forward and, having found it, patted his god's knee as if to say, *There, there . . .*

"At your request, your novices and acolytes serve you blindfolded, only beholding your full glory when they take their final vows. As with our fathers and grandfathers before us, we elders are proud to do so every day until sight fails. By then, we count it no loss."

"Yes, but . . ."

"Shhh. Plan."

Dalis-sar straightened. "Very well, then. Keep the lesser orders in, except for a few of the oldest. We will make do."

"Am I going mad?" Titmouse muttered in Jame's ear. "That's both a Kencyr and a god. But how?"

"I'll explain later, to the extent that I can."

Dalis-sar had swung to face her, the whole room shifting with him. She staggered, blinking, in the full glare of his attention.

"This is all moot without one essential fact," he said. "How do we kill these demons?"

In the old days, water, fire, and their true names would have done the trick. Like the Lower Town Monster, those demons had depended on a core human soul and had fed on others (in the case of the Monster, children), but the dead gods hadn't been a component.

From what she had seen so far of this new breed of demons, their existence was linked partly to dead gods, partly to the fluctuating power of her own temple, and partly to the human souls upon whom they preyed. The loss of feeder souls weakened them, as with the bog monster of the festering lilies. The loss, however, of that special core soul that supported their being could kill them. Witness again the bog monster accidentally stomping his host, also the death by heart attack of the priest who had unwillingly supported the whumping monster.

Was it possible, though, to kill a demon without destroying its core human soul? Therein lay Aden's fate, and perhaps her own if Dalis-sar held her responsible.

"I'll find out," she said, with a gulp, praying that she would.

"You had better."

"I'll stay here," said Titmouse as she turned to leave. "Maybe I can help. At least, I can learn."

On the doorstep, Jame was hit on the shoulder by a shard of slate.

"Psst!" said someone above her. "Up here!"

A Cloudie leaned over the temple's gutter, precariously far out.

"I'm Robin. Sparrow said to watch for you as you were bound to land here sooner or later. Always in the thick of things, he said. What's up?"

This, Jame remembered, was Sparrow's cousin, he who found the Temple District's perilous roofline an agreeable challenge.

"Blood, thunder, and general mayhem," she said.

"Oh, good! How can I help?"

What, in stirring up more?

"We've got a host of demons here, gods galore, and a lot of people running every which way in danger of getting themselves killed. Can you keep track of movement on the streets and report back to this temple?"

"With pleasure! What's more"—here, heads popped up behind him, avid with interest—"my roof-mates want to help."

One toward the rear presented a fluff of fair hair and an enormous grin.

"That's our mate Dandy," said Sparrow, with a negligent wave. "Just one of us, you understand."

"No one lets me do anything," Dandello had said. Now he was back in the thick of things, to his evident delight and the potential cost of everyone else.

Still, good enough, as far as it went, thought Jame as she took again to the district's streaming cobblestones. Now, if she could just figure out how to slay a demon without destroying its stolen soul . . .

III

THE PATTERNS in the street continued to shift.

Followers still crowded in from the greater city, urgent but unsure what to do. Some priests continued to hustle them into the presumed safety of those temples where their gods cowered. Of those gods who ventured out, their people huddled around them, but it was unclear who protected whom. Perhaps it went both ways.

There again, creeping by a wall, was the goddess with her sole childish adherent. Had she already lost her temple? Probably, along with her congregation. Gods, priests, and laity alike tried to call her in to sanctuary but she crept on, one hand holding her cowl over her face, the other clutched by small fingers.

Haunts still hunted in packs for their masters. The lost and the solitary were their prey, or larger groups when they dared to attack them. When they came across one of the wandering bereft, however, they escorted him or her back to the demon that held their soul. The demons, it seemed, also protected their own, if only for their own sake.

"Preserve the larder," could have been their rallying cry.

Some temples had idols of stone or wood or plaster on either side of their steps. These began to stir. Dust or splinters or mortar rattled down from their plinths. A lion roared soundlessly. Many-headed figures yawned and stretched in a wave of gaping mouths. Which side were they on? In Perimal Darkling, the animate and inanimate overlapped. On the other hand, these statues appeared to have been brought to life by faith and a desire to protect. Jame edged by a pair of manticores whose heads turned, creaking, to watch her pass. Their flexing claws crumbled stone.

"Friend," she murmured to them. "Friend."

From ahead came Loogan's voice, raised in exhortation. He stood on the steps of his temple, addressing a tremulous, half-seen crowd of dead gods. Here was a slim woman with the head of a cat; there, a man wreathed with horns; here, a swarm of locusts hopping in agitated unison; there, fluttering fetuses with gossamer wings, younger siblings of the fat urchins who graced the facade of the Res aB'tyrr.

"My lords and ladies," said Loogan, clearing his voice, with a respectful if shy bob in their direction. "This was once your home. Now you return once a year on your feast. You have outlived your worshippers. Your time has passed."

Wings stirred uneasily. The cat-woman made as if to wash her face but paused, hand in the air, the tip of her tongue extended. Horns wove and hooves stomped in hesitation.

"Think who you were, though, and what you did for your people. They served you. You loved them. These are their children."

Back behind them, something huge stirred in the mouth of an alley. A monstrous cloven hoof scraped into the torch light of the street as its owner shifted position.

"Do you really want to prey upon them as demons?"

"Noooo!" came a hollow lowing from the dark of the alley.

"No," murmured the crowd as if in echo. "Not our children's children."

"Well, then," said Loogan as his shoulders sagged with relief. "Go in peace."

They faded away, except for the cloven foot that only withdrew, again clumsily rasping on stone, into the shadows.

Loogan smiled at Jame, looking tired.

An uproar broke out within the temple behind him. Shouts, screams, crashes. Loogan took a step as if to enter, but was thrown back as the door was flung open in his face. He tumbled down the steps. Jame ran to him where he sprawled, half-stunned, on the cobbles. Nothing, at least, appeared to be broken. What was this, though, emerging from the doorway at the top of the stairs in a gray sprawl of limbs? At first, it made no sense to her. A round body, ridiculously long legs, a face with bulging green eyes, contorted as if with unspeakable grief . . .

"Woe!" burbled the image of Gorgo. Water leaked from its eyes, from the down-turned corners of its mouth. Stone limbs grated in stone sockets. Stone teeth gnashed. "Wooooah!"

Dusty figures clung to it, trying to stop its progress. The idol slammed against the doorposts to dislodge first one, then another. Both fragile bodies shattered. Loogan groaned as the fragments of long-dead novices bounced down the steps, here an arm, there a head, still blinking in confusion.

". . . quonk . . ."

The idol's throat sack tried to expand, but was constricted by bonds of stone. It gulped with frowning irritation and scuttled stiffly down the stair, its knobby knees bobbing above its head. Loogan drew back, horrified. Jame could feel the waves of despair that the idol projected. This, truly, was Bilgore's creation, his god of lamentations. Loogan must have suffered such attacks most of his life as the servant of this morbid monstrosity. Trinity, how had he survived?

What use is life? rolled out the gloom, corroding the will of all within its reach. *You will never accomplish anything. You will never be anybody. Abandon hope, therefore, and die.*

A shape lurked halfway down the street, licking its chops—the demon Pathless, a kindred spirit drawn to misery. It seemed to lap up the idol's emanations, waxing and waning according to its source, panting for more. Its outline wavered like a cloak in a high wind. Now it showed the black dog despair, now a cowering man, his much-decayed core soul. Who? Thanks to Pathfinder, he had been stripped of all others. Oh, where was that sage now?

On the threshold behind the idol capered the former high priest Bilgore, urging it on with gleeful, gibbering cries. Was it now a demon? Jame didn't think so, any more than the other temple idols now craning up and down the street to watch the show. It might be Bilgore's creation, but for all of his current animation, the priest was dead.

She drew Loogan back toward the shadow of the alley, feeling oddly protected there.

"Moooo," breathed the shadows as if in reassurance. A soothing, milky odor wafted out of the darkness.

Jame searched desperately for a lost name and found one.

"Abarraden!"

No, that wasn't right, or only half so. Try again.

"Er . . . Gorgiryl?"

Something big and green loomed behind Bilgore. Its wide mouth gaped open. "Quonkkk!" it bellowed over the swell of a full, snowy neck pouch.

Gorgo crouched and leaped, knocking Bilgore over as he did so. The former high priest tumbled down the stairs, wailing, clutching after limbs as they snapped off like so much dry kindling.

The idol turned stiffly. It and Gorgo slammed into each other at the foot of the stair and grappled chest to chest, webbed hands scrabbling. Hieratic remains rolled under their feet, tripping them. They wobbled on the edge of a puddle and fell into it with a mighty splash. It swallowed them both whole.

"What . . ." said Loogan, staring.

"Wait," said Jame.

The water seethed. Gorgo rose out of it, perched atop a broad piscine forehead between two enormous, unblinking eyes. The Eaten One's catfish whiskers fiddled at the puddle's edge.

B-lo-o-o-p, said the hidden mouth, in a frothy welter of bubbles.

Gorgo hopped to dry ground and turned. The monstrous head sank. In its wake, in a flounder of limbs, the idol surfaced. Its weight would surely have dragged it down again, but Gorgo's tongue shot out, wrapped around its neck, and wrenched it to shore. Then he bit down and shook it. Stone became rotting plaster over broken lath. Green glass eyes popped out, followed by jets of salt water. As more bits broke off, more water bled out of the hollow cavity within.

". . . quonnn . . ." it whined, and fell apart. Its remains mixed with those of its master, whose detached head continued to make grotesque faces of frustration.

Jame helped Loogan to his feet.

"You won't tell anyone, will you?" asked the priest, looking anxiously up at her. "His real name, I mean."

"Well, I knew it before. Do I still call him Gorgo?"

"In public. True names are sacred. They hold power and reflect the soul. Surely even you Kencyr know that."

He straightened, brushing down his crumpled robes with an air of decision. "And I can tell you this: the novices, yes, we will gather them up." Indeed, living worshippers were already on the steps, gingerly collecting relics in wicker baskets meant to receive offerings. "My many times great-grandfather, though, isn't going back to his comfortable burial slot in the archives. The pyre for him, and his damned idol for kindling."

"I don't think anyone will blame you. I have to go."

IV

JAME HAD SEEN Pathless slink away and followed him . . . exactly why, she wasn't sure, only that this entire situation enraged her. She loved Tai-tastigon—its complexity, its vitality, its people—and now it seemed to be possessed by demons. Given their way, Heliot and his kind would devour or pervert all that made not only this city but this world so precious. Well, not if Jame could help it.

What she came across first, however, was another of Pathless's victims, if an unlikely one. The centipede demon writhed at a crossroads, its front half all flailing legs and booted, misshapen feet. Its rear segments flopped bonelessly, spraying ichor. It had been bitten nearly in two.

The third Kencyr priest crouched over it.

"My name!" he cried, looking as if he wanted to shake it but not quite daring to lest it fall apart. "My name!"

Jame came up behind him. The sharp smell of the demon's blood made her sneeze again and again. "What is your name?" she blurted out between seizures, wiping her nose.

The priest stilled at her touch, as if in sudden concentration. "It . . . I . . . was . . . Utain. Yes. That is who I was. Am."

The centipede shivered. Its forelimbs stretched out, shuddered again, and went limp. In death, it dwindled and faded.

Utain fell back into Jame's arms. She resisted the impulse to drop him. The flesh withered on his skull, eyes sinking, cheekbones protruding, lips shriveling against bared teeth.

"Free," he panted. "Free." And, exhaling with a rattle, he died.

Jame lowered his remains to the cobbles, into the pool of their own returning shadow. How light they were, like a cricket's shell, as if all but consumed from the inside out.

He might have been the demon's core, but it seemed that ravening hunger had driven the latter to feed upon the very thing that supported it. Perhaps, otherwise, the priest might have survived with his soul intact. That, at last, might be the clue she was seeking. As Loogan said, names had power.

So. Next Pathless, then Kalissan, then maybe Heliot himself, if Dalis-sar didn't get to him first. Her claws were out. She was in the mood for blood.

V

SHADOWY FIGURES scuttled from door to door, admitted by a special knock. Dalis-sar's priests were abroad. On rooftops, beneath overhangs, heads popped up, then down—the Cloudies, spying. So far, though, Jame hadn't seen overall signs of resistance. The gods themselves didn't yet appear to be working together—not that they usually did at the best of times. Too many had overlapping attributes. Who was the true patron of merchants, or healers, or horse-thieves? Who could promise the best lovers? Whose storm was the most powerful? Competition was sometimes fierce. Then too, what could they accomplish while Ishtier and the Kencyr temple continued intermittently to drain them?

A wheedling voice came to her without intelligible words, only with the tone of sly, malicious hunger. She turned another corner, and there was Pathless, confronting Harri sen Tenko.

"Come," the demon crooned, crouching low, a black

mass that smiled as a dog does, all quivering lips and bared teeth. "Only you can save him. Don't you want to?"

His form blurred again, like a wavering cloak. A man was revealed, on hands and knees, shaking. He lifted a stricken face and mouthed, ". . . Harri, don't . . ."

Jame had thought once that the demon's soul was Abbotir's because she had seen them both in the Gold Ringing mansion. Now she realized that it had been Harr sen Tenko's all along. So this was the desperate fate to which the Skyrr noble had been driven.

Pathless could pounce, couldn't he? Perhaps, though, in doing so he could only take the boy's life, not his soul. Then too, Heliot had spoken of willing sacrifices being the sweetest. Perhaps they were also the most potent. The demon looked tattered in flesh and spirit, his core soul hardly less so. The street showed through rends in both of them. Was this another case of one feeding on the other?

Harr sen Tenko reared back on his heels, face contorted, his hands scrabbling to hold himself together against the demon's claws.

"No!" cried his son.

"Ah-ha-ha-ha. You can save him, boy, as I said. All you have to do is take his place. What true son would refuse to do that?"

Abruptly, Jame was reminded of her own father, begging Torisen for release: "My son, my child, set me free." She thought of Ganth these days more often then she had in years, and the sense of loss always surprised her. He had been the monster of her childhood and of Tori's, but neither of them had understood. Fathers, after all, were only people, not gods, not that even gods were perfect. Now she watched Harri struggling with Harr's frailty, with his own possible debt to a man whom he had clearly idolized.

"How could you have come to this pass if the Archiem had not betrayed you?" Harri cried, falling to his knees. "This is all his fault, or ... or is it mine?"

"No!" cried sen Tenko. "I was wrong! I see that now. Son, save yourself!"

Pathless choked Harr back down like a dog swallowing his own vomit. Then he crept toward the boy. "Come," he murmured, licking his lips. "Sweet, juicy morsel, come to me."

Jame edged forward. "Harr, name yourself!"

"I ... I ..." the man stammered, clutching his throat, looking stricken.

"Ah-ha-ha-ha. His name is known, but what is mine? Never mind this diminished manifestation. I am older than any of these newborn demons, even than Heliot, older than the petty pantheon of dead gods from which they have sprung. From the beginning, I have gnawed at man's heart, letting darkness in. Granny Sits-by-the-fire has seen the gleam of my eyes. Her stories have kept me at bay, but not always. I bring death, but myself can never truly die. What am I?"

From their first meeting, Jame had sensed that there was something ancient about this creature. The original identities of the whumping demon and the bog creature and the centipede hadn't mattered, only those of their victims. "Pathless" was just a nickname, a mask worn in passing by something much older. Now, faced with this primordial horror, her mind went blank, as it had on their first encounter. Again the city swirled around her, the maze of its streets unmoored and she lost among them.

I am nothing. I am nobody. I am alone.

"All ends are meaningless," this demon had crooned through ropes of steaming slaver. "What is life but a mindless scramble in the dark?"

Now he grinned and dragged his claws across Harr's chest, disfiguring them both. The demon didn't care. The man writhed.

Jame swallowed against a parched throat. "Pathfinder!" she cried to the midnight street. "We need you!"

At first she thought that the sage wasn't listening. Then the mouth of an alley quivered and opened into a room. People seated at a fire there sprang to their feet, horrified. One of them was Nathe.

"Don't go!" he cried, clutching the sleeve of a white-clad, chubby figure.

Pathfinder gently freed himself and stepped forward into the street. The whites of his blind eyes gleamed.

"Who calls? Are you lost?"

"Yes. Very. This boy is about to sacrifice himself for his father, who doesn't wish it. A nameless demon is involved."

Pathfinder shuddered. "Demons. Not good."

"Shut up," snarled Pathless, crouching. "You have the faith of your followers. Leave us with their flesh."

"Should I, though? You clutch at their souls. Are people flesh or spirit? Admit: they are both."

"So?" Pathless barked. "All are food. Do you not hunger?"

"In my own way. Not like this."

The demon sneered, but also nervously licked his lips. His voice sank to a cajoling whine. "Would you destroy me, little god? Think. What are you without me?"

Pathfinder looked sad. "It is true that I can never ultimately conquer despair, but I can refuse to be conquered by it. Black dog, be gone."

The demon scuttled backward, leaving the rags of Harr sen Tenko on the ground. His son gathered them up. Harr smiled through the ruins of his face and fell apart. Pathless howled. Backing up, he slunk into the shadows, down to a pair of gleaming yellow eyes, gone.

"Until next time," breathed the void, and laughed.

Pathfinder also retreated toward the light of his own fire and his anxiously waiting friends. With the wave of a hand, he turned and was gone, taking the light with him.

Harri was left clutching handfuls of shredded cloth.

The secret name of the demon, Jame realized, was Despair. The name of the god was Hope. And both transcended pantheons.

She watched for a moment, then withdrew. Somehow, she didn't feel bloodthirsty anymore.

VI

THE STREETS were more active now. Before, minor demons and packs of haunts had dominated. Now, New Pantheon gods and their followers also ventured forth to clash on this corner or that with their foes. Here, the deity and demon of earthquakes stomped their feet at each

other, bringing down more temples. Here, a divine
windstorm was countered by an ugly little sprite who
dropped his drawers and cleared an entire street with a
prodigious fart. There, two who fancied themselves clever
traded riddles while their followers hung back, shouting
suggestions. Both of these latter two, Jame noted, were
New Pantheon gods who had apparently gotten carried
away by their ancient rivalry even in the midst of this
crisis.

Jogging through the haze were squads of clerics
lobbing litanies to the distress of demonic ears:

"I will not fear, for my god protects me," chanted one
such group as it trotted past in cadence. "And my family.
And my ox. And my ass. All that is mine he will protect."

"And if he will not," added a little choirboy in a piping
voice, "We will find a god who will. Ow!"

The nearest priest had clouted him on the ear.

Whole congregations were on the streets now, some in
mobs, others in procession, bearing their holy icons and
banners with them like battle flags. Incense and ornate
vestments swirled. Chants filled the air in counterpoint.

Minor demons retreated, no match for such
concentrated devotion, but where were their leaders?
Jame hadn't seen any since her last glimpse of Heliot, and
something about him had been . . . wrong. Why were his
legions holding back?

From somewhere within the maze of streets, a wail
rose:

"They have slain the child!"

Heads lifted. Gods and demons both turned and made
their way, faster and faster, toward the heart of the

district, a roughly octagonal public space, open to the sky, fringed with oddly shaped temples. Over it loured the Master's House, tilted as if about to spill its vile contents upon the city below. To look up at it was to make the whole world seem to shift on its axis. One's head spun.

Jame paused at the precinct's edge. She couldn't see past the heads and shoulders of those who had crowded there before her, but she was slight enough to weave between them and impatient enough to jab with an extended nail at any flank that didn't get out of the way fast enough.

Most of the gods had fetched up against her side of the octagon, demons against the other. Behind both ranks were their followers, far more supporting the gods than the demons. Between them was an open space. Within it, a frost-tipped demon stalked back and forth, flexing its claws, snarling. Ice rimed the cobbles where it moved. Its pace was a haughty strut but also self-conscious, as if it had accidentally crossed some ill-defined line. At its feet sprawled a tiny, broken figure. Jame recognized the child worshipper whom she had seen earlier at the puppet show. Over her bent the black-robed subject of her devotion. The goddess stroked the child's pale face with a rapidly withering hand and straightened her contorted limbs. Then she folded herself over the girl's body. What there was of her melted away, leaving only a shroud.

A moan rose from the gods, and then a growl.

Jame felt the paving shift under her feet, nearly pitching her forward on her face. A ripple of stones swept across the expanse, from the west where she stood to the east, from the gods to the demons, who rocked back on their heels.

The tide was turning yet again. Ishtier had lost control. Both sides rushed toward each other, nearly equal.

Overhead, the House leaned farther forward. Its door gaped. Jame stopped dead, staring up at it. If the Master should emerge . . .

Haaaaa . . . breathed the expanse within.

Then the wind came, shearing off cornices and gables, walls and windows. The entire dream structure was falling apart. Drifts of vapor reached the ground in a patchy, filthy fog.

Jame let out her breath. The Master hadn't come after all, despite Ishtier's invitation. Then, as an anxious afterthought, she wondered, *Why not?*

Indistinct figures buffeted her as they rushed past. Here was the priest from the puppet show, his fists clenched within socks. Here ran whole congregations, scrambling to keep up with their deities. Banners swayed down as their shafts were leveled like spears. Censers swung like flails, trailing incense. Chants became war cries. There went the sen Tenko godling, up in arms but still without his pants. Gargoyles belched holy water and fire down from the rooftops, creating more billows of steam. Cloudies threw slates. Packs of haunts ranged freely, pulling down any god or worshipper that they could, being stomped to pieces in their turn. Toward the edge of the octagon, a huge, dimpled arm swept out of an alley to gather in a knot of minor demons.

"Moooo . . ." said the shadows, gently reproachful even as bones snapped within their embrace.

Where, though, were the major demons? Ah. Here.

Heliot loomed over the fight, in and out of the haze.

Kalissan was there too, although holding back, also others whom Jame recognized from Heliot's sweep down on Ishtier's temple. The red cracks in the sun god's armor defined him against the night while his beard leaped upward in tongues of fire.

At his feet stood a gaudy figure shrunken within its rich robes. Abbotir, surely. So that was who had provided the demon with his soul, the haughty figure Jame had glimpsed before.

But Abbotir was dead.

What am I missing here? she thought.

Heliot's blood fell like rain, igniting the puddles as his feet. The cracks in his armor gaped wide. Again, there was that growing hint of mortality.

Light burst from a side street. Dalis-sar emerged, sweeping aside rubble and shadows. He was at least as big as Heliot, towering over the conflict at his feet but careful not to tread on it. Gods and demons alike scrambled out of his way. He and Heliot met at the center of the plaza, the child's shrouded body on the ground between them.

"What have you done?" Dalis-sar demanded.

"I? Nothing. This creature broke the covenant."

Heliot thrust forward the frost demon, who melted with chagrin into a cloud of icy drizzle.

"No children," said Dalis-sar. "That was the deal we stuck all those years ago on the plain when I saw mere infants among your ranks."

"Oh, please. Holy babes. One, in its blessed innocence, almost killed you."

Dalis-sar ground his teeth. Sparks snapped behind them deep in his throat. "I remember," he said hoarsely, spitting fire. "Instead, I killed it. By reflex. By accident. I will bear that guilt forever. Hence the pact that was my price when the people brought me back to fight you. No children on the battlefield. Ever. The New Pantheon agreed to it."

"The Old didn't."

"You forget. They wanted the deification that your victims' faith had so nearly bought you. Remember: you were still a mortal king then, near death. Your godhood arose out of that covenant."

Heliot pursed his lips. They cracked and bled, unheeded. "Should that coward Death take me when I am so much stronger than he?"

"But you aren't," said Jame, staring up at him. She had caught the echo of Abbotir's defiant words earlier—their arrogance, their fierce denial of mortality. "Dalis-sar beat you. Your followers lost faith in you. You died, both as a god and as a man."

"Never say such things to me!"

His gigantic face swooped down at her, buckteeth bared. His breath stank of what had killed Abbotir, what was now killing him.

Dalis-sar scooped her out of the way.

"Nonetheless, there was an accord," he said, straightening. "One child lies dead at your feet while another stands closer to you even than that."

He indicated a little girl clinging to the demon's ankle, baring baby teeth in a rictus grin.

"Grandma," she had said to the hill matron who hovered near her, making erratic, futile motions and trying to speak.

"Huh, huh, huh . . ."

"What do they matter? You still do not think according to your station. Boy, listen to me. Grow up."

Dalis-sar snorted. "Should I also become a monster? My people have seen one such in Master Gerridon. We hold to what we are. Neither gods nor demons can change that without our consent. You, to convince me? Ha."

Heliot snarled and launched himself. They met with a concussion that shook the environs. Gods and demons alike tumbled aside. Surrounding walls fell. Fire spiraled up in a storm that licked the sky.

Abbotir's robes were burning. Jame threw herself at him under the flaming night. He caught her wrists and bent her backward, panting ash into her face. His grip scorched through her gloves.

"Tell me your name!" she shouted up at him.

His lips peeled back over red-tinged teeth. What began as a snarl turned into a grimace as flesh seared away around his mouth and nostrils. Eyebrows sizzled. Hair floated for a moment in a halo of fire, then crinkled and burned. He looked surprised. How could this be happening to him, of all people?

Jame spat out cinders. Some crunched between her teeth. "Tell me!"

"I am . . . no, I was Abbotir. Lord of the Gold Court. Councilor to the Sirdan. And now I am dead."

That was what she had missed: the soul of a dead mortal could not support a demon, at least not indefinitely. The first two Kencyr priests had shown that when one had died of a heart attack and the other of being trampled. In neither case had the demon immediately collapsed, but soon enough. Abbotir's denial of mortality had sustained both him and Heliot beyond that for a time.

Now, however, the guild lord crumbled in her grasp, his remains black and greasy and stinking. His jaw dropped off. Charred fingers, clutching her, snapped at the knuckles.

Above them, Heliot staggered. Booted feet smashed cobbles. Great gouts of fire fell through the cracks in his armor. He was literally coming apart at the seams but was not yet quite finished. The secondary souls that he had reaped must still be holding him together. How to disrupt those last links?

Jame let what was left of Abbotir fall.

Near at hand was the matron, the last whom she knew Heliot to have taken. She grabbed the woman's arm. Wide, shocked eyes stared back into her own—surely with something human still in their depths. After all, it had been such a short time, barely an hour, since she had been taken.

"Remember your name!" she shouted in the woman's face. "You are Grandma!"

"G—g-g. . . ." She gulped, blinked, and nodded. "Grandma H-hogetty. Yes. Elen!"

Jame let her go. She stumbled over to her grand-daughter and shook her.

"Elen, Elen!"

The girl swayed in her embrace, looking bewildered as if just awaking from a nightmare. She shuddered.

"G-grandma? Granny Hog? Oh, what am I doing here? Was I bad? Never, never again! Oh, please, take me home!"

They were lucky, in their flight, to avoid Heliot's shambling feet. Jame also dodged back and forth as he lurched above her. He bent double and retched out the feeder souls on which he had gorged, that had sustained him. Some were intact enough to stagger away, but most were half dissolved into an acid that ate at his boots.

He turned in desperate search of his consort Kalissan. There she stood not far away, staring at him. He reached out to her.

"Help me, my queen!"

She drew back, hissing in distain at the weakness that he now betrayed.

"Not yours, little man. Never again yours."

Heliot howled and threw himself at her. Flames enwrapped them both as if they were siege towers set ablaze. They fell, grappling with each other, and the earth shook. Incandescent fragments flew. The air was fretted with fire. Jame saw Aden, tiny among their ruins, trying to escape.

"My name is . . . my name is . . ." she mouthed. "Aden, Aden, Aden!"

"Dalis-sar!" Jame cried, but he had drawn back and her voice was lost in the uproar.

Trinity, how to reach the woman? The frost demon had condensed from a cloud into a puddle of misery. Jame stripped off her *d'hen* and sopped up what moisture she could. With it held over her head, she plunged into the maelstrom. Fire rained down on her, sizzling as it touched wet wool. Scorching wind tried to sear her lungs. Pieces of Heliot's armor crashed down around her. The two demons fought each other overhead, tearing, ripping.

What hatred, so suddenly exposed. However, had Heliot valued Kalissan for anything but her lineage and the validation that he thought she gave him? As for Kalissan herself, had she ever really favored this upstart sun god with his human origins?

Bones were falling now, broken, the meat on them smoking. When they hit the pavement, they sank, sizzling, into ice-rimed puddles.

Go on, thought Jame, grimly dodging. *Tear each other apart.*

She had the impression that more such carnage was taking place across the octagon among the demonic ranks. Heliot's fiery vomit seemed to have also loosened their grip on their captive souls. Now they fought each other for the prey that was slipping away from them, taking their borrowed lives with it.

Their dependence on humans, on Heliot himself . . . really, when it came down to it, this generation of monsters was fragile. So much for Ishtier's mighty army.

Aden tottered toward her, clothes steaming. Jame threw her jacket over both of their heads and began to fight her way back toward clean air. Something turned under her foot. She stumbled, losing her grip on the older woman. On her knees in soot-streaked water, she saw what had tripped her: Kalissan's third eye, perhaps gouged out by her former mate. Seen up close, it appeared to be a large uncut diamond, only somewhat dimmed by the ichor that had spilled from the demon's socket.

"Aden . . ."

Jame groped about. The glare and smoke made her eyes ache. Coughing blinded her further.

Then arms were flung around her, trapping the *d'hen* over her head, pinning her hands to her sides. Someone picked her up and slung her over what could only be a shoulder. At least it punched her in the stomach with every stride very much like one.

"Put . . . me . . . down!"

Finally her muffled protest was obeyed, the jacket stripped off. Titmouse hunched beside her with bloodshot eyes, panting. The octagon was what remained of a battlefield. Water burned. Objects sank into it, sizzling. The stench of burnt flesh hung in smoky veils like a pall, under lit by flickers of sullen flame. On the edges stood the gods, dumb with horror. The bereft wandered among them until each in turn caught the scent of its released soul.

"Ah . . ." they breathed in, and stood amazed as life returned to their eyes.

Jame coughed. "Aden . . ."

Titmouse shook his head. "I only saw you," he said hoarsely.

A figure moved through the haze—Dalis-sar, dwindled to near-human stature, a commander in search of the fallen. Most had been too far consumed to return. One could only hope that they had died free. Here he paused, then moved on. There he stopped and knelt. The fire had barely touched Aden although soot had tarnished her veil. He gathered her in his arms and bent over her.

Jame got to her feet more or less by clambering up Titmouse and stumbled toward the god, even as her common sense cried, "Fool! This was his only love, and you failed her."

"I'm sorry," she said, halting at a wary distance.

"Go," he said, over his shoulder. Tears of fire ran down his cheeks. He seemed older than he had before. "Just go."

Jame staggered away.

"I can't begin to understand all of this," said Titmouse, walking beside her. "It seemed like a regular campaign, as far as I understand such things, and then it turned . . . strange."

Jame laughed, shakily. "I'm still struggling with it myself, and I've probably had more experience with such things than you have."

"Your mother being the Dream-weaver and your uncle Gerridon. Yes, I can see that."

Someone tapped Jame on the shoulder.

"Eek!" she said, recoiling in shock. "Master Penari! What are you doing here?"

Her old teacher scowled at her out of clouded eyes. "Blame Rugen the Architect. He just wouldn't leave me alone, nor yet his gargoyle Quezal."

The latter perched on Penari's shoulder, digging into it. Stone weighed down painfully on ancient flesh, on frail bone.

"Is that Abarraden's eye?" asked Jame, regarding the large rock that Penari cradled in his arms. A lacy shawl had been wrapped around it, but had slipped. If any thieves had chanced to encounter him tonight . . .

"Ouch! You little monster, don't. . . . Yes, yes. The one that I stole. The Architect says that I've got to give it back, for his mother's sake, and what's more . . ."

While Jame's gaze had dropped to the half-shrouded

treasure, Quezal had disappeared. He was back in a flicker before she could look up again, bearing its smoky mate in his claws. She relieved Penari of both before he could topple over under their combined weight. He fussed after the one that he had considered his own, but then reluctantly surrendered it, making discontented faces.

"Well, well, let it be as it may. But what, pray tell, is that other one doing here?"

"You told me once that someone else stole it long, long ago. That turned out to be the husband of a friend of mine." Frowning, Penari made as if to count on his fingertips. "Yes," said Jame hastily to forestall him. "It's complicated. He gave it to the goddess whom he worshipped at the time, a nasty piece of work named Kalissan. She made it her third eye. I think it helped her to see the living. The dead she could already see on her own."

Jame looked around. At the edge of a nearby puddle, half in it, lay Kalissan's belt of flayed baby skins. As Jame watched, it slid beneath the surface. The water drained away between cobblestones, seething. It and its mistress were gone, along with all other demonic artifacts. Fragile indeed.

Jame took a deep breath, wondering if she would regret what happened next. "Earth Wife!" she cried across that echoing hollow of desolation. "Mother Ragga, come to me!"

"What?" rumbled a big voice behind her.

Penari and Titmouse both jolted back. Jame turned. The Earth Wife loomed over her, seeming to blot out half the sky. Her hair and dress were as unkempt as always, a mess threatening to entangle the entire world. Her eyes were still pits opening on infinity. How much of Creation's Chain could they swallow whole, Jame wondered, gulping. Why couldn't she keep in mind how terrifying this woman could be?

"I ... er ... have your mentor's eyes." She held out the stones, one balanced on each palm. "What should I do with them?"

The Earth Wife lowered her head, like the moon descending to earth. Her nostrils flared. "Yes. I remember that scent. Like the incense of her sanctuary, it is."

Jame wondered suddenly if Ragga would take the eyes for herself. How tempting, to assume the place of the goddess whom she had worshipped as a child, who appeared to be dead anyway. She was the Earth Wife, after all, whose influence fell over an entire world when she chose to exert it. And she thought that she had betrayed the Old Pantheon goddess of her youth. Would stepping into Abarraden's place wipe out the guilt of Ragga's supposed apostasy?

I betrayed you. Now I am you.

Besides that, Ragga was now blind. If she chose not to be, who could blame her?

Mother Ragga settled on her haunches with a thud that shook the plaza. "D'you mean to raise such questions, girl, or is that just your curse?"

Jame nearly fumbled the eyes. "What did I say?"

"Enough. Too much. Would it make me feel better to smash you flat? I could."

"I know."

"So you do. Yet there you stand."

Yes, shaking in my boots, thought Jame.

"Huh."

The Earth Wife appeared to consider. At least her jaw moved as she sucked on her few remaining teeth ruminatively. Then she raised her head and uttered a long, low call:

"Mooooo . . ."

. . . ooooo . . .

From the mouth of an alley came what could either have been an echo or an answer. Then something emerged into the open. Given the drifting smoke, it was hard to see, more a stirring of the air than a shape. Unlike the demons, it seemed to have little weight. As it approached, Jame realized that she wasn't looking at it properly. What she could make out was a piece rather than a whole. The latter must be enormous, fading up into the sky. What stopped before her, though, was undoubtedly the apparition of a monstrous cloven hoof.

"Well?" rasped the Earth Wife. "Give them to her."

Jame held up the gems. Something reached down and took them gingerly, as if they were grains of sand. Air sighed, or was that Mother Ragga behind her? When Jame glanced back, the Earth Wife was rubbing her eyes. Yes, she had them back. The other looming presence was gone.

The old woman dropped her hands and slapped her knees with an air of finality.

"Well, that's done," she said, climbing to her feet with a grunt. As she rose, she also shrank back to normal stature. "High time that I was on my way. You, girl, stay out of trouble. Ha. As if there were any chance of that."

"Wait!" Jame cried as she shuffled off into the haze. "What about the rest of the Four?"

Mother Ragga turned, now an indistinct, dumpy figure about to unravel into the night. "I don't tell them what to do, nor do they tell me. Fish-face and Blow-hard are probably done here. As for Burny, heh, what do I know?"

And she disappeared.

Wonderful, thought Jame, turning away. Why did she have the feeling that this night was far from over?

Someone approached, materializing nearly where the Earth Wife had vanished. Short, thin, crooked . . .

"Patches! What are you doing here?" Sudden anxiety seized her. "Is something wrong at the inn?"

"You could . . . say that." The little thief paused to catch her breath, bent over, one hand clamped to an aching side. She must have run hard. "Cleppetty . . . sent me . . . to fetch you. The Res aB'tyrr . . . is under attack."

⟨⟨⟨⟨ Chapter XIII ⟩⟩⟩⟩
Night at the Inn
Spring 57

DUSK WAS FALLING, at the end of two very long days.

Rue peered out the front window of the Res aB'tyrr into the square. Torches had been lit in place of the usual light-spheres. In their dancing glare, men were gathering around the fountain as they had the previous night. Then, however, Sart Nine-toes had been there to humor them. He had joked. They had laughed with him, all big men together. Then they had drifted away. That was after four of them had tried to dismember Boo, when their first instinct had been to haul the cat's rescuer out of the inn by her ears. Sart had prevented that. He was a presence, no doubt, however hesitant Rue still felt about that big smile of his. How could anyone honest show so many teeth so often? Tonight, though, he was on duty across town, and she missed him.

Kithra crossed the square to the fountain with a water jug balanced on one swaying hip. The brigands parted, then closed behind her. Rue tensed. Couldn't the foolish girl tell that these men were dangerous? However, they greeted the Skyrrman's young mistress with extravagant courtesy that only turned to leers behind her back. She preened in their apparent regard but nervously, her eyes darting defiantly toward the Res aB'tyrr.

What are you up to, miss? Rue wondered.

Yesterday Kithra had finally managed to slip into the inn while the dancer Na'bim had engaged Cleppetty's attention with one of her increasingly petulant complaints.

Rue had seen Kithra crouching outside Tubain's back apartment, listening avidly at the keyhole. Ghillie had caught her there and had borne her, thrashing in his arms, back down to the kitchen, to Cleppetty.

Such a squall there had been, then, mostly on Kithra's part. Rue had heard it all before: Tubain was being held prisoner by his womenfolk. Abernia was a harridan—no, a demon, to torment him so. Only she, Kithra, could ease his pain with her pretty ways and then he would see, yes, that she was his true champion.

Cleppetty had ejected her yet again, muttering, "Idiot."

The heart of the inn and its greatest secret lay in that back apartment. Rue sensed as much, even if she didn't know what was going on.

"The linen is dry," Cleppetty said behind her. "Help me make beds."

Rue had been lending a hand at the inn since her arrival, not that there was a lot to do with the brigands turning away most of the regular customers. It suited her, though, to keep busy with less time to fret. So Cleppetty may also have thought. Now she assisted the housekeeper in taking down the sheets hung up that afternoon in the stable yard after boiling that morning in a basement tub. Drying power had hastened the process. Cleppetty had a minor talent for domestic magic, Rue had learned, and many such useful dodges. Yesterday had been baking day, with the bread dough rising more rapidly than Rue would have expected, given her limited experience at Tagmeth. Nonetheless, she had offered to help. Cleppetty had turned her down with a sidelong glance and a wry, cryptic comment:

"Your precious lady once helped me quite enough, thank you very much."

Now a load of sheets was dumped into Rue's arms, making her stagger.

"These go upstairs in the back."

Ghillie called to Cleppetty from the hall. She went down to see what he wanted.

Rue took the linens up to the room that she shared with the dancer Na'bim. The girl was there when she entered, clad as usual in one of her diaphanous costumes, discontentedly examining her face in a silver hand mirror that Rue hadn't seen before. A sudden thought stuck her: what if the dancer had gotten it as a bribe from Kithra to distract Cleppetty? What devious turns her mind had taken since she had come to this strange city. Was that bad, or good?

"I'm pretty enough," the girl said with a pout, turning the glass as if to discover a new, more beguiling angle. "Why don't I have an audience of admirers?"

Rue dropped fresh sheets on her bed.

"In case you haven't noticed, the inn is under siege."

"Oh, pooh. They could come in if . . . if . . ."

"They wanted to?"

"No! If Tubain would only spread the word that I was here. A new dancer is always welcome. Always!"

"Was that the case with the B'tyrr?"

Rue sprang the name on her because the girl had begun to irritate her. Everything was her predecessor's fault, whoever that paragon had been. And she had been increasingly snide with Rue too—why, Rue couldn't make out.

Na'bim threw down her new mirror, cracking it. "Ohhh! Look what you made me do! Why do I have to lodge with a scullery maid anyway, when I should have a room of my own? No, a suite of rooms! In the main house!"

"A maid?"

Na'bim contemptuously pushed the sheets onto the floor. "'Do this,' says Cleppetty. 'Do that.' 'Oh, yes, mistress,' you say. 'Shall I lick the plates clean now?' Don't you have any pride?"

Rue regarded her, half amused, half puzzled. She often found people not of the Kencyrath hard to understand. "I have as much pride as I need or merit. Why should I want more?"

"You people! You all think you're so much better than the rest of us! You and your precious Bat-ears, your precious Talis-whosit . . . why should one person be so good at so many things? It isn't fair!"

"Wait a minute." Rue sat down on the chair, staring. "D'you mean to tell me that Jame was both the Talisman and the B'tyrr?"

"Jame! On a first name basis, are you? Wait. You didn't know?" Na'bim crowed with delight, clapping her hands. "Not so smart, are you, after all. And some people say that I'm dim. Ha!"

With that she flung herself out of the room, floundering on the way over the fallen sheets, regaining her balance in a move that, in the main hall, would have gained the applause that she so clearly craved.

Rue sat stunned. Had Jame been such a creature as this, a common tavern dancer? No. Oh, no. And a thief too?

I don't know you, lady. Have I ever? And should I swear to you now?

Somewhere, a cat wailed.

Rue jumped up. For a moment, it was a night before. Sart hadn't yet returned from guard duty. Boo was screaming in the square. She barely remembered what she had done to the would-be molesters, only that afterward, somehow, she had become part of the inn.

Another cry.

Rue plunged out of the room. Yes, it was Boo again, this time plumped down in front of the rear apartment door, protesting stridently that it was shut in his face.

As Rue hesitated, panting, the door opened a crack and the cat oozed inside.

"Good kitty," fluted a voice within.

Rue had never heard Tubain speak. Surely, though, he wouldn't sound like that. She snatched up the extra linen and pelted down the hall. The door was closing. It stopped when she knocked on it.

"Clean sheets . . . er . . . mistress?"

A pause, then it opened again. Rue blinked at the figure before her, at its boots and flounced petticoats, at its half-veiled beard.

"You saved Boo, didn't you?" piped this improbable figure. A pudgy, beringed hand reached out to accept the linen, then returned to pat her on the head. "Good girl."

The door closed.

"Woo," said Rue, turning away.

Cleppetty had said both that the Sirdan Men-dalis was holding Mistress Abernia captive and that he had lost her, in the process losing control of the Talisman whom he had summoned for reasons that Rue still didn't entirely understand. Either way, Abernia shouldn't be here, much less as she appeared to be. Kithra's peculiar expression came back to her. Was this the voice that she had overheard, eavesdropping? If so, whom had she told, and why should that matter anyway?

Rue dumped linen in the other servants' quarters opening off the corridor, most of them unoccupied, and went down to the kitchen.

There, Patches hunched over a bowl of beef stew thickened with barley. "Hello," she said. "How goes the home front?"

Rue sat down opposite her and accepted her own portion of dinner from Cleppetty. "Well enough, as far as I can tell. How goes the war?"

"Oh, on the boil. There are gods and demons and haunts all over the place. Something is definitely brewing in the Temple District, which seems to be falling down, or on fire, or both. Our Talisman has been spotted just about everywhere. I wish I knew what she was up to. How are we supposed to help while she keeps us in the dark?"

That struck Rue as a very good question.

"Was it like this, when she was here before?"

Patches considered. "More or less. Mind you, it wasn't that she set out to make trouble. It's just that around her a lot happened, often very fast."

Cleppetty snorted. She was making stone soup in a cloud of flung spices, with root vegetables trying to crawl out of her reach. Patches scowled at her back.

"You know what I mean. Half the trouble she got into wasn't of her making."

"Ha." Cleppetty seized a pepper pot and applied it liberally. Rue stifled a sneeze. "But as soon as she arrived . . . boom. A match to tinder, that girl. 'Bloody, singed, and dripping wet' she was, that last time, before she and Marc left. I knew then that we were in deep trouble."

Patches laughed. "Well, at least you got your own personal goddess out of it."

Indeed, Rue now realized that the kitchen walls were gently aglow, and not from the evening light or the cooking fires. A sense of beneficence permeated the room like the welcome blush of warmth against a chilled face. She hadn't yet caught a glimpse of the nameless goddess, only the echo, as if in a dream, of her voice. Should she believe in that? Jame had. But Jame was . . . strange. Perhaps crazy. That doubt lingered, even after Rue's experience with the gods of Kothifir. Those seemed, now, like pale shadows compared to the teeming divinity of Tai-tastigon. A shiver ran up her spine. So much about this world was turning out to be beyond the teachings of her elders. That, too, Jame had shown her. How far was she prepared to go down such a path?

Patches was still chewing over what her hostess had said. "Here now. D'you think the Creeper would have gone after Dally if he hadn't fallen in love with the Talisman? Was that her fault?"

"Maybe not. I think, though, that she threatened the Creeper's hold over the Sirdan through her friendship with his brother. Then too, maybe Men-dalis had always been disposed to see Dally as a threat, the gods know why. That boy fair worshipped him."

Men-dalis is a charmer.

Rue blinked. Where had that thought come from? For a moment, she had felt very close to her lady, wherever Jame was.

Although Patches had brought up the Creeper, talk of him seemed to make her nervous. As with a scab, however, she couldn't help but pick.

"Politics. All right. With the Creeper, yes. The Thieves' Guild is lousy with factions. But with the Talisman? When did she ever care about that?"

"Agreed," said Cleppetty over her shoulder, her hands for a moment still. "That was never her game, even when she found herself up to the neck in it. She put her faith in people. What they thought. What they believed. How their belief shaped the world. Much of it was beyond me. Still, she seemed to have her hands on certain levers of power. Like a child. Playing. Did she know where her moves would take her or us? No. If you ask me, it was bloody terrifying."

"It still is," said Rue.

Patches shot her a shrewd, not displeased look. *Mine first*, it seemed to say. *Yours second, if at all.* "She still scares you, does she?"

Rue addressed her supper, grumbling. "Honor is honor. How does being a thief fit into that?"

"Ha. Never stole anything of value, did she? The smallest coin at the bottom of a merchant's purse. A jeweler's practice gem carving before his masterpiece. Even the Peacock Gloves, although I reckon that they were a deal apart."

"What about them?"

Patches fossicked in her bowl, nose down.

"Tell her," said Cleppetty.

"All right! My brother Scramp challenged her to raid Edor Thulig, the Tower of Demons, didn't he? Well, she did it. There was Prince Ozymardien's treasure trove, all the riches of the city, and she only took away a pair of gloves to prove that she'd been there."

"Special ones," Cleppetty said, with the air of doing justice.

"Yes, yes. The man who embroidered them used threads swept up over a lifetime in the city's finest silk warehouse. They were the Peacock Gloves. They were . . . wonderful. I held them once, afterward. Y'see, my brother Scramp claimed that either they weren't the real thing or that the Talisman was lying."

Rue was shocked. "He called Jame a liar?"

"Yes. They fought. He lost. His master disowned him. He hanged himself. The Talisman gave me the gloves to buy my way into the Guild. She didn't have to do that. The point, see, is that she was honest, in everything. D'you know how hard that is, especially for a thief so good that she could have stolen anything? For her, though, it was all a game of skill and daring and . . . and loyalty." Patches stabbed at her stew with her spoon, as if searching in it for words. "She was . . . kind. Oh, you could lose your skin, following her, but that wouldn't be her fault even if she thought that it was. I . . . loved her. I still do. There." She scowled across the table at Rue, her hobgoblin's face defiant. "I've said it. And if all of that doesn't equal honor, be damned if I know what does."

Honor for a Kencyr was a torturous concept wrapped up with always telling the truth. Rue reckoned that she had just heard it.

"Yes," she said. "I love her too, but . . ."

Patches glared at her. "What?"

"Did she have to become a tavern dancer?"

Ghillie barged into the kitchen. "Come and see!" he panted.

There was a concerted rush into the front room. Outside the windows, the darkening square swarmed with men, both big-boned brigands and slight agents of the Creeper. The latter seemed to be trying to organize the former, with limited success. Nonetheless, the whole brimmed with raucous menace. Lights in the Skyrrman went out one by one except at the door where a slim figure stood as if on tiptoe, eagerly watching.

From somewhere several courts away came the beat of drums, approaching. More torches flared. Tumblers entered the square, and jugglers, and people on stilts. Someone breathed out fire, then choked and collapsed, unnoticed, when it recoiled on him. A gaudy party was coming on foot down the street beside the rival inn. Light glinted off plaques of gold and flame washed silver.

"Who . . . ?" Ghillie said, staring.

"That's the Archiem of Skyrr with his retinue," said Cleppetty, "and with him, yes, the Sirdan Men-dalis."

"But isn't Arribek a friend?" asked Patches, staring. "He helped, didn't he, the last time the Five came calling?"

"That was then," said Cleppetty grimly. "This is now. Patches, d'you know where the Talisman is?"

The Townie blinked. "I don't, exactly, but tonight the fires burn hottest in the Temple District."

"Then look for her there. Tell her that we need her. Go."

Patches gulped, nodded, and backed away from the windows. Turning, she bolted toward the inn's rear entrance, away from the firelight and the gathering tumult outside.

"This is insane," said Ghillie. "You remember, five years ago? Arribek sen Tenzi and Harr sen Tenko came here to destroy us. Well, Harr did, anyway. The Skyrrman ended up in flames."

"I think that someone is trying to rewrite history," said Cleppetty.

The newcomers entered the square. Resplendent in cloth of gold, Men-dalis glowed at the heart of the crowd, seeming to illuminate the faces around him. Big men simpered and looked bashful. Small men hid in their shadows, smirking. In the Sirdan's shadow stood the twisted figure of the Creeper like a dark incubus.

"Friends, my good friends," fluted that radiant figure,

and golden light rippled around him except where his shadow swallowed it. "How kind of you all to come, and you especially, my lord, as a representative of the Five."

This last was addressed to the Archiem of Skyrr, who responded with a thin smile. Not for him, apparently, the seductive charms of his companion or the gaudy attire of either retinue.

"This is a fair city, an honest city," Men-dalis proclaimed, casting abroad his beaming regard. "Where else can one look for justice? I ask only that of you, tonight. Come, will you see me vindicated? Shall not the righteous prevail? But first, some entertainment."

He started toward the Res aB'tyrr.

Cleppetty slammed the door in his face.

Knock, knock, knock.

"You have to let me in, you know," said that winsome voice through the keyhole. "It says so, right here in your sacred scroll."

"What is he talking about?" hissed Ghillie.

Cleppetty shook her head. "I don't know. The Innkeepers' Guild has a list of rules, but only Tubain knows what they are. We've never had trouble before."

"Then call him!"

She gave him a harried look. "As it stands, that would only make things worse."

Knock, knock, knock.

"Truly. The Archiem has seen it too. The scroll bears the seal of the Five."

Cleppetty opened the door. Men-dalis stood beaming on the step, a dingy roll of parchment in his hand, Arribek a somber presence behind him.

"My good woman," he said, bowing. "May we enter?"

"You tell me that I have no choice, although I've never heard the like before. And I'm no one's 'good woman' except, maybe, my husband's."

Sirdan and Archiem entered, the latter inclining his head to Cleppetty as he passed. "Mistress."

"That's my lady Abernia," she said tartly, then flushed bright red as if she had misspoken.

Followers crowded in on their principals' heels—brigands, spies, and courtiers, as many as the main hall would hold with more clamoring at the windows.

"Wine for us," said Men-dalis. "Your best. Beer or ale for everyone else."

An interminable time followed full of bustle, loud voices, and the occasional dropped tankard. Rue had never before appreciated how few servants the inn contained.

"Where are they?" Ghillie panted in answer to her question as he passed her coming up from the cellar with another keg of beer. "We had to lay them off when the customers stopped coming. Also, Cleppetty didn't think it was safe here anymore for the youngest ones."

"But you stayed."

"Of course. This is my home."

So too, presumably, was it Na'bim's. However, the dancer glanced in and promptly left with a haughty sniff. No serving wench, she. Let them call her when they were ready.

Rue helped as best she could, although it was very confusing. Who had ordered what? Some, catching the aroma from the kitchen, also wanted to be fed. And the occupants of one table weren't averse to tripping her as she staggered to another, which caused much laughter. She could gladly have murdered them all. The Sirdan and the Archiem sat at a table of their own with a few followers in the middle of the room, Men-dalis chattering, Arribek sardonically listening. What did the Archiem think of this scene? It seemed to Rue that the Sirdan had gotten him at a disadvantage, presumably with the scroll tucked into his golden belt. Then too, she had heard enough of Tastigon politics to know that Arribek of Skyrr and Abbotir of the Gold Court were at odds among the Five, and Men-dalis was Abbotir's master. This, of all nights, was a dangerous time to bring up differences.

"More wine," said a hoarse whisper beside Men-dalis to the left.

Eyes glowed from the shadows there. A crooked hand reached out. Rue fumbled for a glass on her tray. As she stretched it out, skeletal fingers gripped her wrist. Their clutch was very, very cold.

"You, girl, what are you doing here? Your lady is doomed. Your kind is . . . irrelevant. You do not belong. Go."

Rue twisted away, dropping the glass. It shattered, bright shards on black oak. Wine as dark and thick as blood crept over the tabletop and spilled down golden robes. Men-dalis lashed out at her, a blow that she countered against her forearm, spilling more glasses in the process.

"Clumsy, stupid girl! Who are you, to defy us?"

Us?

"I mean, me. No . . ."

He stumbled, glancing not to his left but at the empty space to his right, then quickly away. Rue thought for a moment that someone sat there, a handsome boy who smiled at her.

Help him, said his lips.

Help? *Him?*

The door swept open. Rothan entered, followed by his wife Kithra and their servants. "We heard," he said to Cleppetty. "We came. What d'you want us to do?"

Cleppetty smiled. "It's good to see you again, under this roof. Do? Whatever you can."

Serving became easier and more efficient. Kithra flitted about carrying trays whose size made Rue blink, on a palm raised above her head. There must be some trick to it. While the girl laughed and joked with customers, though, she also seemed to be waiting for something. Her smile was too bright, too brittle. Rothan kept glancing at her with a suspicious frown.

Men-dalis beckoned her to his table. "A glass of metheglyn, my dear."

Kithra looked confused. "Of what, sir?"

"Oh, you can't provide it?" He drew out the scroll and unrolled it, carefully, as it tended to crack and crumble at the edges. "As you see, every tavern is required to stock this ... er ... beverage. Be so kind as to summon your innkeeper."

"No need for that, my lord." Cleppetty appeared at Kithra's elbow. "In the vault," she said to the girl. "Racked under 'mead.'"

"Madam," said the Archiem, "you are resourceful."

"No. I just have an eclectic vocabulary."

Men-dalis stared. Arribek smiled faintly. "Your round, I think, madam."

"Then what about . . ." here the Sirdan consulted his list again . . . "bousa?"

"You mean beer, an old kind so thick that it has to be sipped through a straw if you don't want to choke on the dregs."

Rue noticed that she didn't offer any. Even the Res aB'tyrr apparently had its limits.

Men-dalis affected a gentle shudder. "I thank you, no."

Cleppetty waited a moment, then left him brooding over his scroll.

"What was the point of that exercise?" asked the Archiem.

"Oh, nothing, except . . . well, this *is* an official guild document, stamped by the Five. Lord Abbotir himself gave it to me, by which I assume that he vouches for its authenticity. Would you dispute that?"

"Where did he get it?"

"He didn't say. Of what importance is that? The truth is the truth."

"Huh," said the Archiem.

More demands followed, some reasonable, others not. With each of the latter, Men-dalis glanced to his left at his spymaster. "Make note of that."

"I don't like this," said Cleppetty as Rue paused, panting, beside her. "What is he up to? There will be a catch, somewhere, soon, that we can't overcome."

"Ah," said Men-dalis, his forefinger stopping at an item. "This could refer to the last time you visited this hostelry, my lord. Now, what did you say? 'We have been informed that an exceptional dancer is attached to this inn. Might she be induced to perform for us?' Only you were too polite. This charter gives you the right to any performer on the premises. I mean, the right to see their act. Or did I speak true the first time?"

"That's ridiculous," Cleppetty burst out from the kitchen doorway, where she had overheard. "What host could promise such a thing? Artists aren't slaves, not these days. When were these rules made, anyway?"

Men-dalis smiled sweetly. "That doesn't matter. It says here . . ."

"Never mind!"

Na'bim burst into the kitchen in a flurry of veils, each more gossamer than the last.

"I am that famous dancer, of course. Who else is here? You, boy." This, to Ghillie. "Get your flute. They won't soon forget this night."

"No," muttered Cleppetty. "Neither will we."

As Ghillie scrambled for his instrument, Na'bim fussed straight her crumpled costume—she must have been sitting in it for hours, waiting—and pinched her cheeks to make them glow. Without comment, Cleppetty offered her a stoup of wine. She took it and gulped it down, without thanks. Ghillie returned. A blat of music sounded, in shaky search of a tune, and the audience craned to see what was making the noise. The girl made her entrance into the main hall, hips a-sway, lips parted in an eager simper.

Rue had no knowledge of tavern dancing, but she quickly realized that this was a disaster. Na'bim climbed onto a tabletop, the better to be seen, and set about a sort of languid swooning that, one supposed, was meant to be seductive.

"Like a trout out of water," muttered Cleppetty.

Rue allowed that the dancer had some acrobat skills. Unfortunately, these mostly led to her presenting her barely covered crotch to onlookers. These kept quiet at first, one supposed, out of sheer incredulity.

Then someone snickered. One brigand poked another in the ribs and guffawed. Hirsute faces leaned forward. To say that they leered would be a kindness. They jeered. Someone flipped a sodden bread crust at her, then another, and another. Na'bim didn't seem to notice until one hit her in the face. Beer trickled down between her startled eyes. She sputtered, dashing it away, and seemed for the first time to emerge from her dream of adoration. All of those faces stared up at her, those cruel, laughing eyes.

"You, you beasts!"

She burst into tears. Cleppetty tried to enfold her in her arms at the kitchen door, but Na'bim angrily fought free and flounced away. The inn would not see her again, nor miss her.

Rue was suddenly sure that she had been right about the dancer's fancy (now broken) mirror. Not her home. Never that.

The main hall rocked with laughter. Alone in its midst, Men-dalis was flustered, as if they also laughed at him. "I meant to say, a Kencyr dancer. Yes. Give us that or suffer the consequences!"

Cleppetty looked at Rue.

"Oh no," said the cadet, aghast. "Not me."

"As that fool of a girl said, who else is there? You aren't the B'tyrr but you are Kencyr, and you do know how to dance, don't you?"

"Well, yes. The Senetha. But here? Now?"

"Try."

Rue gulped. She knew her skills to be modest at best and better suited to the cadets' training hall. Besides, how could they please such an audience as this? What was the worst they could do, though? Throw bread crusts? Laugh? No. Burn the Res aB'tyrr to the ground, as they once had tried to do to the Skyrrman. Jame would be horribly upset if that happened. So would Rue.

"All right," she said. "Ghillie, not the flute. Can you beat on something?"

"This is a room full of pots and pans," said Cleppetty. "Ghillie . . ."

"Yes." He dived into a cupboard out of which complicated clangs subsequently emerged. "Go."

"And be damned if I'm going to strip."

Rue took a deep breath and walked out into the hall. No one noticed her at first. Those nearest the door tried to see what was making such a clatter in the kitchen. Others were still poking each other and laughing. Mendalis had leaned back with a satisfied smile. Arribek raised an eyebrow as Rue approached, even more so when she climbed onto the table. Rue bowed to him, then to the Sirdan, then to the audience, hoping that no one recognized the gradations in her salute. As nerves gave way to defiance, the last two gestures had bordered on the insolent.

Be calm, she told herself. *Be serene*.

Even the rawest novice knew that the Senetha was not danced well by anyone in a passion.

Tap, tap, tap went Ghillie's fingertips on the bottom of a pan.

Go on, Cleppetty mouthed behind him.

What kantirs should she choose? Not wind-blowing or fire-leaping: the former took great skill; the latter, more of a specialized warm-up than scurrying about the inn all night had so far provided. Water-flowing? Not after Na'bim's exhibition. Earth-moving, then.

Step, slide, turn, repeat. Step, slide, turn . . .

This was a novice pattern, as she well knew. First, one had to find the heart of one's balance. For her, it fluttered between diaphragm and stomach, easily mistaken for nerves.

Tap, tap, tap went her feet in time to Ghillie's beat. Back straight, knees bent, eyes ahead . . . Oh, but be aware of the tabletop's limited scope. No tumbling off of it into anyone's lap.

Men were watching her now with puzzled frowns, not sure that she was doing. So far, at least, no one had thrown anything.

Ghillie increased the tempo. Taking the hint, Rue shifted to the next kantir in the set: earth shifts, balance in motion.

Step step step turn step step step turn . . .

The trapped air of the hall pushed the hair back from her dampened brow. Her heartbeat quickened. Breathe, two, three, four, breathe, two, three, four . . .

I can lift this hall, she thought, *and throw it to the ground. I know I can. I know I can . . .*

Someone caught her foot.

Off balance, she fell, barely managing to roll upright again. As she tottered on the table's edge, Men-dalis smirked up at her, withdrawing his hand.

"I meant to say, the Kencyr B'tyrr."

Someone started to clap, slowly. The room as a whole turned toward the outer door. It stood open. Framed against the fire-flecked night beyond stood a slim figure with a wry smile. Patches' hobgoblin face bobbed up behind her, then down.

Rue jumped off the table and bowed, in full deference this time.

Jame entered the hall and sauntered between the tables to its heart. As she went, she discarded first her cap, at which her long, black hair tumbled down, and then her sodden *d'hen*. The reek of smoke clung to her. So did her damp white shirt, over small, proud breasts.

Singed and dripping wet, Cleppetty had said, the last time the inn had been in danger. Not this time bloody, at least. So there was hope.

Jame gripped the table and leaned forward. Arms straightened as she found her balance. One leg swung up over her head, then the other. How could anyone's back curve in such a graceful, reverse arc? On her feet again, black hair trailing like a silken sheet, she straightened and spread her gloved hands as if to summon the entire room to her. Men sighed and leaned forward.

Then the B'tyrr began to dance.

Rue recognized the first kantirs of water-flowing but oh, so different from Na'bim's floundering approach. This was the thing itself, as immortal as the ocean deeps, as the waters beneath the earth. How long and fluid those black-sheathed fingers seemed as they winnowed through the thick air and drew all who watched into swaying obeisance. Hands swooped, drawing up power, then casting it forth as if to net souls. The audience groaned. In they drew, and out, and in again. The tide had them, helpless in the grip of its supple strength.

Shall I reap you? Are you worthy?

Yes, oh yes.

Not yet. Watch.

The kantirs moved on. Now the watchers followed through tranquil water, now through turbulence. Down into the whirlpool. Up to the surface again, twisting, turning. A flash on the surface as of bright scales, then down again, into dark, urgently thrumming water. Power coiled within every gyration, drawing tighter and tighter. Oh, for release.

You are mine.

We are yours. Take us.

Rue found herself panting, breathless. This was tavern dancing? Trinity, no. Once or twice she had touched on something similar within the kantirs of her craft. That still heart of power. That feeling, almost, of divinity. But this also felt . . . ravenous, as if it would gladly devour whatever resisted it, and there was her lady in its grip.

"No!" she cried.

For a moment Jame staggered. A hand gripping her ankle couldn't have shaken her more. She blinked at Rue. Her face had been that of a stranger, predatory, savoring the languorous death to come by desire as much as by water. Now her lips quirked ruefully.

I am reminded. Thank you.

The room seemed to hold its breath.

Tap, tap, tap went Ghillie's finger on the bottom of a pot, counting time.

Jame gestured Rue up onto the table.

Oh no, thought Rue, but she felt drawn to rise despite herself.

Jame began again to dance.

Step, slide, turn, repeat. Step, slide, turn—once more, the first kantir of earth-moving.

Had she seen Rue stumble through it? Was this mockery? No. Here, those simple patterns took on dignity, authority. Rue felt herself drawn into them, matching Jame's movements but in the opposite direction. Was this the Sene? When Jame began to clap in time to Ghillie's beat, to the fall of their boots on the tabletop, Rue almost launched into the Senethar. She saw at once, though, that Jame didn't mean to fight.

Rue also began to clap, hesitantly at first. Before, she had concentrated on the mechanics of the form. Now her muscles loosened and she gave herself up to it.

Step, step, step, turn; step, step, step, turn . . .

This was the steady beat of the heart, the throb of the soul.

Their feet left the tabletop together, together came down with a crash that made the furniture jump. They had shifted to fire-leaping. Rue circled the rim of her wooden world, half thinking that she would paint it with flames. Opposite her, she was aware of that dark fire which leaped in Jame's slender form.

Oh, please don't ask too much of me . . .

Ghillie beat faster in time with their flying feet. Someone else was clapping now, strong and steady. The Archiem. Others among the brigands joined him—two, five, twenty—until the very room rocked.

Clap-clap-clap, stomp, clap-clap-clap, stomp . . .

Jame sprang from one table to next, kicking tankards out of her way. A cheer rose even from those who had lost their beer or been drenched by it.

That was wind-blowing, thought Rue, awed. *She flew!*

Jame saluted her across the space between them and stepped back. *Tap*, went a black-gloved fingertip in encouragement against a gloved palm. *Tap, tap, tap . . .*

Sweet Trinity. Rue had danced wind-blowing before, but never in front of such an audience and always aware that others did it so much better than she.

I'm a clod, a mooncalf.

But her blood was up and with it a febrile lick of defiance. She collected her breath, then bowed to the onlookers, who had stilled in anticipation.

The summoning. Hands rise, gathering in power. Heart and lungs swell. The world expands. A breeze raises the wings of one's hair, of one's spirit, and candles flicker. Turn. Flow. Wind rises. Wind falls to rise again. It bends the grass. It stirs the water. It feeds the flames.

Earth, water, fire . . . these also rose up in her, vying for expression. Why had she never noticed before how they overlapped? How did one separate their demands? Were they about to tear her apart?

A pudgy figure wagged a finger at her.

Child, listen to your mother.

Rue's mother had died with her birth in that cold border keep. She did not remember the sound of her voice.

Child, swim with me.

But the waters of her home were far too cold and their catch was not to be trusted.

Child, burn.

Rue gasped. The other powers had seemed distant, already in retreat, but fire swayed outside the front door in the fretted night of the square, lambent cracks opening and closing in the charred skin around its mouth. It was also in the chandelier's candles over her head, dripping molten wax on her head. And it glared from the eyes of the onlookers. The tips of her hair rose in its heat, and singed, and stank.

I am death, oblivion, said the thing on the inn's threshold. *I am the pyre. You will come to me in the end. Why not now?*

"Burnt Man, go away!" Rue heard Jame cry. "This is neither your time nor your place!"

Rue faltered, but light came to support her. A radiance grew around the table, wrapped in an encouraging benevolence, and the darkness outside withdrew. The air seemed to smile.

Child, dance with me.

"Oh," said Rue in wonder, holding her hands out to the inn's nameless goddess. "Oh, yes!"

They moved together in a trance of delight. Earth no longer claimed them, nor water held them down. Fire . . . gone, except for the glow it left behind. Swoop, slide, rise. Were they still on the tabletop or above it? Sway. Bend, just so. All was effortless, the body ethereal. A phantom hand glided up Rue's arm, making the hairs on it rise.

You have served this place, my home, oh, so well, breathed the other in her ear. *I thank you. I love you. A kiss, and then good-bye.*

Air moved across Rue's lips in a blush of warmth. She sank to her knees on the tabletop, so lightly that she hardly felt earth regain its hold. The room was still. Then it erupted into cheers.

"Well done," said Jame, helping her to rise on legs that threatened to crumple under her. "That lady's blessing is no small thing."

Remembering something else, Rue shivered. "That thing outside the door . . . was it really the Burnt Man?"

"Unlike the other Four," said Jame grimly, "he hasn't left yet. Why, I don't know, except that he usually wants to kill me. The Earth Wife said that he would turn up again when least convenient. There was something about him, though . . ."

Ghillie yelped in the kitchen, pots clanging as he sprang up. Cleppetty's voice rose in sharp exclamation. Both were shoved aside by a knot of men dragging someone down the stairs. In another moment, Tubain was thrust into the hall, still trailing wisps of feminine finery.

Men-dalis rose, smiling. "Ah. Mistress Abernia. I am so pleased to see you again."

Cleppetty pushed past them, trying to place herself between the innkeeper and these invaders.

"You have no claim here," she snapped at the Sirdan. "You never did. Archiem, tell him, on your honor as one of the Five!"

Arribek put his elbows on the table and leaned forward over clasped hands. "I must admit," he said dryly, "this situation has puzzled me ever since I first heard of it. What cause had you, my lord, to take this...er... individual in charge?"

"Oh, well, it goes back to the tragic death of my brother Dally. I had reason to believe that the Talisman knew what had happened. I wanted to know where she had gone. All this inn could tell me was that she had returned to her own people, in some place called the Riverland."

"That would seem to have answered your question."

"Ah, but how could I induce her to return? She never favored me—why, I don't know." He spread his hands, smiling winningly. "Why would any honest person refuse?"

"So you kidnapped the innkeeper's wife. As an incentive."

"Perhaps I acted impulsively. What would you do, if your brother had been murdered?"

"As it happens, he was—my elder, the heir, not as with you, your younger, a mere rival. My brother's assassin is now among my most trusted lieutenants. He should be. His son, a sweet, trusting boy, is...er...a page in my traveling court."

Men-dalis smiled again, as if reassured. "Then you understand. Likewise, Mistress Abernia became my guest. I had charge of her for several months, racking up room and board." He drew out the scroll. "It specifies here that a host has the right to retain a customer until they repay their debt, however long that takes. Therefore, I am reasserting my claim now on . . . er . . . her person until my just demands are met."

"That's a ridiculous rule!" Cleppetty burst out. "What's to stop drunkards from living here forever? She was your prisoner. Should we pay a jailor?"

"It has been known to happen," said the Archiem judicially. "And it is written down."

Kithra had been holding back, wringing her hands. "But . . . but," she burst out, "I told you that she was here so that you could take her away. She's horrible! But Uncle Tuby, oh, set him free! Surely none of this is his fault!"

Rothan took her by the elbow. "You fool," he said.

She gaped at him. "What?"

"I'll explain later, if you can understand."

"Master Tubain," said Jame, "what do you think about this rule?"

Tubain had been cringing in the grip of his captors. "I . . ." he stuttered. "I . . ."

"Mistress!"

Abernia straightened, shrugging off the Sirdan's minions by the sheer strength of her resurgent personality. "Let me see that scroll."

Men-dalis handed it over, too surprised to resist. She unrolled it.

"Huh," she said, rapidly scanning to the crumbling seal at its end. "The Innkeepers' Guild issues these every other year and stamps them with the date. This document is obsolete by centuries. Where did you get it?"

"It was stolen from an ancient archive," said Jame, cutting in quickly, to forestall other comment, "along with a book of bad poetry and someone's laundry list."

"What a curious collection," the Archiem said with a smile. "Whose archive, pray tell?"

"Please take my word for this: under the circumstances, it doesn't matter."

"I remember now," said Men-dalis, with an air of boyish delight. "You were there when Abbotir gave it to me, weren't you? 'Do with it what you will,' he said. And I have."

The Archiem examined his cuffs, which were snowy white against dark sleeves. "As my young friend would say, that doesn't matter now either. Wherever this scroll came from, it is now obviously moot. That would seem to cancel your authority here, my lord."

For a moment, Men-dalis looked as if he wanted to punch Arribek in the face. Retainers on both sides stood up with fists bunched, ready to fight. Someone squeaked in a corner—Rue thought that it was Patches, who otherwise, with a survivor's strong instinct, was keeping her head well down.

The Sirdan's smile returned, if a bit lop-sided.

"Not quite," he said, regaining his smooth manner. "There is still the small question of murder."

Arribek raised an eyebrow in polite disbelief. "Whose?"

"My predecessor's, the Sirdan Theocandi, assassinated by this rogue journeyman thief."

Everyone looked at Jame, who sighed with exasperation.

"For the last time, I did not kill him."

"You were there when he died, were you not?"

"That I admit."

"Could you have saved him?" asked the Archiem, leaning forward.

"By then, no. He challenged a force beyond his strength and in his folly, he perished."

"I believe you."

"I don't." Men-dalis drew himself up with pursed lips that tried to twitch at the corners into a scowl. Then he mastered his face again.

"This is solely a Thieves' Guild matter, my lord, both in victim and in perpetrator. We ... I ... have complete jurisdiction here, and I judge this person to be an assassin."

The room muttered. Men-dalis' brigands seemed divided in their opinion, but they were only transients in this city. The Creeper's spies withdrew with a hiss. At that moment, they seemed very much an extension of their master and, in his shadowed post, he was obviously gloating. Jame's friends cried out in protest, but they were outnumbered.

The Archiem spread his hands. "I don't know what I can do," he said to them. "As to jurisdiction, my colleague is correct."

Rue struggled with this. She knew that it was unfair, wrong, but ... but the Sirdan seemed so sure of himself, so persuasive.

He is a charmer.

That thought made her blink, and cleared her mind.

"This is insane," Jame said to Men-dalis under cover of the room's stir. "You brought me here to use me, but like this? How will it help you?"

He grinned at her. There was no other way to describe that rictus expression, those gleaming eyes and teeth.

"Well, I've been thinking," he said, with the air of someone embarking on a cozy, half-whispered chat. "The guild has become . . . restive. I said avenging Theocandi would help me, and so it will. Beyond that, what if you are what anchors my poor brother to this world? He was besotted with you, after all. Hush. Is he here now?"

Jame glanced behind him. Rue thought that, again, she caught a glimpse of that handsome young face, made of shifting light and shadow. It was not smiling now.

"Why don't you turn and look?" Jame said.

"I'm no such fool. The eyes catch the soul. I won't be tricked again. Or, how about this? I threaten to flay you alive unless he leaves me alone. He goes. I flay you anyway."

"There's got to be a catch in that somewhere."

"What do you care? Either way, you will be dead and I will be free."

"Men-dalis. I think you've lost your mind."

He giggled. "Perhaps. But don't tell anybody."

He rose, and the room rose with him.

"What do you say?" he cried. "Shall we lift this curse on our house? Shall we free ourselves of the past? You, and you, and you. What ghosts would you cast off? Come with me, come! To the Mercy Seat!"

Chapter XIV
Several Mercies
Spring 58

I

AS JAME LEFT the Res aB'tyrr, hands bound behind her, in the strong grip of her captors, she encountered a contorted, charred figure sprawling on the doorstep. This, she supposed, was the ill-fated fire-breather. His head had split open with the heat, the brains within half cooked and steaming. Flames still crackled in his throat, around his bared teeth.

The Burnt Man was prone to possess those whom fire had claimed and in doing so to intensify its effect. However, he didn't usually speak.

"I am death, oblivion. I am the pyre."

That sounded more like the blind Arrin-ken known as the Dark Judge, who often kept the Burnt Man company and sometimes spoke for him. Now, there was a lethal link between Rathillien and the Kencyrath. With wind and earth, Jame had felt some affinity. With water, presumably, there was Drie. The Burnt Man, however, remained an enigma. His domain was all of Rathillien. As for the Dark Judge, though, when the Arrin-ken had disappeared into the wilderness, each had chosen a territory. The Riverland was his. The nearby Ebonbane, on the other hand, belonged to Immalai the Silent.

"An unfallen darkling," Immalai had called her when they had met in that high mountain pass and he had passed judgment on her. "Innocent, but not ignorant."

To escape death by a scruple . . . well, she could live with that.

The blind Arrin-ken preferred that she not live at all. No Arrin-ken could enter the House in Perimal Darkling unless accompanied by one of the Tyr-ridan. The Master had only ventured into the Riverland once, to sire Kindrie. Thus thwarted of his just prey, the Dark Judge was prone to pass judgment on those Shanir linked to That-Which-Destroys and probably, in his time, had prevented more than one formation of the Tyr-ridan by slaying its darkest third. She was therefore an abomination to him, and he to her.

"What is the Burnt Man likely to do?" she had asked the Earth Wife.

"Whatever is least obliging," Mother Ragga answered, an understatement if Jame had ever heard one. "He doesn't think. He feels. Mostly blind, insane rage. That's what drew him to that precious cat you call the Dark Judge."

It also helped, the Earth Wife had added, that both had had a taste of fire.

Here was fire now, smoldering on the Res aB'tyrr's doorstep.

Oh, cleanse this threshold, she prayed to the nameless goddess within, and stepped gingerly over the smoking ruin.

Of course, the Judge needn't be here physically. When he and the other Arrin-ken had spoken through Ishtier before, each had been far distant. They had met in the priest's mind by invitation, as it were. For one cat to invade another's terrain without permission, though . . .

The performers outside the inn had scattered, presumably when their fellow had burst into flames. Most, however, hadn't gone far. They emerged from side streets as Men-dalis and his minions passed, with Jame in tow. By the time the company reached Judgment Square, they were cavorting as before, although closer to the protection of the brigands than the latter seemed to relish.

The square brimmed with other revelers. News of the demons' defeat in the Temple District had clearly spread, to general rejoicing. Crowds milled, shouting and singing. The heat of their bodies made the air shimmer. Jame had managed to snatch up her jacket and cap on the way out of the inn before they had bound her hands. Now in this press she was almost sorry. Many roisterers were already staggeringly drunk. Others scrambled for jewels tossed by wealthy merchants like so many baubles or danced in lines that snaked through the tumult. Some had caught haunts whom they played back and forth, from torch to torch, until they stumbled into the flames and ignited, shrieking. The light of their conflagration shone off the gleeful faces of watching children.

Jame also glimpsed gods among the throng, bedecked with flowers, stumbling over festive robes. There went a vast, cloudy deity with children riding on his back among the stars. There, a divine conjuror juggled knives across a circle with his followers. There were Loogan and Gorgo, dancing a jig together.

Slap, slap, squish! went the frog-god's flippers on the pavement, in and out of puddles. *Splash, splash, splat!*

His little priest waved a jug at Jame as she passed.

"Whoop!" he said, stumbling, laughing, and regaining his feet amid the cheers of celebrants. He looked thoroughly intoxicated. Well, no one better deserved it.

Jame nodded to him. However, she didn't cry out for rescue. Her captors formed a small, grim group in this chaotic scene, but they were armed and sober. The folk of both inns followed them in an anxious huddle, Rue and Patches among them. No, she didn't want to risk them either. This was her show now, to manage as best she could.

Others also had grasped the theatrical nature of the scene.

"A play!" someone cried, and was answered by cheers. "Summer's Day is almost upon us and we have survived! Praised be the gods!"

More and more people followed, thinking that this was some sort of religious street theater, with which the city was very familiar. Men-dalis went ahead of them, bowing left and right, his golden robes and face aglow. Did he relish the irony, or did he think his own apotheosis had finally arrived?

The Creeper followed him, seeming to shift so as always to keep in his shadow.

The Archiem walked to one side, looking mildly amused.

If Dally was there too, Jame didn't see him.

The crowd ahead parted. There was the Mercy Seat in an open space at the center of Judgment Square, a granite throne of uncompromising dimensions not built for comfort. Fresh pavement surrounded it. Jame remembered that the original chair had fallen into a chasm that cataclysmic night that she had fled Tai-tastigon. Had Dally still been on it, or by then had Bane replaced him? Where was Bane now? Where was Dally?

A group of richly clad master thieves waited beyond the seat and bowed, stiffly, to Men-dalis as he emerged from the press. He gestured Jame forward and presented her with a sweeping bow.

"My lords, as you see. Here is Theocandi's assassin, brought to judgment."

"So you had promised," said the eldest, a wrinkled little shell of a man, largely bereft of teeth. He stalked up to Jame and spat in her face. "Did you think you could play games with us forever?"

Jame bent her head to wipe her cheek on her shoulder. "I honored my master." Oh, where was Penari now? Probably back in his beloved Maze, grumbling at the Architect about having lost both of Abarraden's eyes. "I obeyed your rules. I did not kill your Sirdan."

"Liar."

Something in her eyes made him step back.

Dalis-sar laughed. "I bring her to you bound, and yet you shrink?"

"Honorable thief—ha!" snarled the old man. "All of our history, our traditions, our craft . . . we weren't pure enough for you, were we? You had to set your own standards. Well, justice has come at last. We wait only for Lord Abbotir."

Should I speak? Jame wondered. Oh, schist. Why not?

"Abbotir is dead, as of two nights ago."

The Archiem smiled. His problem with the Five had just resolved itself. However, shock rippled through the thieves.

"I spoke to him yesterday!" one protested.

"He gave his soul to a demon, hoping for immortality. Such deals are not wise."

The elder sneered. "And this you know, girl?"

"I judge by what I see. What happened to your colleague was . . . unpleasant."

The little man stomped. "We are not yours to judge. Rather, the reverse." He uncinched his robe and let it fall. Beneath, on a wiry frame, he wore tight-fitting black with an assortment of gleaning knives sheathed at his narrow waist.

This, Jame realized, was the guild official known in the streets as "Old Man Skinner." He and his knives had been legends long before she had been born.

He showed his remaining teeth in a ferocious grin. "You wonder: is my hand still steady? I have done this work many times before and I can assure you: these days, it is not."

The crowd cheered. "A sacrifice, a sacrifice! Death and rebirth! Hurrah!".

For the first time, Jame felt the brush of fear. They didn't understand. They would do nothing. Was this how it had been for Dally, when the knives had finally come out?

Canden pushed through the thieves' ranks, Darinby on his heels.

"This isn't right!" he cried. His straw-colored hair stood on end as if he had just risen from bed and his robe was stained, but he seemed to have been shocked reasonably sober. "The Talisman didn't kill my grandfather! She told me so, and I believe her!"

"Now, now," said the others, as if to placate a fractious, embarrassing child. "She played on your good nature. We all know that."

Canden stomped his foot, distraught. "She did not! Oh, you don't understand!"

The opposite side of the circle broke as Patches wormed her way through it, around some brigands, under others who jumped and yelped with the intrusion of her passage.

"You should listen to him," she said, scowling at the assembled elders. "None of you know what really happened."

Old Man Skinner sneered. "And you do, you sorry little imp?"

"A hobgoblin, am I? Well then, I come by it honestly. But I'm also a thief in good standing. You just ask my master."

Sure enough, there was Galishan to the rear of those assembled, trying to look inconspicuous. "You have no reason not to listen to her," he said grudgingly.

Patches snorted. "Right. Then hear this. You've got the wrong end of this business. It starts with Dally's murder."

Men-dalis' shadow snarled. "Girrrrl, shut up."

Patches fell back a step, then glanced at Jame and held

her ground. "I bloody will not! See, you all think that Bane killed Dally. Well, most of you do."

"Oooh, a story!" breathed the crowd, and its foremost rank settled down in rapt silence to listen. The others leaned in over them, passing details back over their shoulders to those in the rear. Beyond them huddled the staffs of the two inns. Beyond that, most of the square continued with its drunken, heedless revels.

"Demons down, gods up!" cried a cavorting matron in flouncing shawls. "Whoop!"

"Master Galishan," snapped the Old Man. "Tell your prentice to be quiet."

Galishan edged to the front, reluctant but drawn despite himself. "Well, no. I want to hear this too. Too much has gone wrong, these past few years. I'm not religious. I won't say that we have sinned and are cursed. But these things have causes, and what happened to your brother, Sirdan, seems to be one of them."

Men-dalis smiled and spread his hands as if to say, "Who, me?" Women in the audience swooned at his charm. So did some men. His expression fixed, however, on a silent figure who had stepped out of the crowd opposite and stood regarding him fixedly. At least, Jame thought that the stranger did. A hood overshadowed his face. Out of its folds, however, light seeped. Her sixth sense tingled. This story had a witness greater than the sum of its mundane parts.

She felt a tug on the cord binding her wrists.

"H'ist," said Rue behind her, and continued to saw until she was free. "The inns will give you cover."

Jame rubbed her hands to restore circulation.

"No," she said under her breath. "I stay here."

Patches gulped, her defiance threatening to give way to nerves. So many people were looking at her, listening so avidly.

"Well," she said with a deep breath, stepping forward. Her attention skated from face to face, settling on Jame's as the one to whom she most wanted to explain herself. "Think back to the night that the gods came untempled, the night that Dally died. See, Talisman, I was waiting in the Moon in Splendor to hear if you and your master had pulled off the theft of Abarraden's second eye. Bet on you, hadn't I, with money that I didn't have. Then Denish barged in, blind drunk, with blood on his shirt."

"I remember him," said Jame. "He was one of Mendalis' thugs."

"Please," said the Sirdan, looking pained. "One of my most trusted servants."

"Right. Splashed beer on me, he did, on this very *d'hen* that my own dear mother made. Then word came that you'd pulled off the job, Talisman, but Denish wouldn't pay up. So I picked his pocket. Then we heard about Dally. On the Mercy Seat. Flayed alive. Denish started shouting that Bane had done it, but I didn't believe that. Y'see, one of the things that I got out of Denish's pocket was this."

She fished a gold button out of an inner pocket and held it up to catch the firelight.

Jame felt her stomach lurch. "That's Dally's monogram."

"Right. And when I get to Judgment Square, there's his *d'hen* draped over the Seat with one button missing. Denish took it as a trophy, I reckon."

"Denish flayed him?" said Darinby. He glanced at Men-dalis, then away again, looking sick. "He can't have, not without orders."

"I've just remembered," said Canden suddenly. "Denish was your grandson, Old Man, wasn't he? You were training him to become the Young Skinner, but he changed alliances from Theocandi to Men-dalis and you disowned him. The point is, he had the skill."

"You deem what happened here 'skill'? Rather, butchery! You, who call yourself Sirdan, was this your doing after all? Practiced on your own brother? In all the names of god, why?"

Men-dalis smiled like a martyred saint, but he had begun to sweat.

"This is a poor, deluded child," he said, spreading his hands in pity, indicating Patches. "Will you take her word over mine?"

The listening crowd seemed divided.

"Whom should we believe?" murmured one man.

"Oh," said several women, speaking in unison. "She is so young and . . . so strange. He is so noble."

"I tell you this," said Patches, going red in the face and shrill with frustration. "On the night of the Thieves' Guild election, I saw Men-dalis and the Creeper take Dally away. I thought, 'Good. He's going back to his brother's fortress, to his own kind.' I never saw him alive again."

Jame stared at her. "None of his friends did. You knew I was upset when he disappeared. Why didn't you tell me?"

"Everybody loved him. You loved him. I was jealous, all right?"

Jame regarded that hobgoblin face, screwed up with apprehension, begging to be understood. Her first flush of anger faded. Could she have rescued Dally if she had known or, like Patches, would she have assumed that he was in the safest possible place? Even now, it was hard to believe that Men-dalis would do such a thing to his adoring younger brother.

"I would like a word with your precious Denish," she said through her teeth.

"Well, you can't have it. He was on Fleshshambles Street that night when your Cloudy friends dropped several tons of stone bull statuary on it. So was I, for that matter, but I survived."

The listening crowd murmured again.

"It could all just be coincidence," said some on the right hand side, speaking together like a ritual chorus.

"D'you really think so?" others to the left asked doubtfully.

Men-dalis spread his hands, which had begun to tremble. "I acted on what I was told—by you, Creeper."

The Creeper hissed and drew himself up in the Sirdan's shadow, a crooked extension of it, with eyes agleam within its hood.

"I only told you what you wanted to hear. He was 'Daddy's favorite,' you said. You resented him. But his charm was purely his own. Yours . . ."

Men-dalis stomped. "Be quiet!"

They circled each other, each seeming to wax and wane by turns according to the fall of light. Steam rose from the collar of the golden robe. Above it, the Sirdan's face glistened with sweat.

Help him, breathed the ghost of a familiar voice in Jame's ear. *Before it's too late.*

"Oh," she said. "Oh! Men-dalis, you're wearing Dally's jacket. Take it off!"

The Sirdan gaped at her. "I . . . what?"

Horrified realization dawned. He fumbled at the studs securing his cloth of gold coat and tore it off. Underneath was Dally's royal blue *d'hen* with one missing button. This, too, he ripped off and dropped, smoldering, on the ground.

The air above it wavered with heat.

"Oh," breathed the onlookers.

A figure had materialized in the haze. Stooping, it picked up the essence of the jacket and slipped it on. Dally smiled at his brother, at Jame, then melted away.

What was left of his *d'hen* burst into flames hot enough to melt the golden threads of the coat upon which it had fallen. Both fell into glowing ash. A sigh from the watching crowd hoisted aloft the embers and scattered them to the night.

Jame realized that she was crying. Oh, Dally, lost again. Men-dalis gasped. "W-what just happened?"

"He saved your life," said Jame, angrily dashing away tears. *But I never cry. . . .* "Then he forgave you."

"I-I didn't want that. I don't need it."

There he stood, shivering in his sweat-sodden shirt, trying to muster defiance, hearing it turn into a petulant, childish whine. With the coat, with the *d'hen*, his glamour had also been stripped away. His once glorious hair hung in lank strands. His chest had sunken and his chin receded under buckteeth. He looked like a rabbit barely left with its skin.

Someone snickered. Someone else tried but failed to stifle a guffaw. The sound rippled around the surrounding crowd, from right to left, from left to right. The brigands shuffled their feet, embarrassed. This was the man whom they had chosen to follow? The inn folk didn't know where to look, as if they had surprised something naked and uncouth.

"Don't you dare mock me!" Men-dalis shrilled, and stomped his foot.

Squelch, it went, in a puddle.

The audience roared with laughter.

"Stop it, stop it, stop it!" That was the Creeper. Like his master, he seemed to dance with outrage, the one mirroring the other, both ridiculous. "I said that I would make you great, didn't I? All you had to do was to leave everything to me."

"This is Honor's Paradox again," said Jame. "Dalis-sar, you recognize it, don't you?"

The figure opposite her pushed back its hood. Light streamed from the sun-god's troubled face, for a moment banishing shadows. The Creeper shrieked and melted into the cracks of the pavement, his fingers the last things to go, scrabbling on lips of stone for a hold on the world of light that he had so coveted. Then he was gone.

"Hello, father," said Men-Dalis with a sickly, ingratiating smile. "I'm all better now. Can you really blame me for what he did?"

"Rather, I blame myself," said Dalis-sar heavily. "We loved your brother, Aden and I. You were . . . charmless. I gave you that gift. Now I see that it came with a shadow. Resentment. Jealousy. Ultimately, it seems, murder and guilt. The glamour and the shadow are both gone now, as is your brother. You are only yourself. Can you live with that?"

Men-dalis turned to his followers for reassurance. The brigands slunk off. Those who had admired him among the crowd turned away. The guild members consulted.

"We think," said the Old Skinner, turning back to him, "that you should leave. Now."

"But . . . but . . ."

Implacable eyes watched him. "Exile would be best," said Galishan, speaking for all.

Old Man Skinner grinned through the gaps in his teeth. "I look forward to our next encounter. Say, here at the Mercy Seat? At sunrise?"

Men-dalis opened his mouth to protest, then closed it again. Reluctantly, he turned and wandered away, glancing back every few steps as if in hope of a reprieve. None came.

When Jame looked again for Dalis-sar, he had also disappeared. They were to have no last words, then. Well, she could hardly blame him. One way or another, she had cost him both his wife and his son—no, both sons. No again. Despite great gifts, Men-dalis had made himself what he was.

"Ahem," said the Archiem.

She had almost forgotten that he was there.

"It seems that we now have vacancies within the Thieves' Guild and the municipal Five. Might I suggest that the late Sirdan's grandson take both posts, at least until the next round of elections?"

Canden gaped at him. "You can't mean . . . me? B-but

I'm just a cartographer. Maybe Theocandi was my grandfather, but he never taught me anything about the craft. A-and I'm a drunk! You all know that!"

"There, there." The guild elders closed around him. "We have had worse—much worse—over the years."

"Remember Sirdan Auffoclus?" said one. "He nominated his pet newt as a master thief."

"Then there was Nominous, who wanted us all to become eunuchs."

"And Sqabulous. The less said there, the better."

"I think the thieves will sort this out to their own satisfaction," Jame remarked to the Archiem under cover of the guild's urgings. "After Men-dalis, they want stability. A lot of them are going to realize, all too soon, how much they fell under Men-dalis' spell and what it made them do. D'you think, though, that the Five will agree?"

He smiled. "Abbotir was a menace even before he died. I, for one, will be happy to deal with someone sane."

"And amenable."

"That too, of course."

"If you want," said Darinby to Canden, "I will assist you."

Canden turned to him like one falling on the neck of a savior. "Oh, will you?"

"And there," said Arribek to Jame, "we have it. I didn't even have to unveil you as the Knorth Lordan."

"Cleppetty already knows. How did you find out?"

"M'lord Harth said enough, before he went away, not that he realized what he was saying. You have some true idiots in your ranks."

"Yes," said Jame. "So do you."

The crowd broke up and began to disperse.

"I told you it was a sacred drama," said one to another. "There was a god in it, after all, and a sacrifice."

"Two, if you count that straggly young man."

"Three, if you count that glowing boy who disappeared. The boggle goes without saying. Ah, modern theater."

The inn staffs came forward in a rush.

"If you are quite through scaring us all half-witless," said Cleppetty, blowing her nose, trying not to fuss, "I propose a celebratory breakfast back at the Res aB'tyrr. You too, Master Arribek, if you will break bread with us, or whatever else we can find after tonight's depredations."

The Archiem bowed to her. "Madam, I would be honored."

Ghillie tugged anxiously at her sleeve. "Have we really got enough for everyone?"

"If not," said Rothan, with a glare at his unusually subdued wife, "the Skyrrman can make up the lack. Mistress Abernia may even join us."

"Go with them," Jame said to Rue. "Get something to eat. Some rest too, if there's time."

Rue looked stubborn. "And when did you last eat or sleep?"

Jame sighed. "I can't remember. We'll be leaving soon afterward, though. First, I have some unfinished business here."

As the inn party withdrew, Patches sidled up to Jame, looking apprehensive.

"You're off again? What about me?"

"You did well enough the last time. In fact, very well. I'm proud of you."

"Yes, but . . . but you saw what happened to the Creeper. Gone. Poof. What's to stop that from happening to me too?"

"Your mother, I should think. You're half human, after all. The other half, well, consider this: there may be some unexplored advantages that the Trinket can use, now that she knows where to look and what to fear."

"Well, maybe." Then Patches gave her a shrewd look in return. "You're upset about something too."

"Not so much that as puzzled. All right, upset too. I was thinking about Dally, or whatever it was that came back wearing his face. It wasn't a dead god, or a demon, or a haunt. I thought at first that it might be a projection of the Sirdan's guilt, given shape by Dally's jacket and his brother's glamour."

"Well, why not?"

"Because it forgave Men-dalis. He didn't see the need for that, although it saved his life. Was he even aware that he was wearing Dally's *d'hen*? I wasn't sure about that myself until just now. Could guilt have been buried that deep?"

"You're saying that Dally really came back."

"His blood on his coat as a makeshift death banner, perhaps? A trapped soul? He was the foster-son of a Kencyr god even if he wasn't Kencyr himself. Perhaps that was enough. Maybe that doesn't matter, though. He and the *d'hen* are gone now. There's only the button."

Patches drew it out. "No blood on this that I can see," she said, flipping it over on her fingertips as one might a trick coin. "I'd like to keep it as . . . as my talisman, if I can't have you."

That seemed fair, as long as Dally was truly free.

"If anything happens," Jame urged, "think again. It occurs to me that I don't know everything about the dead after all. Or gods. Or demons. About anything, really. But then, when did I ever?"

II

IT WAS NEAR DAWN on the 58th of Spring, the eastern sky already dimly alight.

Tai-tastigon had almost settled down, except for the remnant of drunken revelers who continued to stagger through the streets looking for their homes. Some would never find them. The labyrinth had swallowed many such before to add to its wandering tribes of the lost. Pathfinder was likely to find himself much in demand yet again.

However, only two walked in the Lower Town. One was a shadow that slid along the ground as if in mindless search of something. It poked tenebrous fingers into cracks. It fumbled at doorways as if cold for the huddled life within. It paused with what, for another, would have been a sigh. Then a traveler came along, and it followed her.

Jame noticed the darkness on her heels. It trailed after her over trash heaps, between shattered walls, through canyons of ruin, to the threshold of the Kencyr temple where it pooled, shadowy fingers searching after her but stopping short of the portal.

The temple door stood ajar. Inside, the halls were tenantless. Power whispered past Jame as she entered, flowing outward as it had done before—bound, presumably, for the Temple District. Ishtier had said that this was an unnatural configuration, but for whom?

"Hello," said Titmouse beside her, making her jump.

For a big, clumsy man, he could move very quietly, or perhaps that was only due to her distraction. She had left him in the Temple District among the exulting New Pantheon gods. Their exuberance had apparently worn upon him.

"They were too noisy," he said as if, not for the first time, reading her thoughts. "This silence, though . . ."

"Where is everybody?"

"I think most of the priests have retreated to their quarters and locked themselves in. Confusion, dismay, fear, take your pick. Even those who don't support the high priest didn't reckon on this."

"And Ishtier himself?"

"I haven't seen him."

"Or . . . anyone else?"

He looked at her. "Whom did you expect?"

They had reached the temple's central room in which of late the community of priests had danced. How calm it seemed now. How exhausted.

"You know," said Jame with a touch of impatience. After all, her time here was short. "You've seen him about, or at least signs of him. The shadows? The cobwebs? The black beetles? Even bloody footsteps, you said, leading from one blank wall to another. Like those."

She pointed.

The prints started where she had once danced, where power had swirled the mosaic pattern of the floor. Lesser disturbances followed the steps' unsteady tread toward the center of the room and the black granite statue of her god that loomed there. Jame was obscurely relieved that boots, not bare feet, had made the marks. However, each print was rimmed with blood, connected to the next by more gory drops.

A dark figure stood in the statue's shadow, leaning against the black flank of Regonereth, That-Which-Destroys. Eyes gleamed silver in the gloom, teeth white in a sardonic smile.

"Hello," said Bane.

His clothes were cruelly slashed, held together with cobwebs and clotted blood. His thin face was ashen under a tangle of dark, dusty hair. Blood continued to trickle down his side to pool at his feet.

Everything Jame had thought she would say to him at this moment vanished. "You look awful," she heard herself blurt out instead. "What happened to you?"

He laughed. "Have you noticed that every time we meet . . ."

". . . someone ends up bleeding."

"This time," he said, "it happens to be me. What occurred? That is a very good question. I remember clearly, up to a point. So, no doubt, do you. They came for me in the Sirdan's palace. I was stabbed, oh, so many times." He surveyed himself with wonder and fastidious distain. "Any one of these wounds might have proved fatal but then, of course, I didn't have access to my soul. As it is, they don't even seem to have closed. Then my dear guild brothers took me to the Mercy Seat. I was to be flayed alive, I believe. Instead, the earth opened up and swallowed the Seat, with me still on it. Was that your doing?"

Jame uttered a shaky laugh. "You give me too much credit. And then?"

"I crawled here."

He frowned, as if trying to remember. "After that, things are vague. I couldn't die. I couldn't live. I . . . existed."

"What, for five years, bleeding?"

"Has it been that long? Yes, one would think that I would have run dry at least after two or three. Once, I thought I heard you call. You seemed to be in some difficulty, as when are you not? Then there are . . . images. A stony place with things coming up through cracks in the pavement. A man, invisible until I opened him up. A room carved into a cliff face containing a book and a knife. Many swarming insects. Have I missed anything?"

"A campfire," said Jame, her throat tightening, "with the Burnt Man's hand reaching up through it to grip my wrist."

He looked at her, suddenly intent. "You said, 'Your choice, brother.'"

"And you said, 'No blood-price, sister,' although it seems that I didn't kill you after all."

Titmouse had been standing very still, listening. Now he stirred.

"I told you that I came from a strange family," Jame said to him.

Bane gave her a quizzical look. "You explained it to this man, but not to me?"

"Sorry. There wasn't time. We share a highborn father—in fact, a Highlord. Your mother was Kendar."

"Well," he said, bemused, "that's nice to know." His gaze, shifting to Titmouse, became shrewd. "I have watched you in your sleep, priest. Your soul is well guarded. I have also watched you watch over your precious novices. Some nights, I have been very hungry."

Titmouse glared at him, his jaw pugnaciously outthrust. "Why do you prey on children?"

Bane shrugged, "Not so much, anymore. I seem to have lost my taste for them."

"So you were also here in the temple," said Jame, trying to work all of this out. "And, I think, in the Lower Town, wandering, even tonight."

"If I concentrate, I can see the outside of the outer door. I am, apparently, waiting, but can't enter. Could it be that I don't know how? How long have you been back?"

"This is the dawn of the third day."

"So short a time. In that space, I have been . . . er . . . pulling myself together. Consciousness, it seems, can only stretch so far, to so many aspects of the splintered being that I appear to have become. Pray that no one enters your mountain cave in the interim. Why, I wonder, am I here now?"

Somewhere, a door slammed. Hurrying sandaled feet slapped the floor. The next moment, Ishtier burst into the room in a storm of black robes.

"You," he said, baring yellow teeth at Jame. Titmouse, he ignored. Bane, he apparently didn't see at all.

Jame gave him a wary half salute, remembering all the times that they had clashed, all the harm he had tried to do to her. Now he tried again. His claw of a hand rose, clutched at the power in the room, and attempted to draw it down. The light flickered, but remained dim. In a corner, a candle fell over.

Ishtier snarled. "Somehow, this is all your fault."

"What, that your rift between the worlds closed prematurely? That Gerridon didn't come after all? Maybe you forgot to tell him about your plan. Maybe he just ignored you."

This wasn't entirely a goad. She was puzzled, also a bit apprehensive that the Master might somehow put in a late appearance after all.

The high priest rushed at her, fists raised, but she evaded him with a wind-blowing move. It occurred to her that he hadn't danced with the rest of his community. Perhaps . . . oh, happy thought . . . he no longer could.

"Old man, old man. Your priests know now what you attempted to do. Titmouse, here, knows. What will you do next?"

He swung at her again, beginning to pant, and missed. Both instinctively avoided the whorled nexus of power in the middle of the floor, although Ishtier had smeared the bloody footprints and once nearly slipped on them.

"The Priests' College will honor me, or at least the ones with any brains will. Titmouse is an idiot. You!"

He glared up at the statue of his god.

"Most of all, I blame you. You fraud, you coward, you deceiver! I would have followed you to end of my days, a man of honor, but you used, and abused, and abandoned us all. Damn you!"

He struck the rough granite, gashing open his bony knuckles. Mere feet away, unseen, Bane's watchful eyes glowed and his nostrils flared at the scent of blood. Was that the demon within him, or was he remembering how this priest had taken the soul of a trusting boy and betrayed it to serve his own ends? Perhaps both. What had happened tonight was yet another act in that chain of betrayals, yet he did not move.

A thought: was he waiting for Jame to decide? That had happened before, however often she had tried to force responsibility back on him.

"Your choice, brother."

"Your choice, sister."

Face it, she thought ruefully. *Neither one of us trusts our moral compass.*

Ishtier backed away from the statue, glaring up at it.

"At last, I ask . . . no, demand . . . as once your loyal priest: here and now, pass a judgment, my precious lord god, against you yourself!"

"Don't!" cried Jame, but it was too late.

A thrum of power that had not been there before suffused the temple. Triangles of green serpentine, lapis-lazuli, and ivory shifted underfoot. Ishtier gasped, tottering. New patterns swirled around his feet. Horrified, he fumbled at his mouth with bloody fingers, but the words burst through them like scathing vomit.

"TRUST NOT IN PRIESTS, NOR IN ORACLES. WHO ARE YOU, TO CONDEMN YOUR GOD?"

Titmouse had come up to stand by Jame. "The God-Voice," he said, in an awed whisper. "It makes my head ring and my teeth ache. Is that an Arrin-ken?"

"Don't you smell the breath of the mountains? Listen to the dry crunch of snow, the tread of enormous paws. That's Immalai of the Ebonbane, speaking from the fastness of his domain."

"Nonetheless," croaked Ishtier, drawing himself up. "Judgment!"

"WERE YOU THERE WHEN PERIMAL DARKLING BROKE THE CHAIN OF CREATION, WHEN OUR GOD BOUND TOGETHER THE THREE PEOPLE TO FIGHT BACK AS ONE? WHERE WERE YOU WHEN THE DREAM-WEAVER DANCED AND GERRIDON FELL, WHEN WE BROKE THROUGH TO THIS WORLD AND RAISED THE BARRIERS BEHIND US? DARKNESS LIES WITHOUT, ANCIENT OF ENEMIES. WITHIN, WHO KEEPS THE FAITH? PRIEST, DO YOU?"

"You left us none!" It came out in a shriek, in a spatter of sprayed blood from a bitten tongue. "You abandoned us, oh, so many worlds ago! You let evil prosper and good perish. Gerridon rebelled against you, the first with the courage to do so. We would have followed him, yes, even into the shadows. Where else was there the possibility of truth, of honor? Instead you put the false Highlord Glendar over us. I come here into your shameful story, I, and this chit's cursed father Ganth, who led us to ruin in the White Hills, in the Haunted Lands. Dishonor. Misery. Madness. Through all of that, I should still follow you?"

"YOU LACKED FAITH. GANTH LACKED SANITY. WHO IS THE MOST AT FAULT?"

Ishtier lurched, as if violently jerked. His mutilated mouth grinned and stretched over bloodstained teeth.

"ARGH," said a new voice through his unwilling lips, fighting its way out. Teeth splintered before it. "COME TO JUDGMENT, COME!"

Titmouse's nose wrinkled. "That stench . . . singed hair?"

Jame tugged at his sleeve to draw him back a pace, out of the spreading ring of carnage. "That's the Dark Judge of the Riverland," she whispered. "Yes, another Arrin-ken."

"I DID NOT SUMMON YOU, BROTHER."

"WHAT, AM I NOT TO ANSWER A CALL FOR JUDGMENT?"

"THIS IS MY TERRITORY, WHICH YOU MAY ONLY ENTER WITH MY PERMISSION. I DO NOT WELCOME YOU HERE."

"WHY? WHAT HAVE YOU TO FEAR?"

The voices yanked Ishtier back and forth, staggering across the floor. First one side of his mouth spoke, then the other, the corners of both tearing more with each utterance back toward the ears. Blood streamed down his chin. His eyes bulged and also began to bleed.

"Who are you?" he cried, choking, aghast. "What demon speaks through me?"

They ignored him.

Burnt fur, the arid voice of hatred and despair: "WOULD YOU DENY ME MY VENGEANCE?"

"AGAINST WHOM, OUR GOD OR OUR EMENY?"

"IS THERE A DIFFERENCE?"

"ARE LIGHT AND DARK NO DIFFERENT TO YOU NOW?"

"YOU KNOW WHAT WAS DONE TO ME. IN THE MASTER'S HALLS. WITH LIVE COALS. THEN HE LAUGHED. 'BLIND CAT, I LET YOU GO. FIND YOUR OWN WAY OUT, IF YOU CAN.' YOU LEFT ME THERE, TO THAT."

"THE LINK TO THE LOST WORLD HAD BROKEN. WE THOUGHT THAT YOU WERE

DEAD, LIKE SO MANY OF OUR KIN UPON THAT COLD HEARTH."

"WAS I NOT? AM I NOT NOW? ARROO, IS THIS TRULY LIFE THAT I TOOK FROM THE HANDS OF THAT MOCKING APOSTATE?"

"ANSWER THAT YOURSELF."

Ishtier crumpled to the floor and beat it with bloody fists. "Stop it, stop it, oh please stop it . . ."

Bane watched from the shadows, fascinated, Titmouse also, from the light. Jame, no less, wondered where this would end. She had never, ever, thought that she might feel sorry for Ishtier. The room was dim, but two shadows still circled the fallen priest, whose own shade sprawled as supine as his body on the floor. While the cats speaking out of his mouth bordered on civility, their souls spat and struck at each other, in the process tearing clots off the shadow of their unwilling host from either side. His flesh withered. His eyes grew bright with terror.

"IF YOU STILL BELIEVE," the Dark Judge howled, "FOR WHAT DO YOU WAIT? WE SHOULD STORM PERIMAL DARKLING, NOW!"

"WE CANNOT, AND WELL YOU KNOW IT. NONE OF US CAN ENTER THOSE LOST REALMS UNTIL THE COMING OF OUR GOD, OF THE TYR-RIDAN."

"DO YOU STILL EXPECT THAT, AFTER WHAT YOU DID?"

"What?" said Jame, staring.

Both massive, shadowy heads swung toward her, driving her back a step. "BE QUIET," snarled both voices.

"WE HAD NO CHOICE," Immalai growled at the

Dark Judge over Ishtier's prone body. "GERRIDON WOULD HAVE DESTROYED US. GLENDAR WAS OUR ONLY HOPE."

"IT WAS NOT WITHIN YOUR POWER TO MAKE HIM HIGHLORD. THE PRIESTS HAD THAT CORRECT."

Both Ishtier and Titmouse gasped. "We did?"

The Dark Judge bared his teeth, white in a charred mask. He was becoming more of a presence in the room. The mere hint of his claws gouged the floor.

"CAN YOU STILL SAY THAT THESE REMAINING THREE KNORTH ARE LEGITIMATE?"

"YES! THEY ARE OF THE PURE BLOOD, HOWEVER IT HAS DESCENDED. ONE OF THEM HAS TO BE HIGHLORD. WE ARE JUDGES. WE JUDGED THAT GERRIDON WAS NO LONGER FIT. IF WE WERE WRONG, BE IT ON OUR HEADS, NOT THEIRS."

"BUT WHAT IS THE TRUTH? ARE WE TO JUDGE THAT TOO?"

"IN THE ABSENCE OF OUR GOD, YES."

"IN THE MEANTIME, WE EXILE OURSELVES." The dark Arrin-ken threw back his head and wailed. Walls cracked. "YOU WILL DRIVE ME MAD!"

"TOO LATE FOR THAT."

They went at each other, snarling and snapping. Ishtier thrashed in their grip, tearing himself apart with his own hands. Robes ripped. Skin split. Here was his scrawny chest, laid bare. Blood welled. Chunks of flesh disappeared into gaping, shadowy maws. They were ripping him apart to get at each other.

"YOUR PARDON," said one, for a moment drawing back.

"AFTER YOU," said the other.

Bane slid around their tenebrous forms to the priest who lay, gasping, between them. He held a knife. He used it.

"Thank you," gasped Ishtier, and died.

"You're welcome," said Bane, laying him down in the slaughterhouse of his own blood. Only the priest's ravished shadow still attended him. The chamber seemed, suddenly, far more empty than it had been. The Voices had departed, and with them the speakers.

"Where did that knife come from," Jame demanded, hearing her voice shake, "and what did you just do with it?"

"Ah well." Half shadow, half man, Bane smiled at her. "Someone left it in my side. I returned it to its . . . er . . . sheath."

Titmouse let out his breath, looking at the mess on the floor. "Now what?"

"Definitely, the pyre," said Jame. "You don't want him coming back, do you?"

"He could?"

"I have no idea. Let's not take any chances."

As Titmouse departed to summon his fellow priests, Jame turned to Bane.

"What about you?"

He smiled at her, crookedly. "D'you mean, would I prefer the flames too?"

"Something like that. Perhaps Ashe said it best: your state is . . . peculiar. I don't know what you are. Maybe I never did or will, but I . . . care for you."

He touched a strand of her hair that had tumbled down from her cap, wrapping it around his fingers. She wondered if he meant to tear it out by the roots as a keepsake. "Then we have a problem."

"I know your true name now," she said. "That and fire or water would allow you to die. If you want to. This existence must be agony."

"Who told you . . . oh."

"You remember?"

"Vaguely. I was very young, but I must have trusted you even then. So. You hold the key to my soul's destruction or its salvation."

"Sweet Trinity. D'you think I want to?"

"No. It is a serious thing. To kill, to destroy, to annihilate. . . . Something in you draws you that way. It does me too. I don't know how either of us is supposed to deal with that. Our time, presumably, will come. Meanwhile, let's wait, shall we? I would rather not waste everything I am, or was, or will be, before I see the purpose behind it."

If that exists, thought Jame, but didn't say so out loud.

"And then, of course," he added with a laugh, giving her hair a light tug and letting it go, "there is always the matter of honor."

Titmouse re-entered the room. "The keeper of the dead is coming," he said. "Luckily, one of us knows the pyric rune."

Jame turned back to Bane. A glimmer of silver eyes lingered for a moment, then was gone, drawing back into the shadows. Back to dust. Back to rags and cobwebs and scuttling beetles. Back, perhaps, to that verminous cell behind Mount Alban that contained the Book Bound in Pale Leather and the Ivory Knife, whose guardian he had chosen to be until she chose to release him.

"I don't think he will bother you again," she said to Titmouse. "Or at least not on a regular basis. Your novices can sleep safe. And if he does worry them, go into an empty room and whisper, 'Honor.'"

⚜ Chapter XV ⚜
The Anarchies Again
Spring 58

WITH GREAT RELIEF, Jame and Rue emerged among the dried leaves in the subterranean nexus under the Anarchies.

It was hard to tell how long they had been in the step-forward tunnel from Tai-tastigon. Jame was beginning to feel hungry again, despite the breakfast that Cleppetty had urged on her—a jumbled fare based on whatever food was available and safe, the latter still being a consideration, although presumably not for long. The Archiem had looked bemused, but gracious, especially to Mistress Abernia, who had presided over the feast with a magisterial air in her boots and unevenly buttoned bodice not quite covering a hairy chest. Even Kithra had behaved herself. Perhaps she and Rothan would be invited to stay after all.

As far as Jame could tell, the greater city was also sorting itself out.

Ishtier dead was definitely a step in the right direction, likewise Heliot, Kalissan, and Abbotir.

Titmouse had taken over the Kencyr temple, presumably with Bane as an unwelcome, intermittent guest.

Canden had seemed to be in control of the Guild, however shakily, with Darinby at his elbow.

The Five were reviewing their options.

When she and Rue had left, the townfolk had been still busy hunting down those haunts who had not escaped through the north gate to the hills beyond. Even so, pyres would burn for days. Jame didn't like haunts—who did?— but it made her queasy to think of all the sons and daughters, the mothers and fathers, who would wander the streets when dusk fell, ravenous, hunting, in turn hunted by their families with blazing torches.

Enough of that.

Now, Jame told herself, it was time to turn back to what should have been her main concern in the first place, and pray that she wasn't too late. Surely Brier would have left Tagmeth with her cadets for Gothregor days ago. Jame could only hope that her fallback plan would work. Oh, but what a gamble!

She had also hoped to find Chirpentundrum waiting for them. However, the little Builder wasn't there, either below or above in the circle of silently watching *imu* lithons. Had he gone back to Tagmeth on his own? For him, knowing the way, that would be easy. She and Rue would be in trouble, though, if they tried it without him, even with the recovered diamantine panel to give them light.

"Look," said Rue.

At the center of the *imu* circle, last season's leaves were disturbed and the ground beneath them gouged as if from a struggle. Jame picked up a fallen sandal, small enough to fit a child's foot but with unusually long toes. No need to ask whose. Surrounding it, like an infection, was a ring of freckled toadstools.

"Heh," breathed the motionless air. "Heh, heh, heh . . ."

A gray bird landed on a nearby lithon and fanned its wings. The feathered eyes there seemed to blink. With a whir, it flew away.

"Now what?" asked Rue, instinctively keeping to a whisper.

. . . *what, what, what* . . . breathed the resonate stones.

"We follow it."

The city was as it had been before, still, white, barely touched by the millennia that had passed since its inhabitants had died. One hesitated, even, to breathe. The bird ghosted over them, paused to perch and preen, then ruffled its feathers and flew on. More joined it, wheeling farther up against the misty dome of the sky. The light dimmed, then stealthily returned. Had a day just passed as it had before? Too late, though, to turn back, not with that slight slipper tucked into her belt.

More narrow streets, more miniature houses with open, lit doorways, more walls laced with cracks. Here and there were also more patches of fungi, almost as if to mark the shuffling passage of . . . what? Here was an archway. Beyond, within a circle of blank windows bracketed by veins of luminous mold, was what once might have been a sunken courtyard garden.

Had the Builders always liked mushrooms? Here, at least, they ran rampant. To one side were clumps of red-speckled caps, then a spangle of lavender cones, then white buttons strewn like milky stars in tangled nests of rank grass. On the other side, tawny fungoid shelves climbed the skeletons of trees, barely holding together the trunks upon which they fed. The dead leaves above were furry with mildew and seemed, surreptitiously, to crawl. Scaly bracken rustled, stirring the cobwebs that interlaced them. Somewhere, the water of an unseen spring trickled.

"Chirp," Jame called, barely raising her voice. What else, after all, might be listening? Birds landed to line the surrounding eaves, murmuring to each other and flexing their wings. Blink, blink, nod, nod.

Rue made as if to step down into the court's basin, but Jame stopped her.

"Stay here."

"Why?"

"Just do it. Please."

Underfoot, the ground was velvet with spongy moss. It also dipped and swelled like a coverlet pulled over shapeless sleepers. Here and there, fruiting fungi puffed their spores into a low-hanging haze that stirred with her cautious passage. Jame held her sleeve over her face. All too well, she remembered how Torisen had caught the lung-rot that had almost killed him, never mind that that had been in large part due to his exile from the curative powers of his soul image.

"Chirp?"

A small, gray-robed figure moved through the mist, seen, then gone, then seen again. It bent over a hillock and appeared to melt into it. When Jame stumbled over to the rise, she found the diminutive Builder sprawled on top of it. His cloak was covered in a dusting of spores. He didn't appear to have moved in days. When she tried to lift him, something that might have been a bloated hand rose with him, clamped around his wrist.

"Heh. Heh, heh . . ."

Spores wheezed up with each exhalation, so many tiny fungoid mouths pouting and puffing. A broader face broke free of the moss, caked with mold. The hollow sockets of its skull were scabrous with lichen. It grinned. Woodlice swarmed between the mottled buds of its teeth.

"Heh, who, oooh, you. Liddle girly . . ."

Jame dug her claws into what passed for its eyes. It shrieked, a thin, piercing sound, and let go of Chirp to scrabble at its face. She pulled the Builder clear and backed up, supporting his sagging weight.

"Eeeee . . ."

The entire hillock was trying to rise, here a swollen elbow, there a bloated arm. The back of a head, straggly with hair, concave. A chest, bulging not with muscles but with spurting puffballs. Spongy bits of it fell off. Others clung by threadlike tendrils, trying to pull it back together. It floundered, grotesque, monstrous. The birds descended on it.

Rue surged down the steps and scooped the Builder out of Jame's arms. All three stumbled to the other side of the street, opposite the archway. From within came a high, keening wail.

"What in Perimal's name was that?" Rue demanded.

Jame bent over, gasping. Her reinforced *d'hen* sleeve hadn't let much air through or, hopefully, anything else.

"I think . . . he used to be . . . a brigand named Bortis.

This would be the second time... that I've blinded him, but... still alive, here, after five years?"

Chirpentundrum caught his breath with a whooping gasp. "You call that alive? Still, if he lived on mushrooms and they eventually lived on him... Stranger things have happened. I remember, once, a fungoid stag stumbled into the city. Quite a mess, that was, when it fell apart. And there was the case of the orange puffballs..."

Jame looked at him. "You were in there for days. Are you infected?"

"I don't think so... hic!... but I may hallucinate for a while. We did enjoy that aspect of the 'shrooms. It passed the time. Still..." and here he looked mildly apprehensive, "... it may be some while before my dreams are pleasant again, if ever."

To Jame, he seemed even now to be still half within a dream. Emotions flickered across his face—horror, joy, apprehension, wonder...

"Did you find your wife?" she asked him as Rue helped him fumble his recovered sandal back onto his foot.

His expression brightened, then fell again. "I thought that I did. She walked with me in the garden. I felt her hand in mine, but so cold, and her eyes on mine, but so sad. Still, I was sorry when you woke me."

"I may have seen her too," said Jame. "At least, someone in a gray robe led me to you on that mound. What's more, it stirred a memory. I've been here before. The last time—the first time, really—someone acted as our guide, though the Anarchies, through the city, through the tunnels. I assumed that it was male, but I could have been wrong."

Chirp plucked at Jame's hand as though to drag her forward, but was so unsteady on his feet that he clung more than led. His resemblance to a child had never been more pronounced.

"Oh, I see her! There, walking ahead of us. Follow, quick, quick! Oh, why doesn't she look back?"

Some five years ago, Jame and Marc had retreated through this silent city to the circle of *imu* lithons. Her training in Tai-tastigon had made her sensitive to the patterns of streets, and these were more regular than most. Besides, she had remembered a trick from that earlier encounter: if one looked directly at that gray-robed guide, it vanished. A side-long glance, though . . .

"There!" said Chirp.

It had disappeared into a low doorway.

"I've been here before," Jame said, bending to peer within. "Rue, keep guard at the door and don't let anything lure you away, whatever you may or may not hear. We're going in."

Chirp, in fact, already had, at a rapid totter. Jame followed him down a long, low passageway softly lit by diamantine panels. Each step took her an improbable distance ahead over step-forward stones. Here was a familiar room opening off the hall, with a marble table whose legs were apparently affixed sideways to the opposite wall. If she were to enter, however, Jame knew that she would find herself standing next to that table with its litter of small bottles. That was tempting. The last time, she had secured a pocketful of the crystals that had subsequently caused Lord Caineron to float away whenever he got the hiccups. Maybe there was something else here that she could induce him to try, but there wasn't time. What a pity.

Outside, the corridor turned and ascended. While the way looked flat, it felt like climbing an unseen hill.

Finally, here was a familiar door made of ironwood, standing ajar, just as it had before. The room beyond also had not changed. While the rest of the house shone with diamantine light reflected off white walls, here both walls and floor had been hollowed out of dark stone shot with luminous green veins.

A large oval window opened off the far wall, sealed with rock crystal, barred with iron. Chirp stood before it, staring out. When she came up beside him, Jame saw that he was crying.

The sky beyond was a sullen purple blotched by blue bruises. Under it, a deep, overgrown valley plunged down to the remains of a white city half-consumed with vegetation but otherwise not unlike the one in which they now stood.

"That was your homeworld?" she asked him.

He snuffled, wiped his nose on his sleeve, and nodded.

"Lost, lost, so many eons ago. We tried to recreate a fragment of it wherever we went, but only the 'shrooms made it seem real, and only for a time. Then we had to move on."

"I'm sorry. One needs a home."

"No matter," he said. "We still had each other. We are not immortal, but we rarely die. To lose even one is a disaster. To lose almost an entire city, that was catastrophe. To lose one's soulmate . . . there are no words left."

"Chirp, turn around. There, behind the door—no, only look askance."

He stared. "Mohin? Mohie!"

Before Jame could stop him, he rushed forward, then stopped, appalled, as the dust stirred by his advance swirled about the floor.

"She was only fragmented bones when I found her," said Jame, kneeling beside him. "I touched them, and they crumbled into . . . that. Except for a fingertip. As long as I held that, it guided me true, through the city, through the tunnels, home. Then it fell apart."

"Yes, yes, I see. How very like her. Well." He wiped his eyes. "I have found her at last, thanks to you. Now, help me gather her up."

He stripped off his robe—underneath was a much-darned tunic, dingy white—and began to scoop the ashes onto it before Jame realized that he meant this quite literally. Well, ashes were clean. It only remained to scatter them in order to set free the soul.

Chirp carefully wrapped the folds of cloth around them and cradled them in his spindly arms.

"Now we can go back to the oasis," he said.

"And then?" asked Jame, bemused. She was missing something here.

"Give these to your baker. Have him mix them into the bread dough with the flour, a bit at a time, and return the loaves to me."

"Er . . ."

"I will eat them, of course. How else can Mohie and I at last become one again?"

Jame felt her gorge rise. "I . . . huh . . . what?"

"Oh yes, you Kencyr have your own primitive beliefs. To destroy the soul forever, though, what an abomination. How can you deny yourself such consolation?"

Easily, thought Jame. *Would I want Ganth and Greshan and Gerraint—father, uncle, grandfather—to be part of me forever?*

But, of course, they were by blood, if through no such loving communion.

A thought struck her: If souls did indeed hold together the universe, as Loogan believed, did her people's practice weaken it or, at least, the Kencyrath? Was that desire to be set free only a selfish outburst after a life of servitude to their despised god? Perhaps, instead of devouring souls as the demons did, they simply threw them away.

"Is there any soul you would refuse to eat?" she asked.

"Among the Builders? Why should there be?"

He said that with such condescension that her hackles rose. Were they all blameless innocents? Well, maybe they were. At least, they didn't seem to ask themselves many questions. She, however, did.

"I'll do that if you answer me this: a priest in Tai-tastigon told me that all of the temples before Rathillien were designed to draw power out of their host worlds. Was that deliberate?"

He regarded her, wide-eyed. "Why, of course it was. The priests explained it to us. Our god needed that power in its battle against the shadows."

"It never occurred to you to ask why we kept losing world after world?"

"We wondered, of course. Ours was supposed to be a

limited assignment, but it went on and on and on. What are you saying?"

"That your temples drained each world in turn of its ability to defend itself. Through you, we became like demons, sucking out souls, preparing the way for that greater predator to come, Perimal Darkling itself. While you slept and played and . . . and whatever, the Chain of Creation collapsed around you."

He stared at her. "No one, ever, has said such a thing to us before."

"Well, I have. Now."

The Builder looked so confused and stricken that Jame felt guilty.

"There, there," she heard herself say. "We'll sort it out."

Trinity, will we?

Rue met them at the door, wide-eyed.

"Someone called," she said. "It sounded like you. 'Jamie, Jamie, come quick,'"

"If anyone, ever, calls me 'Jamie,' think twice."

"Well, I did, and then it giggled. Heh, heh, heh."

"Dammit. I hoped that the birds would peck Bortis apart. Apparently not. Come on. Let's get back to Tagmeth, and pray that it's not too late."

The light briefly dimmed, then lightened again.

Chapter XVI
What Awaits
Spring 60

I

"THE IDEA," said Cook Rackny, "is to make a dish that looks like something else. You've already played with haslet—dried fruit and nuts that resemble a hunters' feast of entrails. Here." He handed Marc what appeared to be an apple, gold with swirls of green, as if barely ripe. "Taste that."

Tagmeth's steward took a bite, and blinked.

"Dates, raisins, spices, and, yes, veal."

"Eggs too, to make it hold its shape, saffron and parsley for coloring. Mott, over there, is making a goducken—that is, a boned goose stuffed with a duck stuffed with a chicken stuffed, for good measure, with a hard-boiled egg. Then, of course, there's marchepane fruit, omelet owls feathered with flower petals, and a live frog pie, although I don't recommend eating that last raw."

"What's this?" Marc indicated an oddly shaped lump of rising dough.

"My own effort," said the little cook proudly. "Once it's baked, I cover it with chicken liver paté and sliced almonds. A gilded onion for a head with its green spouts upright for a comb, a long tail made of lettuce, parsley, and heliotrope...well? Can you guess what it's meant to be?"

Marc considered. This one took some imagination. "Er...a white peacock?"

Rackny clapped his hands, delighted. "But why am I lecturing you like this? Your own dish should be magnificent!"

"I hope so," said the big Kendar, with a glance toward the headless pig slowly turning on its spit over a bed of coals.

When Cook had announced his idea for this feast, which he had proposed as a friendly competition, Marc had wracked his brains for something to create that wouldn't make him look foolish. After all, he was still a novice in the kitchen, and well he knew it.

The distraction at least had been welcome, as Cook Rackny may well have also thought. By then, everybody had wanted to think about something else, not only because of their lady's mysterious disappearance, but because the nights had become hideous for anyone who tried to sleep. Despite precautions, sleepwalking episodes continued. Some Kendar had attacked others, most often their dearest friends; some had committed acts of mean mischief the memory of which bitterly shamed them when they woke; some would not speak of their nocturnal deeds at all.

Marc had had a narrow escape of his own. He didn't

remember the dream that led up to it, only that he had awoken with a start in the moon-washed courtyard, his hands around the neck of a startled Jorin.

Ha, a gloating voice had whispered in his mind. *Ha-ha-ha. Next time.*

He hadn't slept within the keep since.

Clearly, a dream-stalker lurked in their midst.

Few willingly entered the tower where, chained to a bed, Graykin frothed, much less the room above where that other guest sat, silent, grinning.

Then, perhaps with a spark of prescience, the largest of the keep's pigs had run away, and Marc had had his inspiration, given what else he had on hand. It had taken him days to hunt down the fugitive. The time away from Tagmeth had been welcome, even though he had fallen behind his would-be competitors. Tomorrow, though, all would come to fruition, or rather to a head. Summer's Day was almost upon them.

The spit turned. Grease dripped. Skin crackled. It smelled wonderful, even though roasting had barely begun. The pig's head had already been boned and baked to serve the more complicated part of his project, now residing in the bath chamber under an icy spray of river water.

"D'you think it will keep?" he asked Rackny, not for the first time.

The cook scratched his chin. "Under normal circumstances, no. After all, we've had the thing since the autumnal equinox, but Lady Cyd's little bag of preservatives has worked wonders with the rest of the larder. Even if there's a problem, it will still make a grand spectacle. And there's always the pig."

With that, Marc had to be content.

On some level, though, it bothered him that they were preparing an illusion feast to celebrate the graduation of their cadets at distant Gothregor on Summer's Day. After all, what they had achieved here was real. Everyone had worked very hard to make this keep a success, a home. Now something was trying with malicious glee to tear it apart.

"Look!" called a cadet by the window.

As others flocked to her side, Marc gazed over their heads out into the noonday courtyard and his heart leaped.

Jame and Rue stood by the well, scooping water out of the bucket to drink while Jorin rolled about the flagstones in delight at their feet. Jame looked thinner and more haggard then Marc had ever seen her—Trinity, when had she last slept? Or eaten?—but she also seemed deeply pleased to be back. Her thirst sated, she splashed cold water on her face and shuddered with pleasure.

A small figure in a white tunic stood some few paces back from them, clutching an armful of bundled gray cloth. Rue offered him water cupped in her hands and he leaned forward eagerly to drink, shielding his burden from drops with a long-fingered hand. Marc had heard tales about the small folk in the oasis but never before had seen one. How childlike this one appeared, and yet how alien.

A wail rose from the oasis gate. Girt wandered out of it like a somnambulist, carrying Benj. The infant thrashed in her arms, red-faced and screaming. He hit her face, again and again. She flinched at each blow but didn't protest, as if this was her penance for not being able to appease him. Here were two more who had not slept any time recently.

The little Builder gave his burden to Jame, as tenderly as if it slept. Then he took Benj from Girt's arms.

"So, so, low, so . . ."

At the croon of his song, the child gulped and stopped wailing. His flailing fists wavered, unclenched, and then subsided as he listened open-mouthed.

"Low, low, go slow,
Momma comes with laughter.
Where is her baby-toes?
Here, here, here he goes.
Who will follow after?"

They retreated to the gate and passed through it, the Kendar stumbling, bemused, after the Builder and her suddenly subdued charge. The lullaby faded to a murmur, then was gone.

"Well," said Marc, emerging from the kitchen. "That's a relief." He smiled down at Jame. "And to see you again too, of course."

Jame handed him the bundled cloak. "Give this to Cook Rackny. Ask him to put it somewhere safe and on no account to shake it out. I'm tell him what to do with it later."

Then, as the cadets tumbled out into the courtyard with a cheer, the two old friends moved as one into a tight embrace. Jame dug her head into Marc's chest, feeling the strong beat of his heart, welcoming the scent of his honest sweat overlain with the savory aroma of the kitchen. This, truly, was the smell of home.

"What are you cooking? It smells delicious."

"A surprise for tomorrow's feast."

"I hope there's something to eat before then. We're famished."

"Oh, I think we can find you some stray morsel." He patted her shoulder clumsily with his free hand. "Vanishing like that, though—sometimes, you scare me."

"I'm sorry. It had to do with Tai-tastigon and the Res aB'tyrr. Didn't you get my note?"

Rue produced the scrap of paper, by now very dirty and tattered. Her face flamed. "I . . . er . . . walked off with it. Sorry."

Marc frowned. He didn't know how to read.

"'Away on personal business,'" Rue translated obligingly. "'Don't worry.'"

"That," said Marc, "is not particularly helpful. Still, here you are now."

Other Kendar emerged from the surrounding buildings, calling the good news back over their shoulders to those still inside. The outer ward emptied into the inner, then into the courtyard. More hurried in from the fields. It was a wonder that curious cows didn't follow them. Jame greeted each beaming face by its owner's name, reminded of the last time she had done this during the autumn's eve feast. Names were so important. So was this blessed sense of belonging.

"What day is it?" she asked Marc as soon as the growing throng gave her a chance.

"Eh? You have gotten yourself lost, haven't you? It's the sixtieth of Spring. Just after noon. Tonight is Summer's Eve. You've been gone for six days."

Jame sighed. "Oh, good. There's still time."

"There is?"

"I didn't think I would get back soon enough to leave with Brier. There's another way, though. The folds in the land. Not everyone can travel by them. I only do by the grace of the Merikit and various equines, including Death's-head. If he will take me, maybe I can make it in time." She paused, concentrating. "He's hunting in the wood far above the cataract. It will take him awhile to get here, if he comes at all. He's a cussed beast, and usually annoyed with me. Even so, will this work? I don't know. Then there's you," she added, turning to Rue. "Tomorrow is your graduation day as well as mine."

The cadet gulped and smiled, trying to be brave. "I don't matter. What does is that you get there in time to speak for the future of this keep."

True, thought Marc. Tagmeth's survival depended on its lady. Her brother might be willing to support her—he hoped, based on Rowan's reports, that Torisen did—but he could only do so if she was there.

Jame snorted. "The issue of your worth doesn't arise— or shouldn't. You've proved yourself. Anyone can see that."

"Yes, but we have enemies."

"Who are petty enough to make it an issue. Agreed. Then we must both receive the randon collar or neither."

"But . . ."

Jame overrode her, thinking out-loud. "Let's see. Death's-head probably won't consent to carry both of us, and I once nearly killed Bel on a ride through the folds only half as long. Marc, do we have a suitable mount in the stable?"

"You would have to ask Cheva about that. I think, though, that we do have a spare post pony."

By post, on these tough little brutes, one could travel the twenty-five-odd miles between keeps in close to two hours. No decent rider would push beyond that without a remount. True, the folds were shortcuts, but they were also different each time taken, of varying lengths, through wilderness that no map recorded. Except for the River and New Roads, on the east and west banks of the Silver respectively, the Riverland was largely uncharted territory despite some two thousand years of Kencyr occupation. One might think that the Highborn would have learned something from that. Jame, at least, had.

She smiled at Rue. "You don't get rid of me that easily." And the cadet, with a quaver, smiled back.

Something had changed between them, Marc thought. Before, Rue had idolized her lady without question, without understanding. It had been the blind attraction of a young, naive Kendar to a strong Highborn, and Jame was strong. But she didn't compel. What had she shown Rue to win her over that gulf? What had she shown him that made them so much more than Highborn and Kendar, mistress and servant? Respect. Trust. Love. He was very glad for both of them.

But there was still duty.

"Before you leave again," he said, "I had better tell you what's been going on here. You won't like it."

II

THEY TRIED TO STOP HER. Some argued, quite forcefully, that the tower wasn't safe and, having lost their lady once, they did not propose to do so again, thank you very much. Marc looked worried. Emotions grew heated. Faces screwed up with determination and hands flexed as if to detain by force, if necessary. In the end she spoke to them with words of command, barely tempered with patience. They must let her deal with this. Anyone who came with her would not only be at risk but in the way. Please.

Perhaps, though, in the end it was her cold-edged smile that made them back up.

Now, standing within the outer door that she had closed but not locked, Jame could almost hear the strained silence behind her, could almost feel the weight of all those anxious eyes.

The tower waited, silent. Here was the inner door to Graykin's first-story quarters. She opened it.

He lay on the bed, bound by the wrists and ankles to its four corners lest he hurt himself, they said, gagged so as not to chew off his own tongue. His face was pale and damp as if with sweat, his eyes closed although they twitched under their lids. He seemed to be asleep, dreaming. Should she rouse him?

When he woke, they said, he screamed.

Waking by itself, then, gave no relief.

What appeared to be a lumpy robe covered him from neck to groin, but black heads rose at her approach, sleepily hissing.

"So," she said to the Serpent-Skin Cloak, "it *is* you."

From the Kendars' description, there had been little doubt, as startling as she found the cloak's sudden reappearance.

"Did the Master let you go?" she asked it. "If so, why, and who brought you here?"

Its many heads hissed again, then snuggled back down on top of the sleeper's chest while its joined tails twined and twitched over his legs. Trinity, to be buried alive in snakes . . .

The cloak was a potent healer, though. It had once saved Jame from poison administered by her Senethari Tirandys, but it had fled back into Perimal Darkling after she had recovered. They had a perplexing history. That it should adopt Graykin, though, was encouraging.

Pink showed beneath the black coils. Incongruously, her master spy wore a shabby cerise court coat with coral trim, now much stained despite, no doubt, the Kendars' best efforts to keep him clean. Yes, she could see him donning that to assert his importance even though he knew it would make others laugh. The bastard son of an enemy lord, how he longed for recognition.

"You are mine," she told him, keeping her voice low, almost conspiratorial. "I will give you what I can."

Water dripped from the ceiling. By the stains on the floor, Jame saw that the bed had been moved several times, but always that dismal drizzle had followed it. Now, again, it fell on Graykin's forehead. With each drop his eyelids fluttered and he flinched.

Obscene.

Jame tugged the bedstead sideways, only a few inches—it was quite heavy—but enough for the moment. Then she withdrew.

Here was the second-story apartment, where the garrison had put their second guest. He sat with his back to the door, facing the cold fireplace. She noted the straggly white hair that clung to the sharp lines of his skull, the hands little more than a clutch of bird's-bone that gripped the arms of his chair. His dark robe clung to his skeletal frame. Water ran down its folds to drip into a puddle on the floor and through its cracks into the room below.

She edged around him, peering at what she could see of his face. This hung down, his chin on the sharp bones of his chest, but something about it was very familiar.

"Bender? Is that you?"

"Ah . . ." So a corpse might have drawn breath, painfully expanding lungs in their stiff, scrawny cage, dragging in air. "Ahhh . . ."

"Did you escape, Senethari? Uncle? Have you come to me for shelter?"

"Ahhhhh . . ."

"Trinity, you must know that I will give it to you. Your brother Tirandys taught me honor by his fall. In your resistance, you taught me the master runes. On my bridal night, you gave me the Ivory Knife to fight off the Master. I owe you so much . . ."

The head rose, and grinned. "Ah-ha-ha-ha . . ."

"Bender!"

She touched his shoulder to rouse him, and fell, and fell, and fell.

III

THE FLOOR WAS COLD AND WET beneath her cheek. Her bones ached at its touch.

What . . . why . . . where . . .

That smell, half alive, half dead, so familiar. A hall, lined with faces. A hearth, cold but not vacant.

Rain dripped through the ruined ceiling—yes, she had left that in flames, collapsing—oh, so long ago, it seemed. Water stains ran down the walls into puddles on the verdigris-veined floor. A silent pulse of lightning briefly illuminated the overhanging gallery of death banners.

Most of them had been reduced to bare warp-threads. *Slap*, they went, hitting the wall like wet laundry. *Rustle, fumble, slap*.

Only on a few did vestiges of the weft remain, woven of fibers taken from the clothes in which each had died. A pair of sad eyes here, there the ghostly outline of a face, its hollow cheek half-turned . . .

Shhhh, these went, breathing against stone as if in frightened warning. *Shhhhhh . . .*

Don't panic, Jame told herself to slow her pounding heart. *Think*.

This was the Master's monstrous House in Perimal Darkling, that spanned the Chain of Creation down all of its fallen links. It was both specific in its location and ubiquitous, here and yet there, inescapable on so many levels. In how many forms had she known it? In how many places? Where was she now?

Keral the changer had brought her to this place as a child, when her father had driven her out of the Haunted Lands' keep. She had grown up within these halls although, blessedly, she recalled little of that.

Child, you were gone so long, those ravaged faces seemed to whisper. *Remember those whom you left behind*.

Tirandys, she thought, now dead. Bender. Some debts had indeed been paid but, sweet Trinity, others ...

On one level, then, the House was and had always been a real place.

She had also just seen it as an emanation of the Haunted Lands, if not of Perimal Darkling itself, looming over Tai-tastigon, about to spill its corruption into this world. How real had that been? Enough to do great harm, she guessed, if its master had been present and aware. Ishtier's offer of demons should at least have tempted Gerridon. Perhaps he had been preoccupied. Perhaps he had been here, wherever "here" was, all of that time, waiting for her.

Over and over, the House had been a dream or, more often, a nightmare.

It had also appeared in the soulscape.

She looked at her hand, almost under her nose, pressed against the floor. It was sheathed in bands of rathorn ivory.

Tick, went her extended nails as she flexed them against the cold flagstones. *Tick, tick, tick.*

This could still be a dream.

More likely, though, when she had touched Bender's shoulder, she had been sucked into the soulscape.

"I am not who I am," Bender had said to Graykin, who had told Brier, who had told Marc, who had told Jame. "I would never harm . . ."

Then had come that sly smile, that shift of personality conveyed so vividly even to those who had not seen it: "Jamethiel. Child, I wait."

In Graykin's judgment, this was a trap set in the guise of a friend.

He had been right.

Cautiously, she raised herself onto an elbow. Yes, she was indeed wearing rathorn ivory, at least on the front, with a decided draft up the bare backside. Was she never to outgrow that embarrassing vulnerability? In its prime, though, no rathorn bore armor down its spine. A stallion risked having his primary horn curve around to split open his skull from behind. As a mare aged, though, the body ivory grew to encase her in a living tomb. So it had almost done with Death's-head's dam before Jame's mercy-stroke had freed her. Otherwise, she might truly have proved immortal, but at what a terrible price?

If this was the soulscape, though, this was a soul-image. Whose could it be?

Once she had thought that was her own, that she was the monster which it contained and embodied. Kindrie had unmasked that deception.

"Listen!" he had cried to her. "These banners aren't part of you! Perhaps none of this hall is. It's a trap, to make you think that the shadows still own you, but here you are, in armor against them. Fight, d'you hear me? Fight!"

And she had. And she did.

How strange that she had never before thought that the House might also be Gerridon's soul-image, assuming that he still had a soul. Yes, of course he did: that was what the Shadows wanted and would have if he grew desperate enough to become the One, their Voice. So far, others had paid for his extended life. Someday, though, perhaps soon, he would have to foot his own bill. Everyone did, in the end.

But how decrepit everything here was. The roof had never been repaired. The walls ran with liquid rot.

Luminous mold veined the floor. A soul-image reflected the essence of its source, not how one saw oneself, but how one truly was. Most people never consciously visited it except, perhaps, in nightmares. This place was not loved. Did the Master cherish anything except his own image of himself, and then without understanding what such self-love had cost him? How little she really knew about him, despite years spent under his roof. Trinity, she had never even seen his face.

A whine came from the hearth. Jame rose and went to investigate, already suspecting what she would find. Graykin crouched in the tangle of chains that bound him to the cold fireplace. Arrin-ken pelts lay scattered beneath his feet where he had scrabbled at them trying in vain to escape. His form was that of a scruffy, starveling dog, but his eyes, terrified and pleading, were human.

Jame patted his head. He twisted, trying to lick her hand, and whined again when he could not.

"So you touched him too, did you? Now here we both are."

"A-ha-ha-ha . . ."

Banners shivered against the walls. Graykin cringed.

"Child, I have you at last."

She might not know his face, but she knew that voice, soft and caressing, now underlain with a self-satisfied smirk. No need to see the lips that formed those words; she knew that they curved in a smile. So they had many nights in the dark rooms of her childhood, breathing out of the very walls.

"Oh, I have waited so long. So have you. Welcome home, Jamethiel."

For a moment, she was back in the tower at Tagmeth, anxious faces leaning over her, Marc picking her up. Such a gentle touch for one so strong...

Oh, let this wretched hall be only a dream after all. Let me wake up.

Even so, she couldn't leave Graykin behind, and where was Bender?

"Soon you will see your purpose clearly," murmured the edges of the hall, the corners and dim recesses.

I am in his soul. I am swallowed by it.

He laughed again, as if he had read her thoughts.

"That primitive keep with chickens running about the courtyard, those ungrateful people who have turned on you after so few days...you call that home? What, did you think that you could abandon it and them without cost? I see a room torn from top to bottom, strewn with your pitiful possessions. Why so few? I will give you much finer. I see a dark woman, so angry, so betrayed. Do you blame her? But you never need see her again, nor face her reproach. Who is she, after all, to question you? All of your life, you have questioned good and evil. Here you will know peace at last, and fulfillment, and love. Have I not loved you all of this time, despite what you did to me?"

A shadow moved across the wall, attempting to caress banners that flinched away from its touch. In truth, it was only the hint of an empty glove, flaccid, powerless. Yes, she had hacked off that hand when it had reached out for her through the tumbling red ribbons of a bridal bed. He could be hurt. She would remember that.

"You belong with me. You belong to me. Ever and forever. Oh, I will cherish you as your father never could.

He did not understand what he had thrown away. You are my treasure, my weaver of dreams."

"Don't call me that! I was only a child. What did I know of consequences, of right and wrong?"

Enough, even then, to know better.

"You lied to me, night after night after night!"

She stopped herself, hearing the note of panic in her voice. Once again, forbidden memories had stirred behind the veil in her mind. What crooning lies had he told her? Had there ever been a time in her desolation when she had welcomed them?

Remember Tirandys, she thought. *Remember his brother Terribend.*

Flawed they might have been, the former fallen through love for the Dream-weaver, the latter through some weakness not yet explained, but they had stood by her. Their care, not Gerridon's, had sustained her.

His answer came lightly, almost with a note of flippancy. "Ah, child, you call me a liar. For shame. What, after all, is the truth? Have you not yet learned that each of us creates his own? You think yourself a fierce warrior, no doubt. Behold your armor. But can you truly defend yourself? Shall I run my fingertip down your spine and count the bones? You deem friendship strength, but can you save your friends? Come. For once, be true to yourself. Dance for me."

Jame shivered—oh, this was such a cold place!—but clung to her anger as if that would warm her against the draft of mortality creeping up her back. Was this the time for a berserker flare? No. She had to think before she acted, to consider all she had learned, most recently in that city of gods, Tai-tastigon. There would be no second chance.

"Free my friends and I will dance."

"For so small a price?" He chuckled, pleased to find her still such a child, so gullible. "Done."

Graykin's chains fell away. He slunk to her side and nuzzled her hand. Yes, she could feel that through the ivory that covered it. It was real.

Lightning flickered. Among the faces pallid against the opposite wall was Bender's and there he stood, staring at her. He had been a young man, she realized, when the Master had taken his soul captive. Rain coursed down his shrunken cheeks like tears.

"Jamie, don't . . ."

"You taught me how to read the master runes," she said. Oh, how it hurt to see him like this. "They are neither light nor dark but pure. Truth has no hue. Tirandys, Senethari, wherever you are, you taught me how to fight. Since then, I have learned so much more."

Taking a deep breath, she began to dance. It was stiff work at first in her cold armor, with joints cracking as they stirred into life. And she was scared. Yes, that too. Her entire life, she had been preparing for such a moment, against her people's greatest traitor, against the monster of her childhood. Perhaps Ganth had hurt her more— after all, he was her father—but he had proved to be such a little man. Gerridon . . . well, how to deal with someone who had dared to bargain with Perimal Darkling itself?

But this perverted version of the dance had its own power. This was its home, as the Dream-weaver had first performed it. The air warmed, a patch here, a patch there.

Drizzle condensed. A glimmer kindled in the corner of her eye, lit by the silent play of lightning. Someone moved with her.

Bender stumbled away from the wall. "Oh," she heard him say in wonder. "My lady."

That was why he had weakened and fallen prey to the Master. He, like his brother Tirandys, had loved the Dream-weaver. Poor Bender.

But that first Jamethiel couldn't be here. She was dead. Jame had seen her fall into the abyss rather than doom her children to a similar fate. Love, after all, had conquered weakness. However, this was the soulscape and the Master's soul-image. Could it still be haunted by his sister-consort, his darling? Perhaps. Jame couldn't bring herself to believe, though, that he had ever truly loved anyone but himself. He had used her mother as he meant to use her. That was all. Something else danced behind her, just out of sight over her shoulder. She would not turn to look, however much she wanted to.

"Dear child," the air breathed in her ear, with a low, seductive chuckle. "Dance with me. Dance for me."

She almost turned. "Mother . . ."

No.

That was also his voice framed by smiling lips, mocking in that he did not believe anyone could be as clever as he.

"You know Bender's true name. Say it. Reap his soul for me. Then you will indeed be mine, forever and ever."

The dance tried to twist in her mind, to move her limbs in accordance with his wishes.

"Love. Acceptance. Certainty. Everything you have ever wanted, bought with a mere moment's surrender . . ."

Think.

"You let Bender go," she said, trying not to pant with the effort of speaking back.

"I let him think so, certainly. The fool. As if I would ever simply release him."

"But he did flee, and he took the Serpent-Skin Cloak with him."

Pique disturbed his concentration, and with it his hold on her. "The damned thing never did me any good anyway. All relics of our failed god will be of no use in the glorious world that is to come."

"You lost control of it, didn't you? The ancient objects of power find their own way. The Book certainly did. So did the Knife. One by one, they have slipped through your fingers as if you were never meant to have them at all. You lost control of Bender too, until he got to Tagmeth. Before that, you let him think that he had won free, but in doing so, you also fooled yourself."

The banners stirred against the wall, at least those with weft enough remaining to respond. The dance drew them. Rather, it drew what was left of their blood, bound in the weave of their deaths. This was not only Gerridon's soul-image but his larder, stocked with the last vestiges of the souls that the Dream-weaver had reaped for him.

The effort to resist made her stagger. Never before had the dance been so exhausting, but then it also fed upon her. He would drain her will and strength if she let him.

Think.

The demons of Tai-tastigon lived on human souls. So did the Master. She had asked herself before if he had become another kind of demon. More to the point, did the tactics she had so recently learned apply here? True, Gerridon still had his core soul, but if she were to strip away those others that fed him . . .

She reached out to that wall of yearning faces and cried, "Tell me your names!"

Lorien, breathed one, and disintegrated.

Trinity. Glendar's mother?

Daron, another whispered, falling in flakes that were gone, swirling in the dank air, before they touched the floor.

The father of Tirandys, Terribend, and Keral.

Periel . . .

Mother of Jame's two doomed Senethari.

And on and on. The Master's generation named themselves one by one and escaped. Free, free, free.

A terrible cry rose from the corners of the hall, from its recessed arches and hollow cavities, from the emptiness that was most truly the Master's essence. "What are you doing? Stop it, stop!"

Jame found herself dancing with Bender. He blinked at her and terrible loss clouded his eyes.

"It wasn't the Dream-weaver," she told him. "I am as sorry as you are. What is your name?"

"Terribend," he groaned, and collapsed into her arms.

The walls were cracking. Clots of warp thread tumbled, unable to hold them up. The floor pulsed along widening green fissures. Charred rafters fell.

"Noooo . . . !" wailed the jagged sky.

Jame looked down into frightened eyes set wide in the furry face of her servant. Lyra had scornfully named him "Gricki," Southron for "filth." She, Jame, had called him

"Graykin" after a mongrel dog in an old song, which hadn't been much better. Neither was his true name.

"Woof," he said, and rose unsteadily to his feet, shedding his pelt down to the pink silk of skin. Good enough.

The three of them staggered out of the hall into the rank hills. On these rolled, ever and forever, under a tumbling leprous moon. Everything was in motion but fretfully, with no more meaning than a dream, or perhaps no less. Green light flared behind them out of the House's gaping windows, and the light was also a silent scream. On it went, and on and on, in rage and horror. The hills crested and toppled at its blast. The moon plummeted out of the sky. The whole world around them fell, and fell, and fell.

IV

JAME WOKE WITH A START on a scratchy bracken pallet—her bed, she realized, in her room at Tagmeth, before a roaring fire. She had been so very cold. Now a wave of heat rolled over her, breaking out sweat, and she struggled under a stifling pile of blankets.

Voices spoke. Faces appeared. Rue's. Marc's, furrowed with concern. Jorin jumped up onto her stomach, driving out her breath with a whoof.

"Here," said Marc, lifting her to a cup of cool water.

She drank, inhaled wrong, and sputtered fully awake. Because of Jorin, though, she still couldn't breathe properly.

"What . . . where . . . how . . ."

"You know that better than I do."

Beyond him, she saw her quarters, or what remained of them. Everything had been ripped apart—the meager bits of furniture smashed, the shutters shattered, holes punched in the walls, torn streamers of her already paltry clothing strewn everywhere.

"What . . . ?"

"You already asked that," said Rue, frowning, as if concerned for her wits.

"We found it this way," Marc added apologetically.

"*A room torn from top to bottom,*" the Master had said, laughing. "*I see a dark woman, so angry, so betrayed.*"

"Is Brier very upset with me?"

Marc drew a hand over his beard, considering. "Well, now, you must admit that she had some cause. Oh." He looked around him, seeming to take in the full range of destruction for the first time and, worse, its implications. "Surely you don't think . . . she would never . . . but then odd events have happened here recently. The strain, your disappearance, our guests . . . People have walked in their sleep and done things they would never do when awake. Cadet Wort even cut off her braid."

"She did? Poor Wort. Maybe I should knit her a hat, but it would probably turn into something else."

Just the same, she suspected that Marc wasn't telling her the worst of it.

The Master couldn't visit the Riverland in person without attracting the attention of the Dark Judge. Clearly, he had used Bender as his stalking horse to get within her defenses. Oh, irony: at the same time Gerridon had lurked here through Bender and played his nasty games with the garrison, that dire Arrin-ken had been drawn to Tai-tastigon by the Burnt Man, who in turn had been drawn by Ishtier's attempt to attract the Master's attention. One's full consciousness, as Bane had pointed out, could only be one place at a time.

"My head is spinning," she said. Marc offered the cup of water again. She shoved off a protesting ounce and drank.

Feet clattered up the stair. Graykin burst into the room trailing the fetters that had bound him to the bed below. Hurrah, someone had had the sense set him free. He choked, then impatiently fished the cloth gag out of his mouth.

"Well? Did you kill him?"

No question who "he" was, or that Graykin had come back in full possession of his wits. Was the Cloak to thank for that?

"I don't think so," said Jame, answering his second question. "The Master won't just crumple up and die while he still has his own soul to feed on, or to barter. On the contrary, I may just have made things a lot worse."

Someone below gave a shout of horror. While rain had previously dripped through the floorboards below, now smoke rose.

Jame fought her way out off the bed and pitched into Marc's arms. He set her on her feet. She scrambled down the stairs to Bender's room. He still sat in his chair, but his wet clothes roiled with steam.

He smiled at her out of rising wreaths of smoke. "Free," he said. "Finally. Thank you."

Flames crawled down his arms under his robes and

ignited his fingertips, which burned like candles. Fire crept up his neck out of a damp collar. His white hair kindled. Flesh smoked and blackened. He seemed to shrink within it, his eyes and lips receding over clenched teeth. Bone showed, then it too charred. Inch by inch, he crumbled within his sodden vestments until they too collapsed but did not burn. Neither did the chair.

Graykin was sick in the corner.

The others stared.

Jame cleared her throat, swallowing grief. There would be time for that later.

"What," she said hoarsely, "you've never seen a pyre before?"

"Would you ... er ... care to explain?" said Marc.

"Think of our old songs: 'Once long ago, a randon warrior went to his lord and said, "Master, our enemies hem us in. I can deliver us, but only by such acts as will damn me forever in the eyes of our people and our god. Take thou my soul, so that it will remain untainted, and loose me on the foe. And so it was done. The Three People were saved, but by deeds so foul that no man would record them. Then the warrior reclaimed his soul. Its purity consumed him, as if he lay on his pyre alive, and so he died at last with honor.'"

She continued, "Bane told me that story. He has staked his own redemption on it. Will it come true for him? I don't know. Did it for Bender? I hope so. I also don't know what Bender did that was so foul—perhaps living in the House for so long was enough—but the Master apparently held his soul hostage, untainted, until at last he demanded that I reap it."

"Er . . . you didn't, did you?"

"No!"

She almost asked, "What do you take me for?" but the answer might have hurt. In truth, there were many unanswered questions in her people's long history, even in her own.

Then a thought struck her. "Trinity. What time is it?"

"The third watch of the day," said Marc. "Midafternoon. Death's-head has been in the courtyard for the past two hours, terrifying the poultry. D'you still mean to ride?"

"I have to, don't I? All right: a night of *dwar* sleep is what I really need, but I think that this little nap has done me some good. Rue, you're still coming with me?"

The cadet grinned. "Of course."

"Good. Somebody, find that wretched cloak and stuff it into a saddlebag, or better yet into a hamper with straps. I'll leave it at Mount Alban as we pass to join the Book Bound in Pale Leather and the Ivory Knife. Bane can keep an eye on all three, if he's back. Hopefully it likes insects. Speaking of food, pack us something to eat as well."

While Marc departed to arrange this, Rue plucked at her sleeve. "You're going to Gothregor dressed like that?"

"What's the matter . . . oh."

A Tastigon flash-blade's *d'hen* wouldn't exactly suit her brother's court, or more accurately, the people she would meet there. Moreover, it reeked of the pyre. All of her other clothing, though, had been turned into ribbons thanks, presumably, to Brier.

"When we left," said Rue, "some of your wardrobe was with the garrison being cleaned and repaired. I've asked: both of your court coats are still there and at least one set of common wear. Have I mentioned that you're very hard on your clothes?"

"*I will give you much finer,*" the Master had said, certain that she would be pleased. Once, Caldane, Lord Caineron, had said much the same.

Huh.

"See to that." She sniffed her bare wrist, then a trailing strand of her hair, and made a face. "Death's-head can keep company with his beloved chickens a bit longer. Come Perimal or moon-fall, I'm going to take a bath."

V

MARC ORGANIZED THE KITCHEN, then met with the search party. They had tracked the cloak to its favorite spot, the storage room, and there had cornered it as it hissed and spat at them.

"You grab it," one cadet urged another, drawing back.

"No, you."

Marc gingerly reached down into the seething node. If he gripped it too hastily, would its many heads strike? Worse, might the silver thread that stitched one snake to another snap, or tear through skin? One loose in the keep was bad enough, but the whole lot of them? Sweet Trinity, how could such a thing as this embody healing?

Blunt noses nudged his hands. Sinuous bodies, dry and unexpectedly warm, twined up his arms. When he lifted the dark mass out of the shadows, it flicked his face with forked tongues.

I suppose I should be complimented, he thought,

conveying his burden to a leather hamper hastily converted into a saddlebag.

The cloak didn't fit willingly. The hamper's lid jolted and its seams bulged with rebellious coils. Ancestors knew what the rathorn colt would think of such an unruly burden bouncing against his rump.

Then all was set, or so he thought, but where was Jame?

"She went to the bath chamber," Rue told him.

Sweet Trinity. He hadn't warned her.

Marc charged down the steps into the subterranean stable.

"What?" asked Cheva, staring, as he hurtled past the stall where she was tacking out an ugly little post pony.

At the northern end of the aisle was a door. From the other side came a startled yell that was nearly a scream. Marc flung it open. Spray hit him full in the face, cold enough to freeze his beard. This rocky room was at the prow of the island, open by vents to the glacial onrush of the Silver. Out of its mist loomed a monstrous visage with wide spread horns, glaring glass eyes, and jutting, bared tusks. Peering out from between its jaws was another face, porcine, boneless, squashed.

Jame huddled on the floor by the door, black hair streaming over bare, ivory limbs.

"You do know, don't you," she said when he gently removed her hands from her face, "that the last time I saw that monster it was surging over a river rock, about to decapitate me? Now it's got a pig's head between its jaws. Oh, that's funny."

"Sorry. The idea was to sew the yackcarn's head onto

the pig's roasted body, with the latter's head in the mouth of the former as a fancy touch. I was trying to surprise everyone with a chimera."

She gulped and laughed, still on the edge of hysteria. "Well, you succeeded."

"Steady."

He held her until she stopped shaking.

"You really need to rest."

"Maybe I can sleep in the saddle."

"On that brute?"

"Death's-head might have me for breakfast, but then he always could."

"There is that."

Above in the courtyard, the rathorn waited. He had, with reluctance, accepted saddle, hamper, and halter, but never the bit between his teeth, which was good because he probably would have chewed through it. As it was, his jaws and chest were slathered with grease. He looked ecstatic.

"He got bored with the chickens," Marc explained, looking sympathetic. Poultry, at least in the raw, was not his favorite area of husbandry. "All that squawk, all of those feathers. So he barged into the kitchen and got his teeth into something called a goducken. Cadet Mott is devastated."

Jame stared at him. "You will, in due course, no doubt explain all of that to me."

The post pony was led up from the stables, squat and composed even in the presence of a curious rathorn. Death's-head sniffed his rump. He coiled and kicked. Ivory rang. The colt stepped back, somewhat cross-eyed, shaking his head.

"He'll do," said Jame.

She and Rue swung into the saddles.

"Ride," said Marc, smiling up at her. "Our hopes and blessings go with you."

She grinned down at him. "Be damned if I disappoint you."

They spurred out of the courtyard, of the wards, of the keep, the rathorn running almost sideways as he tried to avoid the hamper lurching at his hip. Dust rose at their heels down the River Road, bound for Gothregor and Summer's Day.

THE END

ᐊᔮ Characters ᐅᔭᐳ

Abarraden	An Old Pantheon goddess of fertility
Abbotir	Lord of the Gold court in the Thieves' Guild
Abernia	Wife of Tubain, mistress of the Res aB'tyrr
Aden	Mother of Dally and Men-dalis, Dalis-sar's love
Argentiel	That-Which-Preserves
Arribek	Archiem or ruler of Skyrr
B'tyrr	Jame's name as a dancer at the Res aB'tyrr
Bane	Jame's half-brother
Beauty	A golden-eyed, unfallen darkling
Bel-thari (Bel)	A Whinno-hir mare
Bender (Terribend)	Jame's uncle

Beneficent	A cow
Benj	A baby, son of Tiggeri and Must
Bilgore	A former high priest of Gorgo
Boo	A cat at the Res aB'tyrr
Bortis	A brigand
Brier Iron-thorn	Marshal at Tagmeth
Burnt Man	One of the Four: Fire
Caldane	Lord Caineron
Canden	Theocandi's grandson, a cartographer
Char	A ten-commander at Tagmeth, in charge of the herds
Cheva	A senior randon at Tagmeth, in charge of horses
Chingetai	Merikit chieftain
Chirpentundrum ("Chirp")	A Builder
Cleppetty (Cleppetania)	House-keeper at the Res aB'tyrr

Creeper	Men-dalis' spy
Dalis-sar	New Pantheon sun god
Dally (Dallen)	Men-dalis' brother (dead)
Damson	A ten-commander at Tagmeth
Dandello (Dandy)	King of the Cloudies
Dar	A ten-commander at Tagmeth
Darinby	A thief
Dark Judge	A blind Arrin-ken
Death's-head	A rathorn
Denish	A thief (dead)
Earth Wife (Mother Ragga)	One of the Four: Earth
Eaten One	One of the Four: Water
Elen	Granddaughter of Grandma Hogetty
Falling Man	One of the Four: Air
Fash	A Caineron follower of Tiggeri

Four, the	Rathillien's elementals
Galishan	A thief; Patches' master
Ganth Graylord	Jame's father (dead)
Gerridon (The Master)	Fallen Highlord
Ghillie	Servant at the Res a'Btyrr
Girt	Kendar nurse maid to Benj
Glendar Arrin-ken	The Highlord chosen by the to replace Gerridon (dead)
Gorbel	The Caineron lordan
Gorgo (Gorgyril)	A rain god
Gran Cyd	Ruler of the Merikit
Grandma Hogetty (Granny Hog)	A pilgrim from the hills of Skyrr
Granny Sits-by-the-fire	An immortal story-teller who translates the "Big Truths" of ancient Rathillien into present reality

Graykin	Jame's spy
Harr sen Tenko	Lord of a Skyrr hill tribe
Harri sen Tenko	Harr's son
Harth	Kencyr lord of East Kenshold
Heliot	Old Pantheon sun god
Himmatin	A Builder
Immalai the Silent	An Arrin-ken from the Ebonbane
Ishtier	Kencyr high priest
Jame (Jamethiel Priest's-Bane)	Lots of things
Jamethiel Dream-weaver	Jame's mother
Jorin	Jame's ounce
Kalissan	Old Pantheon goddess
Kells	Herbalist at Tagmeth
Keral	A darkling changer

Killy	A randon cadet (dead)
Kindrie	A healer; Jame's cousin
Kithra	Rothan's wife at the Skyrrman
Loogan	Gorgo's high priest
Malign	A yack-cow calf
Marc (Marcarn Long-shanks)	Steward at Tagmeth; Jame's oldest friend
Men-dalis	Sirdan or leader of the Thieves' Guild
Mint	A ten-commander at Tagmeth
Mohin (Mohie)	Chirpentundrum's wife (dead)
Monster	Penari's pet python
Mott	A cadet at Tagmeth
Mustard (Must)	Benj's mother, a fugitive Caineron (dead)
Na'bim	A dancer at the Res aB'tyrr
Nathe	A follower of Pathfinder

Nathwyr	A Whinno-hir at East Kenshold
Patches	A thief
Pathfinder	A New Pantheon god, the current manifestation of Hope
Pathless	An Old Pantheon demon with roots more ancient still
Penari	A thief; Jame's master in the Guild
Quezal	Penari's gargoyle
Rackny	Chief cook at Tagmeth
Regonereth	That-Which-Destroys
Robin	A Cloudie
Rothan	Tubain's nephew and heir, master of the Skyrrman
Rowan	Torisen's steward
Rue	Jame's self-appointed servant, a randon cadet

Rugen the Architect	Builder of the Maze (dead)
Sart Nine-toes	A city guard; Cleppetty's husband
Scramp	Patches' older brother (dead)
Sparrow	A Cloudie
Talisman	Jame's name within the Thieves' Guild
Theocandi	Former Sirdan of the Thieves' Guild (dead)
Tiggeri	One of Caldane's sons
Timmon	The Ardeth Lordan
Tirandys	Jame's teacher or Senethari; Bender's brother (dead)
Titmouse	A Kencyr priest
Torisen Blacklord (Tori)	Highlord of the Kencyrath; Jame's brother
Torrigion	That-Which-Creates

Trinket	Patches' nickname
Tubain	Owner of the Res a'Btyrr
Utain	A Kencyr priest
Wort	A Knorth cadet

TIM POWERS

"Other writers tell tales of magic in the twentieth century, but no one does it like Powers."
—*The Orlando Sentinel*

ALTERNATE ROUTES

HC: 978-1-4814-8340-7 • $25.00 US / $34.00 CAN
PB: 978-1-4814-8427-5 • $7.99 US / $10.99 CAN

Ghosts travel the Los Angeles Freeways, and Sebastian Vickery must dodge spirits and secret agents as he seeks to stop an evil from the netherworld.

FORCED PERSPECTIVES

HC: 978-1-9821-2440-3 • $25.00 US / $34.00 CAN

Sebastian Vickery and Ingrid Castine are chased by ghosts and gurus as they rush to save Los Angeles from a god-birthing ritual.

DOWN AND OUT IN PURGATORY

HC: 978-1-4814-8279-0 • $25.00 US / $34.00 CAN
PB: 978-1-4814-8374-2 • $7.99 US / $10.99 CAN

Tales of science fiction and metaphysics from master of the trade Tim Powers, with an introduction by David Drake.

EXPIRATION DATE

TPB: 978-1-4814-8330-8 • $16.00 US / $22.00 CAN
PB: 978-1-4814-8408-4 • $7.99 US / $10.99 CAN

When young Kootie comes to possess the ghost of Thomas Edison, every faction in Los Angeles' supernatural underbelly rushes to capture—or kill—boy and ghost.

EARTHQUAKE WEATHER

TPB: 978-1-4814-8351-3 • $16.00 US / $22.00 CAN

Amongst ghosts and beside a man chased by a god, Janis Plumtree and the many personalities sharing her mind must resurrect the King of the West.